THE
GREAT
UNEXPECTED

Also by Dan Mooney

Me, Myself and Them

THE GREAT UNEXPECTED

DAN MOONEY

PARK
ROW
BOOKS

PARK
ROW
BOOKS

Recycling programs
for this product may
not exist in your area.

ISBN-13: 978-0-7783-0858-4

The Great Unexpected

For questions and comments about the quality of this book, please contact us at
CustomerService@Harlequin.com.

ParkRowBooks.com
BookClubbish.com

Printed in U.S.A.

For granddads everywhere. Most especially mine. Daniel Patrick Mooney and Joseph Keane. I think you'd both have liked this book.

And of course, for Christine. Saint of the Infinite Patience.

THE
GREAT
UNEXPECTED

1

"Miller," Joel whispered across the space between their two beds. "Why aren't you dead yet?"

Miller, in a coma for over two years, said nothing. Instead his knobbly, decrepit old chest just rose and dropped, barely perceptible under the thin cotton sheets.

"Fine. Be that way," Joel told him.

Miller ignored him.

Joel Monroe had objected to Mr. Miller's presence when they'd first brought him in. Not that anyone paid his protests even the slightest bit of attention. A year before they wheeled in the corpse-that-was-not, Lucey had lived in that bed. He had gone to sleep every night knowing she was there and woken up every morning to see her already up and about, dressing herself, cleaning, pottering here and there and chatting quietly with the nurses as they came in and out with breakfast.

She had made living in a nursing home seem bearable, fun even, instead of the parade of indignities and insults it had turned out to be in the aftermath of her death. She decorated the place. Flowers in old vases she had collected from yard sales, photographs of their little family, the three of them at the beach, a tiny little Eva in his arms. She placed brightly colored throws on the beds which cheerfully canceled out the sterility of the place, made it nice. It was what she had been doing all their lives together: making things nice for him. She brought light where she went, and her laugh warmed any room she was in. To Joel's eyes she had never shown any evidence of her advancing years, for she was as bright and energetic as always, a force of nature showing no signs of abating. He, on the other hand, had wasted away slowly while they were there, then rapidly after she had died. It was a cold place without her. Now the photos still hung on the walls, but Joel had paid them less and less mind as time rolled by. Occasionally he might glance at baby Eva in his arms and wonder what he had done to deserve being trapped in this place, trapped without his Lucey.

The ignominy of having her replaced by Miller was an insult that had stuck in Joel's craw. He had told them that he didn't want Miller. He didn't want anyone.

But after a while, Miller was, in fact, easy to get used to. He didn't chew too loudly, didn't care what programs Joel played on the television, didn't engage in pointless small talk, or interrupt the football when it was turned on. Outside of the times when the nurses came in to check on him, move him around and clean him, he was perfectly charming. Shocking conversationalist, but a fine roommate. That didn't stop Joel from resenting the staff for foisting Miller on him in the first place, but at least life was easy between them.

"If you're not going to eat your breakfast this morning, do you mind if I have your eggs?"

Miller, of course, said nothing.

"You talking to Mr. Miller again, Mr. Monroe?" Nurse

Liam asked, as he bustled in with Joel's breakfast on a small foldable table. The orange juice hardly rippled in the young man's steady hands. Youthful, unblemished, not at all gnarled up like his seemed to be.

"Rudest man ever," Joel grunted. "Hasn't opened his mouth since he got here."

Nurse Liam smiled slightly at the joke. It wasn't new. Nothing in the nursing home was. Everything was old and over-used and on the point of breaking. Everything, down to the furniture, showed its age and its weakness. Joel tried not to think about it, but it seemed that wherever his eyes went there was infirmity and uselessness.

"Time for your breakfast, Joel," Liam told him, as if he didn't know.

"I'm well aware of what time it is, Nurse Liam," Joel replied testily. "I've been living here for five years. Eight in the morning has never been anything else other than breakfast time. For over eighteen hundred days and counting, it's been breakfast time at eight o'clock."

"All right, all right. No need to get cranky. Just making conversation."

"Well, if that's your idea of making conversation, boy, then you have a great many things to learn."

Liam sighed and tried to force a tight smile as he nestled the minitable across Joel's lap. He was used to Joel; he might have even liked him. Sometimes. A little bit.

Liam hated to be called *boy*, which naturally enough, meant that Joel found frequent opportunities to deploy the word. It wasn't that he didn't like the young nurse, quite the opposite; he had always enjoyed the young man's company. It was just something about the way that he, and all the rest of the staff at the home, spoke to him during mealtimes, or when the medicine was being dished out, or at bedtime. A sort of false tonality, a singsong quality that Joel was sure was supposed to be upbeat and cheerful but somehow felt like the voice a teacher might use when checking a ten-year-old's homework. He opened his mouth to have another pop, but thought better of it. Nurse Liam was one of the increasingly small number of things about this nursing home that Joel actually liked.

It was sometimes difficult for others to tell when Joel liked something, since his behavior changed not a jot.

Liam was in his mid to late thirties, a full forty years younger than Joel, but had about his face a certain quality of elderliness. It was something about his eyes, a sort of wariness that suggested he'd walked a harder road than perhaps he should have. Everything else about him was ordinary enough. He was a handsome type, with a long narrow face and a ready smile. He was tall but not looming and quite slim without appearing too skinny. There was nothing particularly special about him, except those blue eyes with their aged quality.

His hands moved deftly, with the steady calm and assurance of a man who had worked in his field for years. There was a touch of gentleness about them too, a familiarity with delicacy and breakable things. Joel wondered if he was the breakable thing. He supposed that he was.

Liam seemed to notice Joel biting his tongue, bottling up the urge to needle him further. His tense, forced smile relaxed into a more genuine one, and he cheekily tucked a napkin into the top of Joel's pajamas and then darted out of range before the older man could rip it clear and throw it at him.

"Insolent little…" Joel started furiously.

"I'll bring you some tea," Liam told him, laughing as he backed out of the room.

Joel sulked. To think that he had decided against ribbing the man out of some sense of loyalty, and then the little shit had gone and stuck a bib on him like he was some kind of child. Worse again, he had almost forced Joel into uttering a swear word. Joel despised profane language.

"You believe that, Miller? Can you believe the arrogance of children these days? The disrespect of them?"

Miller breathed. In and out.

"Miller, do absolutely nothing if you completely agree with me."

Miller did absolutely nothing.

He was an agreeable chap in that regard. He frequently agreed with anything Joel had to say on a variety of subjects.

"Nice to have you on my side again, old boy. When he comes back in I want you to give him the cold shoulder like only you can. Don't say a word to him."

"Some tea, Mr. Monroe?" Liam asked as he made his way back in.

"We're not speaking to you," Joel told the nurse matter-of-factly.

After breakfast Joel cleaned and dressed himself. He had been neglecting his appearance lately, which came as something of a surprise to him by the time he realized it. All his life he had been somewhat fussy about his appearance. His clothes were a symbol of his position in society. A small-business owner. A working man. He wore his clothing as a uniform, that passersby might know his rank and station. Up in the mornings to prepare for work, he'd wash, shave and fix his hair, before donning his shirt and tie and making his way to the garage. A shirt and tie, despite knowing that he was going to be pulling on his overalls and getting dirty for his living. The overalls were a symbol of his rank too, his usefulness. A man in dirty overalls is almost never an idle man.

The early stages of retirement had been no different; he had dressed smartly, shaved every day. His rituals had continued unabated. Right up until when Lucey died. Something had happened to him then, a little bit of his life force had left with her, and suddenly Joel found himself in the visitors' room, at five in the evening, in his pajamas and his housecoat, watching soap operas that he loathed, because it was someone else's turn to decide what channel they'd all watch on the common room television. For Joel the only thing worse than the outrageous stupidity of the story lines was the number of people who seemed to buy into them. Hilltop Nursing Home had accrued a small hard-core group of soap opera addicts.

Worse still were the days when he lay abed, not getting up, endlessly cycling through the channels on the small television in his bedroom, never happy with anything that was on, never happy with anything at all. Too unhappy and too unmotivated to just turn off the television and find something else to do.

When he had chanced across his reflection in the sneeze guard on the dining room salad counter at lunch the day before, he had been shocked to notice the fuzz on his cheeks and the stains on his pajamas. His cheeks had appeared extra hollow, skeletal even, despite the fact that he still had some meat on his bones. He hated that reflection. In reaction, he had decided to arrest his decline, and so, after he had eaten, Joel hauled himself from the bed and set about cleaning and dressing with determination.

He plucked his nose hair. He shaved his cheeks. He swept his hair back with the wax his grandson Chris had given him for Christmas nearly six months before. After he was clean, he dressed himself. A white shirt, a simple brown tie and a wool jacket. Brown slacks and brown shoes. He straightened himself up and gave himself a look over. Not bad, he decided. Not tremendous, by any means, but not terrible either.

Joel had never developed a significant stoop. His father, an occasionally vicious man, had been adamant about three

things: good manners, no swearing and fine posture. He re-
warded any display of these three handsomely. And punished
any failures furiously. As a result, Joel stood quite tall, still
approaching six feet. His years of manual work and playing
football had toughened him, and so his frame was still substantial, with only the traces of a paunch showing around the
buttons of his shirt. He still had a lot of hair. For now, at least.
His father had died bald. Joel tried to pretend that there was
no satisfaction in that for him, but that was a lie. He had been
a little bit delighted about it.

"Stay here and guard the fort, Miller. I'm going for a walk."

Around nine in the morning in Hilltop Nursing Home,
the corridors started to come alive as much as they could in a
place where death is potentially around every corner. Having
had breakfast, the residents began their days, and visited each
other's rooms. The nursing staff, having only just started their
shift with the delivery of breakfast, would be full of energy
and enthusiasm. That would wane, of course; it always did.
Some time, after they had to convince Rose that the house
across the street didn't belong to her brother, or when they'd
had their first row with one of the residents' family members over what medication their residents should be taking,
or when they had to change their first adult diaper of the day.
The positivity with which they began every day would fizzle
out. Nurse Liam usually kept his good spirits, and the little
Filipino lady, Angelica, whose laugh could be heard from one
end of the building to the other, was hard to wear down too,
but Joel had seen it a time or two. Given long enough, Hilltop
wore everyone down. Life. Life wore everyone down, didn't it?

And of everyone, this was most terribly true of The Rhino.
Life had made her into something else. Something hard and
unrelenting and, though Joel would never admit it to anyone
else, something a little bit scary.

Florence Ryan, or The Rhino when her back was turned, was both the head nurse and the owner of Hilltop. It seemed something of a misnomer to call such a little woman The Rhino; her size indicated something altogether daintier. Her size was a lie. She was named for her relentlessness and her purposeful charge through the halls that scattered residents and staff alike.

Hilltop had belonged to her parents, and she'd grown up here. Worked here all her life, studied to be a nurse, inherited the family business and now she ruled over the establishment with an authority Pol Pot would have been proud of. Like a blizzard she moved through the nursing home, with a kind of relentless, cold energy. Always threatening to destroy whatever she came in contact with. Even Liam and Angelica stood to attention when The Rhino was on the move, their good-natured smiles replaced with sterner expressions, almost severe, as though old Rhino herself was somehow contagious. The families of residents, vocal in their complaints when dealing with other nursing staff, stepped lightly when dealing with The Rhino, moderating their tones, fawning a little, and when she had finished wringing them out like a wet rag, The Rhino would plunder onward, furiously.

He remembered with a chill the day she had found a family member smuggling in a bottle of whiskey for Old Tim Badger. Joel had watched as she seemed to grow in size, swelling outward, Old Tim's son shrinking before her, contracting into himself until it looked like he might just shrink out of his own clothes. She had brandished the bottle of whiskey like a club. Joel could have sworn she'd grown a full two feet taller by the time she'd finished with him, while Old Tim's son looked like he might actually cry. Literal tears. Joel shuddered at the thought.

He tried to look nonchalant as he scanned the hallways for

sign of The Rhino, but all he saw or heard were the sounds of the residents and staff happily going about their day.

"I don't think she's in yet," Una told him from her doorway.

"Excuse me?" Joel replied.

"You're looking for Mrs. Ryan, and I don't think she's here yet."

Una Clarke had been a resident at Hilltop longer even than Joel had. She had been friends with Lucey. They'd played bridge as a team. A handsome woman, she hadn't yet surrendered to the malaise that seemed to grip everyone in Hilltop at some point, and dressed herself well. She had never been a wealthy woman, and some of the clothes she still wore had once been Lucey's. It set Joel's teeth on edge, but there was nothing he could do about it.

"I was absolutely not looking for Mrs. Ryan. I have no interest whatsoever in the comings and goings of that woman," Joel lied, while trying to surreptitiously check for her out of the corners of his eyes.

Una chuckled at him lightly.

"You're looking very well today, Joel. You scrub up quite well when you bother to get out of your pajamas. What's the big occasion?"

Joel bit back a retort.

Una was wearing a neat navy cardigan with large golden buttons that Lucey used to wear on Saturdays when they would go to the market. Saturday morning was always the market. Lucey dragged him along once, and he had been surprised to find the vibrancy of the place charming. After that he had looked forward to it. A little early morning date with his wife. She in her cardigan and he in his. She'd usually pick up some strange fruit or vegetable and work it into their dinner. He didn't always love that, but complaining to Lucey had been pointless. She'd listened to enough of it over the years that she let it wash off her, smiling at his grumbling and cooking whatever she pleased anyway. That little smile was a beautiful thing.

The cardigan looked well on Una. He hated that it looked well on her. He wanted to tell her that it looked nice on her. He also wanted to tell her to stop wearing his wife's clothes.

"Felt like it," he mumbled instead. Una wasn't the enemy. Come to think of it, Joel was struggling to identify who the enemy was.

"Makes a lovely change. It's nice to see you motivated."

Motivated. He didn't feel motivated. He felt something else.

It was something darker, malevolent but intangible. Something he couldn't explain that seemed to be resting just beyond the edges of his senses, waiting. It wasn't the first time he'd felt it, but there was something more immediate about it now, something more imminent. A bleakness that spread like a cloud around him, thickly, invading his space, his mind. He hoped it would pass.

"Yes. Well. Thought I could do with a shave and all that," he said, trying to come up with a way to end the conversation.

"I remember that jacket. Wasn't that a special occasion jacket?" she asked.

She was clearly thinking back to a time when Lucey had selected his clothing for him. He couldn't remember which of his clothes qualified as special-wear. He didn't want to think about it, or about her adjusting the collars of his shirts as she buttoned them up with her soft hands. She had dressed him for Eva's baptism. He had squirmed under her ministrations, mostly for show, because he loved when she fussed over him, and the more he squirmed the more she fussed. Eva had cooed and gurgled at them from her bassinet.

What a glorious day that had been. Sun shining. Lucey looking as beautiful as ever. Their families and all the neighbors out for the big occasion. It felt so long ago, and the memory of it somehow felt like it belonged to someone else. Someone happier.

"Just a jacket," Joel mumbled as he felt his breath quickening.

"What's on the agenda today, then?" Una asked, noting his sullen demeanor.

"What's on the agenda in this place on any day of the week?" he shot back bitterly. "TV in the common room until they shove us into the dining room like spent cattle? Read a book and listen to Mighty Jim babble incoherently?" He couldn't quite understand why his voice was getting so loud. "Find a corner of a room to doze off in and hope that when you wake up you've killed enough of the day so you don't have to be bored living through it?" The last was almost a shout.

His words took him by surprise. They took Una by surprise. Both surprised, they stood awkwardly staring at each other for a minute. He heard them coming from his mouth, so he knew that he had said them, but he didn't know that he had been thinking them.

"Eh... Sorry. Don't know where that came from," he tried to explain quietly.

"Anything you want to talk about?" she asked.

"No. Really, I must apologize. That came out unexpectedly."

She looked at him with genuine concern.

"Maybe there'll be something good on TV today, eh?" he suggested, trying to force some joviality into his tone, trying to sound normal. "And that show we were watching last week was all right, wasn't it?"

She continued to look at him with concern.

"Maybe we should get Nurse Liam..." she started.

"No, no, no," he cut across her. "I'm fine. Perhaps I'll chance a game of chess with Mighty Jim."

He moved off before she could answer, his long strides taking him out of harm's way before she could insist on getting Nurse Liam. He tried to think about where his words had come from. It might have been seeing Una in Lucey's old cardigan. Or perhaps his quiet fear of Rhino. It could have been his frustration with being treated like a child. But Joel suspected it was that bleak something else that had settled on him. A part of him wanted to analyze it, understand it, but he feared it, feared looking at it too closely. He shook it off and went in search of Mighty Jim.

That afternoon, poring over the chessboard in the common room, Joel tried to ignore the nagging feeling that had been pestering him since his outburst that morning. His mind kept floating back to it as soon as he loosened his grip on his thoughts.

"What I say is relative. It should not become a dead end…" Mighty Jim whispered to himself as he waited for Joel's turn. Joel had long since given up trying to understand what the older man was saying. He'd been a resident here for nearly a decade, and his ancient face was lined, his back was bent, and his gnarled hands were crippled with arthritis. His mind had left his broken body many years before, and now he mumbled nonsense wherever he went, all the while wearing a great big grin plastered across his beaten face.

Joel remembered when Mighty Jim had been Mayor Jim Lincoln. A politician, sharp and savvy, in stylish suits with a serious demeanor and a handshake for everyone he encountered. He was a symbol of strength, authority and command, a totem of manliness. He was unrecognizable now, which Joel suspected was just as well for Jim. The memory of the old mayor would live on as a powerful man, and not this bent old thing with dementia and a warped, semipermanent smile.

The moment he had allowed his mind to wander, the cloud of doom returned, coalescing around his head, bringing its negativity and despair. He felt it almost as a physical sensation. He had felt isolated before; in fact, he had felt isolated since Lucey had left him here, on his own, but this cloud was new, new and terrifying.

Part of it, he concluded, was to do with the look of shocked concern on Una's face. She had been kind to him ever since Lucey's passing. Checking in on him, trying to include him in her Gardening Club, asking his opinion on soap operas and bringing him her unfinished crosswords to ask for his help. Joel had left school at fifteen, to start his mechanic's apprenticeship, so book learning was not his strong suit. He read often, but nothing highbrow. That had been Lucey's area of expertise. He had no answers for Una's crossword questions, but felt a small burst of gratitude that she would think of him anyway, despite his continuing and obvious limitations in the field. He didn't like the idea of upsetting her, after all her kindness. But it wasn't just that. There was more to his unexplained anger than he had managed to put his finger on. Mostly it was the terrible sense of despair that seemed to have crept up on him, a sense he couldn't seem to shake. Looking at it a little closer, a few moments of introspection might have helped, but that sort of thing was well outside Joel's wheelhouse, so he opted instead to try to ignore it again.

Joel moved his knight into position carefully. In hundreds of games with Mighty Jim, he'd never won a single encounter. Whatever terrible affliction had taken hold of his opponent's brain, it hadn't yet managed to get the part of him that remembered how to play chess. Frustratingly for Joel, he had never lost either. Games with Mighty Jim had the predictable charm of repeating the same pattern; Jim would go on the attack, wipe out half of Joel's forces, and then settle back for a stalemate that had no ending. Every time, Joel would tell himself he was done with this stupidity and vow to leave the old man to his pointless shenanigans, and days later he would inevitably find himself back at the table, determined to win this time. Just this one time.

"We simply must reach a greater understanding," Jim told him seriously as he moved his bishop into a killing position.

"Absolutely," Joel replied, as he tried to ponder a way out of the inevitable slaughter.

Behind them a burst of laughter from a gaggle of women, with Una sitting at its center. The laughter set his teeth on edge.

"The hell do they think is so funny?" he asked Mighty Jim testily. Joel did a lot of things testily.

"The romantic lie in the brain," Jim replied sagely.

Joel nodded. He wondered idly how much Jim understood, and how much Jim expected him to understand.

"The laughing doesn't bother you, then?" he enquired.

"Ninety percent of people in the world that have a religion are all wrong," Jim replied, his broad grin breaking through. He laughed a little to himself, delighted, and returned his gaze to the chessboard.

His happiness set Joel's teeth on edge, too. What exactly, Joel wondered, did the old devil have to be happy about? He studied the old wrinkled face across from him for a moment. He seemed happy. Genuinely happy. His smile, crooked sometimes, was not a false effect; he just didn't see or didn't care about the conditions he lived in. He didn't care about his own slow decline or the decline of the residents around him. He didn't care about the mediocre desserts or the constant stream of pills being shoved at him. He was fully senile and fully delighted about it. Ignorance truly is bliss, Joel thought to himself.

Across the room, rapt in front of the television, some of the residents had gathered to watch the soaps again. Joel shook his head at them and looked for his next move. There had to be a way to beat Mighty Jim.

Later in the afternoon, he sat in the common room by a window with a view all the way down the hill. It was a beautiful view, in its own little way, with tall trees that enclosed the gardens and would have been majestic, if they didn't feel like walls too tall to climb over. He flipped through the pages of the crime novel he was reading, enjoying the sensation of being transported away from Hilltop. It was a welcome distraction from the nagging feeling that something was terribly wrong, which seemed to be seeping into his mind, distracting him, infringing on his consciousness. Joel's reading intensified. Somewhere in his head Joel reasoned that if he read the words quicker, then he'd be less likely to be distracted by whatever it was that was imposing itself on him.

He read until he was bored of reading. Then he went for a walk, down the long drive toward the gate of Hilltop and around the path that ran outside the line of tall trees that circled the extensive garden. He walked until he was bored of walking.

In the evening time, at the appointed hour, which was always the same hour, Joel took his supper in his bedroom to watch football on the television. The food was good, though he would have liked to complain about it. He had no doubt that The Rhino had invested her money well when she had hired Cook. The woman obviously loved her work; she had stayed in the nursing home for years, and to Joel it seemed that a woman of her talents could have taken her pick of places to work, places considerably more glamourous than Hilltop. He grumbled at the football as he ate.

"Can't decide if it's bad management, or crappy players, but one way or another, we're one god-awful team, eh, Miller?"

Miller was silent. He never said a word at suppertime.

"Honestly, someone's going to start getting worried about your mental health if you keep talking to Mr. Miller, Joel."

Liam had come through the door with the medication. Again. He would insist on staying while Joel took it. Again. Joel suddenly found this infuriating.

"Just leave it on the stand, please, Liam," Joel told him brusquely.

"That's not how it works and you know it, Mr. Monroe."

Mr. Monroe. It was always Mr. Monroe when he was being told what to do. Oh, it was fine to be all "Joel this" and "Joel that" when Nurse Liam was trying to be all chummy, but as soon as he got to giving orders and dishing out demands, it was suddenly Mr. Monroe. Joel hated the duplicity of it all.

"On the stand, please," he said more firmly.

"Absolutely," Liam replied, changing tack. He put the medication on the stand by the bed and then folded his arms and stood there.

"Help you with something?" Joel asked.

"Nope. Got nowhere to go, and nothing to do."

"Your shift ends in an hour. I can wait that long."

"I'll make overtime out of you yet, Mr. Monroe. I ain't going anywhere until you've taken the pills."

The fact that Joel needed the pills was absolutely irrelevant. That he'd once had a stroke, a tiny one by all accounts but a stroke nonetheless, and the medication was likely the only thing keeping him from having a much more serious event, was secondary to the fact that Joel Monroe mightily hated being told what to do. Regardless of whether or not it may save his life.

They stared at each other. The nurse was implacable with his steady hands and his blue-eyed stare. The argument was pointless. Joel was going to lose. He knew it. There was little value to be had in engaging in the row in the first place, but a sour energy had taken a hold of Joel and made him pugnacious.

He backed down eventually, but refused to break eye contact, even as he reached out for his pills and the glass of water. He didn't blink as he washed them down, but grimaced at the slight nod of satisfaction from Nurse Liam. Joel turned back to his television in disgust.

"Is there something bothering you, Joel?" Liam asked.

Joel again. After he did what he was told like a good little boy, he went back to being Joel.

"Don't know what you're talking about," Joel replied, but in his gut, he knew. He'd been desperately avoiding asking himself that question all day long.

"You're not yourself. I mean, you're cranky and everything, nothing new there, but there seems to be something else."

"There's nothing the matter with me that won't be fixed by a little peace and quiet, boy," Joel said, returning fire.

"Are you sure? It's just that Una mentioned..."

Before he could finish, Joel exploded for the second time that day.

"Well, maybe she and you ought to mind your own business!" he shouted. "Maybe my problem is that it's not enough for all of you to run my life. Eat this, eat that, take these, drink this, drink that... You also all seem to think that you have a right to know what's in my head. Maybe my problem is that there's no such thing as privacy around here and I'm not allowed to have a thought without everyone around here poking at me."

Liam looked shocked, but he was a career nurse, with a long track record working in Hilltop. He'd seen worse, encountered worse. He got past it quickly. His kindly face seemed to absorb the shock.

"I think we both know there's plenty of evidence that there's something going on with you, Joel," he said softly, empathetically. "If you want to talk about it, I'll be here in the morning. In the meantime, do you want a cup of tea?"

He was smooth. Capable of adjusting. If he had taken offense at the outburst, he gave no sign of it. This was enough to infuriate Joel. Did Liam think so little of him that he couldn't even be bothered to be offended when he was being insulted?

"I don't want any damn tea," he lied.

Liam nodded and withdrew. Joel tried to watch the football again. The game was still going on, the players moving here and there, but Joel didn't see any of it. He was trying to answer the question Liam had asked him. What was bothering him?

Joel dozed off in the late evening, after the game was over, without any answers. He was awakened several hours later by the gentle footfalls of Nurse Angelica coming in to turn off his TV and check on him and Miller. He knew it was her from the smell of her perfume and the soft humming to herself that was her calling card. Joel kept his eyes closed and pretended to be asleep. He was still upset that he had lost his temper twice during the day, and was no closer to knowing what had caused the outbursts. He didn't want to make small talk, as he sometimes did late in the night when he couldn't sleep, but he didn't want to insult the soft-spoken Filipino lady either. She had a good nature, and he was worried about giving her the rough side of his tongue.

She killed the TV and shuffled about the room. Then she stopped. He could hear her breathing quicken.

Something was wrong. He opened his eyes, to see her leaning over Miller, checking his pulse. Something was terribly
wrong. She hit the alarm on Miller's bed and ran from the
room. Joel searched his roommate for the telltale rise and fall
of his chest. It was still. He felt a rising panic grab him, para-
lyze him. Silently he begged for the chest to move, for Miller's
ancient old body to twitch or spasm or do anything other than
lie there so dreadfully still.

He remembered the terrible stillness of Lucey's corpse, lying
in that very same bed, the slack look on her face. Without life
in it she looked like something frightening and awful. He had
been paralyzed then, too.

Angelica trundled back into the room with the other nurses,
all action, moving quickly. Alarmingly quickly. Joel watched
as they pulled back the sheets that had covered old Miller's frail
and bony little body, all wasted away from years of coma. He
watched them tear open the cotton pajamas and begin CPR.
Their hands were rough on the spindly little body, pulling at
the sheets and clothes as they had, and then thrusting urgently
on his chest. Miller looked like a little twig; their hands were
like mallets. Joel worried that they'd break the poor man, so
brittle and helpless against their relentlessness.

The frightening part about Lucey's corpse had been its frail-
ness. She had been dynamic, quick to smile, warm, open. Her
dead-still corpse was fragile, looking like it might shatter or
crumble if you touched it.

They continued with the chest compressions, Angelica's
large hands pushing down and up implacably. She paused to
check his airways. Joel felt a spark of hope that died as soon as
it was born when she began pressing on Miller's bones again.

Joel began to silently cry as he watched them try to resuscitate his roommate. He cried for Miller, but also for himself.

The all-pervading feeling that had been bothering him that day was surfacing.

They were frantic now, desperately trying to shove the life back into the little chest, the movement of which had been Joel's only way of knowing that his roommate was a living being. Its constant rising and falling, slight as it was, had been Joel's link to another human, and now they were pounding on it, the little body bouncing up and down in the bed under their rough ministrations.

Nobody had tried to resuscitate Lucey. She was dead the moment she had died, and that was that. Dead and frail and cold and still.

Joel couldn't tell if he wanted them to succeed with Mr. Miller. Maybe the old man was better off? What kind of life were they bringing him back to? If he had a say, would he want them to bring him back? Joel wept all the harder for not knowing if Miller was better off dead.

Still they pushed at the body, pushed as if the life that had left Miller could be squeezed back into him. Joel watched in turmoil, thinking the man was better off dead and silently begging them not to stop, to find a way to bring him back so Joel could watch his broken little chest rise and fall again.

That bed was going to take another life. It was going to take Miller the way it took Lucey. Quietly. Without warning. Sneakily.

Then suddenly it was a moot point. They stopped. Mr. Miller was a corpse now. What tiny spark of life had lived in him was gone, and even though Joel knew that they had tried to save him, he imagined that the nurses had just pummeled it out of the old man.

While Joel tried to control his weeping, the nurses consoled each other with hugs and pats on the back. They had tried, tried their hardest, he knew that, but he irrationally hated them for stopping. His mind was a confused jumble of emotions.

Across the gap between the beds he reached his hand out. He didn't know why. The nurses didn't see him. Miller didn't see him. Instead, Angelica carefully and with reverence re-dressed Mr. Miller and pulled the sheets up over him. The other nurses left to make the appropriate phone calls and ar-rangements, but Angelica stayed, muttering her prayers over the departed. When she was done, she turned to leave, and her eyes met Joel's, the tears still streaming from them. She opened her mouth to say something, but whatever it was died on her tongue as Joel rolled over in the bed, to weep alone.

2

The following morning, Nurse Liam ambled into the room at his usual time, carrying Joel's breakfast. He didn't make jokes, or mess with a napkin. He didn't force the issue of the pills. He took one long look at Joel's eyes, red-rimmed from crying and from lack of sleep, and simply patted him on the shoulder and left.

Joel was grateful for it. A touch was enough, a quiet nod to Joel's desire for privacy, to be left alone to mourn the passing of a friend he had never spoken with. The most agreeable friend he'd ever had.

He ignored his food and stared at the empty bed across the way. They had come for Miller early that morning, taking him away for disposal with borderline alarming alacrity. Now where his silent friend had been there was silent emptiness. They had come for Lucey like that, too. Here, and then gone. He remembered three years earlier, when he had been in the very same bed that he was in now, staring at the same emptiness across the room, where his wife had once been.

She had been up late, couldn't sleep, she said, and when the night nurse had come to check on her, they had whispered so as not to disturb Joel. He had been faintly aware of their chatting, a quiet noise that kept him on the edge of sleep. She asked the night nurse for a cup of tea. The night nurse left to make the tea, a mere three minutes out of the room, and by the time she had come back, Lucey Monroe had quietly slipped away, leaving the shell that his wife had once occupied. A year shy of fifty years married together, and then she was gone, and Joel was left to make his way in life without the captain of his ship.

She had been the real linchpin of the family. He had never had a fantastic relationship with their daughter, and consequently with their grandchildren, but he had enjoyed their visits, and he liked going to their house for dinner on occasion. Without Lucey, all the weaknesses of a distant father had revealed themselves, and so Joel had lost a wife, and for all intents and purposes, a daughter and two grandchildren.

It hadn't always been that way. There had been a time when Eva was small, and Joel owned his own garage and had played with her there. She had talked all day to him, in her little serious voice, and he had been impressed with how clever she was. He could remember moments just like that, a thousand of them, but somehow couldn't recall the moment when Eva had slipped away from him.

When they had selected Miller to be placed with Joel, they had done so with careful consideration for Joel's feelings. They had let him mourn for a year before they placed him with someone else. In a way, Miller had become a transitional friend for Joel. Now he was gone. The same bed that had been his wife's, then Miller's, was now empty again, and Joel, still here, still alive when all the others were checking out, felt every bit as empty.

There were over fifty residents living in Hilltop. Some, like

Mighty Jim, were inaccessible, but most, like Una Clarke, were perfectly fit and healthy mentally. There was a nursing staff of fifteen, in rotation. Nice, kind, caring, considerate people. All told, in excess of sixty-five people, plus guests coming and going, and yet for all of that, Joel realized, he was terrifyingly, cripplingly lonely.

That had been the answer to the questions he had asked himself the day before. That was the creeping cloud of darkness on the horizon of his mind. It had reached him, it settled over him and enveloped him: he was a lonely, scared old man. Worse than that, he was a lonely old man who had lost the will to live.

Sitting up, his tea going cold on the stand beside him as he stared across at the empty bed that once held his wife, Joel Monroe decided he was going to kill himself.

Kill himself before something else killed him.

3

He thought he could do it. He pictured himself trying. Visualizing, he disconnected his thoughts from the emotions and imagined how he might do it. He couldn't see himself hanging. He had heard that men often voided their bowels when hanged, and the thought of the nurses finding him soiled was beyond repugnant to him. Overdose wasn't an option, since the pills were tightly controlled and he was watched. Though if he could get out of Hilltop, he thought he could gain access to a gun. He had hired a man in his garage, a man who still owed him a favor, and he thought he might be able to get a gun from that man. It fit better. He liked the idea of himself with a gun. It was powerful. He'd be like Charlton Heston without the gravelly accent.

The river was enticing to him, too. The thought of slipping below the water, feeling it close in all around him, wrapping him up, carrying him off. He had heard that drowning was painless. He thought he could see that one best of all. Simply step off the bridge.

When he was gone, then he could see what was on the other side.

Joel visualized his suicide until it became firm to him, real. He could do it. He could find it in himself, if it meant leaving this place. It was almost an exciting thought. A sort of queasily enticing thought. He could do it this afternoon if he wanted. His father had always told him that where there was a will, there was a way. His brutal, rigid, mean-spirited father, but apparently a wise enough man. Joel could be rid of this life and this god-awful retirement home by the afternoon, and never again look at the bed that had taken so much from him. Maybe Lucey would be waiting for him.

Lucey.

The thought of her stilled him. If she was waiting she'd berate him quite savagely for killing himself. The thought of his ghost getting a telling-off for bad behavior brought a grimace. He could see her now, her form ethereal, flowing, floating in the netherworld, her arms folded grumpily across her chest.

"What exactly is the meaning of this?" she'd ask, as she had asked so many times before when he'd shirked his responsibilities or mucked about with their daughter until her clothes were ruined.

His ghost would try not to look embarrassed, scuffing its transparent shoes on the floor of the beyond. He smiled a sad smile for the thought of her and her ghostly admonishing. He would wait on his decision. Killing himself could wait… a little while at least.

It wasn't very often that she'd taken him to task during their lives together. When he had spent Sundays watching football instead of playing with his grandchildren, or when he'd scowled at the young men who came calling for Eva, there had been a few tough words, but mostly things between them were kind and gentle and lovely. Some of that, he thought, was because the idea of disappointing her or letting her down in any way was anathema to him.

Instead Joel spent the day trying not to feel. As thought exercises go, it was surprisingly easy to him. He felt a void in his mind, an absence of something, an open yet painless wound. The more he thought about it, the more it felt like he might fall into that nothing and never come out.

He wondered if that was what had happened to Mighty Jim. Had he just wandered into a hole in his mind and never come out? It was a singularly terrifying thought. Worse than death actually. The indignity of it. The terrible fear that a tiny part of his mind might survive in that hole, and never know its way back out. A prisoner in his own body. More alone than ever before.

Joel pulled back from the brink of nothingness and watched television in silence instead. It was a game show he turned on. One he had seen before. He didn't care. He sat there ignoring the empty bed and his own feelings until it was time to sleep again.

"I'll miss you, Mr. Miller," Joel eventually whispered into the black room as he turned out the light.

Sleep wasn't easy coming. Instead Joel slept in fits and starts, punctuated by long stretches of wakefulness in which his mind wandered back to the night before. The thick, meaty hands of the nurses crushing the tiny, unresponsive body of Mr. Miller. The give in the bed as the corpse bounced up and down under the force of their efforts to save his life. He wondered, idly, at half past four in the morning as he stared at the vacant bed, if they hadn't broken any of old Mr. Miller's ribs in their efforts to save him. When the day dawned again Joel's mood had blackened through the night, and he found himself thinking about killing himself again.

The ease of it, the convenience, the finality. He wondered

if, when the time came, he would have the strength to do it. He thought about Mighty Jim, and his plodding descent into senility, and decided he would.

"Are you okay, Joel?" Nurse Liam asked as he brought Joel's pills in their little cup that morning.

"I'm fine."

"You don't seem fine."

"Psychologist now, too?" Joel asked.

"It must be hard for you, especially considering—"

"Don't you have somewhere else to be?" Joel cut him off.

The last thing he needed was Nurse Liam skirting too close to the bone. Now he'd made the decision that he wanted to die, he had to guard the secret closely. They'd only try to stop him if they knew.

"Not at this exact moment, no. You're my priority, Joel. I just want you to know that there are people here for you. I'm sure this must be affecting you. Part of my job is to keep an eye on the mental health of residents here, too. You know that, right?"

"Why on earth would it be affecting me?" Joel asked, ignoring the question. Nurse Liam and his questions and his feelings and his gentle demeanor.

"Because Mr. Miller…"

"Was a corpse when he came in here," Joel barked. "Little less animated than the walking corpses we keep in this place, but a corpse nonetheless. A lousy conversationalist, a terrible football pundit and utterly useless at chess."

He regretted it as soon as he said it. Miller really had been a thoroughly agreeable chap, and Joel supposed that at some point he might have been a nice guy. Maybe even a decent chess player, but Joel was not about to be provoked into expressing his feelings by Nurse Liam and his soft-spoken sympathy.

"That's beneath you, Joel," Liam told him, with something that looked like it might be approaching anger.

Joel had never seen the young man angry. Impatient a time or two—a rare sight indeed—a little vexed by Mighty Jim's rambling insistence now and then, and stressed a few more times by the whirlwind comings and goings of The Rhino, but never angry.

Joel turned his face away and tried not to look embarrassed. He stared out the window and down the long drive to the gate. A slight breeze was moving the tops of the trees in the garden, swaying them ever so slightly. Nurse Liam tried to wait him out, but eventually gave up and left the room. Alone again, Joel decided to watch some television, flicking idly between the channels until he found a sports network showing repeats of classic fights. His mood black, his heart heavy and his patience thin, he couldn't find anything to hold his attention and decided instead to go back to sleep, lying on his side, staring over at the bed across the room.

When he woke sometime later, early afternoon he figured, Joel observed two significant changes. One was that someone had changed the sports to some ridiculous soap opera. The second was that at the head of the bed across the room, there now stood a tall hat stand, populated entirely by scarves, at least fifteen in all. There was a dark navy silk one with sky-blue swirls, a linen bronze scarf with floral patterns, a woolen scarlet scarf, and a white-and-black polka-dotted one. The hat stand swirled in a riot of conflicting colors that dangled down toward the floor. Of their owner there was no sign. Joel regarded them suspiciously for a time before the racket of the soap opera, an old episode judging by the quality of the footage, interrupted his thoughts. He reached for the remote control to switch the channel, only to find that it wasn't on his bedside stand where it had lived for the last three years.

Grumbling, Joel hauled himself from the bed and found it precisely where he feared he might. On the bed across the room. The sheets were a touch unkempt, as though someone had been lying on them; the owner of the scarves, Joel surmised.

He checked the wall clock to discover it was past three o'clock. He had slept for nearly six hours, catching up on his restless night the night before no doubt, and in the meantime, an interloper had sneakily arrived. As he climbed back into his bed, changing the television station on his way, there came a loud guffaw of laughter from the room next door, followed by the sounds of many voices all at once. He recognized Nurse Liam's good humor among the laughers, and Una's genteel chuckle; several others were unrecognizable, but louder than them all was a man's deep and booming laugh. It was a reverberating baritone, a laugh of comradely friendship, and it had no place in Hilltop, not at such a sensitive time anyway. Joel knew it for the laugh of the interloper. He didn't know how he knew; he just knew.

It would be his luck to get trapped in the same room as that laugh.

Joel settled back into his bed to watch the sports channels and placed the remote control on his bedside stand, where it rightly belonged, wondering whether or not he could get away with chaining it to his side of the room, and set to waiting for the newcomer. He tried to listen to the conversations coming from the room next door, but it was garbled and unintelligible to his admittedly less than perfect ears. From what he could hear, though, it sounded good-natured, friendly even. He maneuvered himself in the bed, leaning out the side toward the open door.

Unfortunately for Joel, he greatly overestimated his own dexterity and began to slip from the bed. He reached out for balance, his arse sliding out from under his sheets, all thoughts of the interloper vanishing as he desperately tried to keep himself from spilling onto the floor. His arms windmilling to find purchase on anything that would steady him, he knocked over his bedside stand, only righting himself when he managed to catch the frame of the bed.

The stand going down had also taken with it the remote, his unfinished tea from the morning, his glass of water for his pills and a framed photograph of Lucey, which all smashed on the floor. The crash alerted the gaggle next door, and the silence in its immediate aftermath was followed by the sound of them rushing into his room. Joel righted himself in the bed and adjusted his pajamas and covers before they could get in to him, trying to look as nonchalant as possible. His dignity reflected in his cool demeanor.

"Everything okay there, Joel?" Liam asked as he bustled over to Joel, fussing at the blankets and checking over him for injuries.

"I'm perfectly fine, thank you."

"What happened?" Una asked, regarding the smashed glass and cup and the spilled liquid.

"Nothing," Joel replied, before realizing how appallingly stupid that sounded. Too late to back out, he decided to stick with it.

"Nothing?" Liam asked skeptically.

The interloper looked like he was trying to stifle a laugh. Joel turned to him coldly.

"Something amusing?" he asked.

"Nothing," the interloper replied, almost giggling.

Una suppressed a smile; even Liam looked like he might giggle. Joel clenched his jaw and fixed the interloper with a steady look of disdain. He wasn't a tall man, nor was he particularly short. Average, and yet not average-looking. He had aged well; his face was lined and wrinkled like every other resident of Hilltop, but there was a youthfulness about him, a certain quality of energy and vitality that seemed to make a lie of all the wrinkles. His gray hair was still somehow shot with streaks of dark brown, and it was wavy, almost girlishly long, swirling down around his ears and the nape of his neck. He was, in truth, a handsome sort of fellow. His suit was obviously old and of poor quality but clean, complete with waistcoat that housed a small pocket watch. The word *popinjay* was the first to spring to Joel's mind, and he said so:

"Popinjay."

"No, sir," the interloper replied. "I am Frank de Selby." He paused after he said it, and then added: "Yes. *The* Frank de Selby."

He stood there waiting, as if for applause. Una beamed at him encouragingly, and Liam smiled tolerantly. Joel withered him with another look, but if de Selby noticed the disdain he paid it no mind; instead he continued to wait for the ovation he apparently thought he deserved. Joel wondered how much of this lunatic's brain had gone missing on him. His moment, however, was ruined by the timely arrival of The Rhino.

"Mr. Adams?" she enquired, no nonsense, as she approached de Selby.

De Selby coughed, embarrassed.

"Yes, well…de Selby is my stage name. Yes. I am Frank Adams." He offered his hand.

Joel snorted his laughter at the popinjay. De Selby indeed. What an ass.

Frank's discomfort lasted but a moment, and suddenly he was back into his dash and charm. He beamed a huge smile at The Rhino and kissed the back of her hand as she took his to shake, and extended one leg to bow with a flourish. The Rhino cocked an eyebrow at him.

"I take it the belongings in the hallway outside are yours?"

she asked, ignoring the kiss and the popinjay and his stupid bow. She didn't wait for de Selby or Adams or whatever he was called to answer. "If you need a hand carrying them, ask Nurse Dwight to help you with them. Nurse Dwight, see to this spillage, please, and then assist Mr. Adams with his belongings, and tuck in your shirt." She demanded impeccable appearance from all of her staff.

Not bothering to listen for an answer to that either, she departed as abruptly as she'd arrived.

"Well," Adams noted, with a raised eyebrow, "she is going to be tremendous fun."

Then he winked impudently at Una, who laughed at his flirtation.

Joel stared balefully at him again. No one had consulted him. Again. No one had asked his opinion, or sought his permission or even given him a moment's warning. Again. Just as they had after Lucey had died, they shoved the next person on the waiting list into his room without so much as a by your leave, and of all the people, this eccentric upstart with his fifteen scarves and his winking at Una and his soap opera nonsense. It was a complete insult to Joel. But before he could voice his opposition, Adams bent over—still surprisingly limber for an old one—and picked up the photograph of Lucey. Pulling an embroidered handkerchief from his pocket, he gently cleaned the frame of the spilled tea and water and polished the glass on the front, and tenderly placed it on the shelf above the bed. Even his handkerchief was over the top.

"Your wife?" he asked Joel without a trace of his impudent, irritating smile.

"She was."

The past tense was obvious and awful.

"Sorry for your loss," Adams told him, with complete sincerity.

Joel scanned the man's face for signs of mockery or cruelty. There was none. He was taken aback. There was sentimentality in the act, and genuine feeling. It felt alien to Joel. Perhaps the interloper could be tolerated. The soap operas could not be, though. There would have to be a discussion about that.

"Now, Nurse Dwight, be a doll and fetch my things. I believe Ms. Clarke here is trying to get me on my own for a minute," Adams told Nurse Liam, lapsing back into his foppishness. "We'll draw a curtain so you don't have to watch, old boy," he finished, turning to Joel with a long wink.

"Oh, you're just terrible," Una laughed again.

Just terrible. Joel agreed with her.

4

The Terrible Frank Adams—Joel was determined not to refer to the man as de Selby—turned out to be a talker. After two years of sharing a room with the most agreeable of roommates, Joel suddenly found himself being bombarded with questions.

"What do you do for fun, Joel?" he asked jovially, after they had been formally introduced in the common room at dinner.

"Fun? Here?" Joel asked incredulously. "This is a nursing home. We don't do fun."

"Everyone else seems to be enjoying themselves," Adams replied, glancing around the room where the residents and nurses chatted amiably among themselves. Mighty Jim was wolfing down his dinner, pausing every now and then to smile broadly at no one in particular. Some of the residents had finished their meals and were playing cards. Some of them read in the old but comfortable armchairs that were scattered about the room.

"Everyone else is kidding themselves," Joel told him, in no mood to be corrected.

"Ever get any of those youth groups coming in singing? Nothing like a good singsong."

"Yes. We get them. Church groups with their phony smiles."

"Don't like the church, Joel?"

"Never mind," Joel told him, remembering years of attending mass with his father. Obligatory. Followed by years of practically forcing Lucey to attend with him. Wasted years.

"Anything you do like, Joel?" Adams asked him with a smile.

"I like eating in peace," Joel replied, returning to his dinner with determination.

Later that evening, sitting in front of the television in their room, Frank started again.

"Sports, Joel. You like sports, surely? There was sports on when I arrived this morning."

Joel sighed and tried to ignore him.

"Me, I like dramas."

"I don't care."

"Dabbled a little in television. Never got to play the parts I wanted. Got a few minor roles in the movies. Went close a couple of times. Ended up on a soap opera."

"Figures," Joel grunted.

"Ever watch *Glory Days*?"

Joel clenched his jaw. Lucey had loved *Glory Days*. Watched it religiously every night. He had often watched it with her, though more often than not, he simply read while she watched. He liked just being in the same room as her. They had sat in their living room, him reading a book, little Eva lying flat on her stomach, Lucey with her tea and her smile, and *Glory Days* had played for them. The Terrible Frank Adams had probably graced their living room. He remembered those times, when Eva was his little girl and Lucey his wife and felt a pang in his stomach. Better times. He glanced at Lucey's photo sitting on the bedside stand again. She would probably have enjoyed Adams's relentless chattering. She probably would have asked him all kinds of questions about being on television, about the show, about what the actors were really like.

"Don't watch soaps," he said, instead of telling Adams any of that.

"Not much of a fan myself. Classically trained. Don't mean to be snob about it, but give me hard drama every day of the week."

"You were watching them this afternoon," Joel corrected him.

"Reliving the glory days," Adams told him, with a grin. "If you'll pardon the pun."

Joel tried not to smile, but failed.

There was something about the chatter of the man. On the surface it seemed inane, pointless, but there was a quality about Adams that seemed to suggest he was too smart for this insipid small talk. He seemed, to Joel, to be laughing at a joke no one else could see, and all the talking, all the probing, all the questions were a means to an end. It made him interesting in a way that Joel couldn't quite put his finger on.

"I like football," Joel told him eventually.

"Me, too. Tremendous drama in football."

Drama? In football? Nonsense.

"It's not about the drama, Adams," Joel corrected him. "It's about the athleticism."

"Ah, stop, who do you think you're kidding with that? Do you watch track and field events?"

"What? No…" Too late Joel spotted the trap he'd fallen into.

"See. If it was about the athleticism you'd be all over that like a rash, but it's not. Oh, it might be a part of it, sure, but it's the drama that makes sports interesting. The ups and downs of it all, the great reversal, the inspiring underdogs, the swagger of the champions…"

As he spoke his voice rose and fell, a storyteller's voice with the delivery of a performer.

"…There's villains and good guys, and sometimes the heroes win and we love it, and sometimes they lose and we love that too, even if we're heartbroken for them. Tremendous drama. Better than any soap opera."

"But it's mostly about the athleticism," Joel told him obstinately.

"Good God," Adams groaned in despair. "Are you going to turn out to be one of those people who'll tell me it's not raining while we're outside getting soaking wet?"

"What? No."

"Sure you are. That's what it is, isn't it? You're a contrarian. If everyone else says black, you'll say white."

"Don't be ridiculous," Joel spluttered.

"Oh yes. I know your type. Sinatra? Good or bad?"

"A gangster."

"I'm not asking about his personal life. A good singer or a bad singer?"

"Good," Joel told him from between clenched teeth.

"Ha! You wanted to say bad, but then you'd prove my point, and you're so contrary that you couldn't even agree with yourself, so you said good."

"Are you this annoying everywhere you go?" Joel asked him, feeling his irritation rising.

"Are you this cranky everywhere you go?"

"I don't go anywhere. So there."

"So if you don't go anywhere, and you're always this cranky here, I can logically declare that you are this cranky everywhere you go."

Joel turned to shoot an angry retort at his new roommate and realized the man was deliberately goading him, with a great big grin on his face. He had been winding Joel up, and enjoying every second of it. Someone had once told Joel that arguing with some people was like wrestling with a pig; after a while you realize that the pig is enjoying it. Instead of biting back, Joel shifted to face the television again and turned up the volume.

"Oh, don't be like that," Adams told him, laughing to himself.

Joel raised the volume a little higher. If it bothered Adams, he didn't let on but chuckled to himself and picked up his book. It was an ancient old thing with a battered cover, something pretentious and over the top, Joel assumed. Just like the man reading it.

Joel woke the following morning as Nurse Liam was delivering Adams's breakfast. It was the first morning in three years that he'd woken up without silence all around him. His first reaction was to be irritated by the presence of the interloper, but the feeling was immediately followed by something else.

It was relief. Joel felt relieved. The feeling irritated him.

"Loud enough, aren't you?" he asked of Adams and Liam.

"Pfffft. You're one to talk. Snored all night like a fella sawing logs."

"I do not snore," Joel told him indignantly.

"Clearing your throat for eight hours, then? It's a good thing I don't need much sleep."

"Well, what are you complaining for, then?"

"Merciful hour, is that Joel over there complaining about someone else complaining?"

"How dare you?" Joel asked without venom, adjusting himself in the bed. "A man I barely know."

"I've been here less than twenty-four hours, and I already feel like I've known you too long," Adams replied, also without venom.

Nurse Liam smiled at them both.

"What are you smiling at?" Joel growled.

Liam's smile just widened. Like Adams, he had a terrible habit of looking like he was in on a joke that no one else was.

"I'll get your breakfast, shall I, Joel?" he asked patiently.

Joel grimaced at the younger man, drawing yet another smile from him. He turned to Adams before he left.

"Anything for you, Mr. de Selby?"

Adams smiled a false smile and shook his head. It was a patently false smile, not like the day before where he was so cheery it was cloying. That at least had looked convincing. This smile was something else. It had a sickly quality to it.

It was a curious thing, the false smile. The sickliness of it. In less than a day Adams had shown himself to be easy in everyone's company. Even The Rhino, who was imposing, sometimes even terrifying, hadn't knocked a stir out of him, but there was something in the smile, something uneasy. Joel wondered at it.

"Don't like Nurse Liam?" he asked.

"Oh, I know you don't, Joel. You don't like anything," Adams replied drily.

"Hey. I was talking about you. I actually do like Nurse Liam."

"Really? Wow. You have a funny way of showing it."

"You wouldn't understand. You haven't been here long enough."

"I don't imagine many of the residents will be here for long enough," Adams replied with a laugh.

Joel didn't smile. He wasn't going to be here for too much longer. He wouldn't have to tolerate Adams and his questions and jokes. He was going to whatever was waiting for him when his life was over, and whatever it was, Joel reckoned it was better than here.

The comment was also too close to the reality of living in Hilltop. Death strolled about the place casually, picking whoever it chose, whenever it fancied. Not Joel. Joel would pick death before Death could pick him.

"Sorry," Adams said, the roguish look gone again. "I forgot about the last fella. Miller wasn't it? That was insensitive."

"Hmm. Sensitivity doesn't seem too high up on the priority list for a fella like you," Joel told him, as though Adams hadn't cleaned the photo of Lucey so delicately the day before.

"I am what I am, and what I am needs no excuses," Adams replied, and the twinkle was back in his eyes, the sardonic smile playing across his face again.

"Miller was a strange friend to have," Joel told him, though he didn't know why. "Never said a word. Didn't move, didn't laugh, didn't sing, didn't read pretentious books, didn't do anything. But there was a comfort to having him here. And now he's gone."

"And now you're stuck with me," Adams replied, smiling.

"I am. God help me."

Adams chuckled at that, and Joel found himself smiling slightly. There was another wave of relief, this one without the irritation. A pleasant feeling of camaraderie, something he hadn't had in a while. It was a good feeling, one he tried to hold on to. He couldn't. Joel couldn't even keep a good mood alive. He felt it slide off him. He hoped it didn't show on his face, the sliding off. He sat there with his grin fixed. If Adams noticed, he didn't mention it.

The next morning Adams was awake before him again. Sitting up in his bed, reading from his cache of pretentious books and loudly laughing to himself. This one was about

theater and Joel was convinced that the man was only reading it to be seen reading it. No one could possibly want to
read a book on theater.

He considered telling the popinjay, but before he had the
chance, a visitor arrived.

Una Clarke.

Once again she was well turned out, in a pink jacket over
a white blouse and black trousers. She always wore some of
what little jewelry she possessed even when she was just am-
bling about Hilltop, pearl earrings and various necklaces her
children and grandchildren had given her as gifts.

"Oh heavens, my dear," Adams cried, in his most performative voice. "But you cannot come in here when we're in
such a state of undress. We're positively unseemly, made all
the more so by your radiant presence."

"You old rogue, you." She smiled at him. She had seen the
flattery for what it was, but enjoyed the compliment nonetheless. "I just came in to see how you're both doing, and to
see what kind of mood Joel was in."

"The life and soul of the party has recently awakened, and
is already brimming over with good humor. He's scowled at
me twice and I think he farted."

Una reddened at the joke. She was terribly prudish that
way. Joel thought it was a sort of charming quality about her.

"I think that's more likely than him being in good humor."
She smiled.

The joke was made lightly, and Joel forced himself to smile
at it. The gall of her, accusing him of being without a sense
of humor. He bristled inside at the insult.

"Old Joel knows how to smile, my dear. He's just sparing
with his gifts is all," Adams told her with a grin.

"Did I hear rightly that you used to be on *Glory Days*,
Mr. de Selby?" she asked.

So this is why she came in, Joel thought wryly. To kiss up to the D–list TV star.

"Please, Una, Frank will do."

"And his name is Adams, not de Selby," Joel chimed in.

Rather than be outraged by the interruption, Adams leaned over in the bed, stuck his tongue out at Joel and blew a raspberry at him.

Joel spat out a laugh in spite of himself. It was a curious moment. He couldn't remember his last laugh.

"Old fart," Adams told him, before returning to Una. "Yes, my dear, I spent two years on the show as the local shopkeeper, Andrew Duggan. It was back in the eighties, I doubt a woman as young as yourself would remember so long ago."

"Oh, I remember all right. Now that you mention it, I think I see the resemblance. Why did you ever leave?"

"They killed me off. Heartlessly, ruthlessly, murdered me. Death by writing. They gave me a heart attack."

"Oh, what a shame."

"Not at all, my dear," he assured her. "I was done with it. I must admit to not being much of a soap opera fan. I wanted to get back to the boards. Where I absolutely excelled. To the theater. My true love."

"Besides yourself," Joel chimed in again. The conversation was happening whether he liked it or not. His room had been so bereft of it for so long, it was a curiosity to find that he was pleased to hear it again.

"Joel, don't be unkind," Una told him firmly.

He took it on the chin.

"Not at all, Una, not at all," Adams said, rescuing him. "I'm learning to take the rough with the smooth with Mr. Monroe over here. So far he's proving to be quite fun. And do you know, I think he likes me."

"I do not," Joel spluttered, caught off guard. Grudgingly,

for this was the only way that Joel Monroe would admit anything, he had to accept that Adams wasn't entirely wrong. He wasn't the most awful thing Joel had ever encountered.

Nurse Liam bustled back in to save Joel's blushes with breakfast and pills. Multivitamins, cod liver oil, beta blockers, thiazide diuretics. A cocktail provided by doctors over the course of years to stave off the stroke that everyone except Joel just knew was coming. Joel didn't even know what he was taking anymore. They simply dropped them off, and he shoveled them down.

"Now, Joel," Liam announced cheerily. Too cheerily for this hour of the morning. "Time for breakfast, and of course…"

Joel felt his hackles rise again.

"You can just leave them on the stand, please, Liam," he said, locking eyes with the young nurse.

"Mr. Monroe…"

Mr. Monroe again. Always bloody Mr. Monroe when there were orders to be given.

"I said leave them on the bloody stand, Liam," Joel barked.

"Joel…" Una began.

"No. Don't Joel me. I'll take the damn pills all right. But I'll take them when I want."

"I'd listen to him," Adams interjected. "Woke up on the wrong side of the bed this morning. Mind you, for Joel I think they're both the wrong sides."

Joking again. Bloody joker.

"Joel," Liam pleaded, "this isn't like you. You know the drill by now. I'd leave them with you, but I have to make sure you take the pills. This isn't optional. This is for your own good."

As if these people knew what was good for Joel Monroe.

"Well, it bloody well better get optional quick. I'm not having you, or this bloody joker over there telling me what to bloody do," he told them, thrusting his finger at each of them in turn.

"Mr. Monroe," Liam said, trying to take the firm route. Joel could see the hint of anger beginning to creep into his normally gentle eyes. "This isn't acceptable behavior. Now, please, take your pills and eat your breakfast."

Do this. Take this. Eat this. Sleep now. Wake now. Die now. Joel had had enough.

"I will in my fucking hole," he barked, surprised by his own use of profanity.

Una and Liam gasped. Adams laughed his deep, booming belly laugh. And then they stood and sat there locked in a standoff. It was too late to turn back now. Joel faced them all, refusing to budge. He could beat them by pure determination, by a pure gut refusal to bow to them, and just when he thought they might crack, she walked in.

The Rhino, bustling as she did in her matronly clothes, immaculately turned out, her hair pulled back into a severe bun.

"What's all the commotion in here?" she demanded.

Liam balked. Whatever personal row he might be having, he knew that no one wanted to be on the end of a blast from Mrs. Ryan, and he didn't want to leave Joel in it. Joel saw the hesitation and regretted his anger. Liam could have thrown him into the soup, but was now desperately trying to think of a way to keep Joel out of it. He decided to save him the bother.

"The commotion is," Joel replied, trying to mollify his tone in her terrifying presence, "that I'm sick to death of being told what to do all the damn time, so I'm not taking any of that medication until I decide I want to."

For such a diminutive little woman, her commanding presence was nothing short of incredible. Joel felt the worm of fear creep up in him.

"Mr. Monroe," she said, her voice low, calm and threatening. "You will take those pills and you will take them this instant, or shall I call your daughter?"

Call his daughter. Like he was some kind of errant child.

"I'll take them when I want," he replied, furrowing his brow and bracing himself for the backlash.

"Look," Adams interjected again, "I'm here, I'm not going anywhere. Say we just leave the pills here and I'll make sure he takes them."

"Stay out of this, Mr. Adams," The Rhino snapped. "Mr. Monroe, take those pills this instant or there will be hell to pay for this behavior."

There it was again, the kind of tone used to discipline a child, not a man of seventy-six years. He knew it too well. He had used that tone on Eva when she was supposed to clean her room, or do her homework or go to bed.

"Fuck off," he growled at her, shocking himself even as he said it.

"How dare you…" she began.

"No," Adams suddenly barked. "How dare you?"

The whole room turned to regard the little actor.

"How dare you talk down to the man like he's some kind of child?" Adams continued. "How dare you dismiss me as if I'm unworthy of common courtesy? You ought to be ashamed of yourself."

His tone was commanding, a challenge issued in defiant ringing tones, the voice of a performer of caliber. Joel was stunned by it. By his own challenge to her and by Adams's willingness to get himself involved. Una looked stunned by bloody everything.

"I can see," The Rhino announced calmly, "that putting the two of you in the same room may have been a mistake."

"Or maybe not," Adams declared dramatically. "Joel, my

old pal, would you be a dear and take those pills for me? I should hate it if you caught ill."

Joel turned to his new roommate in admiration. He was offering Joel a way out. He checked the man for signs of condescension; he saw none. Instead he saw the smile playing about the edge of Adams's lips and recognized the feigned outrage for what it was. He really was a joker.

"Certainly," Joel said eventually, as if the rest of the room didn't exist. "I'd do anything for you, Frank, my old friend."

He reached out and popped the pills into his mouth calmly and quietly. Then slowly and deliberately poured some milk into his tea. The Rhino regarded them both coldly, then swept from the room. Liam visibly relaxed, though he shook his head in disappointment at both of them before leaving with a sigh of what Joel assumed was relief.

He had been saved. Adams had done it, hiding a smile as he did. Joel felt an enormous surge of gratitude for the man, and a warmth for him that he thought he had forgotten somewhere along the road. He smiled broadly in spite of his shock, and the horror of his casual profanity. When he finally trusted himself to look up from his tea, Frank was grinning broadly at Una, who chuckled lightly despite herself.

"The two of you," she said to them both. "You're both just terrible."

5

"A bold move from Monroe," Frank told the room in a loud dramatic whisper, "scratching his nose like that, as if we can't all tell that he's secretly trying to pick it"

The handful of people sitting about the common room sniggered at Frank's running commentary. Joel just tried to ignore him. Over the first couple of weeks of Frank's life at Hilltop, Joel had found himself warming to the retired actor more and more. Ever since the incident with The Rhino, the two had found themselves in each other's company with increasing frequency.

Alarmingly for Joel, after what had seemed like an eternity of passing politeness to his fellow inmates and the staff, he found himself beginning to converse. Not the one-sided conversations with Mr. Miller, but really talking. Initially he found it difficult, but within a mere fortnight, Frank Adams had managed to worm his way into Joel's affection, so that the grim monotony of his existence seemed somehow more bearable. Joel didn't care to think too deeply about how long it had been, but he suspected that Lucey was the last person with whom he'd had a conversation that lasted longer than five minutes.

What Joel might have called routines, minimal as they were, were interrupted by Frank's presence and, with it, his constant energy. He moved a lot; his hands, his head, his shoulders, always moving, as though stuffed with a vigor that he couldn't contain. Joel found it both amusing and irritating in equal measure. He gesticulated when he spoke, he nodded animatedly during conversation, his shoulders rocked up and down every time he launched into that loud booming laugh of his. This energy somehow acted as a bulwark against Joel's cloud of despair and his suicidal thoughts. They stalked him still, creeping up on him in moments of quiet, forcing him to pine for the days when he was just plain old miserable instead of miserable with a terrifying desire to kill himself.

Adams somehow repelled that cloud that followed him, scattering it with a never-ending parade of stupid questions and inane jokes.

The jokes were another thing. They flowed through Frank as constant as his endless moving. They were usually dry, sardonic jokes, told in low tones as the two of them sat abed at night, watching football or reading, but Frank could tailor them to fit his audience, and so in Una's company they were much more socially acceptable, with just a hint of sauciness designed to make the prim and proper woman feel edgy. It was telling how quickly he could change shape to fit his crowd. Nurse Angelica hooted with laughter and then snorted every time Frank impersonated the other residents. Every time she snorted, it sent her into fresh gales of laughter, and she wasn't the only one. Frank's popularity was such that nurses, cleaning staff, even other patients' visitors were coming to visit Frank and Joel's shared bedroom. Joel found the irritation to be small; it was nice to see the spirits raised a little. He still found it hard to look at Nurse Angelica's hands however; they were still meaty, too meaty for the thin chest of Mr. Miller. He saw them crush that little chest every time she laid a tray down, or checked his pulse, or did anything really. He tried to put it behind him, but it was catching him unaware from time to time.

Joel shook his head to clear the thought and then placed his knight carefully.

"Monroe with a move so stupid that it must be a trap for the wily Mighty Jim to walk into," Frank told the room.

"A face that toils so close to stones is already a stone itself," Mighty Jim told Joel happily.

If Jim had been paying even the blindest bit of notice to Frank's commentating skills, he showed no sign, but continued to smile and carefully move his pieces from square to square, always obedient of the rules, but without any apparent forethought.

"The champion taunts his opponent with a piece of wisdom about stones that's clearly a reference to Mr. Monroe's testicles," Frank announced.

Someone started choking on their tea laughing. Joel tried to wither Frank with a look. His look. A personal trademark of Joel's, designed to flatten people who irritated him too much, or tried to talk to him when he wanted to be left alone. Because of Joel's dominating frame and generally cranky manner, most people stepped lightly around him when he shot them this patented look. Frank did not. He smiled ever broader, glad to be getting under Joel's skin.

"Mind your language," Joel growled at him.

"Monroe beginning to show signs of cracking under Mighty Jim's relentless mind games. He's determined to show the whole world how old and stodgy he is by objecting to the word *testicles*, as if old Mrs. Klein over there isn't giddy from hearing the word."

Mrs. Klein laughed and Una chuckled guiltily. The women of Hilltop certainly loved Frank. Una was by his side daily, the two of them slipping in and out of the room in the early mornings when Joel was just beginning to wake. She had often visited Joel before, and she continued to check on him, as though attending to a task, but Joel knew it was Frank she was there to see. He wasn't jealous exactly or, at least, he hoped he wasn't, but there was something about Una's relationship with their new resident that made him feel like an outsider, like *he* was the interloper.

The most surprising relationship that had failed to improve in the days since Frank had moved into Hilltop was that of him and Nurse Liam. Frank didn't crack jokes with him. If there was company present Frank was performing certainly, but when Nurse Liam pottered about the room on his own, or came and went with the tea or the drugs, Frank remained conspicuously silent. He averted his eyes, or returned to his reading, and on more than one occasion he simply pretended to be asleep. It was so unlike him to miss an opportunity to impress someone with his incessant babbling. It stuck with Joel. In that little mystery, Joel thought he could unlock the truth of Frank Adams.

The joking, the performances, the constant merriment and mocking humor, even the occasional self-deprecating comments all hid something. He wore his masks, and he slipped them on or off depending on where he was and whose company he was in. Joel watched and waited for the hints of the man under the masks, for there were many, and thought he saw the first signs of something else in the distant, almost cold attitude that his flamboyant friend displayed toward Nurse Liam.

"Ooooooooh," Frank told the room. "Mighty Jim looking to rub salt in Monroe's already exceptionally salty wounds with that maneuver."

Joel snapped out of it again to realize that Jim's bishop had moved in and effectively boxed his queen. Nowhere to go. It would be stalemate in five or six turns, depending on how Jim played it.

"Dammit, Jim," Joel grumbled.

"The workman of today works every day of his life at the same tasks," Mighty Jim told him cheerfully.

"And I think that's it, ladies and gentlemen, and Mr. Robins, of course," Frank told them. "Monroe looks ready to accept his inevitable and soul-crushing defeat. Withered once again by the most electrifying entertainer to ever grace Hilltop Nursing Home, and still undefeated champion of not losing but not winning either, Mighty Jim Lincoln!"

He brought his announcement to a rousing crescendo. There were tolerant smiles, and a scattering of slight applause. The effect was ruined somewhat by Mighty Jim's vacant, slightly confused look as if he had just noticed Frank for the first time.

"Just walk beside me," Mighty Jim told him.

"Absolutely agree, old chap," Frank replied solemnly.

Joel had had enough. He'd passed another hour; his time with Jim had served its purpose. Get the day out of the way, so that the evening time could get done quicker, and he could go back to bed, back to sleep.

His sleep, at least, wasn't populated by thoughts of killing himself. It remained untouched. That was perhaps the worst part of his sudden shift, the vividness of it all. Ever since he had first visualized it, Joel couldn't stop imagining it. Down by the river, one step over the edge, pulled away by the current. No more missing Lucey. No more taking his damn pills. No more being treated like a child. In his idle moments his brain found ways to think about how he might kill himself if he ever managed to get out of here.

"Where are you off to?" Frank asked as Joel turned for the door.

"Outside I think. Some fresh air."

He didn't wait for a reply. He knew Frank would follow him whether he waited or not. It just seemed to be in him to follow Joel wherever he went.

He walked toward the yard without any great sense of purpose. He had no pressing need to be there, just a sense that being there would be better than being inside, better than being in the company of Mighty Jim and the other residents, blissfully living out their remaining days in a purposeless haze of nothing. Behind him he could hear Frank following after with tremendous purpose.

"I'll come with you," his new friend told him.

"Why?" Joel asked. "There's no audience out here."

He said the words without any great malice, but recognized them all the same for what they were. Nasty and hurtful. He'd been a bit of both lately. Side effect of wanting to kill himself, he figured. It didn't take a genius to figure that out; he was a lonely, isolated, pointless old man who couldn't stop thinking about how he might just be done with it all. Something, he concluded, had grabbed a hold of him, and he didn't know how to shake it. Worse again, he didn't think he cared to. What would be the point?

"Audience of one was ever enough," Frank told him pompously as he fell into step beside Joel.

"Jesus, you never get enough of the performing, do you?" Joel asked him.

"Life is a cabaret, old chum," Frank replied airily.

Outside, the gardens of Hilltop reared up to intimidate. The main building was a large and sprawling thing, built a century or more before his time, and extended here and there over the intervening years. It rested on a small plateau midway up a tall hill, surrounded by gardens that dropped down from the front of the building and climbed up the rest of the hill behind it. A long winding driveway meandered from the home down to the tall iron gates at the foot of the hill. Through those gates was the outside world, but the rest of the property was ringed with massive trees that hid the elderly from society. Here and there little flower beds sat, well maintained by the grounds staff and several of the green-fingered residents of Hilltop's Gardening Club.

Joel had no interest in gardening. The small garden he and Lucey had kept had been tended by her careful ministrations and, in a fashion typical of her, was as lovely as it was wild-looking. After long days at the garage they owned, Joel would come home to find Lucey's hands dirty from soil and torn here and there from the prickling bushes and occasional stubborn weed. He had always thought there was a lovely symmetry to their hands, his stained with oil, hers with earth.

Their days together had always been full. He had worked and scrimped as a young man to put the money away, and when the time was right he had opened his own garage. She had been a teller at a bank—that was where he had met her for the first time, sitting behind her counter. He had been immediately fascinated by her and had found excuses to visit the bank. He made his deposits twice weekly instead of once, so that he might chance to be at her till again. He hadn't the charm or the wit to ask her for a date, but she knew regardless, and one day she casually dropped into conversation that she might be attending a dance.

Joel still remembered the evening of that dance. The scrubbing of his hands to get the grease and dirt off them. How she had held his scrubbed hands as they danced. He remembered with a grimace how she had stood there while he made a perfect fool of himself trying to summon the courage to ask her for a kiss. She knew what he was working toward but had cheerfully let him blunder his way through it. Joel had simply never been what anyone would have described as smooth.

After that their days were working and gardening and laughing and raising their daughter, and before he knew it, Joel had grown old with Lucey. They had grown old together. Then she had left him. The thought of it twisted his face bitterly in the weak morning sunshine.

He walked into the garden and aimlessly took up the small gravel path that ran by the trees at the farthest edge of the garden. Someone inside was watching the two of them, he thought; someone was always watching at Hilltop.

"Want to talk about it?" Frank asked.

"There's nothing to talk about," Joel told him. "I just fancied a walk."

"Nonsense. You don't fancy anything."

"Something to do, isn't it?"

"We could have played chess. That's something to do and you don't have to be outside in the cold."

Frank adjusted his scarf as he spoke. It was brisk for a day in May, but certainly not brisk enough for a scarf. Not that it mattered to Frank. He often wore a scarf even when in his pajamas and dressing gown. They were a part of his image, his brand.

"You didn't have to come," Joel replied.

"I thought you might want to talk about it."

He was dogged. Joel was obstinate. They walked in silence for a bit, but remaining quiet for any extended amount of time was beyond Frank Adams.

"I think Una fancies you," Frank said eventually.

"Shut up, Frank," Joel told him.

"No, really. I think she does."

"Yeah, well I think she fancies you. It's not me she's coming to see in the mornings."

"Good lord, no, you're at your very worst in the mornings. If it wasn't for my endless charm we'd have no visitors at all."

"I liked it fine enough when we didn't actually."

"Liar," Frank replied immediately.

There was a tone in his voice, something that lacked his usual merriment. Joel wanted to be indignant about being called a liar, but it was true. He knew it. He liked the people coming and going. Something about their presence distracted from whatever it was that had taken hold of him lately. He didn't want to like their presence; he wanted to be fine on his own, but there it was. Frank sensed something in the silence.

"Was she pals with your wife?" Frank asked tenderly. It was in his tone, something from inside him, from underneath the masks and the performance. It was "real Frank," if such a thing existed.

Joel scanned his new friend's face for a sign of mockery. He couldn't have borne mockery, not when discussing Lucey.

"Yes. She was," he said eventually. "Still wears some of the clothes that Lucey gave her. Hurts me to look at it sometimes."

"Might hurt more if she stopped," Frank told him astutely.

"It would," Joel replied, feeling a lump coming to his throat. He missed Lucey. He missed Miller. What a ridiculous thought. He missed Miller. A man who had never spoken a single word to him.

"It's just so fucking pointless without her," Joel snapped after a moment.

"What?" Frank asked, clearly surprised by the outburst and the vehemence behind it.

"I fucking hate it. Pardon my language. I hate the room without her. I hate seeing her clothes on someone else. I hate that we sold our home for this. Can you believe that? Sold our old home so that we could retire here? I hate that walking in the garden for half an hour is somehow part of my day. You want to know why it's part of my day, Frank?"

Joel's intensity levels had crept up now. It was the week before all over again, startling Una the way he had in the hallway. Frank didn't look startled, though. He looked excited.

"Tell me," he almost whispered.

"Because it kills half an hour. No other reason. That's all I've got without her. Time to waste and to throw away because what's the fucking alternative, pardon my language, but what the fuck is the alternative?"

"You could play chess against Jim," Frank told him, but Joel knew that statement for what it was, provocation. He wanted more. And fortunately for Frank, Joel was in no mood to stop.

"This is what I spent my working life building for, to be shunted off to the side, to be stuck playing chess with an imbecile, to have them nurses and The Rhino tell me when to eat, when to sleep, when to empty my bowels, when to take my damn pills. What am I taking the pills for anyway? To prolong my life? Why the fuck would I even want to? Pardon my language, but why the fuck would I want to prolong this fucking life?"

"Maybe you just have the wrong perspective—" Frank started.

"Shove your perspective up your arse, Mr. TV Star. I built a business, a home, a marriage, a family. For what? So I could end up here with some scarf-wearing smart arse, pardon my language, making jokes about my balls and sleeping in the bed that my wife used to sleep in. I once went to the bookies, on my own, met my colleagues, went to the beach with my wife. I did things. I went places. I didn't sit here rotting. I was in charge of my life, you know?"

He ran out of steam toward the end, and his near-shout trickled down into a murmur. He checked guiltily about the gardens for some sign of one of the nurses. He knew he was being watched after the outburst just a few days before, but there was no one in earshot.

"No one can hear you," Frank told him, reading his mind, but he also checked.

He looked a little shook himself, as though he hadn't just poked the bear for a response. Joel just ambled on, regretting the outburst now, regretting shouting and telling Frank all about how much he hated his life. He barely knew the man, knew almost nothing about him. Someone had told him once that a problem shared is a problem halved, but Joel trudged along the garden path feeling as though the burden had doubled. When they reached the small bench near the bottom of the garden, just alongside the long driveway to the gate, he sat himself down heavily and sighed.

"I want to tell you it'll get better," Frank told him. "But I don't think you'd believe me."

"And you'd be right. I'm sorry. I shouldn't have told you any of that. It's not your problem."

"A problem shared is a problem halved," Frank said, reading his mind again.

"Bullshit," Joel replied.

"Pardon your language," Frank finished for him.

Joel barked a short laugh at that. The mask was back on again, the little twinkle in the eye, the pretend person covering the real one.

"How come you hate Nurse Liam?" Joel asked. He wanted to change the subject. And to satisfy his curiosity.

He saw a flash of Frank as he was caught off guard by the question. Joel knew there was something he was missing, and that Nurse Liam was key, but the mask didn't stay slipped. Frank was a practiced hand at faking how he felt.

"You know yourself, old pal," Frank said casually, "these kids and their youthful exuberance. Gets under my skin."

"Now who's the liar?"

"I haven't the slightest idea what you're talking about," Frank said, dismissing him, but he was blushing.

"Yes, you do," Joel asserted, sensing a weakness. If conversation could be chess, he was boxing Frank in, cutting off his avenues of retreat.

"Playing the psychotherapist, are we? Going to ask me about my feelings? I thought better of you, old pal. I thought this mushy crap was beneath a man of your stature and dignity."

He was trying for casual offhandedness, but it wasn't working. What was more was that Joel sensed something else about Frank, a sort of duplicity. He had something he wanted to say. He just didn't want to say it.

"He's a nice young chap, you know, but stuffy maybe from time to time, but not a bad old sort," Joel continued, prodding.

"Wow. Coming from Joel Monroe, that's quite the compliment."

Frank had a sort of mocking smile on. A disconcerting sort of smile.

"The other inmates love him." Joel used the word *inmates* without even thinking about it.

"Well, why don't you all just get a room with him, then?"

"Go on, you may as well tell me. I'm not going to let it go. You got your kicks provoking me a little while ago. Turnabout's fair play. Why do you hate Nurse Liam so much?"

The mask slipped again; Frank's best efforts to preserve it had been insufficient from the moment the question caught him off guard, and it was pointless to try to pretend otherwise. Instead he sighed deeply and stared out the gate of the nursing home and into the quiet street outside.

"I don't hate Nurse Liam," Frank told him, in a voice that Joel had never heard before. A real Frank voice.

"You absolutely—" Joel tried to cut in.

"Let me finish, you vicious old bastard," Frank snapped.

It was one of only three times that Frank would ever call Joel vicious in either of their lives.

Joel wanted to be insulted by the word, but found a strange kind of attraction to it; there was an energy about the word *vicious* that he had been lacking in his life. He almost smiled at it, but instead just waited for Frank to finish. They sat in silence for a moment.

Joel watched Frank wrestle with something. He was practically squirming with the need to say something. Joel waited for it.

"I don't hate him," Frank said eventually, and then, more quietly, almost whispered, "I like him. I like him quite a bit actually."

It took Joel a long minute to realize the implications. The subdued tone, the grim, determined facial expression, the defiant tilt of the head. Frank was a homosexual. Joel didn't have anything particularly against gay people, but he had never had a gay friend. It was a very uncomfortable feeling. *This is what you get for asking fool questions*, he thought to himself through the shock.

The two of them continued to sit there staring straight ahead, out of the gate, at freedom denied.

"You're gay," Joel said eventually. It wasn't a particularly clever thing to say, nor was it in any way profound, but it was literally the only thing that Joel could think of.

"And you're a genius," Frank told him sarcastically, still staring straight ahead.

"You're not gay about me, are you?"

"No, you shriveled-up, cranky old bastard, I'm not *gay about you*."

"Been gay for long? Like, when did you decide?" Joel asked.

"For fuck sake," Frank muttered in exasperation. "You don't decide to be gay, you imbecile. You just are."

"Ever tried not being gay?" Joel asked. He regretted opening the line of questioning. He was massively uncomfortable. The mask of Frank de Selby, he decided, was better on than off.

"All my life," Frank replied seriously, and Joel felt like a proper fool.

Frank sat there staring straight ahead, peering through the bars on the giant iron gate at the front of Hilltop, his lips pursed, his face rigid. Joel thought he could see small tears forming in his eyes.

That was what the mask was for. Frank de Selby was a gay actor, a one-time minor television star, a flamboyant, carefree, debonair senior citizen. Frank Adams was a man who wished he wasn't gay. Joel had guessed at something in the man's personality, something hidden. He had not expected this.

"So you *really* don't hate Nurse Liam, then?" he asked finally.

Frank burst out laughing.

"No. I don't hate him. He reminds me of someone I knew once…" The laughing trailed off. "I'm sorry, I suppose I shouldn't have told you that. It's not something I tell people about."

"A problem shared and all that bullshit. Pardon my language."

Joel was trying to reassure Frank, but he knew it wasn't working; he knew Frank could sense his discomfort. He slipped his de Selby mask back on, and with a broad, forced grin he stood up and dusted off his trousers that didn't need dusting.

"I think that's a sufficient amount of time killed for me. I think I'll retire to the retirement home," he joked.

"Well, I've not finished my walk, if you want to…" It was a halfhearted effort to cover his uneasiness, and Frank sensed it for what it was.

"No, no, you go on ahead, roll that boulder up the hill. I'm going to watch some soaps."

With that he nodded once more and made his way back up the long driveway, head held high, chest out, performing the part of a man not even a small bit heartbroken and alone.

Joel felt like a fool and a coward. In Frank Adams there was a very lonely man, an isolated, vulnerable creature, just like himself, and in the moment that the man reached out, Joel had recoiled out of a sense of disquiet about the man's sexuality. Lucey would have berated him, but it was too late now. Frank was a shade more spritely than Joel and had covered half the length of the driveway in his long purposeful stride.

They were pathetic. Both of them. Joel hated how pathetic they were. Lonely and isolated and terrified. But underneath the contempt Joel felt something warm, something unexpected. He felt kinship. It had been so long he almost didn't recognize it for what it was. Without knowing how, without seeing it coming, Joel had bonded with Frank. He had seen the de Selby mask and the Adams underneath it, and he had felt something give in himself in the unloading of his own anger, then something else entirely in the unloading of Frank's guilt, and Joel realized that he had a friend. A new friend. At seventy-six he didn't think that was possible, but there it was. And he had driven that friend away by being a vicious bastard.

Joel sat on the bench at the bottom of the hill and let the

regret gnaw at him, even as he marveled at the idea that there was a part of him left that still knew what a friend looked like.

That evening, and for the first time since Frank had moved into Hilltop, he didn't eat his supper with Joel, preferring instead to sit at a table with Una, Mrs. Klein and Mighty Jim. Jim seemed to have finally become aware of Frank's existence and babbled at him incessantly; Frank nodded good-naturedly, though clearly not understanding, and cracked jokes to make the two women chuckle. Joel watched all of this from a table on his own across the room. He wore his best cranky face to discourage others from joining him, so that he might figure out how best to proceed with his new and faltering friendship.

It worked a treat; they all avoided the cranky face.

Nurse Liam watched from the door, his blue eyes scanning the room and noting Joel's isolation, Frank's decision not to eat with his roommate.

"Anything the matter?" he asked, approaching Joel and ignoring the look.

"Nothing at all," Joel lied.

He studied Nurse Liam a little more, noting that the young man was handsome in his own way. He wore his uniform well. He had a little pin on that Joel had never noticed before. Or if he did, he hadn't cared. The pin was in a rainbow.

Liam was gay, too. Joel had missed it.

"Should I be worried about you, Joel?" Liam asked earnestly.

"Absolutely not, and let's not start all that pill nonsense again. I'm taking the damn things, aren't I?" he said, to cover up his shock.

"It's not about the pills, Joel. It's about your mood. I just…"

Whatever he wanted to say trailed off in the face of Joel's flat, unfriendly, uncompromising stare. Joel hadn't time for this. He'd hurt his new friend, isolated him, and it was both ering him. Nurse Liam nodded after a moment.

"Please know that I'm here if you need to talk. What happened last week—"

"Happened and so be it," Joel cut him off. He was sick of thinking of the rough hands all over poor silent Mr. Miller.

Nurse Liam took the hint and moved off. Joel considered sitting at the table where Frank and the others sat, but he had little energy for dealing with Mighty Jim, or with whatever it was he felt for Una Clarke. Instead he took the small plastic cup of jelly he had been given with his dinner and walked over to Frank, placing it by his tray.

"Didn't fancy mine," Joel said gruffly.

"Awwww," said Mrs. Klein. "Isn't that nice?"

Joel found himself blushing a deep red. Frank, the real one hidden underneath the false, nodded at him, and Joel left.

He'd never given a man jelly before. In retrospect it seemed a somewhat ridiculous sort of apology for being heartless.

When Frank finally made his way to bed that evening he found Joel sitting up reading. He moved stiffly, almost formally. The fundamental change in him was apparent. Once he'd shown what was under the mask, he knew he could never get it back, and in his isolated vulnerability he tried to cover that with what he felt was left of his dignity. Joel felt tremendously sad for him. He recognized in Frank's behavior a mirror of his own. A cold aloofness that would do in place of feeling lonely. It wouldn't do, Joel decided, for them to continue like this, and to even the scales he decided to tell Frank.

"Frank?" he said quietly.

"Joel," Frank replied seriously.

"I have to tell you something."

"No, you don't. Look, earlier on, I shouldn't have—"

"No, you look, this is serious. I want to tell you, because I like you."

It occurred to him that what he was saying could be misconstrued, and he flushed with embarrassment. When Frank cocked an eyebrow at him, he blushed even deeper.

"Not like that," he assured his roommate. "Not in a gay way or anything."

"Jesus fucking Christ," Frank muttered.

"No, really. I need to tell someone."

The immensity of what he was about to say hung in the room between them, and Frank couldn't help but feel it. He sat down on the edge of his bed, slipping his shoes off with a grunt.

"Go on…"

Joel took a deep breath.

"I want to kill myself," he said.

It was a perfectly profound and deeply unsettling moment for them both. Joel had finally vocalized it, and in doing so confirmed to himself that he really wanted it. It wasn't an idle thought dredged up by the death of Mr. Miller and the continued mourning for his wife, but a concrete and real desire. He no longer wished to be alive. He wanted out. Frank sensed the gravity in it, the sincerity, the resolve of his new friend. He paused, his shoes still half off, and stared across at Joel.

Joel thought back to his imagined suicides. His hanging, or his overdose. Maybe Frank could help him with it. Whether he did or not, Joel desperately hoped that the other man recognized Joel's need to confide for what it was. He did like Frank. He didn't understand how it might be possible for him to like anyone, much less the eccentric that shared his room, but there it was. He liked him so he told him. To balance the scales.

Joel had exposed himself completely, and in that moment the awkwardness and discomfort between them vanished. The playing field was level, each man now as honest with the other about themselves as they possibly could be. Frank tried not to reel under the weight of the moment, tried not to blink as his friend held his breath waiting for a reply. One was required. He had to say something. Joel tensed.

"I think that's a wonderful idea," Frank told him.

For the second time that day Joel found himself at a loss for words.

"You what?" he asked flatly.

"I think it's a wonderful idea."

Joel hadn't known what to expect in reply to his simple ambition, but it certainly wasn't this.

"You do?" he asked, confused now.

"Absolutely. It's a powerful expression. You hate where you are, you want change, no one will let you change now, not in here, not in our circumstances, so why not? Take control. Master of your own destiny. Captain of your own soul and all that."

Joel sat back in his bed and pondered that. He found the thought exhilarating. It was the first time he had felt exhilarated in a great many years. His heart was pounding in his chest; he tingled at the thought. Master of his own destiny. It was an alien concept to a man who didn't know the four-digit code to get out of his own bedroom at night.

"How will you do it?"

Joel could hardly believe the conversation.

"I don't actually know," he confided guiltily. "Thought about hanging maybe? Feels wrong, though. Maybe I shoot myself?"

"Hanging? Lord, no. Did you know that you shit yourself when you do that?"

It was a thoroughly disgusting thought.

"What I'd really like is to go off the bridge, I think."

"Undignified," Frank told him.

"What? Why?"

"Man of your stature? An ignominious end, I think."

Joel didn't know what the word meant, but he knew he didn't want people to describe his death in long words he didn't understand the meaning of.

"I'll think of something," he said lamely, still reeling at how surreal the conversation had become.

"On the other hand..." Frank mused, continuing to undress for bed.

This would be bad, Joel thought, this is going to be the deflating part of the evening.

"Go on," he told Frank.

"You want to do this right? I mean, really want to?"

Joel looked across at Frank, lit only by the lamp that was attached over Joel's bed. In the dim light, his erstwhile morose friend looked energized, excited. He looked how Joel felt.

"I do, Frank. I really do."

"If you're going to do it, it has to be right."

"How do you mean *right*?"

"Like, not tacky, or classless. Not something undignified or messy. It has to be great."

"What do you mean *great*?" Joel had no idea where Frank was going with this.

"Don't slip off a bridge. It sends the wrong message."

"I'm sending a message?" Joel asked.

"Absolutely, you are," Frank told him. "You're making a statement. You're saying to the world, this is my choice. This is what I want, and I'll do it because you lot have been trying to tell me what to do for too damn long. Joel Monroe doesn't take orders from anyone. Joel Monroe will not do what he's told."

There was a passion in the speech, something alive and almost frantic about it.

"I will not do what I'm told," he murmured.

"It has to be profound, theatrical, wonderful, encapsulating. Something that will leave a mark. Something that will make them talk, and keep them talking."

Joel had never been a man for the limelight. He was practical, functional, pragmatic, but something about the idea of people talking about his death long after he was gone appealed to some dormant theatrical part of him.

"Like what?" he asked.

"Ye Gods, man," Frank said, aghast. "Will there ever be a more personal decision than this in your whole life?"

"I mean it's not that personal. I'll take suggestions is what I'm saying."

"Don't be daft," Frank told him crankily. "This has to be you. That's the whole point. It has to be all you, and only you."

"But I really liked the bridge idea…" Joel started.

"If you're going to end it, you better make it big. No slipping off bridges. It's undignified for men of our vintage. Go big or don't bother," Frank told him with a note of finality.

"You'll help, though, right?" Joel asked, suddenly feeling his isolation all over again. It felt right to tell Frank, somehow it felt as though the man ought to know, that he owed his new friend that. Joel realized with a start that this was the only person for whom this was true. After a paltry two weeks in the man's company, Frank had already claimed a place that Joel had left unoccupied since his wife died. There was no one else he would have dreamed of telling. It was a terrifying feeling.

"Of course I'll help," Frank told him loftily. "You haven't the imagination to pull this off without me. But, like I said, it has to be you."

"It has to be me," Joel confirmed, relieved to have his friend on board. Relieved to not be on his own.

He lay back on his bed, satisfied with himself. He would do it. He would make his final statement and exit the world on his terms.

"Thanks, Frank," he whispered as his friend climbed into bed.

"No," Frank replied. "Thank you."

Joel killed the light in the room and closed his eyes. It was soothing to know that he had a plan, soothing to have a purpose again in life. A statement, the only huge and profound statement he was ever likely to make to the world. Then he could go, and be damned with the consequences.

"Good night," he whispered to the other bed.

"Good night, my friend," the other bed whispered back.

6

Frank was writing in a moleskin notebook as Joel's eyes opened the following morning. Frank had an expression of deep concentration. Joel's sleepiness may have been affecting him, but in that moment he thought that Frank looked every inch the scholarly theatrical writer, with his knobby old hands sticking out of his overly fancy dressing gown and poised delicately over his notebook. Not even out of bed and the man already had a scarf fashionably wrapped around him. His eccentricity went all the way down into his bones.

"What are you writing about?" Joel asked him around a yawn.

"You," was the reply.

"Me? What on earth are you saying about me?"

"Don't get a big head or anything, but I want to document you. There's a play somewhere in this story. Maybe I'll come out of retirement to perform *The Outrageous End of Joel Monroe*."

"That's what you're calling it?"

"Working title," Frank told him, scribbling again.

"And you'll be playing me?" Joel asked.

"Who else?"

"Someone taller, for a start."

"Short jokes. I would have thought such things were beneath you. Not to worry, I'll perform on stilts, and stuff my shirt full of pillows to fill out that fat gut of yours."

Joel checked his perfectly normal-sized gut and scoffed. Perhaps he was a little soft around the middle, but "fat gut" seemed a stretch. He opened his mouth to object only to spot the small half smile that was quickly becoming Frank's trademark. He changed tack instead.

"Don't you think it's a little risky to be writing that stuff down? I don't want…"

He looked around conspiratorially before continuing.

"…I don't want Nurse Liam to find it. God forbid, he'd bring it straight to you-know-who."

"Don't be stupid," Frank told him dismissively. "It never mentions you. If they ask, I'm writing a play, and no one will be any the wiser."

"Don't let them see it, all the same," Joel insisted.

He had a vague sense of what he wanted from the end of his life, and the idea that The Rhino would discover his plan, and worse again, tell his daughter, wasn't part of how he saw his remaining days panning out.

"Any further thoughts? Regrets? Change of heart?" Frank asked.

"None," Joel told him firmly.

"Good, good," Frank replied, though his heart hardly seemed in it.

"Look, you don't have to be involved if you don't want to," Joel told him, trying to mask his disappointment.

"Pffft. If I wasn't, you'd probably only botch it, and then

I'd end up writing *The Outrageous Stupidity of Joel Monroe*, and surely everyone in here has seen that one before."

Joel pretended to be offended, but only to cover his smile. He had never thought of himself as a quick wit, but neither had he seen himself as some kind of slouch, until he met Frank Adams. Too quick by half.

"So," Frank continued, "you've had no inspirational ideas?"

"Nothing really. I mean, just some ground rules stuff."

"Like?"

"Like I don't want anyone else to get hurt."

"You're going to publicly kill yourself, Joel. I'm afraid not everyone is coming out of this without an emotional scar or two."

"I meant physically. No one gets out of anything without an emotional scar or two. Let them suck it up."

"Heartless, but direct," Frank said, making a note in the journal.

"Why are you writing that down?"

"Character notes for when I play you."

"I'm not heartless…"

"Okay, tiny shriveled black heart and direct. Noted. Continue."

Joel was nearly sure that Frank wasn't writing what he was pretending to write, but he craned his neck to get a look anyway. Frank just laughed at him.

"Well," Joel said, giving up, "I want it to say something about me and society."

"You mean your place in society?"

"Something like that."

"Give me an example."

"Maybe in my favorite football jersey, you know? That says that I cared about something, but it wasn't enough. Is that good?"

Frank buried his head in his hands.

"In a football jersey? You think you're making a profound statement if you kill yourself wearing your football jersey?"

"Well. Profound for me."

"People sleep in those, you know."

"So?"

"So they'll think you killed yourself in your pajamas, you dolt."

Joel recoiled. He definitely didn't want people to think he killed himself in his pajamas. He wore the pajamas too much. He wore them about the common room sometimes. They were starting to weigh on him, as if somehow they were linked to his increasing isolation and loneliness. No, he definitely didn't want to go in his pajamas.

"Maybe a smart suit, then. Like a very nifty one you'd see a movie star in."

"No one says nifty anymore."

"I do."

"You don't count."

"That's the problem, I think," Joel surmised.

"The suit thing isn't a statement, it's just saving the undertaker the job of picking out your clothes."

"I'll think about it," he told Frank.

"Do."

Joel pondered profundity for a few moments until his thoughts were scattered by the arrival of Nurse Liam.

"Morning, gents," he told them as he brought tea and pills. "What are we discussing this morning?"

Joel began to panic. What if he'd heard? What if he knew?

"I'm writing a play," Frank told him, cool as you like.

How readily and easily he lied. Joel would have been falling over his words, Frank sold them as genuine.

"Oh, interesting. Coming out of retirement, are you?" He

was behaving very calmly for someone who might have just overheard two old men plan a suicide.

"Considering it only," Frank told him with an easy smile.

They were the first easy words that Frank had given Liam. Joel marveled at him. He was either lying with his whole body, lying with his demeanor and his attitude, or the spell that Nurse Liam held over him was somehow broken. Joel watched Frank carefully, studying his face and his hands as he and Nurse Liam spoke to one another. Searching for a clue.

"What's the play about?" Liam asked as he placed the pills and tea and milk on the bedside table.

"It's about a cranky old bastard that no one likes," Frank told him. He didn't look at Liam as he spoke, but seemed to address a spot somewhere just over the tall nurse's head. That, of course, answered Joel's question. Frank could lie readily, but there was a tell. Small, not immediately noticeable, but there it was. His face gave away no other feelings regarding Nurse Liam, no hint of what emotional baggage he was carrying.

"Where on earth do you get your inspiration?" Liam asked sarcastically, his eyes flickering toward Joel.

"I'm sitting right here, you pair of insensitive asses," Joel barked, more to play his part than with any real malice.

"Oh, he's inspirational all right," Frank told Liam with a broad wink.

The wink also gave him away. Too broad, too performative, too de Selby, not enough Adams. His mannerisms, his body language, everything spoke of an easy comfort with the nurse that Joel now recognized as false. He admired the ability in his friend to simply turn it on and off at will, but felt a twang of pity for him, too. How would anyone ever know him? How would anyone ever know who Frank Adams was? It was no wonder he was so alone.

"Looking forward to the visit today, Joel?" Liam asked.

"Visit?" he asked, confused.

"Yeah. It's Sunday. Don't your daughter and grandkids come on Sundays?"

He had forgotten about that. He was so excited about getting on with the process of dying that he had completely lost track of what day of the week it was.

"One grandchild," he corrected Liam sourly.

"I thought you had two? A boy and a girl?"

"Only one comes. They take turns. Why should both of them have to suffer? That's probably why everyone begged off last week."

He knew he shouldn't blame them. He was hardly sterling company at the best of times, but he remembered holding them as small children, long before they had become the adults they were today. He remembered them loving him, playing in the small garden. He remembered their young laughs. How he had walked them through their small neighborhood, showing them off, delighted to be a grandfather, hoping to bump into Mr. McCarthy down the street so he could see how bright and clever they were.

What they had become was sullen and unresponsive. He supposed he should shoulder some of the blame for that one. He had withdrawn from them even as they had from him. He had done nothing to bridge the growing gap between them. He had Lucey do that for him. Joel ignored the look of pity on both Liam's and Frank's faces. For a moment he considered having another fight about pills, just to get rid of the pity faces, but he decided against it. He had bigger fish to fry now, and a purpose, and the fight just seemed like a waste of energy anyway.

"Well…" Liam said awkwardly. "If you need me, you know where I'll be."

He patted Frank on the arm companionably, and Joel saw

the other man's jaw tighten. His hands twitch slightly. Another tiny glimpse under the mask.

"Do you think he heard?" Joel asked after Liam had left.

"No. He'd be doing something about it if he did, but we'll have to be careful. No more talking about it here."

"Where then?"

"I don't know. The pub, I suppose. Somewhere in the city, away from here."

"In the city? Are you mad? I can't leave this place."

"Why not?" Frank asked incredulously.

The absurdity of what Joel was about to say struck him before he said it. The unfairness, the childishness, the wrongness of it. He said it anyway:

"I'm not allowed."

Frank gaped at him.

"Don't look at me like that," Joel snapped. "I had a fainting spell once."

He looked down at his lap, embarrassed. It wasn't a full lie. He had collapsed. Not fainted. And the collapse had been brought on by a TIA. The transient ischemic attack was the reason he wasn't allowed out. A warning sign, the doctors said, that he could have a stroke. It had been dubbed enough to get him locked up here. A TIA was almost always a precursor to a larger stroke. Hence the pills. The never-ending stream of damn pills.

"Eva decided that I wasn't to be let out without supervision," he almost whispered in mortification.

Frank gaped even harder.

Joel tried to remember that he had some dignity left and looked up from his lap, rather than staring at it like some scolded child. It was ridiculous, and he knew it was.

"Well," Frank said finally, "fuck that."

"Excuse me?"

"Fuck that. Out of the question. We're leaving here. Today."

"And how do you think we'll manage that exactly?"

"When your daughter gets here. Eva? Is it? When she gets here we'll get her to tell them that you're allowed to leave whenever you want, and if she doesn't, we walk out the damn gate like everyone else does. We're grown men, dammit. We'll do as we please."

The thought sent a little thrill of excitement through Joel that stayed with him all day. He dressed early in anticipation and began watching the long curving driveway for her car. Deciding it appeared unseemly, he shifted his focus to the Sunday football. His team won, and he felt excited for the first time in a long time for the arrival of his daughter.

When she finally arrived, she came wearing her Sunday best and her most forced smile. She wore that for him, not a nasty thing of faked camaraderie, but a brave face for the maelstrom she expected whenever she encountered her belligerent father. She planted a kiss on Joel's cheek. Her daughter, Lily, did the same, before she picked her mobile phone from her pocket and buried her consciousness in it.

"How are you, Dad?" Eva asked, fussing with the lapel of his jacket.

She was still so little to him, his imposing figure still towered over her. Her short-cut blond hair had been hastily tidied, her makeup hastily applied, and yet she still looked lovely. Motherhood had always agreed with her. She was slim, like her mother, with the same green eyes and a touch of something earthy about her. She had inherited few, if any, of her father's physical features, perhaps a bit of him in her cheeks and strong jawline, but had most certainly learned her stubbornness from him.

A willful child in her youth, she had often been in trouble, and every time that Joel was called to discipline her, it would come with a warning from Lucey. "Don't be too hard on her. She gets it from you."

Joel smiled at the memory. Eva was tough. She had raised the two children on her own, with minimal help after her waste-of-space of a husband had left them for a younger woman, who promptly left him for a younger man. Joel had been tremendously proud when Eva had sent him packing after he had tried to come crawling back, but the strength to stand on her own had come at a price. For several years she had no love life, no social life, no outlet until her children had turned into adults. When the recession bit, she had been left with almost nothing and, in her stubbornness, had refused to ask for help. By the time she had run out of options, she was so far in over her head that selling Joel's family home was the only way to get her out. Joel had never wanted for much, but he had never been a tremendously wealthy man either. It was a fair trade-off—their old family home for their daughter and grandkids. And truth be told he had once enjoyed living in Hilltop. He didn't regret it until she trapped him here.

The sale, however, had been the turning point for her, for which Joel was grateful. Since then things had been picking up. She had even met someone. Joel was pleased for her, even if he thought Tony was a gigantic ass of a man.

"Good now, love," he told her with a smile. "How's Tony?"

"He's fine. He was asking after you."

Joel was fairly certain he had not been.

"Oh yeah? Tell him to come up next time. I'd love to see him."

Joel would not love to see Tony.

Eva smiled at her father, surprised by his unusually pleasant demeanor.

"I heard about poor Mr. Miller," she told him sympathetically. "You must have been devastated?"

He could still see the tiny body rocking up and down as Angelica tried to beat the life back into it.

"It was his time, I suppose," Joel told her, nodding to reinforce his point, desperately trying not to think of the little skeleton in the bed, pulverized, its meager hold on life long gone. His ghost now wandering Hilltop like all the other ghosts.

"Just his time is all," Joel repeated casually.

Eva was looking at him in surprise; even Lily had put down her phone to examine him. This was not the same Grandpa Joel that she remembered from the last time it had been her turn to visit. Joel felt a wave of regret. He must have been ruder than he thought to startle them so much with a couple of soft words. He tried to think of something else to say. Nothing came, so he sat into the small armchair in the corner of the room and picked up his tea, just to have something to do.

The awkwardness descended on them, and Lily went back into her phone. Eva stood there looking at him.

Before it could get any worse, Frank sauntered in, fully dressed under his dressing gown and sporting a black and red scarf in twirling patterns.

"Well now," he said, turning his charm up to ten. "What on earth did you do to deserve so lovely a pair of visitors, Joel old boy?"

The tension in the room evaporated in his presence, his air of general calm dissipating it with ease. He smiled his old smile at them and extended a hand.

"Eva," Joel's daughter told him, returning the smile. "Eva Monroe."

"Monroe suggests that you're the daughter he told me so much about, but your beauty suggests that your mother must have dallied with the postman, since you couldn't possibly be this old creature's child."

It was his delivery that Joel reckoned he would never be

able to emulate. From anyone else this would have seemed smarmy, but his easiness and obvious charm defused the words, making them soft, lovely and funny. Eva laughed at him, and Lily put her phone down again.

"And who might you be?" Eva asked, almost mimicking Frank's grandiose tone.

"Frank de Selby," he told her, kissing her hand. Even his voice had changed, a warmth in it, a tone of confidence and friendliness. He sounded like a different person.

Lily stepped forward, to introduce herself. Joel was struck again by how adult she had become, and he felt his ancient-ness from his toes to the tips of his almost fully gray hair. She was twenty-two, tall, stylish, borderline overdressed, with the same dark brown hair that Joel used to have, and her grand-mother's wide toothy smile.

"Now you on the other hand," Frank began, appraising her, "have managed to inherit only the best parts of your grand-father, and have none of his obvious deficiencies."

"You think I look like Grandpa Joel?" Lily asked with a smile.

"Only the handsome parts of him, my dear," Frank replied, kissing her hand also.

It should have been cloying, it should have seemed false and perverse, it should have made them uncomfortable, and yet they were disarmed.

"Lily," Joel's granddaughter told him. "It's nice to meet you."

"And you my dear. I am the misfortune that's been as-signed to live in the same room as the snoring machine you call a grandfather."

"Well, that's nice," Eva said without thinking.

"Debatable," Joel told her.

"Nonsense. He's very fond of me deep down," Frank said.

They both looked skeptical.

"I was hoping," Frank continued, "to take him for a pint in the local bar hereabouts this evening, to see if some stout might mellow him in any way, shape or form, but he tells me that you are the gatekeeper for such things."

Eva looked taken off guard. The charm offensive Frank had planned might have worked on someone else, and it was clear that she was impressed with him, but Eva Monroe was a formidable woman, and all the charm in the world couldn't change her mind once she set it.

"I'm not so sure," she replied dubiously. "Liam tells me you've not been yourself lately, Dad, and I think he's a little worried. Mrs. Ryan said you had a shouting match with her last week."

There it was. Joel felt his excitement and optimism vanish as he realized he was to be punished for bad behavior.

"It was nothing," he protested. "Just a minor disagreement."

"Mrs. Clarke said she was becoming a little concerned, too. Though she did say that you had been in much better form lately."

"I'm fine, Eva," Joel told her. He tried to sound as reassuring as possible. He tried to sound reasonable. Calm. He tried, and failed.

"You don't seem it, Dad," she told him with a concerned look. "Is there something you want to talk about?"

Out of the corner of his eye he could see Frank wince, and retreat a step. He was a quick study. A quicker study than Joel's own daughter. He could see the signs of Joel's temper beginning to fray.

"I don't seem it, do I not?" he asked, with deceptive mildness. "Is my word that I'm fine not good enough?"

"It's not like that, Dad. I just want to know if something's wrong. Last time you were out and about you had a stroke in the middle of a pub. They all thought you had dropped dead, do you remember?"

How could he forget? It was highly embarrassing. Someone had started to try performing CPR without checking to see if he was actually breathing or not.

"It was only a tiny stroke, and I don't see how that's got anything to do with anything," he told her through clenched teeth. "The point is that I'm a grown man capable of making my own damn decisions, and you're treating me like a child."

Frank looked horrified at the words *tiny stroke*, but he tried to cover it up.

"You wouldn't take your pills last Monday and threw a temper tantrum," Eva told him, her cool begging to slip. "If you don't want to be treated like a child, try not acting like one."

"I will not be held prisoner in here..." Joel urged.

"Oh, don't be so dramatic. You're not a prisoner, Dad. For Christ's sake, this place is the lap of luxury!"

"Oh, it is, is it?" he asked, infuriated now. "Then why is there a combination lock on my door that I don't know the code to? Why am I locked in here at night? Why does that nurse have to force pills down my throat? Hmm? Lap of luxury, my arse."

"That's for your own safety and you know it."

"Safety? What exactly are these people trying to protect me from? What dreadful threat is waiting out in the hallways that a locked door is going to keep me safe from? Do they think a locked door can keep a stroke out?"

Eva stared at him furiously. She had no answer, not that it mattered. Joel knew he wasn't getting out. She simply wasn't going to allow it.

"How about I come up next week with Tony and we take you out for a bite to eat?" she asked, trying to modify her voice to sound more reasonable.

Dinner with Tony was not what Joel might have called a consolation. A chore, a punishment, an atonement, penance. These were all closer to the mark.

"Fine," Joel told her anyway, through clenched teeth. Maybe Frank wasn't kidding about trying to walk out the gate.

It was irrelevant anyway. If he could think of something clever and profound enough, he wouldn't even be alive next week. Even through his impotent fury there was a small thrill at the idea of taking a shortcut to life's exit. Freedom from this, the safety of a locked door at night and from the relentlessness of a daughter who trusted him not a jot.

He sulked in his chair. He knew it was sulking, and he knew it was unbecoming and that it played right into the idea that he was behaving like a child, but he didn't care. As he withdrew from the conversation, Frank filled the void with his gentle banter and considerate, polite questions.

"How did you meet Tony? Oh, very nice. What does he do for a living? How very interesting. Do you drive a nice car? Isn't that great. Is the neighborhood you live in nice? Well, how wonderful. Any plans for the summer?"

It was all so banal and pleasant. Eva was calming down, clearly grateful for the presence of the charming Mr. de Selby. He didn't stop at Eva either, but probed at Lily, too.

"How's university? Hmm, I'm sure. What did you study? Fascinating, absolutely fascinating. Where are the cool nightclubs these days? I see, I see."

She answered him with an interest that Joel found disconcerting. It was a little alarming for him to see how much his family clearly enjoyed the company of his new friend. They hadn't enjoyed a trip to Hilltop this much since Lucey was alive.

Eventually they left, after an excruciatingly long conversation with Frank during which Joel had to continue sulking, bidding their goodbyes with promises of a trip to a restaurant the following week. They were no sooner out the door when Frank was up and moving.

"Let's go, you can sulk later," he barked with urgency.

He was spry, moving quickly for a man who must have been in his early seventies, grabbing both of their coats as he headed for the hallway.

"Where are we going?" Joel asked as he followed.

"Out to dinner with your family," Frank told him.

7

"What?" Joel asked him, confused.

"Just shut up and follow my lead."

Frank stepped behind one of the doors midway down the corridor and, poking his head out, checked for sentries. Joel stepped in behind him. There was a furtiveness to Frank's movements that was almost alarming.

"What are we doing?" Joel asked in a whisper.

"We need to get out the front door without them seeing our coats," Frank told him in a low voice.

"Why?"

"We just do. Can you shut up for a minute?"

Down the corridor one of the nurses crossed from the main reception into the common room, and as soon as she passed from sight, Frank was moving again, down past the reception in a brisk walk with Joel stepping guiltily behind him.

"Can you try to look more relaxed, please?" Frank asked him in exasperation.

"I'm not a retired professional liar," Joel replied irritably.

They stopped just short of the reception, located in a recess a mere ten feet from the front door. Frank checked around the corner. Joel watched behind them.

Fishing in his pocket, Frank produced a mobile phone and his fingers flicked over the touch screen with a familiarity that Joel found surprising. He pressed the phone to his ear. Around the corner, the telephone in the main reception rang, and as it did, Frank grabbed a startled Joel and hauled him along on quick, quiet feet.

At the reception, Angelica stood from her seat and turned to answer the phone behind her. She missed the two elderly men sweeping past her and out the front door.

"Hello?" she said into the phone.

Frank clicked off the mobile as they stepped into the afternoon sunshine looking very smug and pleased with himself.

The theatrics were probably unnecessary, the secrecy irrelevant, but Frank put such gusto into it that Joel found himself carried along by the enthusiasm. He checked both sides as they darted out the door; in fact he was so busy looking side to side that he almost plowed into Una Clarke, who had materialized from thin air and startled both of them.

"Hello, gents," she said pleasantly.

Frank looked less smug but smiled at her, his best smile, aiming for relaxed and confident. Joel just stood there, looking guilty.

"Going somewhere?" she asked with a smile.

"Yes," Frank told her casually. "Joel's daughter has graciously invited us to dinner on this fine May Sunday."

"Mmm," Una said, a smile playing about the edges of her lips. "Do the staff know?"

"Not yet," Frank told her carefully. "But they will soon."

"Better get moving, then," Una said. "You don't want to be late for dinner." She was eying the coats in Frank's arms, one eyebrow raised slightly. She knew.

Frank nodded politely to her, while Joel grimaced, and the two made their way out into the garden.

"The front gate is that way, you know," Joel told Frank as they picked up the small gravel path that led to the back of the garden, up at the top of the hill behind the main house.

"We have a phone call to make first," Frank told him.

They picked a spot on a stone bench at the back of the garden, hidden from view of the house by the tall trees that circled the expansive property.

Frank cleared his throat. His face changed, his lips pinching as he got into character and dialed again.

"Yes, hello there. My name is Tony Patterson, I'm Eva Monroe's partner. Yes, very well, thank you. Oh good, that's wonderful. Is it possible for me to speak to the supervising nurse today?"

The voice coming out of his mouth was barely recognizable as Frank's. It could have been a different person. Joel looked at him in alarm when he asked for the supervisor. It might well have been The Rhino. He opened his mouth to protest, and Frank shushed him with a flapping hand.

"Mr. Dwight, how do you do? Tony Patterson here, Eva Monroe's partner. How are you this evening?" He paused and Joel could faintly hear Nurse Liam's voice as he replied. "Oh, delighted. That's great news. Eva was telling me that there was a bit of a row last Monday, and that Joel's spirits have been a little low lately." He paused again. "Mmm. Mmm-hmm. I see. Of course. We were discussing it on the phone just a moment ago, and we both think that Joel and his handsome friend Frank de Selby might benefit from joining us for dinner."

He actually called himself handsome. Joel stifled a laugh despite his nervousness.

"That's right. If you don't mind I'll pop over and collect him right now? Okay. Excellent. Not to worry. We'll have them back before night. I'll tell them to wait for us down at the gate. Okay, many thanks. Yes. Thank you. Bye bye."

Frank smiled triumphantly.

"Hard part done," Frank told him jubilantly.

"Keep your gay pants on," Joel replied, trying to smother his own exuberance. "How are we going to get Tony to come and collect us?"

"We're not," Frank told him, dialing again.

"Oh. Okay. We're not. Anytime you feel like letting me in on the scheme I'd love to hear all about it."

Frank's flair for the dramatic was showing. His face opened up into a mysterious smile. A smirk, actually.

Joel was nervous, all the way down to his toes. They'd duped the staff. Sure, Frank had made the phone call, but Joel was an accessory, and they'd used his daughter and her irritating boyfriend as pawns. It could yet go all wrong. Joel wasn't sure if he didn't want it to go all wrong. The practical man inside him abhorred the duplicity of the plan, and the fact that his daughter, stubborn and unrelenting as she was, had been somehow implicated didn't sit right with him.

A much louder internal voice overrode the first one. *Get out of here for a while*, it said.

"Good afternoon," Frank spoke into the phone. It was his own voice again, but with some added authority. "I need a car, but not just any car. I need a silver Primera. Do you have one? Excellent. I need a pickup at Hilltop Nursing Home. You know the one? Very good. Now this next bit is crucially important— when your driver gets here and buzzes at the front gate, I need him to tell the nurse that his name is Tony Patterson. Is that clear? Tony Patterson. No one gets paid unless Tony Patterson comes to collect. Excellent. I thank you."

He clicked off the phone call and looked at Joel with a bright, mischievous grin.

"Shall we go and wait for Tony?" Frank asked.

"Who did you phone?"

"Tony," he replied glibly.

"No, you didn't."

"I phoned a car company. Don't be such a Nervous Nelly all the time." Frank grinned at him mischievously.

Joel found himself grinning back, a bundle of excitement mixed with a tingling of fear. It had been one year and six months since he'd been outside without a chaperone or supervisor. One year and six months of being under the watchful eye of a pack of people who treated him like a child. There was no way he was stopping now.

"Let's go," he said, rising to his feet with purpose.

The two of them made their way back down the garden, this time taking up the main driveway toward the gate. They passed Una en route, and she smiled at them and shook her head. Joel made a mental note not to underestimate her again. She was sharper than ever he had realized. As they walked he kept expecting someone to shout at them. Nurse Liam or Angelica maybe, running out the door and calling them back with admonishing words and condescending tones, but no one came. All the way down the drive the two of them walked, grinning from ear to ear until they sat down on the bench at the front gate.

Joel hardly dared to speak even when the silver Primera rolled up to the gate and the driver leaned out and pressed the buzzer. He almost held his breath until the gate doors swung open and the car rolled in. Both he and Frank stood as the car pulled up alongside them.

"Stop looking around, you dolt, you're making us look guilty," Frank snapped.

"Well, we sort of are guilty," Joel hissed back as he opened the door.

"Well, try not to look like we are," Frank ordered him before sighing. "Amateurs. I hate amateurs."

They sat into the back with Joel staring directly forward, his false smile cramping his face.

"Just reverse out, will you?" Frank asked. "The last thing we need is them getting a look at that face you're pulling, old man."

The driver smiled at them in the rearview mirror. He couldn't have known what they were up to, but he knew shenanigans when he saw them.

"Mind if I crack a window?" Joel asked, now practically tingling with nerves and excitement.

"Be my guest," the driver told him.

Joel sat in the back of the car letting the mild May breeze ruffle his hair as they swept away from Hilltop and into the city.

8

On the busy street corner where their driver had let them out, Joel heaved a great sigh. The sidewalk was packed with people, busier than most Sundays he could remember. He found the crowds intimidating and oppressive. Frank, on the other hand, seemed to love it. He was shrugging his shoulders excitedly and rubbing his hands together. Joel guessed that most of the source of his anxiety was the fear of getting caught. Their alibi was tight, though what if Eva decided to go back to the nursing home for some reason? Or called to check in on him? Or wanted to have another chat about his changing mood?

He looked anxiously at Frank.

"Pint?" Frank asked.

"You buying?" he asked.

"Don't be ridiculous. The last time I had money was 1993, I think it was a Saturday, and I spent it all on cider."

"I paid for the cab," Joel complained.

"I arranged it, so we're even on that front."

"Fine," Joel grumbled, forgetting his anxiety in his irritation.

Money was a problem for Joel, not a significant one, but a problem nonetheless. Had been for some time. Owning the garage that he had worked in since childhood had been fulfilling in many ways. Financial reward was not one of them. Eva's wanton husband had ruined more than Joel's daughter's marriage; he had broken their entire family financially. Selling the house was the only means of addressing that. He didn't mind it really; he wanted the best for her, and a retirement in a home wasn't a jail sentence if Lucey was there. With Lucey, everything was glorious. Without her, everything was garbage.

He didn't regret their decision for a minute, but the idea of spending hours toiling and saving and pinching pennies, taking mediocre holidays and tightening his purse strings year on year to end up locked inside a bedroom at night with no more authority than a small child, rankled with him. He had envisioned a retirement with Lucey on a beach somewhere, or on a cruise ship. Not that he would ever get on board a cruise ship; it was too full of asinine morons and faith-healing believers. He also hated crowds. But they had been nice daydreams, payoff for a life of sacrifice. He fished around his pockets for his wallet.

"F—" he almost swore. "I mean, blast."

"Problem?"

"My cards are all back at Hilltop."

Frank treated him to a long unfriendly expression.

"Do you have cash?"

"Just the change that the taxi man gave us."

"How much?"

"Ten."

"That's enough for two anyway."

"Barely. How will we get home?"

"Ah," Frank exclaimed happily. "That's Future Frank and Joel's problem."

"Not exactly solid financial planning."

"Well, look where all your millions got you? We're standing on a street corner, and you've barely a penny to your name."

"That's barely a penny more than you have."

Frank shrugged.

"What do you fancy doing with your newfound freedom?" he asked Joel.

It struck Joel as something quite sad that for all his complaining about freedom, the second he had it he had no idea what to do with it. He looked blankly at Frank.

"See, this is your problem," Frank told him pompously as he began to walk, "your imagination is underutilized. It's been allowed to atrophy to the point of uselessness."

"Can you even hear yourself talk?" Joel asked, following.

"And of course your attitude stinks, but I suppose that's your lot in life."

"Where are you taking us?" Joel asked, rather than arguing.

"See, you're a glass half-empty kind of guy, my old flower," Frank continued as he moved. "You fail to see the opportunities."

"What opportunities?"

"There are certain things available to the fine men and women of our age that are denied to the younger generation. We're supposed to be a generation of thinkers, of innovators. Without the internet we relied on our wits and our imaginations to take us places, to find chances to take, to think—as they tell us in business—outside the box. Sadly for you, I'm concerned that you're unaware that there even *is* an outside the box, and so you never consider what things we might be denying ourselves, when we have a chance to do something we might fancy doing."

"Like?"

They rounded the corner at the end of a busy street, bringing the river into view just in time for Frank to point dramatically.

"Like that," he said gesturing at the castle. The old fortress sat on the riverbank overlooking the oldest quarter of the city. It was huge and dominated an entire bank of the river. Two bridges ran across it, heaving with traffic and propelling people in and out of the city.

An ancient reminder of what the city once was, flanked on all sides by modernity and progress, and yet the castle itself stood resolute against those changes. Proud. Strong. Respected. And absolutely packed with tourists. If there was one thing Joel disliked more than crowds of people, it was crowds of tourists.

"We're going to take the castle?"

"No, we have an access that the kids don't."

"Castles are denied to young people?" Joel asked, unimpressed.

"No, you bitter old goat," Frank told him witheringly. "Entry for OAPs—we old age pensioners—is free. We're going to go visit the castle. Won't that be nice?"

The last question he asked in the simpering voice used by some of the younger nurses at Hilltop. Used once and once only. After seeing Joel's reaction to the voice, it was seldom used a second time.

Joel shook his head at his friend as they made their way along the riverbank through the throngs of tourists taking photos of the river or the ancient old building or each other. Couples that walked arm in arm. Young and full of energy and enthusiasm for the years ahead of them. Not suicidal.

Joel's eyes strayed occasionally to the river and the bridges. To slip off and into the waters would be easy. So easy. Instead he walked alongside Frank, who positively beamed to be part of the crowd.

At the visitor's center entrance Joel somehow expected to be stopped. Irrationally he thought that maybe the staff might send him back to Hilltop, that they knew he was on the lam, and they would act on the nurses' behalf and send him packing, but in the outside world, beyond the tree-lined nursing home, no one seemed aware of the indignity of his living situation. The receptionist smiled at them and waved them through. Joel tried to pretend he had every right to be here. Frank sauntered casually. Frank did most things casually.

In the courtyard of the castle sat an array of old weaponry— canons, catapults, ballistae, as well as a score of attractions for visitors. A mock-up smithy and tannery, staffed by bored-looking students in costumes, rattling off their learned lines at the small huddles of interested guests.

Frank tsked at them as he walked by, shaking his head.

"No love for their art," Frank told Joel disappointedly,

"Well, would you love it if you had to do that all day?" Joel asked.

"I would, and I did."

"You did?"

"Worked here for several tourist seasons."

"When you were young?"

"Nope. About ten years ago, I'd say. I was younger, but I don't think any of those kids would have considered me young."

"Why? I thought all you actors were rich?"

"Exactly how many actors have you met, Joel?" Frank asked drily.

"Well, just you so far, but Lucey used to read about them all the time. She read the Sunday papers from cover to cover every week. Even the bloody financial pages. I just assumed when they give you a TV show you get to be a millionaire."

"Sadly not. I didn't do badly, did quite well for a time actually. Had a fancy little car. Used to drive it around London when I was on the West End."

"Let me guess, a convertible?"

"How did you know?"

"You're the type," Joel sighed.

If Frank took it for the dig it was intended to be, he showed no signs; if anything, he seemed to puff up at the idea of being the type.

"What happened?" Joel asked him.

"Runs out eventually. Get a little older, starts getting harder to get parts. Fall in love with the wrong boy, spend too much money, move out of the apartment you can't afford, take smaller and smaller roles. Before you know it you're an old man living in a nursing home paid for by the state sleeping next to the snoringest, crankiest donkey that ever wore human clothes."

He delivered his speech without even the faintest hint of regret. He mentioned his decline as if he had been talking about what he ate for lunch. With his hands stuffed in the pockets of his old suit and his longish hair he still managed to look quite grand, a stark contrast to his reality, but Joel guessed that was important to the man. Appearances had to mean something.

"Sad," Joel said out loud in summary of his thoughts.

"Not really," Frank disagreed. "Sometimes you're up, sometimes you're down. I enjoyed myself when I was on top, and now I'm down here with you peasants, I'm having a fine time of it, too."

He smiled as he spoke the words to take the sting away. Joel resisted the urge to cuff him across the back of the head.

"Aren't you ever sad that you let all that money go on nothing?"

"It wasn't on nothing. It was on a convertible and a self-ish young man and about fifty other things that I thoroughly enjoyed spending it on."

"But now you have to live in a nursing home," Joel told him, incredulous at the cavalier attitude.

"And aren't I having a wonderful time while I'm at it. Making new friends, listening to a wild animal snore all night long?"

They stood there in that moment, with Frank beaming at Joel as he rocked back and forth slightly on his heels, a man at ease, entirely comfortable with himself despite being practically destitute. Joel wanted to tell him he was a fool, but he couldn't think of an argument that could trump Frank's easy comfort at his situation. So he just gaped.

"By the way," Frank continued, "I'm hugely impressed that you managed to not even flinch when I mentioned falling in love with a boy. I was sure that one would rattle you."

Joel was surprised at himself for even missing it.

"You underestimate me," he lied, but gave it away by turning a bright shade of red and squirming on the spot.

"It's pretty up here, isn't it?" Frank rescued him as he wandered over toward the high wall that overlooked the river.

"I think the catapult looks nifty," Joel replied clumsily, unsure of himself, unsure of the protocol.

"It's not a catapult. It's a trebuchet," Frank insisted with exaggerated patience.

"I know that," Joel snapped at him, promising himself to look up the word *trebuchet* at the next available chance.

Frank just laughed at him.

"If you're worried about me because I'm broke, don't be. If you're horrified at me for wasting my money, don't be. I'm sure you were a proper bean counter when you were making your money, and the two of us ended up in the exact same place. Except I'm not constantly stressed about it. You should try it. It's fun. Just stop worrying about everything for five minutes and enjoy the feeling of being outside, of freedom to choose, the fresh air, all of it."

He gestured vaguely around him, at the walls of the castle and the sky above them, the excited babbling tourists posing for photos with one another, crowding the fake smith and photographing themselves with him. It all seemed to hum with a positivity that Joel was certain had abandoned Hilltop decades before. He smiled at it all, feeling the casual easiness of the people around him, an easiness he coveted but lacked. He smiled at Frank too, urging Joel to relax, to live a little.

"Now what would you like to do?" Frank asked eventually.

Joel looked about at the crowds of people and the bored-looking actors and the trebuchet.

The fake smith had a little printing machine with him, and he was churning out little coins. His very own personal mint. The coins looked like the shoddiest tin, and the printing machine was doing all the work so that the tiny pieces lacked any form of artistry, and yet the tourists and day visitors crowded the little hut and collected their pennies with pleased smiles, displaying them proudly to one another.

Such a tiny thing to be happy about. A cheap knockoff thing. A thing without skill or craft work to it. And yet, they all smiled as they received their toys from the "smith."

"I'd like to get one of them," he told Frank.

"What? One of the coins?"

One of the coins. As if owning that thing that made other people smile might somehow make Joel himself happy, to boot.

"Yes, please," Joel told him. "And then I want to go to the pub."

"An excellent choice," Frank told him. "Though I don't think they accept fake coins for pints."

The walk back into the city center from the castle was a study in theatricality by Frank de Selby. Even on a bustling street corner in a packed city center he performed for his crowd, his walk much more of a swagger than anything else, his scarf cast rakishly over his shoulder. He moved confidently, comfortably, as if all the world was his, and even though Joel knew that there was a part of this man that was broken and frail and vulnerable, he still believed the performance, and drew strength from it. What could be gained by worrying about Hilltop? Why should he worry? This was his life, his to control, and he would walk it every bit as coolly as Frank did. Feeling a surge of giddiness brought on by his newly discovered freedom, Joel powered up the street behind his friend, idly playing with his new coin as he turned it over in his fingers. So far it had failed to make him any happier.

They wound their way confidently down one long street, crossing over and turning down a narrower one before turning again onto yet a smaller street and taking the first available left. It was only when they ended up back on another wide busy main street that Joel realized Frank had no idea where he was going.

"Where on earth are you taking us?"

"I'm getting a feel for the place," Frank replied loftily.

"Get a feel quicker. I'm not built for swaggering around the town like some damn peacock."

Joel's exuberant sense of freedom was inhibited by his joints, which creaked and ached unfortunately.

"You have no sense of place, Joel. That's your problem."

"My first problem is that I don't even know what that means, and I'm not certain it means anything at all."

"Of course you don't, you have the soul of a potato."

Joel admitted to himself that his soul was more potato-like than he would have wished for it, but life's like that sometimes.

Eventually they wound up sitting at the bar of a small pokey pub midway up a small pokey alley off the main street. It was old; it must have been. The walls, in dire need of a lick of paint, were still stained with cigarette smoke, and the tiny windows offered little in the way of natural light. The low ceiling, with its thick beams, seemed within easy touching distance for Joel, less so for Frank. Other than its smoky walls, the place was in good nick, tidy and clean. The barman was young, though not insultingly so.

Joel had never been much of a drinker. He had enjoyed a beer or two at home while watching football, with the occasional drop of whiskey when the mood took him. He had nothing against the drink, but had seen its grip on others, seen the effect of that viselike hold on employees and friends and their families, and he had swerved to avoid such a trap. Every time he had indulged he had found Lucey a more than enthusiastic supporter. When Eva was still young Lucey had practically pushed him out the door on Friday nights to have a drink with friends. He would, at her encouragement, head off to the local bar, picking up a neighbor or two as he walked. They were easy with him, and he with them. Friendly, but not friends. Enjoyable enough company, but temporary. It wasn't until after she had died that Joel realized that, all those years ago, she had been trying to make friends for him. He had once thought her enthusiasm for his rare drink was because she liked having some bonding time with their small daughter, but as the years passed he concluded it was because his wife was worried that *he* wasn't having any fun. What Lucey had missed was that he was having all the fun he wanted. The terrible lack in his life was that he didn't want more. He had never succumbed to fun or to booze.

He grimaced at the thought as he played with his coin, and then grimaced again when Frank stuck a finger into his ribs.

"What?" he snapped irritably.

"The man asked you a question."

Joel looked embarrassingly at the barman.

"Two pints of stout, please," he told him and sat himself down to prop up the bar.

"Senior moment?" the young barman asked impishly.

It was never intended to be anything more than playful ribbing, the kind of casual barroom banter served up by impudent barmen all over the globe, but Joel found it insulting.

"Ever had your teeth knocked out by a seventy-six-year-old?" Joel asked in a deceptively pleasant voice, placing his solitary note and his coin on the countertop before him.

"Sorry, we don't accept those here," the young barman joked nervously.

Joel put on his trademark "look."

"Merciful hour," Frank grumbled as he took his seat. "Do you practice that look in the mirror?"

"No. We don't all love mirrors as much as you do."

The barman looked from one to the other before shooting Frank a look of sympathy.

Senior moment indeed.

No respect for his elders, that was that kid's problem.

"So now we can get down to brass tacks," Frank said.

"Think it's safe to talk about it here?" Joel asked. Suicide was a sensitive topic.

"Have you always been such a Nervous Nelly?"

"I'm not a Nervous Nelly," Joel objected. "I'm just not as

reckless as you are. Every now and then it pays to think ahead, you donkey."

"Donkey?"

"Mule. Ass. You," Joel told him.

Frank smiled blandly at his friend as the pints of stout were delivered, then licked his lips in anticipation.

Joel understood his eagerness. The pint was pure freedom. No matter how it tasted.

"To your perfectly timely death," Frank proposed grandiosely, because grandiosely was how he did most things.

"Good health to you," Joel countered.

It had been a long time since he'd had a pint, and he was surprised to discover he still enjoyed the taste of it, the thick creamy head coming away on his upper lip so that he had to scrub it away with the back of his hand. He knew that it didn't really matter if it had been the world's worst pint; he wasn't tasting the beer, it was something else. The sitting at the bar with his friend, sipping his pint on his own time. Here no one would tell him what he could or couldn't do, and the utter pointlessness of his existence could be forgotten in amiable conversation and the thin buzz he knew he'd have after he'd finished his pint.

"So, you can see my point about the football jersey, right? It's a dreadful idea," Frank told him.

"I don't see why."

"It lacks class and dignity."

"You think there's a classy way for me to kill myself?"

"Now you're being deliberately obtuse. I'm saying that your death should be a statement. A statement about your life. When we die, the people we leave behind talk about all the various things that we did and that's how we're measured. By all those little actions we've taken, by our attitude to life, by our personalities. If you shoot yourself in the head wearing a football

jersey they'll either think you killed yourself in your pajamas
or they'll think you're a martyr for a football team, and honestly I can't tell which one is sadder."

"Football's one of my things, you know. It's a thing people
know about me."

"It's undignified. You're a dignified man. Your death needs
to be a reflection of that, and it needs to be a commentary
on society."

"Like what?"

"I mean, like it needs to be a statement about how you view
the world. Something artistic."

"I'm not an artsy person."

"Nonsense. Everyone's an artsy person. It just varies by
degree."

Joel let that sink in a little. He didn't disagree with the position exactly. Lucey had dragged him to museums and galleries,
and they had admired paintings together. He never pretended
to understand the things like Lucey did; he just liked looking
at them. While she talked about the artists' specific attention
to detail on faces as a way to force people to focus on them,
Joel stood there thinking about how pretty the paintings were.
Modern art annoyed him. And then it hit him.

"Got one," he told Frank.

"Go for it," Frank replied, sipping again from his pint.

"I used to look at art quite a bit. I mean, not like you would.
You've probably been in every damn museum for fifty miles.
Twice. Bloody fancy scarf and all that. But Lucey used to bring
me and it was mostly nice. Except for the bloody modern art.
I thought I understood the why of the whole thing—I mean
you can only paint so many pictures of flowers before you
have to start branching out a bit. Otherwise everyone is just
going to say you're a cheap imitation of a dead fella from a
hundred years ago. So they started getting all experimental,

but nobody reined them in, so suddenly you've all these men and women making art and it's basically just whatever they say it is, because there's no rules anymore. Then I go into a museum with Lucey, and I sat down on this bench this one time, while Lucey is talking about brushstrokes and primary colors and all that. This security guard comes running over. 'Oi!! You can't sit there!' I got confused.

"'Why not?'

"'Because that piece is worth thousands, it's not for sitting on.' I'm telling you now, Frank, it was a bench. A pretty ordinary-looking bench. I probably should have twigged something was wrong because it was a garden bench, and apparently that was very important to the artist, but it was just a regular bench. So I started to look around. What else here is art? There's a crisp wrapper over there in the corner and there's a velvet rope around it, and I honestly couldn't tell if it was art or not. Stuck up on one of the walls was the word *THIS* in giant carved wooden letters, and I get that one. This is art. Literally saying 'this' is art. All I could think of was, no, it's not, pal.

"No, it absolutely is not.

"Now I'm no artist, I know that, but I feel like art isn't for me anymore. It's for young people, and fakers, and bullshitters, pardon my language, and I think I can say something about that. I'll get that gun I was going to get for the other one. I can get a gun, by the way, no problem. If I need one like. I'll dress myself up really nice. As nice as I can, and I'll walk into that museum…"

In his mind's eye Joel could see himself walking into the City Gallery of Art, wearing his nice pin-striped brown suit, with the matching waistcoat and extra-polished shoes. He could almost feel the weight of the revolver in his jacket pocket. He saw the beautiful red-haired young woman who worked at the reception, and the curly-haired man who was the curator who bustled from room to room with special honored guests. He looked like he could have been a theater actor, too.

He could see all the fancy know-it-alls and fakers oohing and aahing over the various pieces of crap that someone had stuck to the walls.

In his imagination it played out: he walked through the gallery and came to a stop right in front of the "this" and turned to the people in the room with a broad smile worthy of Frank de Selby.

"This is not art," he told them.

And then he shot himself in the head and his body slumped onto the ground. The various gallery attendants would argue for the rest of their lives that his suicide had itself been both a commentary on art, and art for its own sake. He marveled at his own creativity.

"What do you think?" he asked Frank when he had finished.

Frank had his little journal out, and had been scribbling as Joel spoke, as though trying to capture the moment.

"Crap," he said without hesitation.

"Why?" Joel asked, deflated.

"It's too…" He paused looking for the words. "It's too 'angry man.' You're going in the right direction, it's just not quite right. It's the work of a crank. A man petty enough to kill himself because art had become something he didn't like. That's what they'll say, this angry old man is so arrogant that he's going to kill himself because young people don't make art specifically for him anymore. Its lasting impact, if it has any, will be that Joel Monroe was a bitter, angry man, and that's not what we're going for."

Joel sighed. He had thought it a perfectly fine way to go, but Frank was right. He didn't want his legacy to be as an angry, bitter man who hated art. His suicide must be something that was hated and loved. Loved for its statement, hated for its brutality. It must be brutal, but not bitter.

He hadn't always been an angry, bitter man. He didn't want to always be remembered so.

At the end of the quiet bar, the young barman was staring at them incredulously. His towel held loosely in one hand, the glass he was polishing forgotten in the other. His jaw slack with shock at their conversation.

"What?" Joel asked him. "I didn't say I was definitely going to do it."

The barman stared at them and tried to laugh nervously again before going to find something else to do.

"You might not do it?" Frank asked casually.

"I didn't say that," Joel replied. "I'm definitely doing it, just not doing it that way."

"Why so adamant?"

"You going to try to talk me out of it?" Joel asked pugnaciously.

"No, not at all. I told you I think it's a powerful statement. I just want to know why you're so adamant."

"I've had enough, Frank. And that's all the reason I need. I've had enough of this."

He gestured vaguely around him. He heard his own words and heard the authority in them, felt the need to remove himself, brutally, awfully, but something diluted his anger.

Sitting in the bar with Frank, having a pint, away from the nurses and his daughter and Mighty Jim with his pointless chess games, it was difficult for Joel to drum up the depth of feeling he had known since he watched Mr. Miller die. Somehow that feeling was removed, like it was far away, like he had left it behind in the bedroom he had shared with Lucey, and far away as it was, it couldn't reach him here.

Instead it waited for him to come back to it. It wasn't going anywhere. Its absence a temporary relief.

"All right," Frank told him with a wave of his hand, "it's a good decision. I already said that. Powerful statement. I know better than to tell you otherwise."

"What would you do?"

"I already told you, Joel, this has to be you. Only you."

"But why?"

"You'll figure that out on your own, too."

"Bloody mystery man with your mysterious statements."

"Bloody lazy simpleton who wants everyone to do the understanding for him."

Joel chuckled at that. Frank remained unfazed by casual insults.

"Soon," he told his friend.

"How soon?"

"My birthday's in June. Three weeks. Seems an appropriate time."

"Poetic. Out on the anniversary of the day you got in."

Joel had never thought his birthday was important. It reminded him of times when his mother had made a fuss while his father had rated him to see how close to a man he measured. He had never measured up. He had always been found wanting. Even when he eventually outgrew the man, towered over him, broad and powerful, his father had still found a way to look down at him.

"That's it, then," Joel announced.

An end. Finally. An end.

9

The two escapees finished their pints in silence. Frank happy to sit and sup at his leisure, Joel at a loss for how to express himself when he felt both comfortable and full of dread all at once. When they were done, and had peed in the tiny men's room at the foot of the stairs to the basement, they nodded their goodbyes to the barman, and the two slipped back out into the early evening sunshine. The sun had come around on its way down and lit the small alleyway that the bar sat in pleasantly, though Joel knew that the light and heat wouldn't last. Sunset was not far off.

It had been only one pint, but the fact that they had skipped dinner for their escapade meant it hit Joel about as hard as he was expecting, and he found himself buzzing ever so slightly from the Guinness. The freedom and the alcohol and the sunshine and the thought of his impending death combined to make him giddy. Too long since he had walked about the town on his own time, he found himself excited by his consequence-free afternoon out from under the watchful eyes.

"We'll take the bus home," Frank suggested, adjusting his superfluous scarf.

"With what? We've barely the price of a bar of chocolate after the pints, and I don't think they'll accept fake coins any more than that obnoxious young barman would."

"Then we'll get a bar of chocolate and take the bus home."

"Are you listening to me? We've no money for a bus."

He found that he didn't really care that they were stranded.

"We're OAPs, remember? Free transport for the elderly."

He wasn't wrong. It had never occurred to Joel that government legislation might work in his favor for once. All OAPs traveled free in possession of ID.

"I've no ID," he said as realization struck. "It's with my wallet."

"Then you get on the bus, and you pretend to be dithery and the bus driver just lets you sit down."

"What?" Joel asked.

"Pretend to have a senior moment. Act goofy. Like Mighty Jim. Smile too much. Drool a little if you can. Nod incessantly. The bus driver'll be too embarrassed to question you, and you just take your seat."

"He'll know we're having him on."

"He might suspect, but he's not about to go interrogating an elderly man in front of other passengers, and if he does I'll raise a stink. He won't be long sitting down."

"I'm not an actor like you," Joel protested, but in his giddiness he thought it might be fun to try.

"I'll coach you. This'll be easy."

The walk to the bus stop took them across the wide bridge that held itself loftily above the broad river surging through the city, and Joel felt a remarkable sense of peace and easiness in its presence. He looked at Frank, stepping lightly beside him in that relaxed and easy manner of his, and envied his friend his casual attitude even as he admired it. Along the way Frank spoke at length about the performance required on the bus; he jabbered about tilting your head just so, and about slowing your rate of speech, about looking the driver straight in the eye. Joel took in some of it, but mostly he just enjoyed the leisurely stroll.

"Have you been listening to a word I've said?" Frank asked him when they reached the bus stop which stood in front of a small convenience store not far from the river.

"Not really," Joel admitted, forcing himself into Frank's airy way of speaking.

"Right," Frank sighed, "practice run."

"Practice run?" Joel asked, a little alarmed.

"Into the shop there," he said, gesturing at the convenience store. "I want to see you bamboozle the shop assistant."

Joel felt the airiness drain out of him and his mouth dry all at once. It was fine to talk about it, but another thing to put it into practice. He looked back at the small shop. There were no customers inside; it looked quiet. A bored young woman fidgeted with her phone as she stood at the counter in her shop uniform, one hand idly playing with her hair.

"All right," he said reluctantly. "What do I do?"

"Go in and ask the girl if she knows where you are."

"I know very well where I am, thank you very much."

"I know that, you dolt. She doesn't. I want you to get in there and give her a senior moment that she'll never forget."

"What are you going to do?"

"I'm going in to grade your performance. I'll be your audience. Critique to follow on the journey home."

Joel looked at the shop once again. She may have already seen them. Then it struck him that they may not have even registered with her. Just another two old men. He took a deep breath and walked in.

He tried not to stand up so straight. He put a little hunch into his back, and he smiled a broad, clearly false smile. He took smaller steps, faltering almost as if unsure. As he walked in he tried not to look up immediately. It would give the game away, and instead he looked about him as if confused. He made for the refrigerator and then stopped. He made a small noise of confusion and ambled in the direction of the aisles before stopping again. This time he looked up at her, and smiled broadly again. She was staring straight at him with genuine concern. He instantly felt bad. She wasn't some snotty teenager whom he might feel comfortable despising; she seemed like a perfectly lovely person. Before he could change his mind and walk out, Frank strolled in and nodded, as if in passing at a stranger before immediately making for the aisles himself, like he was on a mission.

"Can I help you?" the young lady asked in a perfectly friendly and helpful voice.

Joel took a look over his shoulder to see where Frank had gone, only for the young woman to mistake it for confusion.

"Over here, sir," she said, loudly and slowly and annoyingly. The same voice the new nurses used at Hilltop, but only the once.

Joel felt his irritation rise again. He hated when people did that.

"What?" he said to her, practically shouting his confusion.

"Can I help you?" she said again, louder and slower and more annoyingly.

"*What*?" he definitely shouted this time, still looking confused.

She forced a smile at him through gritted teeth and made her way out from behind the counter to help him. The guilt kicked back in again. That was a nice gesture; she could have just given up.

"Is there anything I can help you with?" she asked, taking him by the arm and leading him toward the counter.

"Do you by any chance…"

Before he could finish, he spied Frank over her shoulder. The actor was grinning from ear to ear and gleefully stuffing his pockets with bars of chocolate. He treated Joel to an exaggerated wink.

Joel didn't know whether to bark at his friend or burst out laughing, standing there, delighted with himself as he picked chocolate bars indiscriminately from the stands and stuffed them into various pockets. The shop assistant caught him looking in Frank's direction and made to turn.

"Do you know where I am?" Joel barked at her, causing her to jump in surprise. He hadn't even bothered to pretend he was confused anymore.

"Excuse me?" she asked slowly. It was dawning on her that she was being played. Joel swallowed. Improvisation was an actor's talent, and Joel was learning quickly that he was no actor. The only actor in the building was still stuffing his pockets with chocolate.

"Eh… Here?" he asked stupidly.

She narrowed her eyes at him.

"You'll have to forgive this one," Frank interjected smoothly, leaning past her and taking Joel by the shoulder. "He's a resident at the nursing home I live in. Heaven knows how he got out on his own. Sadly he's not all there in the head."

The look he gave her oozed sincerity. She regarded them both suspiciously.

"I'll take him home," Frank stated without missing a beat. If he was even remotely ashamed of the ruse or the pockets bulging with chocolate, he gave no indication. He began guiding Joel toward the door. Imminent safety gave Joel heart, and he leaned back into his role with renewed vigor.

"I think I once peed up against this door in 1967," he announced loudly.

Timing being on their side, the bus rolled down the street and came to a stop at Frank's beckoning. Joel was ready, after his matinee performance, to wow the bus driver.

As the bus pulled up to the curb he put on his simpering smile and tried to look vacant. Frank pretended to be his personal minder. Painfully slowly he climbed on board and looked straight at the driver and to his massive disappointment the man waved them on without even bothering to ask for ID. After his shaky, but ultimately successful raid on the shop, he had been hoping for a chance to impress, and the bus driver, bored of seeing another elderly citizen climb on board, had robbed him of that. He was beginning to see what Frank enjoyed so much about acting. There was a rush to it. As they trudged down the aisle to find their seats, Joel found himself bubbling over with excitement. His first acting performance at the tender age of seventy-six. He looked at Frank and saw his own excitement reflected there.

"Over-actor," his friend told him, as they both began to chuckle.

Joel's sense of elation stayed with him as the old city bus trundled out of town and into the suburbs. The small crowd of Sunday travelers thinned out stop by stop, many of them smiling at the two elderly gents who chuckled all the way home, sharing a bar of chocolate between them. Joel nodded at them as they went, feeling how infectious his own smile was.

Outside a small school that sat at the bottom of the hill, the two men disembarked and made their way to the gates of Hilltop. Joel could no longer tell if his good mood was the lingering effects of his solitary pint, or the excitement of pulling off a heist, but he didn't care. He pressed the buzzer.

"Hilltop, can I help you?"

The voice ran his blood cold. It was The Rhino.

Joel froze but Frank did not.

"Frank de Selby and Joel Monroe returning from day-release, Warden," he told her impishly.

The gate buzzed open without further ado; her silence at Frank's humor seemed to transmit itself through the electronics so the gate swung wide in front of them in an almost ominous fashion. Joel's excitement evaporated as he scanned the long driveway and front car park for a sign of his daughter's car, or that insufferable partner of hers.

As he had guessed, his sense of dread was waiting for him inside the swinging gate. Like something in the air around Hilltop that seeped into his bones. He tried to force the smile onto his face as they climbed the small hill, Frank's easy gait now an irritation. Did nothing flap the man?

At the top of the hill Nurse Liam was loading something into his own car. He turned to look at both of them as they made their way toward the main door. Joel was trying to gauge if the man looked like he suspected something or not.

"If you don't stop looking so damn guilty, they're going to figure us out," Frank told him out of the corner of his mouth, still smiling.

"How do you do that?" Joel asked, trying to replicate it.

Frank burst out laughing, causing Nurse Liam to stand up straighter and narrow his eyes at them.

Inside the main door Head Nurse Ryan waited for them, her look cool, composed. A tiny, petite woman in her mid-forties, she carried herself with the authority only years of experience in nursing can give you. Her uniform was immaculate. Joel scanned her face for signs of something, anything that might tell him what was in store. She gave him nothing.

"How was your dinner?" she asked in a tone loaded with suspicion.

"Marvelous," Frank told her with a smile, looking her dead in the eye.

"Your daughter didn't drop you home, Joel?" she asked, turning her attention.

"Tony did," Joel told her. "I asked him to let us out a little early. For the walk, you see."

"I see," she said, clearly not believing a word.

She looked from one to the other slowly. Frank stood casually, smiling lightly, his whole demeanor a sort of challenge—"just try to make me take you seriously," he seemed to say without opening his mouth. Joel on the other hand took everything seriously; his body language said he wasn't for budging, and you'd need a bulldozer to do it if it took your fancy.

If anyone was up for these challenges it was The Rhino.

"I've been meaning to talk to you Mr. Monroe. Privately if you please, Mr. Adams."

"No. It's fine," Joel told her. "He can stay." He wouldn't have liked to admit it, but he needed the backup.

She said nothing for a moment but looked him up and down coolly. Frank offered her a bland gaze and planted his feet. It amazed Joel how unaffected his friend was by her icy presence.

"As you will," she told him after a moment. "Nurse Dwight and your daughter have both spoken to me about your recent behavior. Your mental well-being has become a matter of concern for the staff."

He didn't like where this was going. Maybe Nurse Liam had heard him talking about his suicide that morning. Maybe he'd told her.

"And?" he said, trying for Frank's bland look but feeling like a bug about to be squished underfoot.

"We'd like you to speak to a counselor or psychologist," she told him. "Considering your recent loss, we feel it's prudent."

Joel tried not to look horrified. They must know he wanted to kill himself.

"Do I have a choice?" he asked.

"Yes, Mr. Monroe, despite your belief to the contrary, this isn't a prison."

"Then I choose not."

Her glare got colder, if such a thing was possible. A deep and sustained freeze. She wasn't used to being defied.

"Mr. Monroe, this is a retirement home and a nursing home, but we don't have the facilities or the staff to care for someone whose needs are complex and psychological. We can help you only if you let us, but should you choose not to, then perhaps we'll have to move you on to somewhere that can cater for you. I strongly recommend that you speak to the counselor. For your own benefit."

Her tone was cold, a deep and profound cold, and the threat was barely veiled. Comply or leave.

"So I don't have a choice?" he asked her bitterly, thrusting his hands into his pockets.

"Mr. Monroe, regardless how you may feel personally about the staff here, I can assure you that we all have your best interests at heart. Me included."

He found that hard to believe. His best interests, he was sure, didn't include being treated like some kind of trucu-lent child.

Inside his pocket his fingers struck his lucky penny, and he felt some of the bitterness drain out of him. She couldn't take his taste of freedom away from him.

She took his silence for acquiescence and turned on her

heel and marched back down the corridor, her footfalls echo-
ing as she moved.

Joel watched her leave in mixed resentment and relief. He
had time. He hoped he had time. He didn't need much. Just
enough to decide how he wanted to die.

"Let's go count the loot," Frank said eventually, when he
was sure they were out of earshot.

The two made their way to their bedroom, with Joel's
mood somber but lightened by a sense of accomplishment.
He rubbed the penny in between his fingers as he walked.
They had done it. He had left. Taken control. Disappeared on
his own steam and had his own day. He looked at his friend
gratefully as Frank unloaded fifteen different types of chocolate bars from his pockets.

In a spur-of-the-moment decision, without really thinking, Joel dropped his penny on his bedside table, walked across
the room and threw one arm over Frank's shoulders, embrac-
ing the smaller man in a sort of awkward side hug. Frank just
laughed.

"What have you got there?" came Una's voice as she walked
into the room.

Joel remembered that he was grateful to her, too. She clearly
knew, before they left, that they were up to something, and
just as clearly she had let it go without comment. He realized
to his surprise that he was glad to see her.

"We brought you a gift," he said, brandishing as many
chocolate bars as he could.

10

Joel had nightmares that night. It might have been the booze, or maybe the chocolate.

In it there were skeletons, hundreds of them, and all of them were Mr. Miller. They ambled aimlessly here and there in a hilly, barren wasteland. In the distance Frank pursued him, but his nightmare version of Frank was a therapist who wanted him to sit down and talk. At the foot of the largest hill he found a huge rock that he tried to hide behind, but as soon as he put his back to it, the thing started rolling out of his way. Therapist Frank was gaining on him, and if he could just get the damn boulder to sit still, he knew he'd have somewhere to hide.

"Joel," Therapist Frank called out in The Rhino's voice. "I'd like a word with you, please."

The cursed boulder kept rolling and rolling, and he kept trying to hide behind it. The skeleton army of Mr. Millers began to converge on his position, and he shooed them away in case they gave away his hiding place. He could hear Therapist Frank getting closer and closer, and he tried to edge around the huge boulder, until he realized he was stuck behind it. If he let it roll back down, it would crush all the bony Mr. Millers. He heard Therapist Frank's footsteps in the rocky soil and tensed.

Coming into view, first his feet, then his too-wide pants that didn't quite fit him, then it suddenly wasn't him at all, but Lucey, standing in front of him.

"What on earth are you doing?" she asked curiously.

"Fuck," he exclaimed as he started out of sleep.

"Fuck," he said again, as he came face-to-face with Mighty Jim, who, for reasons unknown, was nose to nose with Joel and examining him in his sleep.

"What on earth are you doing?" he asked the older man angrily, brushing him away as he tried to right himself in the bed.

"I should have put him in his proper place," Jim muttered, as he shuffled out of reach, looking chastised.

Not for the first time, Joel wondered just how much of what was going on around him Mighty Jim could really understand.

"Don't bark at him, you old crank," Frank admonished from across the room.

"He was watching me sleep."

"Sure, we all do that. Take it in turns, too."

Mr. de Selby was awake early it seemed, and Mr. Adams still fully asleep.

Frank was sitting up in his bed, happily eating one of the leftover chocolate bars that hadn't been devoured or donated the night before. Wearing a scarf of purple and green and blue.

"Want some tea?" Frank asked him.

"Not off that traitor," Joel replied.

He had decided some time the night before that both his daughter and Nurse Liam were traitors. Especially Liam. Frank and Una's point about him just doing his job was well wide of the mark for Joel, and he imagined a conversation between

The Rhino and the two traitors where each of them thought up ways to punish him for not doing what he was told all the time. Nurse Liam had been a friend, and it was probably unfair of Joel to assume the worst of the man, but he felt aggrieved. A bloody psychologist just because he wasn't all sunshine and roses like the great Mr. de Selby? It stuck in his craw, and as was Joel's wont, he worried at it until it got worse and worse.

"He's not a traitor and he's not working today. It may come as a surprise to you to remember that this is his place of work, he doesn't live here and he doesn't spend his time plotting ways to make you even crankier than you already are."

"What's Jim doing here?" Joel grumbled, letting the Traitor Liam moment pass him by.

"No idea, old boy. He just wandered in here to see you. You okay? You were tossing and turning there for a bit."

Joel remembered his nightmare and the Therapist Frank chasing him around a hellish landscape. He looked over at Frank, in his pajamas with his scarf on, dipping Turkish Delight in his tea. He laughed at the absurdity.

"Something funny?" Frank asked with a raised eyebrow. It added to the comic effect, and Joel laughed even harder.

"Nothing," he said.

Jim was smiling again, regarding Joel and Frank pleasantly, patiently.

"I think he's looking for a game?" Frank suggested.

"All right then," Joel announced hauling himself from his bed.

As he rolled out, he saw the coin, his lucky penny, sitting next to his photo of Lucey. He smiled at it.

His bare feet struck the old linoleum floor, as they had done most mornings for the last five years, but for the first time, Joel found an odd satisfaction in the sensation. The cold on his warm feet. He wiggled his toes and wondered what could have made him so chipper. He was not, as Frank had pointed out to him in his first week at Hilltop, a morning person. There really wasn't much doubt where his positivity had come from, a whole day outside the prison walls, the delicious forbidden pint, the freedom. He remembered the threat of the psycho-therapist, but decided that he wasn't going to be put off by it.

There were aches, of course. Minor ones, but many of them. It had been a while since he'd walked for as long as he and Frank had the day before, and he hurt. His knees were the worst, but the pain was all over. A reminder that his body had been in slow decline for some time now.

"Can you wait a minute for me, Jim? I just want to make myself presentable."

"You'll need more than a minute," Frank de Selby quipped.

Joel, bare chested, washed himself quickly in the shared washroom, then wet and combed his hair. He studied the re-sults. Time had been kinder to him than it had to others, but it was hard for him to look into a mirror and not see this aged creature. In his head he hadn't changed. In his head he was still the man he once was.

The meager handful of dark brown hair was more of a mockery of what it had been, and while his shoulders were still broad, they had sloped a little. He had never been a very vain man, but he had known that he cut an impressive figure in his youth. Even past middle age he was still formidable, the kind of man that people called "sir." Now old, he saw only his gray chest hairs and the sagging of the skin around his jaw and chin. He had aged. He sighed at himself and re-buttoned his pajamas.

Outside the washroom Mighty Jim waited patiently, his small pleasant smile unwavering.

"Enjoy your date," Frank told them as they left.

"Try not to ruin the sheets with chocolate," Joel shot back.

As they made their way slowly through the hallways for the common room, Joel nodded and smiled to the passing staff and residents. They moved at Jim's pace, which was slow, bordering on a snail's. Joel's typical impatience at Mighty Jim's excruciatingly slow pace was conspicuously absent this morning, and he clasped his hands behind his back as they crept along. Through the corridors they walked, and Joel had to remind himself that Hilltop was a prison and that a prison, comfortable or not, was still a prison, and that being told what to do, when to eat, what to eat, when to sleep and every other minor command they gave was another erosion of the life he had built for himself, a life that he had surrendered for reasons he now couldn't recall.

He found it odd that he had to remind himself of this. It was usually at the front of his thoughts, but today seemed different, more colorful. Even the bleak nightmare that had dogged his sleep was forgotten in the bright light of day. He checked for the presence of the cloud of suicide and depression that now typically shadowed his steps through the hallways of Hilltop but couldn't find it.

"Cheek against the stone," Mighty Jim told him.

"Certainly," Joel replied with a tolerant smile.

For all his happy-go-lucky nature, Mighty Jim certainly knew how to wipe a smile off someone's face. Over two hours they played to stalemate three times. The third time Joel thought he saw a window, a tiny moment where he might sneak past Mighty Jim's mighty defense, only to see the door slam shut on him. He also thought he saw a twinkle in Jim's eye, a hint that the old man had left that door ajar for him to aim at, only to close it on him for his own amusement. Though Mighty Jim, being fully senile, surely wasn't capable of such subterfuge.

His early-morning good mood mostly squandered, Joel

made his way back to his room to watch television, and kill
another few hours. Frank was already present, reading some
ancient Greek tragedy, presumably in the hope that someone
would notice that he was reading an ancient Greek tragedy.

"You win?" Frank asked, smiling to himself as he saw Joel's
scowl.

"No. Only this time I think he was making fun of me."

"You think that Mighty Jim, the man who hasn't spoken a
coherent sentence in about a decade, was making fun of you?"

"Sometimes I think he knows more than he's letting on."

"And the nurse is a traitor?"

"Yes," Joel said obstinately, though he could see where
Frank was taking this.

"Have you ever heard of paranoid delusions?" Frank asked,
without looking up from his book.

"Have you ever heard of broken teeth?" Joel threatened
back idly.

"Maybe you do need to see that therapist," Frank told him
with a laugh.

It wasn't intended to hurt. Joel was certain of that. Neither
the de Selby mask nor the real Adams would deliberately hurt
him, or anyone really, but it stung all the same. He hadn't
made a friend in a long time, and he didn't want the one he
had to start thinking he was crazy just because he wanted to
kill himself so badly he could almost taste it.

Worse again were the consequences of being sent to the
therapist. He might end up confronting his own hopelessness,
his own utter unhappiness with the world around him and end
up being moved away from the first friend he'd made since
Lucey had left him behind.

Maybe they'd even put him into the psychiatric ward and
drug him heavily, and as far as Joel was concerned, that was
a fate worse than death. To have even less freedom than the

meager amount he still held to. The fear of it was a palpable
sensation that quickened his breathing and choked him all
at once. He tried to cover as he sat on his bed, tried to mask
the breathing and whiteness of his face that he knew must be
there; he had felt himself blanch. Suddenly Frank was by his
side, helping him into the bed.

"It's okay," he said soothingly. "It's okay."

Joel nodded his thanks at him, but didn't trust himself to
talk.

Frank shoved a piece of chocolate into Joel's mouth.

"There you go now, old boy, that'll help. Deep breaths.
Deep breaths."

Joel slowly composed himself, mortified that the mere mention of a therapist was enough to set him off.

"I can't," he finally mumbled at Frank. "I can't go to that
therapist."

"Okay, okay. No therapist."

"Promise me," he insisted. It was irrational, he knew that.
Frank could promise no such thing; Joel just wanted to hear
someone say it.

"I promise, I promise," Frank told him.

"We can hold them off until my birthday, can't we?"

"We can," Frank said reassuringly.

"It's just three weeks. We can hold them off for less than
a month."

Frank Adams opened his mouth to say something but
thought better of it. He closed it again.

Neither of them spoke as Joel sat upright in his bed, Frank
attending nearby, hovering worriedly. Joel took deep breaths.
No one had ever explained to him whether or not a panic attack might result in a stroke, but he had been having one the
day the TIA struck him. He didn't want another one.

Frank sat into the seat by Joel's bed as Joel steadied himself.

He flipped through the channels on the television. There was a comfort in the familiarity of sitting alongside one another and watching TV. It soothed Joel, he was surprised to find.

At one point Nurse Karl came in, a well-built chap with a jocular manner, short-cut blond hair and an occasionally straggly blond beard. He covered Liam's days off, and shifts for the other nurses here and there. Joel liked him, but as he came down from the sudden and overwhelming panic attack, he couldn't bring himself to face the young man, and so he ignored his greeting save for a slight nod. Joel worried it would make things worse. He worried that Karl would report back that he had failed to engage, that he had seemed withdrawn. The sliver of hope was that Nurse Karl was temporary; perhaps he wasn't in on the betrayal.

When Joel eventually felt well enough to talk again, it was a simple enough two words across the room.

"Thank you," he said to Frank.

"Not at all," de Selby replied munificently.

He recalled with a jolt his nightmare from the night before. The sense of doom, the sense of being chased, the skeletons of Mr. Miller following him, and worst of all the low, oppressive, terrifying clouds. He thought he had been safe in his sleep, but apparently not. If that cloud could follow him into his dreams, there was nowhere safe. He was sure that had contributed to the panic attack.

He needed a suicide. He needed a good suicide and soon.

11

"You think it should be funny, don't you?" he asked Frank.
"What?"

"My death."

"Depends on whether we're laughing with you or at you. My preference, well known, is to laugh at you, but in this case maybe that's not what we're aiming for."

"Have you ever answered a question like a normal human?"

"Normal humans are frighteningly dull, old boy. I prefer to avoid connection to them."

"Jesus," Joel almost groaned at the pomposity, "funny or not funny?"

"Funny is good."

"Maybe I should kill myself in a clown suit?" Joel mused.

Frank treated him to a long-drawn-out stare. It was flat with its lack of enthusiasm.

"I don't mean like that would be it, just maybe I should be in costume when I do it."

Frank shook his head disappointedly.

"Well, if you'd tell me what to do, we could avoid all this,"

Joel complained as he tried to imagine himself dressed as a clown, detonating an explosive in a tiny car. He smiled in spite of himself.

"Do you know what 'pithy' means?" Frank asked.

"No."

"Pity," Frank replied and then chuckled at his own cleverness.

Joel let him have his moment.

"I probably won't kill myself in a clown costume," Joel told him eventually.

"Good to know," Frank said, returning to his book.

Joel watched his friend out of the corner of his eye. There was a depth to Frank that he had underestimated, a soul in him that Joel found himself almost envious of. He couldn't remember at what point he had given up his soul or, at the very least, surrendered it to the idea of his death, but it was gone now, and in its place just this need to be done. This need to cast off. Frank simply sat, in his scarf reading his book. For all his depth and worldliness, he seemed unperturbed by the terrible finality of life.

"Now what shall we do today, old boy?" his friend eventually asked. "What adventures shall we have?"

Joel glanced around at the walls, and half-longingly out the window.

"Watch TV more?" he suggested.

"We'll call that a maybe. Any visitors coming today?"

"No. Eva visits on Sundays with one of the kids. That's it. How about you? Any visitors?"

"No," Frank replied with a rueful smile. "I'll get no visitors."

Joel wanted to kick himself for his own selfishness. In all the time since Frank had moved in, it had never occurred to ask him about his family. Once the gay thing had been mentioned, Joel had let Frank keep his personal business to himself; he had asked for nothing and nothing had been volunteered. Joel knew, beyond doubt, that Frank would never volunteer personal information. He would preen and talk and impress everyone with his de Selby mask, but he wore it strictly for the purposes of keeping people out. It seemed wrong to Joel, that they should be on such uneven ground, as if Frank's confession to him had come full circle. Now he was the one left out.

"No one?" Joel asked, feigning casualness.

"Ha!" Frank laughed. "Don't try to pull that one on me. I invented that one."

"What one?" Joel asked indignantly. Frank had seen through him immediately. He was too sharp for his own good.

"The offhand inquiry one. I invented it. I've been doing it to you all week."

"No idea what you're talking about," Joel shot back.

"Sure you do. You're no slouch either, but you do have a tell. Sticking out your jaw like that when you're embarrassed is one of them."

"I do not," Joel said, trying to tuck his jaw back in without appearing to try.

Frank just laughed at him. It was a good-natured laugh, not the loud booming de Selby laugh, but a low chuckle. It was warm. After a moment the laughter stopped, and Frank just stared straight ahead, apparently looking right through the television. Joel changed tack; he didn't probe, he just turned to his friend, his lonely, vulnerable friend and waited. Frank continued to look through the television; Joel continued to wait.

"You know," said Frank, finally acknowledging him, "for a vicious old bastard you've a remarkably compassionate streak. Though it might just be nosiness."

That was the second last time that Frank ever called Joel vicious.

"You don't have to talk about it if you don't want," Joel told him grumpily. "I just don't want you thinking you can't, you know."

"Merciful Jesus," Frank muttered, "we've changed places."

Joel tried to think of something philosophical and witty to say. He came up blank.

Suddenly Frank was talking and Joel didn't have to think of anything.

"When I was eighteen I kissed a boy for the first time, and someone who saw us told a man who knew a man, and that man told another man who knew a different man and that different man knew my father. When he found out he beat me quite badly." Frank was wearing his de Selby mask and only a slight twist to his lips could have given away how much he was hurting as he spoke.

Joel didn't know how to respond. He knew himself that he lacked the tact and subtlety to say the right thing. He sat in his bed, like a fool, while Frank emptied his soul into the space between them.

"I think my brothers beat up the misfortunate boy I kissed. Didn't know him. I was drunk and we'd just finished doing a show. A play. Terrible that I can't remember the boy but I can remember the show. *Romeo and Juliet*."

He let out a short, angry laugh as he recalled.

"I didn't have a lot of friends growing up. Not until I found the theater. See, I always found myself attracted to boys, and I was terribly afraid they'd find out. I was safer with girls, but the more time I spent with them the more people wondered about why I was in their company but didn't have a girlfriend. A stupid time to grow up, when we were kids. I mean, I'm sure it's not easy nowadays either, but imagine being that afraid, all the time. I was terrified my father would know, and so I just pretended I didn't like boys. I pretended that I liked girls and I avoided everyone. For fear of my father."

Joel recalled his own father, the rough discipline of the man, the vicious streak in him, the barely contained fury when Joel failed to live up to expectations. He recalled his own private delight when he had outgrown the man and watched him wither under his old age. He understood, and his heart broke for Frank.

"When we moved into town and out of the countryside, I joined the drama society. New life, new opportunities. No more sitting around on my own. I was determined," Frank continued, a wistful note entering his voice. "And things were different. I fell in love, instantly. I performed, I sang. I don't have a terrible voice, let me tell you, and I was good. Everyone knew it. Suddenly I had friends and people were telling me I was special. When we performed *Romeo and Juliet* with another school, I met a boy, and when the show was finished we all drank stolen booze in the dressing rooms and then down little laneways in town, trying to sneak into bars. I kissed him then. Can hardly remember it, though. My first kiss."

The last words were bitter, and the de Selby mask slipped off, showing Frank Adams, angry, hurt and somehow still confused by the events all the years later.

"My father beat the shit out of me. My mother sobbed the whole way through it. I remember begging her to intervene and she standing there watching. Turns out she wasn't sobbing because he was beating me, she was sobbing because she didn't want a gay son. She watched the beating happen because she honestly thought it was for my own good. The saddest part of all, my dear," he told Joel as he tried to slip back into the de Selby mask, tried and failed, "the saddest part was that I started to think it was for my own good, too. I went to college. I got a room in a house and studied something or other. I didn't really pay attention. I joined the drama society.

"They came to visit," he continued, his voice becoming cold, distant, his eyes hardening. Joel almost held his breath, his heart breaking further with each word.

"They came unexpectedly. They didn't catch me in the act or anything, but they knew. Me standing in underwear looking shocked and frightened. They knew. I tried to fight back that time. Can you imagine it? Me? He beat me to a pulp. She didn't cry that time. She just watched. He made shit of me, Joel. He smashed my face, broke several ribs, shattered an arm. For my own good. All of this for my own good."

Joel felt his fury join with Frank's. He had been on the receiving end of beatings from his father growing up. Beatings handed out for his own good. It was the way of parenting at the time. Spare the rod, spoil the child and all that. He resented his father for it, maybe even hated him a little, and feared how much of that man made up who he had become. But he had never had the very makeup of who he was be the focus of a rage so profound that his own father would try to beat it out of him. He had been a vicious bastard, but not that vicious. A lump formed in his throat, and he felt the stirrings of tears.

"She came to see me in the hospital too, but I'll tell you this, and I'll swear it to anyone who listens. Nothing gives you confidence like performing on stage. Nothing will help you to slay your fears quite like performing for an audience. It wasn't like the first time he hurt me. I was angry now, and confident and fed up. And then there was this tall nurse, with these lovely blue eyes…" He trailed off for just a moment.

A tall blue-eyed nurse. A description of the man who cared for them five days a week. The pieces clicked into place.

"My mother came to tell me that if I promised not to be gay anymore that I could come home, but that father dearest was still very upset. She wanted to know if I felt bad about making daddy feel upset? Can you imagine? I was full of my anger, and I was in love with a nurse and I hated them, and I think, I hated myself a little, too. Don't ask me to explain that to you. I've had the best part of sixty years with that one, and I still have no idea.

"I told her to go fuck herself. I looked her dead in the eye, just like I had when I was begging her to stop my father from beating me up, and I told her to fuck off. She slapped me in the face, and I slapped her right back. I still remember the look she gave me.

"That was the last time I spoke to any members of my family. I assume that I was the great shame of my family. I assume they went back to their parochial little lives and their bigotry and just pretended I wasn't their son. I changed my name to de Selby and pretended they didn't exist. Every now and then I get a twinge, and I wonder what it would be like to have a family, but then I remember his big fat fists smashing my face, and I move on."

"You never heard from them again?" Joel asked, almost breathless. Frank de Selby's life was a tragedy.

"Never," Frank told him.

"What about the nurse?"

"We lived together for a while," Frank told him, sniffing as if he could hide the profound pain he was feeling in a performance of indifference. "He was a beautiful person, inside and out. We broke up eventually. I don't want to be one of those people who blames his father for absolutely everything that ever happened, but I wonder about it. I was afraid to hold his hand, you see. Afraid to kiss him in public. Afraid of showing off too much of myself. Isn't that silly? Me? Afraid of showing off?"

There was a slight catch in his voice. A threat of tears. His face slipped between Adams and de Selby. Showing one, then the other.

"I'm sorry, Frank," Joel told him earnestly.

He understood the reaction out on the bench when they had first spoken. It had taken a lot to bare his soul that day. He had made no peace with who he was. What he needed was instant support; what he got was instant outrage. Joel kicked himself internally again for his insensitivity.

"Hardly your fault, old boy," Frank replied, trying to force his de Selby mask to stay on. "If you don't mind, I think I'll take a nap."

Joel wanted to tell him not to. He wanted to tell him that between the two of them, they could talk their way through it all. That together they could find a way through Joel's own hopelessness and isolation, through Frank's loneliness and self-loathing. He didn't say it though, because he knew it wasn't true. A conversation might help them both, but it would fix nothing, practically speaking. He sat, powerless to come to his friend's aid, feeling every bit the useless old man when suddenly an idea came to him, a light bulb moment that would equally fix nothing, but would help, at least soothe the hurt.

He waited until he knew that Frank was asleep, and reached into the nearby chest to retrieve his contact book. Carefully, he stole from the bedroom in his slippers and dressing gown to make his way to reception.

Nurse Angelica sat there with her beautiful skin and fleshy hands. She smiled nervously at him. So she knew as well, then. Knew he was sick. They were all in on it. That probably included Karl. He made his best smile to comfort her and asked if he might make a phone call. Eva had given him a mobile phone for his birthday the year before, top of the range by all accounts, but it lay in its box, in a deep recess of the cubby in his nightstand. He preferred the landline at reception, an old

Bakelite with its spinning dial. There was something about the feel of a landline, the weight of it, the realness. The fact that it still worked, still existed was tantamount to the sense of permanence it had. Not like the mobile phones, transitory things, gone and replaced by something better as soon as you had it in your hand.

He thumbed through the old moleskin book until he found Lily's phone number and dialed it, pulling at the old dial and listening to the satisfying click click click as the dial rolled back. She answered promptly, the number for Hilltop being saved into her phone.

"Grandad?" she asked quizzically.

She sounded sleepy. He remembered Eva's propensity for sleeping late and bit back the admonishment.

"I need a favor, Lily, my dear," he told her confidentially.

When he was finished on the phone with Lily, he turned to Angelica. She was clearly still uncomfortable with him. He decided he could use it to his advantage.

"I'd like to have a movie night," he told her.

"Ooooh, very nice," she replied, in her soft accent. "When would you like to have it?"

"Tonight."

"Well, that's very short notice, Mr. Monroe. Perhaps next week?"

"Tonight," he said firmly, and he put on the face.

Angelica swallowed hard. He felt like a schoolyard bully. It surely wasn't Angelica's fault, but to Joel's mind a line had been drawn, and however she felt about it personally, it had become a case of them versus him, and she was firmly in the "them" camp.

"Well…" she said uncomfortably shifting in her chair.

"Well?" he asked, making the face even harder than he had before.

"We'll see," she said.

"I have a daughter," he told her in uncompromising tones. "I know what 'we'll see' means. I also know that it's what we use as adults to fob off children in the hope that their short attention spans will lead them down another road. Do you think I'm a child, Angelica?" He added a dangerous soft note to the words.

"No, Mr. Monroe, not at all…"

"Because I can behave like a child if you want? Do you want me to throw a temper tantrum and shit my pants?" he asked with a smile.

Her uneasy smile faltered now, and she looked at him as if seeing for the first time what the others had been talking about.

"Shall I throw all my toys out of the pram, Angelica? Do you want to see me screaming and crying, Angelica?"

The smile vanished, replaced by a guarded look that was part nervousness, part surprise.

"A movie night?" she said. "No harm in a movie night."

Joel dropped his false smile and replaced it with a real one.

"No harm at all," he assured her. "After dinner, maybe? In the common room?"

She nodded at him, looking relieved that he had gone back to smiling pleasantly. His victory was tainted more than a little by the rising guilt of behaving like a bully.

He thanked her and left, moving on to find his next accomplice, but when he arrived at her door he found himself unsure. His old-fashioned sensibilities kicked in as he tried to summon up the courage to knock at the entrance to Una's tiny slice of Hilltop. A little voice told him that this was unseemly. Him going into the private room held by Mrs. Clarke, a friend of his deceased wife. It was the memory of poor Frank's story that pushed him forward. He knocked gently on the door, but then worried that his knock might sound like an elderly person's knock, so he knocked again but louder this time. The result was a pounding on the door that he had definitely not been going for. Now he felt embarrassed he'd knocked timidly once, and shook the door the second time.

Una arrived at the door looking vexed, until she saw him, and her expression was replaced by one of pleased surprise.

"Joel," she greeted him. "Come in."

She stepped back to let Joel in.

The room was decorated precisely the way he expected it would be. Little porcelain and china knickknacks, small framed photos and paintings of various birds, brightly colored bedsheets, not the standard prison-issue ones, but ones that her family had brought in from the outside. A little bookshelf on the wall was piled high with various books, and more sat on the floor underneath it. He had never realized she was such a voracious reader.

"I need your help," he told her.

She smiled warmly at him.

"Anything for you," she told him.

He told her that Frank was feeling down, though he skipped over the why of it all, and that he had a plan. She laughed at him when he rather guiltily told her that he had bullied Angelica. "You're terrible," she told him fondly.

Her laugh was a little tinkling thing like a small bell ringing. It was, he had to admit to himself, the first time he had been comfortable in her company since Lucey died. Karl popped his head in at one point to check on her and tried to cover his obvious surprise at Joel's presence. Joel hoped that it would go some way to mitigating against threatening to shit himself. When he finally left her room, Joel had regained the morning's good form, but found that Frank remained a little withdrawn. Joel tried for a reassuring pat on the shoulder that made both of them uncomfortable.

Throughout the rest of the day, he tried to contain his excitement. Lily dropped off the package with a smile, heartened, he felt by seeing an energy and enthusiasm to him that was typically lacking. And this of course was the secret to Joel. When he had a purpose, regardless of what it might be, Joel was a ball of energy, a relentless perpetual motion machine, directly, inversely proportional to the energy and enthusiasm he could muster when his days were a long pointless march into night.

"You're all fired up today," she told him as she handed him the box.

"I'm a force to be reckoned with," he replied fondly.

She smiled at him in a way she hadn't done in as long as he could remember. Like she was seeing him for the very first time. Seeing a person underneath the cranky thing that had replaced the grandfather she had grown up knowing. An adult seeing another adult, seeing the person inside. He hugged her extra hard before she left.

The potential spanner in the works arrived when it was time for dinner.

"I'll just take it in here with the telly," Frank told him, putting on his best de Selby fake smile.

"No," Joel told him, "you won't."

"Oh, won't I?" Frank replied irritably.

"Your company is requested," Joel replied, channeling his inner de Selby.

"I politely decline," Frank replied firmly.

"I'm not asking," Joel replied determinedly.

"Neither am I," Frank shot back.

Then the two of them stared at each other, borderline

malevolently, until Frank finally sighed and got up to dress himself, muttering all the while about stupid pigheaded stubbornness.

Dinner couldn't pass fast enough, and when it was finally done, Karl arrived in to roll down the large projector screen, and dim the lights.

Frank looked all about him in confusion.

"What's going on here?" he asked.

Joel just smiled at him, delighted, for once to have managed to pull off something that even Frank couldn't see through. It was a good feeling to know that the old actor didn't have all of the answers all of the time.

As Karl fiddled with the projector and the box of DVDs, Una stood up and tapped the side of her drinking glass to bring the room to a hush. All the residents, some of them in on the ploy and some not, went quiet.

Una took them all in with a sweep of her gaze. Lit softly by the lamps in the room she appeared grand, majestic even, in her hand-me-down clothes and calm, dignified manner. Joel smiled encouragingly at her.

"Ladies and gentlemen," Una announced in her most pronounced speaking voice. "Thank you all for coming this evening. Tonight's entertainment, courtesy of Joel Monroe's granddaughter, Lillian, is a celebration of the work of one of Hilltop's most talented residents."

The penny had dropped with Frank, and to Joel's delight, he could practically see the fog clearing from around his friend as he sat up straighter in his seat and adopted a modest pose.

"His primary works include theater and film, but most of you will know him from the long-running soap opera *Glory Days*. Tonight we will enjoy a viewing of this talented actor in season four of the series, one of his strongest seasons, if I may say, in honor of this wonderful performer. Residents and nurses, I give you Mr. Frank de Selby."

The room burst into applause, and Frank graciously stood up to accept. He bowed a little, smiled around the room, mouthed the words *thank you* over and over again. He could have been accepting an Oscar or a lifetime achievement award. Joel realized that if he'd seen such a display a week or two beforehand, it would have instilled in him a deep loathing for this flamboyant character, this gallant creature, but now he just smiled at his friend, and watched him enjoying another moment in the limelight.

They settled in to watch each episode, and Joel found himself enjoying them, much to his own disgust. He could never tell Frank that, of course. Frank for his part smiled at the television and, sitting between Mrs. Klein and Mrs. Clarke, filled the audience in on little titbits from each episode. What actors were drunk on set, who was having affairs with whom off camera, ad-libbed lines and broken props. He basked in his moment, his cares forgotten for another day. In this moment he was the de Selby he had renamed himself to be, not the Adams that he loathed.

It wasn't a fix, Joel knew that; nothing could fix Frank now, just as nothing could fix him, but it would help, somewhat, to ease them through another day. He smiled as he sipped his tea, enjoying the happy murmuring about the room, and the air of positivity that had come with it.

How comfortable some prisons can be, he thought to himself as he looked about at the inmates.

12

They strolled through the grounds of the nursing home, Joel in a sharp tweed suit (which seemed, he felt, to add an air of dignity to him, something of the old formidable man he used to be), and Frank in his pajamas, dressing gown and a silk scarf with tiny golden fringes.

"That was nice of you last night," Frank told him as they ambled.

Neither of them had spoken much in the early part of the morning. When Joel woke, Frank was already awake, reading his pretentious literature. That's the word Joel reckoned Frank would use. He wouldn't say book. He'd say *literature*.

They had sat in the common room in companionable silence and afterwards, without discussion or planning, had both retired to the garden for a morning stroll. Together they had walked down to the front gate, circled around on the small pathway that led them under the stand of trees that imperiously stood watch all along the borders of the prison home.

"Well…" Joel mumbled, uncomfortable with the compliment.

"Not like you," Frank said airily.

Joel was grateful for the dig. He was a man unused to, and massively discomfited by, praise. The easy good-natured ribbing between them was much more his pace. It was a language that men of his generation had grown up speaking to one another. A language he'd inherited from his father who displayed his love for his children by patting them on the head from a reasonable distance and saying "well done." Joel was about thirty when he heard a man say *I love you* to another man. It had startled him. He wasn't aware that men were allowed to do that. He tried not to think about the ramifications of that. How that lack of affection, that derogation of language, could have left him here in this isolated place, how such language, such culture, might have made his friend an outsider. He was too old to change his ways now.

"Think I might be in a spot of trouble over it when The Rhino hears about it."

"Oh?"

"I may have threatened to throw a temper tantrum."

"I see," Frank said, the start of a grin appearing on his lips.

"Might have told Angelica that I'd shit myself."

The peal of laughter that burst from Frank startled several birds from their branches overhead. He watched them take wing as he wiped a small tear from the corner of his eye.

"The poor woman. I think she's half-afraid of you already, you know," he said finally, when he'd composed himself.

"Can't say this'll help," Joel commented.

"What'll you tell The Rhino?"

"Don't know. Didn't plan that far ahead, to be honest."

"You worried?"

"A little."

"The psychiatrist thing?"

Joel let the worry wrap itself around him again. The cloud

that was never far away, always waiting for his mind to wander back to it, so it could envelope him, coalesce where he was and blur his ability to think straight. Every bit the prison that the walls of Hilltop were. They would send in the psychiatrist who would know. Joel couldn't hide it from him like Frank might have. They would know, and then they'd send him to a psychiatric ward to strip away the last of the dignity he held on to.

"They'll send me away, Frank. They'll ship me off to some shit hole, pardon my language, and pump me full of drugs and I'll die there not knowing who I am."

"Jesus, Joel." Frank looked at him agog. "And they call me dramatic."

"Don't make a joke out of it. It's not funny," Joel said, ignoring the de Selby mask and talking straight at Frank Adams.

"All right, all right."

"What'll I tell her?"

"You're sorry, for a start. You are sorry, aren't you?"

Joel checked internally to see if he was sorry. He found a morsel of regret. Angelica was a nice woman, kind to him in her own way, and sweet with everyone else. She laughed a lot. He found her particular in-your-face brand of religion irritating, but she hardly deserved to be bullied. The tiny morsel of regret was born of the knowledge that if he wasn't an inmate in Hilltop Prison Nursing Home he would never have behaved in such a way.

"I suppose I am a little."

"Good place to start. Keep her off your back."

Joel worried at it as they walked, kicking through the branches and twigs, pine needles and moss that blanketed the pathway under the trees around the end of the garden. This would be less of a problem if he was dead, he realized. He assumed corpses didn't worry about the pointlessness of their existence, and they were singularly unconcerned if you were offended by them. If he had followed through with the plan when it first occurred to him, if he had swallowed all the pills, or fashioned a noose for himself from the cord of his dressing gown, he wouldn't have to worry about whether or not he had upset the head nurse. He wouldn't look at tall trees and think of sentinels guarding against his escape. He'd be free. Free from worry, free from the pointlessness.

He was lost in his thoughts until he kicked the root of a tree and looked up. He had never, he realized, walked this path before, and was surprised to see the wall dip a little, enough for him to see over into the backyards of adjoining houses.

The property that Hilltop occupied was large enough that several houses butted onto it, and in the May sunshine he saw children playing on swing sets and kicking footballs as they romped on little stocky legs under supervision of au pairs or child minders. He smiled as he watched them at play and for a moment forgot about dying, or nurses or guardian trees and just enjoyed the feeling of being a man walking in the woods.

"Over here," Frank barked at him.

Joel had almost lost his friend in the small tangle of woods that marked the edge of the nursing home. Frank hadn't wandered off, however, but moved into the corner where the walls marking the east and south of the grounds met. There, shaded from sunlight and damp from it, sat a large rock, propped up against the corner.

It was an opportunistic rock. A rock of convenience. It sat, a little weathered, with a natural groove in it that looked like a little step, the prefect height for either of the two elderly men to climb up and perch on the wall. The wall was built around the thing, as if perhaps, at some point in the history of the old grounds, there had been a point to being able to climb up on the wall and survey the surroundings. Presumably before someone had built a house next to it. The top of a flat garage roof was visible across the top of the wall, with its perfect stair-rock. Its only drawback were the thick brambles that blocked access to it.

From looking at the various gardens they'd passed, Joel knew the drop on the far side would be high. Too high for either of them, but the rock called out to be climbed, and the wall beckoned to be sat upon. There might be a way down the other side if they could get to it.

Joel looked at Frank who was peering skyward, craning his neck this way and that.

"What are you looking for?" Joel asked him.

"I feel like now would be the appropriate time for a ray of sunshine to pop through the branches and illuminate our little ladder over there."

Joel scowled at him.

"That's the problem with you, and the sky," Frank told him. "No sense of romance. Come on, help me clear out these brambles."

Frank hitched up his dressing gown and started kicking at the brambles, but delicately in his slippers. With his clothes pulled up, his scarf around his neck and his delicate, clumsy attempts to remove the thorny, tangled mass, he looked like something that had escaped from a cartoon, and Joel found himself breaking down in laughter.

Frank regarded him coldly for a moment, a sharp jab waiting just behind his lips to put the laughing Joel in his place, but Joel's laughter infected him, and a slow smile spread across his face as he looked at his fancy slippers amid the mud and brambles and the smile turned into a laugh, sheepish at first but growing as Joel wheezed through his own mirth. The two of them stood in the little clearing, next to their newly discovered rock, and laughed until neither of them could breathe properly.

Eventually the laughter subsided, and Frank picked his way carefully toward the rock, studying it closely, his smile still stretching across his old lined face. "What are we going to do?" Joel asked Frank in between little aftershocks of laughter.

"Right now? Nothing. We're going to go back to the room."

"Later?"

"Later we're going to do some gardening."

That answer was enough for Joel to know that Frank was done talking on the subject for the moment. He was planning something. Scheming, as was his way. It wouldn't do at all for Joel to probe too hard into the inner workings of the little genius. Besides, it would ruin his grand reveal.

And so they wandered back to the nursing home, with thoughts of a stair-rock replacing thoughts of suicide. Joel thought they might look a little preposterous walking together, the tall man in the sharp suit next to the little man in his dressing gown and scarf, but instead of being embarrassed by it, he stood a little taller next to his pal, and smiled in the early morning sunshine.

That afternoon the repercussions of the day before came back to haunt Joel. The Rhino stood in front of him, in her immaculate uniform and her stern, unflinching face. Joel met her calm outrage with a brick wall of obstinate, one-word answers. Anything more and he feared he'd betray the fact that he was afraid of her. She might already know, but he didn't want to give her the satisfaction of showing it.

"You threatened to defecate," she said. It wasn't a question. Just a loaded statement.

"Yes."

Joel felt it was a little unfair; it hadn't been intended to be taken seriously. He just didn't want to be fobbed off. What little dignity he felt he had left was worth clinging to, and he would certainly not throw it away by soiling himself for a dirty protest over a movie night.

"You threatened a member of staff?" she asked this time, the slight shift in her tone at the end taking the steel out of the words.

"No."

"No?"

"No."

She locked eyes with him again.

"You didn't tell poor Angelica that you were going to scream at her?"

Poor Angelica. Joel scoffed at the idea of poor Angelica. The Rhino didn't care a jot for "poor Angelica." She just enjoyed having leverage on Joel.

He still struggled with the nurse, though. Nice, friendly, warm and caring she may be, but it was her hands, big against the tiny frame of Mr. Miller, that he still saw when he closed his eyes to go to sleep at night.

He said nothing, but instead tried to return the look with interest. He hoped she'd back down before he lost his nerve. He hoped the nerves weren't showing all over his face.

"Can you understand, Mr. Monroe, why this would be a problem for us?"

"No," he said, though he was dismayed by how reasonable she sounded. And how much sense she was making.

"You've been here for five years, Mr. Monroe, and while you're not famous for your wit like Mr. Adams here..." She threw a withering look at Frank in the bed across the room. She also loaded the word *wit* to make it sound as if it was a mortifying venereal disease that someone might contract. "You were still always regarded as a polite, calm, respectful resident. In the last few weeks that seems to have changed."

"No one was forcing me to take medication a few weeks

ago," he replied. It was a poor excuse, he knew, but he didn't need her digging at him, he didn't need her finding out just how unwell he really was.

"We didn't have to force you a few weeks ago, Mr. Monroe. You were happy to take the medication then—medication, may I remind you, that you very much need to take."

"Before I realized that noncompliance would mean I was labeled as some kind of lunatic."

"No one thinks you're a lunatic, Mr. Monroe." Her reasonable tone was infuriating. She was doing it on purpose, he knew. "But the sudden death of Mr. Miller, all things considered, may have had an impact on your mental health."

Joel thought that the relentless monotony of a pointless existence, imprisoned by his own family as he mourned the death of the love of his life may have something to do with it too, but he decided not to say that out loud. Instead he, somewhat childishly, turned his face away from her, and stared out the window at the long drive down the hill to the front gate.

He had no reply. She had him cornered. He wasn't well and she knew it, and the consequences of her knowing that might very well be a worse prison than this one. Another home, away from Frank, or a psychiatric unit. Constant surveillance. No chance to end it, no space to pull off his personal great escape. The pointlessness exacerbated by the even more tightly confined space, by having to share that space with those who had been beaten down by life, their minds destroyed by it. He'd have to kill himself before they got the chance to move him.

He looked down the driveway and racked his brain for a worthy suicide.

She remained where she was, her very presence a demand for answers.

"Probably my fault," Frank said out of the blue.

Mr. de Selby had been awfully quiet for the start of the conversation, held in check presumably by The Rhino's all-encompassing authority. He found his voice in Joel's moment of need.

"Excuse me?" The Rhino said, turning her gaze on Frank.

"I must have gotten him all riled up," Frank told her.

They hadn't been friends long. It was almost hard to believe in a way, Joel felt he knew the other man. Knew him well. Knew his soul. In the short time of their friendship he had learned to distinguish between Adams and the de Selby mask. He had learned when the showman was preparing for his cue, and when the real man was slipping out from behind the mask to let the world see his sad face, however briefly.

Joel knew his last comment was pure de Selby, intended to be performed, not said. It came from the blue to startle a response. Joel knew precisely what his friend was looking for. A two-man show.

"You did no such thing," he practically squawked with false indignation.

"Sure I did," de Selby replied casually, arrogantly even. "You're easily upset. I came in here and upset your routine. Knocked you out of kilter."

"Don't flatter yourself, you preening jackass," Joel shot back. He tried to keep his performance natural, believable. Just the right level of disdain. He had enough practice at it over the years; he should know how.

"Ah, look," Frank said, patronizingly. "It's happening again. Getting all cranky."

"I'll go over there and cranky you in a minute," Joel shot back.

If she was buying their performance she gave no sign of it,

but the distraction was keeping her from bringing all of her guns to bear on Joel.

"You know what this cantankerous old so-and-so needs, Nurse Ryan?" Frank asked her grandly.

"I'm positive you'll tell me," she replied drily.

"He needs a bit more exercise."

She paused, frowning. She may not have been buying the two-men-fighting routine, but this was an angle she didn't see coming.

"Oh, you know what I need, do you?" Joel threw in, to keep her off balance.

"Certainly. Perhaps tomorrow I could take him out and show him some of my green fingers. I kept quite a garden back when I could be bothered to keep quite a garden."

Gardening again. The old rascal had something up his sleeve, but what planting flowers and cutting the grass was going to do for them, Joel had no idea. The Rhino frowned doubly hard.

"I'm not doing any bloody gardening," Joel said, rolling the dice.

The frown eased out a little; she weighed him up.

"Perhaps a little exercise is wanting for you, Mr. Monroe. I've often heard that exercise is good to lift one's spirits. I'll arrange for you to join Hilltop's Gardening Club tomorrow. Mrs. Clarke is a friend, isn't she? I'm sure she'll be delighted to have the extra pair of hands."

Joel pretended to sulk. He turned his face away from her and looked back down the garden, only this time he wasn't looking at the gate; his eyes strayed into the corner in the southeast, where the rock waited for them.

He stared at it as she made her exit, and when she was safely away, he turned to Frank who treated him to a broad wink and a wide smile.

★ ★ ★

That afternoon Mighty Jim beat Joel to a stalemate again, while Frank provided commentary to the amusement of the common room. Una greeted the news that Joel and Frank were joining the Gardening Club with a warm smile that Joel thought contained just a hint of suspicion. Joel could keep nothing a secret; his face was an open book for anyone who cared to read it, so he felt he was best off not knowing what Frank had planned, but Una Clarke, Joel was beginning to understand, was no one's fool, and she saw the twinkle in his friend's eye for what it was. Mischief.

Long after lunch was done, Joel was sitting in the armchair by his bedroom window when a familiar little red car drove up the hill. Sitting inside were Lily and Chris. As they wound up the long drive, his granddaughter waved at him, and his grandson shot him a weak smile.

The time when he was the favorite was long gone with both of his grandchildren. He had doted on them outrageously when they were little. He brought them into the garage and tried to teach them how to fix cars, just as he had done when their mother was little. They were too young, but he didn't care; he just wanted to be in their company. By the time he had realized that there was a gulf between them, Joel found himself at first sad and upset, but increasingly ambivalent as the years rolled by him. Without Lucey it all just seemed so irrelevant. A pattern had revealed itself, but Joel was too self-ish or too stupid to see it. He had allowed that gap to open up, first with Eva, then with Lily and Chris, and it would have taken so little to bridge it, but he had allowed it to grow into something huge and unfixable. He wondered if there was still time before he went.

Now, underneath all the ambivalence, and for the first time in a very long time he found himself excited to see them.

Lily a little more than Chris. She had been such a willing accomplice the day before with the DVDs. He wouldn't have
known where to even start sourcing such things, and yet she
had delivered in a mere afternoon. He found himself grateful to be wearing his suit, so that they'd not see him wrapped
in his bed clothes, sitting morosely again. For his part, Frank
seemed absolutely unmoved by the idea of spending the day
in his bed clothes. Unlike Joel, he didn't look depressed when
he wore his dressing gown. He wore it with a certain panache
that made him look comfortable and casual, instead of depressed and borderline suicidal.

"Have you come for the DVDs, love?" he asked Lily as she
walked into the room.

"Hello, Grandad," she said, hugging him. So many times
before the hugs were perfunctory, a necessary chore to show
the minimum amount of affection, but this one was real, and
warm. He hugged her back.

"No, I want you two to keep those. I actually bought myself some copies. I wouldn't mind getting them signed by
Mr. de Selby?"

"Mr. Adams," Joel corrected her lightly.

"Leave my public alone," Frank admonished him. "I'd be
delighted to sign them for you, my dear. And who's this strap-
ping lad?"

Chris grinned at him. Joel reckoned Frank and Chris would
get on well. The same devil-may-care attitude. The same mischief and trouble twinkling in their eyes. His grandson had
Joel's height, with more growing to do, and though he still
had some of the gangliness of youth, Joel thought he could
see the boy filling out into a broad, imposing young man.
He was already a young man really, at eighteen, but Joel had
found that the older he got, the higher he raised the bar before he considered someone an adult.

"I'm Chris," his grandson told Frank, extending his hand.

"I swear, Joel, your grandchildren hit the genetic jackpot. All of the handsome bits about you, without any of your glaring flaws. This one could be cut out of you."

Chris and Lily beamed. Joel sniffed loudly to make his displeasure clear.

"What brings you two here?" he asked, settling back into his chair as Chris plonked himself down on the edge of Frank's bed. It was familiar territory to the young man; he'd perched on the edge of that bed many times during their more frequent visits to see Lucey.

"Just thought we'd pop up and say hello," Lily told him as she casually moved about the room.

"A pleasant surprise," Joel told them.

"Yeah. Like that phone call yesterday. I think that's the first time you've called me since Nana..." Lily trailed off as she realized the impact that her words would have. Joel tried not to let it show, but it stung. He forced a smile anyway, to let them know he wasn't upset.

"Anyway," Chris continued, trying to cover the awkwardness. "We just thought we'd swing by. See how you were getting on. Just check in, you know?"

Joel's excitement at seeing them faded. They weren't here to see him. They were spies. They were here to check up on him. The conversation between Liam and Eva had come to this. A "casual" visit to check on his mental well-being. Did they think he was so feebleminded that he wouldn't see through this? Did they think so little of his intelligence? He stifled the anger, the outrage at the chicanery of it all. Their report would be immaculate. They'd return to his daughter empty-handed. He may not be a champion liar, but for this, he'd outperform de Selby.

"Check in. Of course. Well, as you can see, all's perfectly well with the world."

Considering Joel's track record of cranky reticence, this was practically revelatory. Positive. They were sure to be shocked by it. Joel took a small delight in the idea. He could hoodwink all of them. He'd show them all.

"So," Lily tried. "DVD night last night? That must have been good?"

"It was marvelous, Lily, my dear," Frank told her, while Joel fixed his smile onto his face. "I was in my pomp in season four. The writing team, the other cast, the good directors. Honestly, it's a wonder I ended up here and not in some Beverly Hills mansion."

"And you organized it all, Grandad?" Lily asked, not distracted by Frank's efforts.

"With a little help," Joel told her, still smiling politely.

"Lovely," she said, though he reckoned it was more for something to say.

"Cards?" Frank asked. Clearly he had read the room; he knew Joel was shutting them out.

They settled in, made themselves comfortable, covered up their real reason for being there with friendly chitchat. Nightclubs, bars, college work, shopping, football. Banal conversation disguising a deeper motive. It rankled with Joel that he should have so many people prying into his life. That he could have nothing for himself, not even his own misery. He played a hand too, Forty-Five. He wasn't a bad player, though he should have guessed that Frank would be the supremo of the foursome. Joel played to hide from them, to keep them from knowing what he had no intention of giving away, until eventually they called it quits.

Frank was busy grinning through his victory as they began to gather their belongings.

"Grandad," Lily told him seriously, as she put on her coat. "It's nice to see you coming out of your shell a bit."

He nodded at her with his polite smile in the most paternal manner that he could. A poker-faced smile.

"Nice to see you, love," he told her.

"Must come up for a game again," Chris told Frank, in his confident, easy manner. If there wasn't fifty plus years between them, they could have been friends.

"And, Grandad," Lily added as she stepped in for a hug. "Please, please, give me a call anytime you need it. For anything. Okay?"

Maybe she meant it. Maybe somewhere in her she wanted to reach the man whom her grandfather had been. Maybe she had felt the same spark of recognition that he had felt the day before. A connection between family, long lost but not forgotten. But all Joel could see was more interference. More policing by his daughter. More intrusion into his head.

As he hugged his granddaughter he found himself thinking that it would be tough to leave her behind, to leave all of his family behind. Tougher still, he thought, to have to stay here with them.

After they had left, their casual probing done for the day, Joel stretched himself out on his bed. Frank remained suspiciously quiet beside him. Not normal for the gregarious performer.

"Something wrong?" Joel asked.

"Thought it was nice of them to visit. You didn't have to go all cold on them."

"I did no such thing," Joel lied.

"Don't pull that crap with me. I saw it. As soon as she mentioned your wife, you clammed up."

"Actually, I clammed up when they told me they were here to spy on me."

"You're being paranoid."

Joel thought about it. There was a chance, a slight one, that they had really come to spend some time in his company, but it wasn't enough. It was too much like the control that had been exerted over him in recent years. Too much like the control he had lost of his own life for him to be comfortable with it.

"Maybe I am, Frank," he sighed. "Maybe I am, but it doesn't matter. If I am, then it's because I can't trust anyone to treat me like a grown man anymore. I can't trust anyone to let me be. To make my own way, to not live day-to-day in this pleasant little hellhole."

Frank was silent beside him, absorbing. It was a philosophical moment for them both.

"I can trust you, can't I, Frank?"

It was a galling kind of question to ask. More because in the moment of asking it, Joel knew he needed to be able to trust his friend. To have one person who would let him live, or die as he pleased. Who would help him if he wanted it, and leave him alone if he didn't.

"You can trust me, Joel. I promise."

The relief for Joel was almost palpable. He sighed with it. Before he could thank Frank, Nurse Liam bustled in.

"Have I interrupted a moment?" he asked.

"Not at all, old boy," Frank told him, slipping into de Selby mode quickly. "We're contemplating mortality."

"Morbid," Liam admonished them, though he had the sense not to poke at it. Silly to tell two elderly men in a nursing home not to talk about death really.

"I understand Nurse Ryan spoke to you this morning, Joel?"

"She did," Joel replied. He still hadn't entirely forgiven Nurse Liam for the chin-wagging behind his back, but in that moment of relief, of knowing he had someone, an important someone to help him, Joel was not in the mood to take it out on the young nurse.

"I hope you're not mad at me. I'm just worried about you."

"I know you are, and I appreciate it. Can you appreciate that your concern, all of your concern is suffocating me?"

Liam looked at him for a moment. A long moment. Joel could see the young man trying to reach a conclusion, stretching out to put himself in Joel's shoes, to understand what this elderly, cranky man was feeling.

"I think I can," he said finally.

"Then me and you will do fine, Nurse Liam. Sometimes I just want to be allowed to paddle my own canoe."

"I get that. You..." He hesitated for a moment, uncomfortable, in new and unfamiliar water. "I know what it's like to have people try to force something on you that's not you."

As he said it the nurse glanced in Frank's direction. A small thing, a flicker of the eye really. He understood. Somehow he knew what Frank was going through. On some level or other he understood it. Frank assiduously avoided eye contact, though something now hovered in the air between them. Joel thought he might understand it, too. Liam was what Frank had lost, because he had never allowed himself to be what Liam was. Gay and open and unconcerned about what any of these elderly folks thought about it.

In showing his intuitive understanding, Liam telegraphed to Joel that he'd have the same sympathy when Joel finally executed his plan. Now there were two people at least who would understand why he did it, after he was gone.

"So me and you will get on better, then?" Joel asked Liam. He loaded the question and hoped Liam understood what he was implying: Will you let me be the grown man that I am?

"I'm sure that we will," Liam said gently, and now he was

looking at Joel strangely, the way Lily had. Seeing something stir and come alive inside the elderly man where there had once been a shell. How ironic, Joel thought, that they could see the life stirring just on time for him to snuff it out.

"Live and let die?" Joel asked him with a smile.

Nurse Liam nodded slowly at them both and walked out.

Joel stewed in the moment before he finally turned to Frank.

"What's the plan for tomorrow? I know you've got something up your sleeve," he said as he looked across the room at his friend, stretched out on his bed.

Frank smiled a small secretive smile.

"The plan for tomorrow is that we're busting out of here, and we're going to find a place where we can plan that final farewell of yours. How about that?"

The old actor leaned as far across the gap between them as he could without falling out of his bed and whispered his idea.

13

Early the next day Joel and the other prisoners of Hilltop's Gardening Club made their way out into the cloudy May morning. Frank, extra energetic and enthusiastic, had dressed in his finest, a waistcoat and tweed suit; his long hair, curling naturally at the end, bounced around his scarf. The Gardening Club members looked at him askance as he walked onto the grass in his clean leather shoes. Mrs. Clarke tsked and shook her head, but said nothing.

That morning at breakfast in the common room, she had smiled knowingly at the two of them from across the room. Joel had offered her a serious nod of his head in return and hoped that she didn't see the guilty apprehension all over his face. He still couldn't quite make up his mind about what exactly Una Clarke meant to him, but recently he had found himself happier in her company than he had been for a long time. He wondered if it might be hard to say goodbye to her too, when the time came.

It was the thought of his impending end that snapped him back into the moment. He had work to do. The plan was not complex, but it required a little timing, and a little luck. If Frank was right, no one would be paying attention to what tools they carried, just two old men out gardening for the day. When the moment was right, they'd need to strike. Since the Gardening Club had twenty members, Frank surmised that the comings and goings of the two of them wouldn't really be noticed.

Joel tried to keep the sense of nervous excitement under control as he stood alongside Frank while Una explained all of the various jobs. Frank nodded his way through it, as if he understood everything. Joel could practically feel The Rhino's eyes on him from somewhere back inside the nursing home. In his imagination she was standing at a window, staring at him. Only at him.

When the briefing was complete, the gang headed for the storage shed that sat up against the west wall behind the home itself. Inside they picked garden shears and hoes and thick, heavy-duty gloves. Frank looked so ludicrous in his old, shabby finery with the thick gloves and the hoe slung over his shoulder that Joel had to smile at him.

"And what jobs would you gents like this morning?" Una asked them as the groups began to break away to their tasks.

"We were thinking," Frank told her, "that there's a little patch down by the front gate, just inside it, that could do with some attention."

"All the way down at the front gate, eh?" she asked.

"We're less likely to be in anyone's way down there," Joel put in.

"Indeed you are," she replied. She was smiling broadly now.

"A fine day for it," Frank told her. "I've an itch to be about my work."

She looked him up and down patiently and absently fixed his collar.

"Try not to get into too much trouble," she told them as she moved away. "And don't ruin any of my flowers," she added as an afterthought.

She might know they were up to something, but she had no plans of stopping them.

"Let's move," Frank told him tersely. He might have done a fine job of appearing casual, but Joel could see signs of the same nervous energy about Frank that he had himself.

They moved down the driveway, acting nonchalant, and made some show of fussing about the flower bed down there before surreptitiously checking for watchers and dodging into the trees.

"So what happens when we have it cleared?" Joel asked as he made his way through along the path, littered with its pine needles.

"We'll cross that bridge when we come to it," Frank replied, carefully picking his way across the ground so as not to scuff his shoes.

Joel had, at least, gone for the most serviceable apparel he had. Once upon a time he had owned overalls for working in the garage, and pairs of jeans and sturdy boots. He had retired them when he had retired himself, but still among his clothes were sensible trousers and stout shoes, and a warm wool sweater. He, at the very least, didn't look ludicrous for a man preparing to be about the garden. As they moved along the wall, passing the back gardens of neighbors' homes, Joel thought he could feel the rock calling to him. The perfect little ladder, secluded, out of the way, something he missed in all of the walks he had taken, in all the ground he had covered in his years at Hilltop, this little gem lay buried. He figured he owed Frank some thanks for its discovery, but he'd reserve that until he saw how much work the man was willing to put in to accessing it. Joel suspected it might be less than strenuous.

Then they were upon it. It looked a little slipperier than the day before. He suspected there might be no sunlight in this little corner of the property at all, but it still looked majestic to him. The brambles in front of it looked less so. They were thick, gnarled, their roots deep, but Joel found himself grinning at his friend, and found Frank grinning back as he hung his suit jacket on a branch and loosened his collared shirt. Joel rolled his sleeves up, and they slung their tools into the task. It was, Joel felt almost instantly, lovely to be back at work. To have something to do. A job, a purpose.

They sheared at the thicker brambles on the outside first, chopping with an energy that Joel thought he had left behind him some years before, and when the worst of them were cut away, they started to hoe at the ground around the base of some of the thick bushes.

The first phase of the plan was not complex, just shear and hoe a path through the brambles so they could reach the rock. It took them the guts of an hour and a half, but when it was done, when they had shifted enough of the thick undergrowth to be able to make their way through it, Joel found himself as excited as he had been since he moved into Hilltop.

Without speaking, the two of them pushed their way through the little path they had cut, and with Joel moving first, they both climbed up the small little stairs. His arms were weary from the work, his joints ached. His body was letting him down badly. The spirit was very much willing, but Joel's advancing years told him he was weak. He ignored the protests and awkwardly, uncomfortably swung himself up on top of the wall and sat himself down. Smaller than he, Frank merely folded his arms on top of the wall and rested his chin on them.

Beyond the wall was a significant drop. Close to ten feet from the ground. High enough, in fact, that Joel was level with the roof of one of the neighbors' garages, and close enough that he could have almost reached out and climbed onto it, if he trusted his own body enough. It was perilously high, and Joel reveled in it. He let his feet dangle over the neighbors' backyard along the side of their garage, and he sat there.

The neighbors' yard was clean, well kept. A small conservatory jutted from the back of the house, stuffed with children's toys and coloring books and crayons. He hoped that none of them decided now was the time for play. He feared they'd be frightened by the elderly men poking their heads into the back garden of their home.

At the bottom of the wall, flush against it and just a few feet from where Joel was sitting, a wide coal bunker sat. One of those plastic, impermanent things. He measured the height with his eye.

"It's too high for us to drop down," he told Frank.

"Too high for you to drop down," Frank corrected him.

"Oh, you think you can make it, do you?"

"Well, I'm still spry. You, on the other hand, are second-hand parts."

Joel felt like he was secondhand parts, rusty ones that didn't quite fit together the way they should, but Frank didn't have to put it so bluntly.

"I still think it's too high."

"And I think you're a fraidy-cat, but that's a problem for down the line. It's time for phase two."

Reluctantly, and slowly because of the pains and cramps he was feeling, Joel swung himself back over the wall and into the grounds of Hilltop once again. For a moment only, he had felt free, but stepping down from their perfect little rock, Joel felt the walls close in around him again.

"What's phase two again?" he asked.

"We hoe the flower patch at the front, then we rejoin the rest. They'll be waiting for us. We go back up, we eat or have tea, or whatever the others do, and in the afternoon we come back…"

"Why are we hoeing a flower bed?"

"Because if someone comes down to check on us, we have to make it look like we were productive, and if we don't move now, they'll be down on us like a flash. If you think she's not watching…"

He trailed off, the threat more than implied. There could be no doubt who "she" was.

With every step away from the rock Joel felt a little more trapped, but equally determined. There was no way he could make the drop, but Frank was confident, and if Frank could get down, well, they could figure something out.

They hoed at the flower patch, weeding it, flipping the soil, rearranged some of the flowers, and were just getting done when Nurse Liam and Una arrived to check on them, and bring them back up to the house for tea. Both men were sweating heavily and showed all the signs of their labors deeper into the tree line, but if Una or Liam suspected anything untoward, they showed no sign of it.

Joel drank his tea and listened to the idle chitchat about gardening as patiently as he could manage. The rock was still down there, and the wall, and beyond it another taste of freedom. Another chance to escape the drudgery. A chance to feel like a man again, on his own, with himself and his friend for company, deciding things, doing things, being someone, and he had to sit here and listen to their idle banter. It was almost more than he could bear.

His joints ached, and yet he felt more alive than he had felt in a good many years. The pains in his knees and feet and hands from hoeing the ground were balanced by a sense of vitality and energy that had been obviously absent only weeks before when he looked into a sneeze guard and saw a skeleton's reflection looking back at him.

It seemed that in his rush to get dead, he was really living it up.

"You look agitated, Joel," Liam told him as he fixed Mrs. Reddan's IV drip.

"Just keen to get back to work," Joel told him, truthfully.

"Good. That's great. It's good to see you with some energy, some enthusiasm."

He sounded genuinely pleased. Joel resisted the urge to scoff at him. As if mere bloody gardening could offer him some kind of release from the monotony of Hilltop.

Frank remained calmer, of course he did; the performer didn't know what pressure was, always relaxed, always cool, but as the Gardening Club began to gather themselves to return to the tasks at hand, Joel could sense the anticipation off him. He had taken a moment during the tea break to dust himself down and tidy himself up, and looked, once again, completely immaculate, and utterly ridiculous.

"You ready?" he asked Joel as they stood up from the common room table.

Joel nodded.

"Good, start down the hill now, bring the gear with you. Wait for me at the rock. If I'm not there in five minutes, wait longer."

Joel had to laugh. In all his nervous excitement, he didn't think he had it in him to crack jokes, but nothing ever stopped Frank. He made his way down the yard, toting two hoes and two pairs of shears and the heavy-duty gloves as if he was planning an extended excavation of the main gate, but when he was alone at the bottom of the hill, he propped the tools up against a tree and made a deliberately clumsy effort to hide them. Anyone who came upon them would think the two had tried to hide them and then somehow slipped out the front gate in all the commotion.

He checked around him before he ducked into the tree line. They would eventually twig that the two men were missing, but with luck it would be a while before they noticed it.

Joel was halfway along the canopied route to the rock in the corner when the commotion started. The fire alarm pealing out in the still, early May afternoon. Joel chuckled to himself. He could practically see Frank standing on his bed, lighting a little slip of paper and wafting it under the detectors. The alarm would start certain protocols into action, and the nurses would be deployed to search rooms and round up the residents. In the hubbub of it all they'd make their escape, and when the dust all settled, the staff would check the emergency exits along the west wall at the back, and not down in their newly discovered southeast corner. Phase Two continued to pierce the air with its shrill but unnecessary warning as Joel leaned on the wall and waited.

The sound of the alarm was insistent and awful, and Joel felt bad for the unnecessary anxiety they were causing the other residents but they needed the distraction. They needed a way out.

He waited and waited and began to get nervous when Frank appeared through the trees, picking his way delicately as he went.

"What kept you?" Joel demanded irritably.

"Had to go back for the book."

"What book?"

"My notebook. If we're going to plan your suicide, I'll need to take notes. *The Unfortunate End of Joel Monroe* isn't going to write itself."

"So you made me wait while you fetched a damn notebook."

"Waiting is good for you, Joel. It builds character. You're in too much of a rush to get everything done anyway."

"Know what else builds character? A rap in the teeth."

"Why is it always violence with you?" Frank asked as he brushed by to mount the rock stairs. "All that aggression can't be good for your chakras."

"My what?"

"Never mind. There's no point in making fun of you if you don't understand what I'm saying."

Joel winced. Double hit. He was being made fun of, and he didn't understand it.

"Two points to you," he admitted grudgingly.

"We're keeping score now? That's good to know. Here, help me down."

The smaller man had, despite his advancing years, managed to shimmy himself up onto the wall, but had to squirm and wriggle as he tried to position himself to be able to drop down onto the coal bunker.

"What do you want me to do?" Joel asked, puzzled.

"I want you to sort of…" Frank gestured vaguely. "You know?"

"No. I don't. How on earth am I supposed to help you down?"

"Jesus, Joel, it's not that hard, you just sort of…" He squirmed and gestured at the same time.

"I don't know what that means."

"Fucking hell. Just get over here and grab me and kind of…" He began to gesture again, but there was more squirming this time.

"I'm going to throw you off the wall if you don't explain yourself."

Behind them the alarm shut itself off. Both men turned to look in the direction of the big house.

"We better start making a move," Frank told him seriously, "just come over here and grab me."

Joel climbed the stairs and reached out to his friend. He felt awkward, ungainly. He tried to tell himself that Frank's sexual orientation had nothing to do with his discomfort, but that would have been a lie. He forgot about Frank's uncanny ability to see into his mind.

"Stop feeling me up, you pervert," Frank told him, "I need you to just…"

He squirmed and gestured.

Sighing, Joel finally understood, and with significant reluctance, he sat himself down, so that Frank was positioned in between his legs. He became uncomfortably aware of how intimately close they were as he placed his hands under Frank's arms and began to slowly lower the smaller man down. For his part, Frank reached out with his short legs and braced them against the side wall of the garage to slow his descent and take some of the weight from Joel.

Halfway through the operation, Joel found the urge to giggle rising in his throat. He tried to stifle it, but found it bubbling up through him. His arms and chest shook with the need to laugh. If the owners of the house, or any of the kids walked out now, they'd spot two men into their seventies, one halfway down a wall, trying to escape a nursing home with the last echoes of an alarm still hanging in the air.

"Stop laughing," Frank gasped, his legs still propping him up against the side wall of the garage. "You'll drop me."

"Can't," Joel breathed in between stifled giggles.

Frank managed to release one leg and probed beneath himself for the top of the coal bunker, his toes grazing it.

"Little more," he choked as he continued to try to keep himself airborne.

Joel lowered him farther as the need to burst into tears

laughing crept up on him. He was nearly dizzy from it. He tried not to think about the chance of getting a stroke from laughing. It would have been outrageously ironic if he died during the act of escaping to plan his death. That would make a nice finale to *The Unfortunate End of Joel Monroe*, but a crappy ending to his life.

Suddenly the weight was gone from his hands, and for a terrifying moment, he thought he might have dropped his friend, but Frank had landed safely, and stood on the coal bunker scowling back up the wall at Joel.

"I've a good mind to leave you up there," he said in a hoarse whisper.

"Why are you whispering?" Joel asked, composing himself.

"Because if there's someone in that house we're getting arrested, you jackass."

That put a stop to Joel's gallop. What if they got arrested? It was, he noted to himself, a ludicrous thought. He was on his way to plan his own suicide. So what if he got arrested? Yet the nervousness never left him.

"How do I get down?" he asked eventually.

"I don't know. Give me a minute."

"What do you mean you don't know? They'll be looking for us right now."

"Yeah, but they'll be looking by the fire exits or the front gate. That was the whole point of Phase Two."

"Well, they'll move on quick enough. I need to get down."

Frank turned and searched about the neighbors' back garden, checking windows to make sure no one was staring out at them. It seemed all quiet. After a few minutes, he reappeared with a stepladder.

"Found it in the shed," Frank told him, as he threw the ladder up next to the bunker.

"I have to assume that what we're doing breaks several

laws?" Joel asked, as he delicately stretched his feet out looking for purchase. He was careful, so careful. Falling from a
ladder would be a worse death than stroke. He didn't know
why that was true, but it was.

"Not any big ones," Frank assured him, grasping the steps
to hold them in place.

When Joel got his feet back on the ground the two of them
looked at one another for a moment, and laughed. Without
thinking about it, Joel reached out and pulled his friend into
a hug.

"Let's get moving," Frank told him after they'd stopped
laughing.

They stowed the ladder back where it belonged and casually, as if they had every right in the world to be there, headed
for the front gate of their neighbors' garden. Joel waited for
some kind of a shout. Someone calling at them, "Where do
you think you're going," or something similar, but it never
came, and so the two of them simply walked out.

Joel paused to observe the conservatory, stuffed with children's toys of every shape and size. Teddy bears strewn lazily by
the bodies of dolls and trains and trucks here and there. Stuck
to the wall beside the door that led into the main house was
a collection of pictures and drawings. The artist had signed
every image, and Joel found himself picturing two loving parents looking fondly on their little prodigies as they hung their
handiwork on the walls.

So many of the toys were creative things, building toys,
making toys, fixing toys, that Joel saw in his mind's eye the
kind of dedication and love that he had never given to Eva.
Her mother had been her playmate, her father a stern thing,
a quiet thing. She had spent hours in his company, but only
where he wanted to be, in front of the television watching
games, or in his garage while he worked. He had dedicated

no time that he could recall where she had decided what they did or where they went. He struggled to remember a single toy that had belonged to her, and the realization of his distance from his child caused a lump in his throat.

"Problem?" Frank asked, peering through the window at the mountain of toys.

"No," Joel told him.

"Lucky kid," Frank observed.

"Lucky parents," Joel replied, and moved away.

They made their way through the estate, a small collection of suburban bungalows with flower boxes and big gardens and driveways big enough for two cars, before emerging onto the long road that led to the gates of Hilltop. It looked far away, but not so far that someone out searching for them wouldn't be able to spot the two old men.

The bus stop where they waited was painfully exposed, up against the wall of the local school and in plain sight of the front gate of Hilltop, though still some distance away. Joel carefully watched the gate of the nursing home for signs of someone coming to get them. No one stirred; the gate didn't move. Nonetheless, he felt an almost overwhelming sense of relief as the bus pulled in to whisk them into town.

"I hope you brought money this time," Frank told him, as they took their seats next to one another, midway down the bus.

"Did you?" Joel fired back.

"I don't need to. I'm the brains of the operation. You're the muscle and the money."

Joel patted himself down, finding his wallet inside his jacket's inside pocket.

"Brought it."

Frank smiled at him as Hilltop vanished behind them.

14

The bus rolled toward the city center in no apparent hurry, and Joel enjoyed the lack of urgency as he sat with Frank in a comfortable silence. He wondered what the other passengers might be thinking of them. Two elderly gents out for a jaunt. Did his guilt and nervous apprehension show itself? Could they see his fear of getting caught? Or did the other passengers think anything of them at all? Were they invisible in their own way? Just another two old men going from here to there.

"Where to?" he asked.

"Where do you fancy? World's our oyster."

"Do you know, I've never had an oyster."

"You want to go for oysters?"

"No, just that I've heard that expression a million times and I've never understood it."

"That's almost philosophical of you, Joel. If you're not careful we'll uncover an artist in you."

"Pfft." Joel scoffed at the idea outwardly, but had to admit he had enjoyed his little acting roles under Frank's watchful eye. He thought the show they had given The Rhino the day before had been particularly masterful.

"Oh, you can pretend you're indignant all you want. I bet you've been quietly begging for a leading role all your life."

"I worked all my life. That's what I did."

"You regret it?"

"Yes and no," Joel admitted. "I think I neglected Eva because of it. Makes me a little sad to think of it."

"I'm sure she understands."

"I'm not. I don't think I'd have to sneak out of a nursing home if we were closer. I think we'd be closer if I'd been a nicer dad."

"You're too hard on yourself."

"I suppose at the end it makes sense to look back on all the mistakes."

Frank didn't reply to that. Joel would admit that talking about your suicide is typically a conversation killer. Instead he allowed his mind to wander back to his garage. It was most of his adult life and a portion of his childhood, too. He'd been apprenticed at fifteen. At the time that was considered old enough, but now he wondered. What had he missed out on in those intervening years?

"Let's go to my old garage," he suggested.

"You think there's inspiration waiting there for you?"

"Maybe, but mostly I just want to look at it."

"Excellent. We break out of a maximum security nursing home so we can go stare at a garage. Have I admonished you on your frightening lack of imagination before?"

"At least once. Maybe more. I don't often pay attention to you."

"Well, try to recall the last lecture and come up with something better than your garage."

Joel let words wash off him. He had been lying, of course.

He hung on almost every word Frank said. It was hard not
to, they were performed so well. This time though, he really
wanted to see that garage. He wanted to look at the building
that had taken so much of him, and not just his time and energy. His money, his emotional well-being, his status in society had all rested on that building and the people who went
in and out of the place, and after all that, here he was, sneaking out of a nursing home because he wasn't allowed to walk
around without supervision in case a stroke killed him.

"No. I want to see it."

"Interesting," Frank mused. "You seem quite certain of
yourself here. What's going on in that block of cement you
call a head, Joel?"

"I gave a lot to that place. I feel like…" He paused, trying
to find the words, trying to sum up the tangle of feelings in
his head. "I feel like it owes me something."

Frank said nothing, but when the bus stopped just a couple
of blocks from the old garage and Joel made a move to go,
his friend slipped out of his seat behind him and nodded encouragingly at him.

The two of them made their way calmly along the quieter streets just outside the city center, passing people rushing
here and there as they took their time. It was all so familiar
to Joel. So much of his life had been lived in this neighborhood. Sometimes he'd go for lunch in one of the local diners, or have the occasional after-work drink when one of his
employees had talked him into it. He'd driven to this garage.
These streets had been his streets, and his feet remembered
them as he walked. Frank strolled with him, offering nothing, but Joel caught him glancing every now and then, as if
trying to measure his reaction.

Around the corner it revealed itself, standing at the end
of the street, dead ahead. It was his, but it was not. Someone

had painted it for a start, and added slick signage that gave it a modern look. It looked well, but somehow alien to him. It was jarring.

As they approached it, Joel didn't bother to slow his pace; his feet moved him independent of thought, and he simply walked into the building without hesitating as he had done for decades.

It wasn't his. The alien effect was tenfold inside. Cars being worked on had laptops attached to them, the mechanics poring over the diagnostics. They wore their overalls but looked clean somehow, or at very least cleaner than he would have expected. Loud music played, and the men shouted over it at one another.

He scanned the room for anything familiar. A face, a piece of equipment, an old decoration but found nothing. It was all new. All so different. He tried to remember how he had laid the place out, and found the memory hard to reach. Like a dream after waking, it was intangible, just out of his reach. He could recall little touches, some of the decorations and affectations that Lucey had added to the place over the years to try to make it more comfortable for him and his customers, but he had scoffed at them. He wished now he could recall them. He wished he had appreciated them at the time.

It wasn't his. He'd dedicated decades to this place. Its permanence, its endurance had been his. His home, his marriage, his livelihood had been this building, and now it was something different: a stranger in place of a friendly face.

"Help you?" a voice asked him, bringing him out of his reverie.

"No, thank you," he told the man absently.

"Well, is one of the cars yours?"

"No. I just wanted to look."

He tried to think of a way of explaining that he had practically built this place and that the young man addressing him was standing in a spot where he had worked on countless engines and drive shafts and wishbone bushes, but the words eluded him.

"Well, I'm sorry," the man told him in condescending tones, "but you can't just stand around here, pal."

Another one. Another person who thought they could talk to Joel Monroe like he was a child.

"Can do whatever I want," he told the young man, sizing him up. Joel was delighted to find himself looking down on the man.

"Yeah, I don't think so, buddy. This is a garage, not your living room." He made a move to usher Joel out.

"Don't even think about putting your hands on me," Joel told him ominously. He drew his shoulders back and puffed his chest out.

Work all around the garage seemed to stop as the mechanics all looked at him. The atmosphere in the room had become charged. The temperature seemed to drop. Joel was, he decided in that moment, making quite a fool of himself. He wouldn't have tolerated a complete stranger standing in the middle of his garage when it was his. He might have handled it with more tact, but he certainly wouldn't have brooked the implied threat. He was about to back down when Frank saved him. Again.

"Gentlemen," he intoned to the room. "I humbly beg pardon, but my pugnacious friend here is the former proprietor of this establishment, and unfortunately he's dying of cancer, likely to pop his clogs any minute now. He wanted one last look at the old dear before he goes."

The mood changed in an instant, and the young man who had been confronting him looked suddenly mollified.

"Sorry to hear that," he mumbled.

"Not your fault," Joel told him, in what he hoped passed for a magnanimous tone. "Just wanted to nose around."

He shot Frank a grateful look before he scanned the room again.

It wasn't his. It was someone else's now, and he was an invader in their space. In a way it was a sort of liberating feeling. One less tie to the old life that was holding him back. This look around would suffice as a goodbye. A farewell to the building that he had given so much to. Where his daughter had played, and his grandkids. He thought there was something poetic in saying goodbye to it.

He patted the young man on the shoulder and turned to make his way out into the sunshine.

And there it was. Hanging up just by the door. His scan hadn't taken in the full 360 degrees, so he'd missed it. A little sign. "My Tools, My Rules," it said, printed on an old license plate. Lucey had bought that for him. Told him it fit him. She had hung it up, too. Not where it was hanging now of course; he seemed to recall it hanging in his office. It had been her gift to him. Now it hung on someone else's wall.

"Can I take this?" he asked no one in particular as he began to unhook it from the screw that loosely held it in place.

He wasn't doing it particularly deftly, and the plate scraped uncomfortably against the wall, scarring the paint.

Frank stopped alongside him.

"Right, there, pal?" he asked, doing that trick where he talked out of the corner of his mouth. "Can we speed this up a little? This isn't my favorite kind of audience."

Joel shot a glance back over his shoulder to see all of the mechanics and floor staff staring at him.

"Used to be mine," he called out to them.

They continued staring.

"I have a strong feeling they're considering returning it to you," Frank told him, still smiling, his lips barely moving, "but I don't think you'll enjoy the reunion the way they'll do it."

Joel twisted at it a little more, and it came away from the wall.

"Thank you," he told the room as he made his way out the door.

His tools, his rules. He had forgotten that somewhere along the way. He wouldn't again.

"I'm going to put up one of those signs back at Hilltop," Frank told him outside. "'Days Since Joel Offered to Do Violence to Someone.' Gonna start a little pool. I bet you can't make it to three."

"Sorry," Joel told him, subdued by the ordeal but glad to be leaving with this hidden and almost forgotten little piece of Lucey.

"I didn't know the place meant so much to you," Frank told him, dropping the amusement from his voice.

"I guess I didn't either. Just so many years went into it, you know. And for what?"

"Joel, I know this is going to hurt, but literally everyone has the exact same thought. When it's all said and done we've given decades to doing the same thing every day, and very few people are lucky enough to have something to show for it besides a few scars and, if they're lucky, some savings."

"I guess I thought it would be nice. I don't know. Pleasant to see the old place. But it wasn't. It was awful. Like I'd never been there before."

"I'm sorry, pal."

"Me, too. I wish…" he trailed off wistfully. He didn't know what he wished, but he was certain that it wasn't what he'd just experienced. At the very least it was a goodbye. He stared down at the little sign. His rules. His way. Master of his own fate. The garage was no longer his. That life was no longer his. All ancient history. But at least he was still in charge of something. At least he could still end it any way he wanted.

15

"What about if I hung myself from the clock tower?" Joel asked as they sipped pints of stout at the bar.

"Hanged," Frank told him, brushing the head from his lips.

"What?"

"Hanged. The past tense of *hang* is *hanged*."

"No, it's not. I hung loads of things in my day. It was always hung."

"No, you hung loads of things, but anyone who got hanged wasn't *hung*."

"That doesn't make any sense."

"The past tense of the verb to hang someone is hanged. The past tense of the verb to hang something is hung."

"You're making that up."

"No, I'm not."

"Fine. What if I hanged myself from the clock tower?"

"Doesn't sound right, does it?"

"Well, you were the one who insisted it was correct."

"I meant it doesn't sound like a good suicide."

"What exactly does sound like a good suicide?"

"I told you this was your baby, not mine. You're not cadging me for ideas. Why the clock tower?"

"I don't know, something about being out of time?"

"Jesus," Frank groaned disappointedly.

"Maybe in the clown costume? Or something else—what if I was dressed as a priest?"

"Good lord," Frank groaned again.

They had wandered and meandered their way through town until they had arrived at a bar, Frank leading the way again, leading as if he knew where he was going, though Joel suspected he was as clueless this time as he had been less than a week before. He didn't mind; there was something pleasingly familiar about the streets they walked. It had been a while since Joel had taken time out to just stroll, and he found himself feeling right at home as he ambled.

Inside the bar, sconces illuminated the beige wallpaper, old but clean, and reflected from the highly polished dark wood bar top. A small handful of patrons sat here and there at the collection of low tables with their accompanying soft-topped chairs, an eclectic mix of social classes and styles of dress and states of inebriation. Behind the counter the barman flicked through his form guide while the low drone of the horse-racing commentator intruded on the room from the television.

Joel and Frank had taken their places at the end of the bar, staring up the length of the place, their pints of stout resting on the now damp beer mats, "My Tools, My Rules" resting nicely alongside them. Joel liked the vibe of the bar, the sort of everybody welcome atmosphere that saw suited elderly gentlemen sit with down-and-out-looking middle-aged men with a handful of young kids, not even twenty, dressed like idiots, drinking ironically.

"What's so wrong with that idea?" he asked Frank indignantly.

"It's ill conceived."

"Is it possible for you to say anything without overcomplicating it?"

"It's a stupid plan."

"Why?"

"Because it's ill conceived."

"God dammit, Frank."

"All right, all right, here it is." Frank took a breath. "If you're arbitrarily picking landmarks to hang yourself from, then you clearly don't understand the point of making a statement. If you had told me that the clock represents the inexorability of aging or death, or the false sense of progress achieved by the passing of an hour, then I'd have told you it was fine..."

"Okay then, that's what I meant," Joel interjected.

"No, you didn't, you fraud!"

"Maybe I just don't express myself as well as you, but that's one hundred percent what I meant."

"Liar. You can lie all you like, Monroe, but you're not fooling me, and you're certainly not fooling yourself."

Joel opened his mouth to retort, but the popinjay was right. Worse than being right, he wasn't even being smug about it, just quiet and tolerant. Joel took a swig from his pint and sighed morosely.

"I'm running out of time, Frank. I really am. That's not a joke about the clock."

Frank barked a short laugh.

"Of course it's not. You're not clever enough to have come up with that."

Joel shot his friend a most unfriendly look.

"A bloody psychological examination. They'll send me away, or worse, lock me up."

"You're doing a fine job of hiding it so far," Frank assured him.

"Not really," Joel replied, thinking of all the recent run-ins with the staff, and the presence of The Rhino in his bedroom. "It has to be done before they get their chance with me."

"Maybe you'll get away with it, you know. I don't want to see you rush this."

As he spoke Frank scribbled notes into his journal of ideas, his thin wrinkly hands a blur as he scratched out his thoughts. Joel envied his mind, his creativity.

"Ach," he said, "you just want me to stay alive so that you can get more of that play done."

"No. Not even close, but I'll tell you this for absolute certain. When the right idea comes, when it really hits you, you'll know all about it. When you finally get it, you'll really get it."

Joel let that thought marinate as he called for two more pints. He thought about Frank and his creativity and his plays and his acting, and wondered what that life might have meant for him. He could have worn some scarves and spent his days with theater folk drinking in the afternoons. He might have had friends then, more than just his wife, though she had certainly been friend enough for long enough.

"Good health," Frank said, proposing his toast.

"Or not?" Joel replied, lifting his glass.

"Excuse me, gents?" a low voice piped up from behind them.

Turning on their stools, Joel and Frank found themselves looking down at two elderly men, one in his Sunday best, the other, rougher around the edges, and both well into their seventies.

"Help you?" Joel asked.

The man with the wrinkled and spotted shirt lifted a deck of cards.

"More fun with four?" he said.

Frank was moving before Joel, sliding out of his stool and positioning himself at the lower table; his face was already breaking into the wide grin of the de Selby mask, preparing for a show. Joel smiled at his friend, ever ready to meet new people, ever ready to engage, always on stage. Joel still ached a little from the act of lowering Frank down onto the coal bunker. He had realized some years before that aches and pains were generalized now, a sort of all-body aching. He was slower than Frank to climb down from the stool.

"Name's Roberts," the dapper one said, extending his soft, wrinkled hand. "Leonard Roberts."

"Joel Monroe," Joel replied with a brief handshake.

"This is Darcy. Mick Darcy. Most people call him D."

Joel shook the other man's hand, a harder, tougher hand. It was like shaking his own hand.

"De Selby is my name," Frank told them.

"Adams is his name," Joel corrected.

"Frank de Selby," Frank continued, unperturbed.

Roberts and Darcy watched him press his hand to his chest in introduction with amused glances.

"You get used to him," Joel told them.

They smiled even wider.

Joel felt the afternoon slip by him in a pleasant reverie. They drank pints together, all four of them, and Darcy became D, and Roberts became Leonard, and by the time they had reached pint number five, the barman was bringing their round without being prompted. Joel felt like he was the lord of the manor. The other customers came and went, but for four or so hours the four men played five-card stud and gambled for pennies. Joel covered Frank for the gambling, and was surprised, though perhaps he shouldn't have been, to watch his friend scoop hand after hand.

It was the casual way he played, still regaling the table around him with the made-up antics of his youth, full of bullshit stories about the women he'd chased. In his stories he was the hero, and his lack of anything approaching modesty should have been off-putting but wasn't. Joel knew them for the lies they were, but he wasn't about to interrupt, and despite knowing them for false, he found himself caught up as Frank recalled a time when he had his face slapped by three women at a dance, only for all three of them to wind up arguing over him by the end of the night. Mick and Leonard lost their money in good grace, caught up in the "de Selby Show." Joel just enjoyed the moment.

Around the end of pint five, the moment had passed. There was no incident, just a simple unspoken acknowledgment that their time together had come to an end. Leonard and D slipped on their jackets, and with hearty handshakes and warm smiles, they bade farewell, with an invitation to do it all again next week.

Joel and Frank sat back to finish their pints.

"You think we're in trouble when we get back?" Joel asked eventually.

"Almost certainly, but what exactly are they going to do? Ground us?"

"When do you think might be a good time to go home?"

"Whenever we want. We're masters of our own destinies. Captains of our own souls."

"So no rush, then?" Joel asked.

He had felt his trepidation and worry almost leak out of him as the day wore on, the fear of being caught dwindled as Hilltop had vanished from sight behind them on the bus. In its place was the certainty that they'd be facing a verbal firing squad when they got back to the home. Typically this was the kind of thing that Joel Monroe worried about. His love of obeying the rules and being honest gave him a distinct anxiety about transgressions, but since he was planning on killing himself anyway, he found it harder to muster up the worry that he'd usually have for such incidents.

"Perhaps a pint somewhere else?" Frank suggested.

"You don't like here anymore?"

"Variety is the spice of life."

"Even I've heard that one before," Joel told him.

"I'm sinking down to your level," Frank replied loftily as he swung his scarf over his shoulders and marched out the door.

Outside, the afternoon sunshine stabbed at them, and the fresh air threatened to make a fool of them both after five pints each. The street bustled with people in the afternoon going to and fro, shopping, meeting friends, running errands. Joel found himself smiling at the bustle of it all, the energy around him; he enjoyed the feeling of being a little drunk among a crowd, the sense of being part of a vibrant city. Most of all he was enjoying the sense of not being cooped up, of not looking at life from the outside, hidden away at the top of a hill with nowhere to go and nothing to do with his day.

He was enjoying it right up until he heard a voice call out.

"Dad? Is that you?"

16

"Be cool," Frank told him under his breath and smiled welcomingly at Joel's daughter.

She was walking down the street toward them with Lily, both burdened with shopping bags. She looked well, Joel idly thought, with her blond hair hanging loose, in smart clothes with two lovely little earrings. She also looked angry.

"What are you doing here, Dad?"

"We're just out for a…" Frank started.

"Excuse me, Mr. Adams. Dad, what are you doing here?"

Joel cursed his inattention. The pleasing familiarity of the street had tricked him. It was the street where Eva's work place was located; her office must have been no more than a hundred yards away. He had been enjoying his stroll so much he had completely forgotten, and his sense of comfort had come not from his fresh sense of perspective on the world, but from the fact that he had walked this street often enough in the years before.

He could have kicked himself.

"Having a pint," Joel told her coolly to cover his disappoint-

ment. He checked his words after he said them for any sign
of slurring. She didn't need to know how many they'd had.

"Did the nursing home let you out for the day, Grandad?"
Lily asked, a small smile playing about her lips. She wasn't
angry; she was impressed. Joel got a lift from it. At the very
least his granddaughter didn't think he was some kind of imbecile.

"Yes, they did, my dear," he told her warmly.

"Time off for good behavior," Frank added.

"Did Nurse Ryan tell you that you could leave, Dad?"
Eva asked, clearly angry.

"Not in so many words," Joel hedged.

"Did she or did she not?"

"It doesn't matter whether she did or not," Joel replied,
feeling his temper beginning to fray.

"I think it does," Eva replied.

"Well, it doesn't. I don't need to be told by her, or by anyone else when and where I can go."

"Dad, this is ridiculous, what if something was to happen
to you?"

"Like what?" he replied hotly. "Like I enjoy myself for an
afternoon? Heaven forbid."

"Do you not remember what happened last time?"

Joel recalled the TIA. He had been dizzy. He tried to recall
if he had eaten anything that morning but couldn't. Something very temporarily restricted the blood flow in his brain.
Deprived of oxygen for just a few moments, brain cells began
to die. Joel lost his balance and went down. The next thing
he remembered was a crowd around him, a man's mouth all
over him and another man hurriedly phoning an ambulance.

They told him the next one might kill him. Two years later
and he was still painfully alive.

"Well, you once threw up in a shoe shop and you're still allowed out shopping," he bit back, as if these two things were comparable.

"I was eight, Dad."

"So what? Things happen. Doesn't mean I have to be a prisoner all my days."

"Not this again. You're not a prisoner, Dad. The home is a nice place, with nice people, not a prison."

"They could be the loveliest prison guards in the world, but if I'm not allowed to leave and they lock me into a room at night, it's still a prison."

His temper was really boiling now. A perfect little afternoon ruined by a chance encounter. He would have had to face the music anyhow, but now he'd be shuttled home immediately. It wasn't fair.

"Don't be so bloody dramatic," Eva snapped at him.

"Don't you take that tone with me, young lady."

"Okay, easy now, Joel," Frank said, trying to calm him. His smile had slipped into an uneasy grimace. Lily's, too. They were both hugely uncomfortable with the showdown unfolding in front of them.

"I'm not a child, Dad!" she snapped back.

"Oh, would you look at that. An adult who resents being treated like a child. What a surprise."

"If you didn't act like one, you wouldn't be treated like one."

"Well, if you didn't act like such a bitch, I wouldn't treat you like one either."

As soon as the words were out of his mouth, he regretted them.

It was a nasty, low, rotten thing to say. A verbal slap. The kind of one that he hated. The words had stung her, too. His little Eva. His daughter. She looked furious and hurt and startled all at once. He thought about apologizing. Thought about it and then discarded it. He wouldn't bend now. She'd backed him into a corner.

She stared at him for a long minute, holding his gaze. He stared right back. Lily and Frank shuffled awkwardly on the spot.

"Lily," Eva eventually said, in a low furious voice, "wait here with your grandfather. I'm going to get the car so I can take him back to the nursing home."

"I'm not going anywhere," Joel replied.

"Yes, you most certainly are."

Her will was iron. He could see it in her. She had always been a stubborn child. He remembered her refusing to leave his workshop when she was ten. She couldn't be told what to do, or where to go, by anyone. Lucey had despaired. When Eva had become a young woman she was uncontrollable. A rebellious, stroppy child. Joel had watched Lucey tearing her hair out in frustration, yet he had done nothing. That, he thought to himself, might very well have been the beginning of the gap that grew between them. He let his wife try to tame their errant child, and he worked. That was his contribution. Work. Nothing more.

Now he had no work and his willful stubborn child was determined to lock him up.

"Perhaps we ought to head back, pal," Frank offered uneasily.

Joel wanted to bark back. He wanted to say no, to take off and head for a new pub, to enjoy being part of a society again, and not separated from it by virtue of his age, but he recognized the pointlessness of it. He also knew that whatever trouble they were in would only be compounded by standing his ground now. And trouble might mean the psychologist. He just needed to hang in there for another few weeks.

"Go get your bloody car, then," he told his daughter. She

nodded, in satisfaction, and turned smartly in the direction of the car park.

The drive back to Hilltop was conducted in silence, with Joel and Frank sitting in the back and Lily and Eva up front. Frank tried to add some levity once or twice as he climbed into the car but quickly gave up, dropping the de Selby mask and sitting in the uncomfortable silence.

Joel's furious sense of injustice was tempered somewhat by his granddaughter. He could see her face in the wing mirror next to the passenger seat as his hands played with the sign he'd lifted from someone else's garage. The tilt of her head and the sparkle in her eye suggested something to him. Amusement, certainly, she found the whole thing quite hilarious, but wouldn't risk her mother's ire by laughing; but there was something more. It was a feeling more than anything else, a sense of something that had been lacking. He thought it might be respect. He hoped it was. If he had still been a praying man at that time of his life, he would have prayed for it.

Unlike her mother, Joel thought, she may not see the cranky old man who won't simply do as he's told. She could see something else. Something she liked. Something she might even admire. He clung to that feeling to keep the humiliation of being escorted back to his prison from eating him up.

He glanced sideways at Frank and found him clenching his jaw in a bid to keep from smiling. Frank too felt the wrath of Eva was not something he should draw upon himself, and so he stifled his amusement, but it was plain to see. Between Lily in the front seat and Frank in the back, Joel found himself almost caught up in the humor, and like several hours before, suddenly discovered that there was a laugh bubbling up from his stomach. He looked in the rearview, catching the reflections of his daughter's eyes, still hard and furious, and found that equally funny. The laugh bubbled up to the surface, and he coughed to cover it. It didn't work. Some of it found its way out.

Frank, who had been working hard to keep the smile from his face, was caught unaware and he snorted a laugh, which he tried to cover by fetching a handkerchief from his inside pocket. Lily was entirely unprepared for Frank's snort, and her shoulders now twitched as she tried to keep the laugh in.

She turned her head entirely to one side, so that her mother wouldn't see the smile that she could no longer stop, and her shoulders began to gently rock as she laughed a silent laugh. Joel watched Eva's head turn incredulously to her laughing daughter. The outrage Joel saw there caused him to guffaw out loud, which caused Frank to crease over, his loud booming delight filling up the whole car. Eva opened her mouth to admonish them, but suddenly Lily erupted, no longer able to contain herself.

The three of them sat in the car in hopeless gales of laughter as Joel's daughter waited impatiently, furiously for them to quiet down. She was determined to have her say on the matter.

"I'm glad you all find this so massively amusing," she told them icily, just as they had composed themselves.

That set them off again, fresh peals of laughter and tears from the two elderly gents in the back. Eva harrumphed in disgust.

"What if you had fallen down, Dad?"

"What if you had fallen down?" he replied in between giggles.

"Don't be so childish…"

"No, really," he said composing himself, "anyone can fall down anywhere. I could, you could. It's a stupid argument to lock a man up."

"For Christ's sake," she fumed, "you are not being locked up."

Her words weren't helped by the broad, forbidding gates

of the nursing home looming before them. She noticed it too and turned away so she could call up to reception and have them opened.

"Hilltop Nursing Home," the voice announced. The receptionist. Mark. A young man. Dry and funny. Joel liked him, inasmuch as you could like any of your jailers.

"Eva Monroe," his daughter snapped into the machine. "I believe you're missing two residents."

"Uh, ah, Ms. Monroe. Of course. Buzzing you in."

The call disconnected, and the buzz started, soon drowned out by the noise of the two huge gates opening ponderously before them. Joel stared up the long, winding driveway. He knew what he was about to see, but it didn't help to know. She would be coming for him.

Sure enough, as the car wound toward the small parking spaces at the top, the diminutive but commanding figure of The Rhino bustled out from the main entrance. Everything about her was menacing, her body language, her thunderhead expression, her tightly controlled fury evident in her every step.

Joel steeled himself as best he could.

"Mr. Monroe," she began, her voice ice-cold. "Do you care to explain yourself?"

The giggles had just passed, and her fury was terrifying, but five pints of Guinness makes an excellent insulator against terror and more than emboldened Joel.

"Not really," he told her casually as he stretched his still slightly aching body. The toil of the morning remained in his bones.

She flattened him with a look. It was all he could do to keep his feet against her. He schooled his face to nonchalance.

"Mr. Adams," she said, turning her attention to Frank. "Do you care to explain yourself?"

"Madame Ryan," Frank began, his de Selby mask on. "I humbly apologize and fervently beg your forgiveness. A weakness took over me, a wanderlust you might say, and with my feet itching, I decided to see the world. Joel tried to stop me, and eventually only came with me to try to convince me to return. I'm afraid I've led the boy astray, and for that I'm so very sorry."

Eva snorted at Frank, and Lily, standing alongside her mother, pursed her lips to keep from laughing all over again.

"Have you two been drinking?" The Rhino asked incredulously.

"Imagine that," Joel retorted, "two grown men having a couple of pints. The horror of it."

"Mr. Monroe, I'll thank you not to take that tone with me."

"And I'll thank you, Ms. Ryan," Eva interjected, "not to lose my father again."

The Rhino turned her baleful eye on Eva. Sizing her up. Joel thought she looked like a tiny lion considering how it might eat an entire giraffe.

"I shall not, Ms. Monroe, but I shall need your father's cooperation. It's something that's been sadly lacking these last few weeks."

Eva regarded Joel for a moment.

"Do you think maybe the death of Mr. Miller may have affected him more than we thought?" she asked.

"Perhaps. The counselor we had been discussing might be a better idea after all. Hilltop is not adequately staffed to offer your father the kind of psychological help he might need."

They were deciding his future. They talked about him as if he wasn't there. They spoke to one another right through him, as if he, standing there right in between the two of them, was some kind of ghost, a shade. Joel saw Lily looking at him sadly, with tremendous pity. Somewhere inside her she knew, he could see she knew, that their ignoring of him was a tremendous insult to him. He felt his temper flare at the sight of her pity. He thought, for a brief, lovely moment, he thought she might have respected him, and now she stood there pitying him for being ignored.

"Don't you dare," he almost shouted. "Don't either of you dare attempt to discuss me or my mental state as if I'm not here."

They looked at him, both a touch shocked.

"How dare either of you think you can decide what's best for me, while I stand here, without even looking at me?"

"Dad..." Eva began firmly.

"No. No, no, *no*! I won't have it. I won't stand for it. You'll look at me when you're speaking to me." His anger was mixed with alcohol and grief, and tears sprang to his eyes, a lump jumped into his throat. *My Tools, My Rules.* "You'll include me. Don't you dare exclude me."

His voice rose to a crescendo at the end. Performative, but fueled by anger. Frank was looking at him almost proudly, Lily with a small delighted smile playing on her lips. Some residents, enthusiastic types who were still finishing their gardening, stood up from what they were doing and looked over.

The silence in the aftermath of his outburst was loud. The Rhino and Eva both stood there. Neither looked particularly chastened, but neither did they take him to task for shouting. They simply regarded him quietly.

"He is almost entirely detached from his life and the world," said the voice of Mighty Jim as he ambled over to Joel's side. The only noise in the yard.

The silence stretched out, the three of them locked in it, completely.

"A game of chess, old man?" Frank eventually asked quietly, ignoring Eva and The Rhino as they had ignored Joel.

Joel stilled himself. They were still boring holes into him with their eyes, but neither had spoken. It made sense. He had raised a daughter as pigheaded as he himself was, and he knew it. The Rhino was a whole new level of unrelenting. He wasn't going to win any staring contests. He wasn't sure he wanted to anyhow.

"Sounds lovely," he replied. "Jim, care to join us?"

"A heavy yet measured step," Jim told him calmly.

"Couldn't agree more," Joel replied. The three of them walked toward the main building. Joel noted with some satisfaction that the other residents were still looking at him, but as he passed them, he saw the looks they were offering. Supportive. One or two nodded encouragingly as he passed.

Inside the main hallway the trio met Una Clarke, dressed for the evening and out of her gardening clothes. She carried herself, as she always did, with great dignity, but there was a twinkle in her eye again, a hint of the same mischievous smile as she had offered them that morning.

"I thought I told the two of you to stay out of trouble," she admonished them gently.

Joel loved the twinkle in her eye, the smile, the calm tone she had with him.

"Where's the fun in that?" he asked, with a wink worthy of de Selby.

It was later that evening before the full consequences of their actions became apparent. Joel and Frank had arrived back in time for supper and sat in the common room eating with the hunger that only comes from a belly full of drink. Mrs. Clarke and Mrs. Klein sat with them, eager to hear tell of their adventure.

"How did you get out, though?" Mrs. Klein asked for the third time.

"Top secret," Frank told her, for the third time.

"How though?" she asked again.

"We tunneled out with spoons," Frank replied.

"You did not?" she asked, aghast.

"Something tells me they're not going to tell us," Mrs. Clarke said wearily. "We found your gardening equipment down by the gate. You hardly climbed over?"

"We could have climbed over," Joel told her. "We're spry." His muscles screamed at him in protest.

She looked at him disbelievingly.

"You're in good shape for a man of your age, but something tells me you're lying."

"I thank you for noticing," he told her, pleased to see her blush at his comment.

Frank covered a smile by shoveling in another forkful of potato.

Joel found his confusion regarding Una Clarke to be dissipating, and to his surprise and pleasure, found himself enjoying her company more and more.

"How did you get out, though?" Mrs. Klein asked again.

Before he could answer, Nurse Liam walked into the room, his face somber, no-nonsense.

"Joel, when you get a minute I'd like to speak to you in your room."

Joel's appetite vanished. There would, he realized, have to be consequences for their behavior. This was it.

"Let's go," he said to Liam brusquely, dropping his fork and trying not to appear dismayed.

They walked through the halls to the bedroom in silence. His shoes popping on the tile floor, Nurse Liam gliding before him. When they reached the bedroom, the nurse took his place by the television stand, no trace of his usual humor or good nature showing. Joel sat on the edge of the bed and steeled himself. He looked to his bedside table for inspiration. His sign leaned against the wall behind the photo of Lucey, where his new lucky penny sat. "My Tools, My Rules," it assured him. He felt his resolve stiffen.

"We need to know how you got out, Joel," Liam told him sternly.

"Top secret," Joel replied, poker-faced.

"This is a health and safety matter, Joel. We can't have residents wandering off whenever they like it. Now how did you get out?"

"I walked," Joel told him.

"How?"

"On my legs," Joel replied.

Nurse Liam sighed. Joel could tell he didn't like being in this spot. He wore his feelings in every expression of his face. He hated being the bad guy.

Joel searched for any sign that the young man knew of their rock. They must have searched the gardens. They surely saw the fresh digging and hoeing and chopping that Joel and Frank had set themselves to. If he did know, and was looking for confirmation, he gave no sign of it.

"I don't think you understand the seriousness of this, Joel…" he began.

Joel again. Because Liam needed something. Not the Mr. Monroe he used when he was giving orders or admonishing Joel like he was some kind of child.

"We walked out the main gate," Joel lied.

"No, you didn't."

"How do you know?"

"There are cameras, Joel. We checked them. Please don't lie to me."

"We flew over the walls."

"Joel, please…"

"We built a trebuchet out of gardening equipment and flung ourselves to freedom."

"I'm trying to help you here."

"I don't think that you are, Nurse Liam. I really don't think that you are."

"I am. I want to be on your side, I really do, and I know that you think I'm somehow against you. I promise you I'm not." He paused for a moment, agonizingly. "There's been a discussion, and a decision. You just haven't been yourself lately, and we're worried about you…"

Joel snorted his disbelief at that.

"…Nurse Ryan believes, and your daughter agrees, that if you don't cooperate, they'll have no choice but to relocate you to somewhere that better suits your needs. If you don't speak to someone about what's going on, we really don't have a choice. I know you can't see it, but we're worried about you."

Joel had felt this was coming, but was still unprepared for the feeling of it. Like a kick in the stomach.

"So I'm to be treated like a crazy person for wanting some independence."

"No one is treating you like a crazy person."

"Oh, you all say that. Who else do you send for psychiatric evaluations except for crazy people?"

"It's just that your behavior has been so erratic lately, we need to know if something is wrong, and if you won't cooperate with us, we have to use other means to find out. Please, Joel, I promise you, I'm trying to help."

Joel felt like spitting at him. It would surely only make matters worse. His sincerity was clear. He really thought that he was helping.

"When is this evaluation to take place?" he asked instead.

Liam sighed heavily.

"You're so hostile all the time, Joel. Why?"

"When is it to take place?" Joel demanded.

"As soon as we can arrange. Maybe in a week."

In a week. Joel didn't even try to suppress the shudder at the thought. A week. No time at all.

"Is that all?"

The nurse nodded at him almost sadly, before withdrawing from the room.

A single, solitary week, Joel thought as he dressed himself for bed. He had just seven days to kill himself.

17

That night Joel dreamt again, another hellish dream of a wide open, barren landscape dotted with boulders and hills where an army of Mr. Miller skeletons ambled aimlessly. Joel walked among them, trying to talk to them; they ignored him completely

At the foot of a huge hill, sitting down with his back to a large boulder, one the exact same shape as the rock they'd found at the foot of Hilltop, but massive in size, sat Therapist Frank. He had his little notebook open, and he was scribbling in it relentlessly. Joel tried to tiptoe around Therapist Frank, sweating profusely, desperate not to draw attention to himself, when a voice called out from the other side of the boulder. It was Lucey's voice. No, it was Una Clarke's voice. He couldn't tell which. This frightened him.

"Over here, Joel," the voice of Una or Lucey called him. "Over here, my love."

Therapist Frank looked up at him.

"Ah, there you are, Mr. Monroe," he said in The Rhino's voice. "Lovely to meet you. My tools, my rules."

Joel woke from the dream with a start, confused and dis-orientated.

"You okay?" Frank asked from across the room.

He was sitting up in bed, reading again, still dressed in his pajamas with the polka-dotted scarf draped around his neck.

"No," Joel told him, trying to orientate himself.

"Nightmare?" Frank asked, climbing from the bed.

"Nightmare. Don't want to talk about it."

The room, it seemed to Joel, had shrunk, collapsed in on itself. It was smaller in a way he couldn't put his finger on, the walls closing in.

The night before he had told Frank about the meeting with the psychiatrist. His friend knew about the dread he was feeling.

"It'll be okay, pal," Frank had told him consolingly as he stood by Joel's side.

"They're going to know," Joel told him in dismay.

"Maybe it's for the best. Maybe you could do with talking. Maybe there's more going on than you're willing to face."

"You promised, Frank. You promised I'd never have to see them."

He couldn't explain the fear. He didn't even want to. He wanted out, and every day that they forced him further into a corner rushed him toward his inevitable death. He just had to find a suitable way to go. If he couldn't find it, maybe just any suicide would do.

"Okay, okay, no therapist. So, what do you want to do?"

"I don't know," Joel replied helplessly. "I need you to tell me what to do."

Frank looked at him for a long moment. Joel could see the wheels turning in his head.

"A week, maybe two if you're lucky," Frank mused. "A thought. I know this is going to be anathema to you…"

Joel nodded, pretending he understood what *anathema* was.

"…but maybe we need to just behave ourselves?"

"Meaning?"

"It's time for you to put on a show. Behave yourself. Play nice. Do as you're told. If you give them a nice show, be the good dog, they might let the psychiatrist thing go?"

"But what about my…"

He couldn't quite bring himself to say it. He wanted to say *suicide*, but the word hung on the end of his tongue, blocked by some part of him, some old, sensible part.

"If you're dead set on it, pardon the terrible pun, there's no reason to stop planning, but we'll just have to be a bit more low-key. You need time to get this right, and as near as I can tell, the only chance you have of getting more time is to be the best little boy in the whole of Hilltop."

Joel mulled it over. The idea had potential. There was a chance. Two weeks of toeing the line, of kowtowing to them in exchange for his freedom? Could he do it? Before the thought had fully taken hold, he remembered Lily's face, outside the car the day before, when he had taken his stand and shouted them down, and her smile when she and her mother had caught him and Frank red-handed. He loved that face, that pride, and respect and admiration for a man she knew, a man whom she valued.

He remembered Chris's face too, the tinge of something around his nose and his lips. Disgust, or discomfort, or some other mixture of things that Joel didn't know. He hated that face, hated what it represented. He hated what he saw in those eyes: another used-up, spent old man. To be visited because that's polite, but of no value.

To kowtow was to accept the face of Chris, to accept his position and tell them all that he could take the absurd, pointless existence that he had been passing time in for five years, and if he did it, it would mean he would have to remember that face that Lily had shown him, however briefly, and it would stab at him for the fraud.

Frank, with insight that Joel now considered typical of the man, saw all the cogs turning in Joel's head, and smiled a small, wry smile.

"I know that Joel's not for turning, but it might be the only chance you have?"

"No. He is not," Joel admitted. Could he do it? Could he fake it that he was happy living out this miserable existence?

"I'll try it. God dammit, I'll try to do it, even if it shames me."

Joel suspected that his good boy behavior would last all the way up until he saw Lily or Chris again. That's all it would take. One adult to treat him like he still possessed his own agency and he'd throw the whole act out the window.

"So what shall we do now?" Frank asked.

"We plan my suicide," Joel replied determinedly. "We just do it quieter and quicker than we had before."

"You are, without a doubt, the most pigheaded, most stone-stubborn creature I've ever met. And I'm glad I know you," Frank told him lightly.

He hugged Joel without warning. And Joel hugged him back.

18

Joel Monroe, as previously stated, was a man of tremendous energy and vitality, when he had a purpose. His purpose now, under the threat of removal or evaluation, was death. As Thursday ticked on by, he read, he even pawed through the snooty, pretentious crap that Frank read, looking for inspiration. He had convinced himself that everyone in theater killed themselves, all the time, and that the inspiration for his final liberation would come from a theater play. He read Shakespeare, and something called a Sophocles, and leafed through thick hardback tomes whose names he didn't even bother to learn. He read in the morning and through the afternoon. He read with his lunch in the common room and with tea out in the garden. Once or twice his eyes absently strayed down the hill to their rock, and he found himself thinking of outside again, and wistfully he'd remember just how much he had been enjoying himself, before they were arrested as it were, by his daughter.

He also tried to ignore the questioning looks he was getting from the others around. Mighty Jim looked positively perplexed by the arrival of literature into Joel's life. Nurse Liam dropped in and out of the room in the early evening about five times more than was necessary just to check if Joel was still reading. Pleasingly, Una Clarke was looking at him askance, too. Having been in her room some days beforehand, and seen all of the various books she was reading, he thought she might appreciate seeing a more scholarly side to him, and he tried not to smile as she swept into their room in the early evening, ostensibly to have a chat.

"What on earth has gotten into him?" she asked Frank, aghast, as Joel read *The Lonesome West.*

Frank, for his part, had spent the day with his notebook, scribbling, whipping through pages, glancing occasionally at Joel, as if to measure him for dialogue or action. He put down the book to address Una, with a warm smile.

"Took me a mere couple of weeks to train the man, I'm pleased to say."

"You did a fine job. Really, though, what's wrong with him?"

Joel tried not to hear them. Everyone was acting as if something was terribly wrong with him. He tried not to let the irritation show. Though a grain of worry popped in that so much reading would only reinforce the opinion that he was going insane.

"There's nothing wrong with him," Frank replied with a laugh. "Well, nothing more than usual like."

"You'd tell me if there was, wouldn't you? I promised his wife I'd look after him."

Her words made Joel sit up straight. It had never occurred to him that his wife might have been planning his life without her. She had slipped away so suddenly that it seemed like she couldn't have. That was why Una was always so nice to him. That was why she looked after him, and took an interest in him. He had been downright rude to her at times, he knew that, and regretted it doubly now. He felt an extra twinge as he realized that perhaps that was the limit of her interest in him.

Probably for the best, he thought, since the finish line loomed so close now. He did think it might be nice to go out with a kiss, though. Something romantic, something warm. It had been too long since he'd shared that kind of moment with anyone. He had thought that maybe Una might…but now it seemed it was something else.

How lucky he had been, though, to have had a wife so concerned, so loving, so giving. It made his heart swell again with pride for her, and break a little more for her absence.

"She was a great woman," he said, without looking up from his book; he didn't need them to see the tears forming in his eyes. He suspected Frank knew anyway.

"I should like to have known her."

"You'd have loved her," Una told him without taking her eyes off Joel. "A warm woman. Kind to a fault. Welcoming all the time."

"I got lucky," Joel said, in the understatement of his life.

"You did," Frank told him, and in his voice a trace of wistfulness. A hint of something missed.

"She was terrific," Liam said, as he came through the door. He had heard it all.

"Pills?" he asked.

There was a tone in the question, one that had been missing lately, one that Joel appreciated. It wasn't a demand, it was a request, and kindly offered.

"Please," Joel said, laying the book down.

Nurse Liam placed a glass by the bedside and dropped the pills next to his lucky penny and his "My Tools, My Rules" sign. A show of trust. He wasn't going to stand there and babysit. Joel nearly smiled. Nearly.

"And for you, kind sir," Liam said to Frank, laying the pills out.

"Thank you," Frank said, his eyes dropping, as they did in Liam's presence.

"No," Liam said kindly, lingering by the bed for just a moment. "Thank you."

Joel was watching the interplay between the two when he caught Una's reaction, a quiet, satisfied nod. An indication that she saw something she needed to see. Joel didn't have the depth of understanding for people that Frank did, but he caught the significance in her look all the same. She knew. He had underestimated her again. Did she know Frank was gay? She surely knew that Liam was. She had been here long enough, and as Joel had eventually learned, she was too sharp to miss that. She saw something pass between them. Joel checked to see what it was. Frank hadn't looked up, his de Selby mask was still on, but there seemed to be something of Adams showing in the small, almost frightened smile on his face. Joel couldn't have recognized what had passed between them, but if it was making Frank happy, he was in favor of it.

Joel smiled at his friend across the room.

"Think I'll turn in now," he announced to them. "While the going is good."

19

"I have to tell you, Joel, we're really happy with you these last couple of days. And Nurse Ryan seems to have come around, too," Nurse Liam told him on Saturday morning.

He had come in as Joel sat with his book on his lap, his eyes vacantly staring down the long drive to and across the gardens to where the rock was. He was thinking about it.

Joel had spent all day Friday reading again, turning pages of Frank's collection looking for inspirational suicides. He had been quiet as a mouse. The absurdity of being praised for quietly looking up ways to make a statement by killing yourself wasn't lost on him, and Joel chuckled at Liam as he offered him breakfast.

He was thoroughly uninterested in knowing that his docility had earned him a gold star from the jailers and the respect of the warden. He wanted to spit out his pills just to spite them all, but more and more he thought he saw someone on his side in Nurse Liam. A man who wanted Joel to be happy, to have what he wanted out of his remaining years, but was caught between his duty to his job and his desire to see his residents thrive.

"I'm glad," Joel told him, as if it mattered to him in the slightest.

Liam patted him encouragingly on the leg as he prepared to withdraw. He couldn't know that Joel deeply and bitterly resented the patronizing pat on the leg. A pet for a good doggie. He stomached it, because that's what he said he would do.

"It was a nice thing you did the other day," Joel told Liam as he turned to leave.

The nurse glanced at Frank's empty bed; the raconteur had left to have breakfast in the common room with Una.

"What's that now?" he asked, feigning ignorance.

"What you did for Frank."

"I didn't do anything really."

"I don't fully understand it, but I think it was a nice thing. It lifted him."

"You're a pretty surprising guy, Joel. Sometimes I think you live in a little world of your own, but you don't miss much, do you?"

"I miss too much, to be honest, but not that one."

"It's pretty amazing seeing you two together. How close you are already. You really love him, don't you?"

Joel was hugely uncomfortable with the word *love*. Especially where it related to a gay man he shared a room with. Liam saw it, and laughed.

"But then you're also you, aren't you?" he said.

There was a trace of bitterness in the question. A hint that for all his own comfort in his own skin, Liam had encountered a thousand Joels, a thousand times. Each Joel bringing his own level of discomfort or distaste into Liam's world, hurting it with chip after tiny chip into the man's personal defenses.

"Only thing I've ever been," Joel told him. He tried to

sound contrite, sorry for the way the world was, but it came out sounding privileged, authoritative.

Liam nodded at him with a wry smile.

"You're all right, Mr. Monroe."

"Am I?" he asked, trying not to let his anger show. Another compliment on his good behavior, on what an excellent house pet he was now that he was casually accepting his place.

"I know it's hard for you, Joel. I know that," Liam told him. "We're not trying to make it hard for you. The exact opposite. And I'll do everything I can to make you as comfortable as you can be."

While you wait for me to die, Joel thought to himself. But he stayed quiet and forced a smile.

Joel plunged back into his suicide research, reaching for something that would inspire him, that would show him a way to do something profound so that those left behind would pause, and wonder if maybe there was a better way to care for the other residents, that there was a better life to be offered to them. A lesson in his passing that would stand the test of time that he himself could not. All the while the threat of the psychiatrist loomed behind him. It was his greatest fear, that he'd be found out, that someone else would delve inside him and find within him the lethargy, the fury, the hopelessness and the thin, occasionally wavering wedge of desire to end it all. And that when they found it, they'd lock him up for real. No rock at the end of the hill, no Frank, no Una. It terrified him to his core.

In the early afternoon, sometime around three o'clock, Joel sat in the common room, fighting to another stalemate with Mighty Jim.

"He goes back down to the plain," Jim told him earnestly as they drew to the game's inevitable conclusion.

Joel sighed heavily as he placed another knight. He could already see it. Four moves, maybe five. His only hope now was a calamity from his opponent. A calamity he knew was never coming.

"He can wholly understand why he is being sent to jail," Jim told him with a cunning smile.

It was clear and sharp. Lacking the vacancy around the eyes that typically marked Jim Lincoln.

"Are you in there, Jim? Is there something on the surface there? Something I could maybe talk to?"

"The workman of today works every day in his life," Jim told him, the cunning smile gone, the vacant, empty eyes returning with a heaviness that almost hurt Joel to look at. A moment of lucidity perhaps? Or perhaps a nothing.

Frank sauntered into the room, still in his pajamas, with his dressing gown on and his scarf, this one mostly white with a thin pattern of brown waves running through it. As the old man took his place, Nurse Liam arrived, his coat on, ready to finish his shift.

"Half day today?" Joel asked, still playing the good dog.

"Back in tonight for the night shift," Liam told him.

"No rest for the wicked and all that," Frank said conversationally.

His body language had changed toward Liam. Something about it spoke of an ease and a comfort, but Joel recognized the de Selby mask even if his friend was wearing it a little looser. Whatever had passed between them had been lovely, warm, but not enough to erase decades of defenses.

"This is for you, from the staff," Liam told him, presenting him with a neatly wrapped box.

"What's this now?" Frank asked, genuinely surprised.

"Just a little birthday gift. Enjoy yourselves."

Joel kicked himself as the nurse made his way out the door.

It was Frank's birthday. He didn't know, and couldn't have known, but there it was. His friend's birthday and he hadn't even mentioned it. Perhaps birthdays were nothing to Frank. Years without a family to celebrate them, without a wife or a husband or anyone to bring him cards or make him dinner or throw him a party. Perhaps birthdays were just another reminder that he lived an isolated life. It was an awful thought to consider, and Joel hated it. He wanted to make it better. Show the man that he had someone who cared now.

Almost wistfully Frank unwrapped the present and removed it from the small box. Joel knew what it was long before the lid came off. Some presents are just too perfect for some people.

Delicately Frank lifted the silk scarf from the box, smooth silver material with roses in white and maroon woven finely into it.

"I'm sorry, Frank, I didn't know," Joel told him.

"Not to worry, old boy," Frank assured him, still admiring the scarf. He handled it carefully, almost reverentially.

"What age are you?"

"Seventy-nine."

Joel tried not to let his shock show. Frank was older than him. Something about his debonair attitude, his casual nature had made Joel think he was a younger man. A much younger man. That he had three years on Joel had never occurred to him.

"Now I feel bad. I got you nothing."

"I didn't want a fuss made. If I wanted a fuss made, I'd have been banging on about it. You know me."

The opportunity was there to perform, to play the victim, to turn in another trademark de Selby performance and condemn Joel for his thoughtlessness in a tirade of cutting, hilarious remarks. Frank ignored the opportunity, and let him off the hook. Joel couldn't decide if the decision was out of deference to Joel's fear of impending examination, or his determination to see himself out the door of life, or because the de Selby mask was off and in its place stood a lonely, isolated Frank Adams, opening a birthday present for the first time in a long time.

These thoughts were repugnant to Joel. He didn't want to be deferred to, or wrapped in cotton wool by the man who had become his best friend; nor did he wish to see that man lonely, neglected.

Joel glanced about the room. All he could see was neglect. Old furniture still useful but in bad need of repair or restoration. An old television set, donated so long ago that Joel was certain its like couldn't be found in any shop. He knew that was in his head. He knew some people were happy at Hilltop and the rot and ruin that marked the place for him was a symptom of his own impulse to suicide, but that didn't change his opinion of the place a jot.

The neglect that he saw was so much more than the building or the furniture; it was the people. The nurses didn't neglect them. Society did. It was as depressing as it was infuriating. He looked at the wistful, happy smile on Frank's face. It seemed all at once so pathetic. This gift, this sop from the staff who were complicit in hiding them away from the world. He felt his anger and his frustration as an energy inside himself, a galvanizing, cavalier force that ignored his fears, that ignored his trepidation.

And all at once Joel had an idea. A dangerous idea, but a fun one.

"Why don't you and I go to town and have a pint to celebrate?" he asked.

Frank's face lit up a little, but he quickly extinguished his excitement.

"Probably not a good idea. We've been doing well. Keeping a low profile. It's been a lovely quiet little world for the last two days, why rock the boat?"

"Don't be daft. It's your birthday. We should be celebrating."

"Joel, I don't mean to question your already feeble grip on sanity, but don't you think that's a little nuts?"

There he was, Joel thought, there was Frank. Sharp. Witty. Jovial.

If Joel got his way they'd never get to spend Frank's eightieth with each other. He'd be done. Moved on. His mortal coil shuffled off. This would be his last chance to spend a birthday with the best friend he had newly acquired.

"No, as a matter of fact I don't," Joel told him. "My tools, my rules."

"You're about one more outburst from a psychiatric evaluation that might see you locked into a mental institution for good, and you want to go poking at the bear?"

"I don't want to poke any bear. I want to have a pint for your birthday."

"Joel, dear boy," Frank started, lowering his voice to conspiratorial levels, "all things considered, and taking certain future plans into account, don't you think this will just be bringing unnecessary attention down on you?"

As he mentioned future plans he drew a rather exaggerated thumb across his throat. Joel smiled at it. There was a point to what Frank was saying, no doubt, but all Joel could think about were the faces, the look of pure disappointment on Lily's face, the casual discomfort on Chris's, the withering condemnation from both his daughter and The Rhino. He loathed the faces, he loathed the power they held over him. He had agreed to be the good dog, to lie down and do what he was told, and he'd taken the pats on the head for his good behavior, though uncomfortably, as if somehow he owed to these people a performance of good behavior, as if he should simply accept the control over his life and learn to stomach it. He felt an almost animal growl begin deep in his belly.

"I will not have my life dictated to me by anyone. Not on my friend's birthday."

Frank looked at him, really studied him for a moment, and his face broke into a large and mischievous grin.

"You should never underestimate the sheer pigheadedness of some people," Frank told him, adjusting his scarf. "How do we do it?"

Joel felt the excitement in him begin to bubble. He would earn back the smiles and the flicker of respect he'd seen from his granddaughter. He would do what he wanted, what he chose to do. He would act on his own agency and not the patronizing, relentless monotony of life at Hilltop.

"Out the window, after supper, when they do the first nighttime round."

"They lock the windows," Frank told him.

"We ask someone to open it now. Some fresh air into the room. Then we stuff the catch. When they close it, it'll close all the way, but if it doesn't catch we just open it again and climb out."

"It's pretty narrow."

"You calling me fat?"

"I've a far greater vocabulary than that. If I was going to insult you, I'd use words like portly, or stocky, or thick."

He was back. His friend was back. Nearly three days of being shamed and bullied into being something they weren't evaporated in a moment of shared excitement.

"I'll fit, don't you worry."

"It'll be getting dark by then—think we'll have a problem making it through the trees?"

"We'll be fine. Have a little faith. You're the one that's supposed to be the optimist."

It was at that moment that they both realized Mighty Jim was still sitting right next to them. He was smiling patiently. Waiting to return to the endgame.

Joel and Frank looked at one another.

"You'll keep our secret, won't you, Jim?"

Mighty Jim's smile widened.

20

The execution of their plan was nonchalant. Sitting in their shared bedroom as they read, they asked Nurse Karl, in passing, to open the window and let some air in. After he'd left the room, they stuffed the catch on the window with toilet paper.

Frank busied himself in his wardrobe, selecting his attire for the evening, while Joel flipped through pages of a book, not really reading, too excited and nervous to take in the words. Suppertime crawled toward them, painfully slowly, and when it finally arrived they took to the common room eagerly, rushing in, trying to act casual and failing miserably.

Inevitably, it was the eagle-eyed Una Clarke who spotted something. She had sat with them through supper, making idle conversation and casually observing them with sidelong glances. As they fell into their desserts, she caught them unawares.

"I don't know what it is you're both up to, but I assume it's going to get you both in trouble again?"

Joel stopped dead with a spoonful of ice cream hovering

inches from his lips. Frank simply raised a casual eyebrow before realizing Joel had given the game away with his shocked reaction.

"You have absolutely no sense of calm about you," he muttered at Joel.

Joel recognized that this was probably correct. He still hadn't eaten the ice cream.

"Same again? Vanishing act?" she asked.

"It's Frank's birthday," Joel told her lamely.

"Oh, very nice," she replied. "Happy birthday, my dear."

"Thank you." Frank smiled broadly. "I take it you're not going to dob us in?"

"I take it you'll both take care of each other wherever it is that you're off to?"

"Take care of each other," Joel spluttered. She wasn't his mother.

"Yes, dear," she told him, reaching out to wipe some melted ice cream from his chin. "I've grown quite fond of both of you, and I don't want anything happening to you."

Joel blushed at her words. A smoother man than he might have had the courage or the wherewithal to tell her how fond of her he had become. Instead he ate another spoonful of ice cream.

"You seem remarkably composed about this," Frank said.

She remained quiet for a moment. Pushing her dessert around its bowl with her spoon. Joel watched her pick her words carefully, but when she delivered them she assiduously avoided making eye contact with him.

"He's a different man since you got here," she told Frank. "He's happier. More open. He's more like the man that moved in here some years ago. A little more adventurous I'd say, more cavalier if you like, but it's a nice change. I've worried about him. I've watched him become a shell of a thing. It's nice to see him come out of himself. If you both get a scolding for it, what of it?"

Joel allowed himself a smile. He wanted to reach out to her, take her by the hand and thank her. Instead he ate yet another spoon of his ice cream.

"Want to help?" Frank asked.

She returned his smile with a grin of her own.

Shortly after supper, as they lay in their beds pretending to wind down for the evening, Nurse Karl made his rounds, bringing angiotensin receptor blockers and cod liver oil and tea. He closed the windows as he did it, and it was all Joel could do not to stare at it. He accepted the medicine and the tea without qualm, earning a satisfied nod from the nurse. Just more evidence that he was being a good boy. Ten minutes or so later, they heard the faint chimes from inside Una's room, a call for attention. They listened, almost holding their breath as Nurse Karl made his way into her room, and heard the low murmurs of Una begging a favor.

Nurse Karl would be carrying books up to Mrs. Klein's room for the next twenty minutes or so.

Full to the brim with nervous excitement, the two men bounced from their beds and began to hurriedly dress themselves. As Frank put the finishing touches on his attire, including his new scarf, Joel walked to the window.

Tentatively he pushed it.

The window opened at his hand, letting in the evening air. Joel sucked in a great big breath of freedom and allowed himself a grin.

"What on earth are you waiting for? I haven't got all day," Frank told him, as he approached the window. The rascal was well dressed for the occasion. His best suit, in navy, still a little old and worn-looking on his sloping shoulders, with a crisp white shirt and a pair of brown leather shoes. His birthday scarf was tied into an elaborate but loose knot at his neck. Joel was more soberly dressed, but still cut a dashing figure, he rather modestly thought.

With a careful grip and a measured, quiet step, Joel hitched up his suit pants and carefully climbed out the window. The thrilling feeling of being out of bounds had him again, and the giggles that had afflicted him the two previous times threatened to overwhelm him, but mixed in with it all was a terrifying fear of getting caught, and just a tiny desire to be caught. If they didn't make it off the property, the trouble was likely to be less.

Frank stepped out behind him, carefully lowering his foot into the gravel. They made their way down the garden on the grass, to limit noise, but when they were approaching the tree line, lights blinded them.

In front of them, pulling up to the gate, preparing to start his night shift, was the car owned by Nurse Liam. Without thinking the two men ducked as low as they might, and broke into a shambling half run. The twist in the road just before the gate was in their favor, and if luck was on their side, Nurse Liam would be digging through his rucksack for his magnetic pass, or pressing the buzzer or looking somewhere else.

They shuffle-ran to the tree line, as quick as they could, Joel waiting to hear a beeping of the horn or a call out from behind to announce that they had been spotted in the fading evening light. He kept his eyes locked on the car and waited for the alarm to be sounded. Midstride he thought he saw the nurse look up at them, Joel was almost certain that he had, and he braced himself for the shout to stop. None came, and when they hit the tree line they were home and free.

The two stopped behind the bole of a huge evergreen to catch their breaths. Chuckling to himself, Frank sucked in deep breaths, while Joel, a little less out of breath but feeling the palpitations of terror still wracking him, craned for a look at the car as the gates swung open. As the car pulled up along the driveway, he saw Nurse Liam's profile, carefully, almost obviously looking away from them. He had seen them, Joel was sure, but it couldn't be, because the car pulled up the driveway and slid slowly into his staff parking spot.

"Let's get out of here," Frank told him.

The second significant obstacle of the night, obviously, was the wall. They reached the rock, carefully sheltered from sight in the trees, and climbed it easily, and found themselves again overdressed and sitting on a wall too high for men their age.

"It's higher than I remember," Joel told Frank.

"No, you're just older."

"By three days?" Joel asked.

"Older is older. Let's not quibble about numbers."

"Same again?" Joel asked.

Frank nodded at him, still wearing his broad, ridiculous grin.

And so the two men positioned themselves clumsily, with Frank's feet scrabbling at the side wall of the garage, carefully trying to lower himself onto the coal bunker. When they were half the way down, a light came on. They froze.

The source of the light was the conservatory in the back garden, the one that had been filled with toys. In the dimming evening light, with the inside light on, it was unlikely that the occupant would be able to see them, but the two froze anyway.

If it was possible to double freeze they would have done that, when they spotted the room's occupants. Inside the glass, picking up toys and chatting amiably to a small boy, was The Rhino.

Out of her uniform and in her casual clothes with her hair tied back in a loose ponytail, she smiled easily. Something the little one was saying tickled her in a way that brought a hearty laugh that even Joel and Frank could hear through the thick glass.

Joel remembered the feeling of envy when he'd passed that little room with all its toys just three days before. The feeling that this must be a wonderful parent. He could hardly believe his eyes. She looked normal. And nice. Like someone you'd want to be friends with.

In his shock he forgot about Frank, and it was only when his friend let out a strangled gasp that he realized he'd been holding him up by the scarf, practically choking him.

"Sorry," Joel whispered as he continued to lower the smaller man down.

When Frank's feet found purchase on the top of the bunker he rounded on Joel, still atop the wall. His strangled whisper could hardly be heard, but Joel was fairly sure it heavily featured the words *bastard*, *idiot* and *asshole*.

He nodded his way through the tirade.

"Get the ladder," he whispered eventually, cutting Frank off just as he was describing Joel's mother in unflattering terms.

"We can't. Not with them in there."

"Well, how do I get down?"

"Here," Frank said, doubling over.

Joel nearly laughed out loud. He was going to have to lower himself down, and literally use Frank's back as a stair.

"Don't fold up on me," he told the smaller man.

"Try to think unportly thoughts," Frank shot back.

Gingerly, hoping he wouldn't laugh out loud, Joel lowered himself onto Frank's back, and into The Rhino's garden. His eyes darted from Frank's hunched back to the conservatory building, obscured only slightly by the corner of the garage. Whatever the little one was doing, she seemed engrossed by it. His feet landed on the yielding back of his friend, and for just a moment, he thought Frank would crumple under his weight, but the smaller man held his ground, grunting only slightly in protest. Joel kept as much of the weight off him as possible, by trying to hold himself up with his arms.

When they'd finally landed on solid ground, they stood in bewilderment. She hadn't seen them, or heard them, and continued to play with the small child, still smiling broadly, still looking like a normal person.

"Let's go," Frank whispered.

The two of them sidled up the pathway at the side of the house, away from the conservatory, and eventually had to pass the kitchen window. The light was on inside, and a man pottered about putting away dishes. He looked normal, as well. Pleasant even. Was The Rhino married to this man? He looked happy, not like someone who was tortured every day by his decision to marry a despot. What life had she carved for herself that she could be happy here and so cold and aloof up in Hilltop?

The shock had worn off Joel by the time they reached the bus stop, but the surreal nature of it all was still a lot to take. He mentioned this to Frank as he brushed his own shoe marks off the smaller man's suit jacket.

"Guess you never really know a person, do you?" Frank told him, still checking himself over for spots of dirt from the trees or the coal bunker, or Joel's shoes.

By the time the bus had arrived, Joel had let the moment slide behind him altogether and, instead, allowed the excitement to take over. It was fast approaching nighttime. It was getting to the point where he'd be out on the town on a Saturday night. He had barely gone out on the town on a Saturday night when he lived in his own home, and a part of him felt that there were some experiences he had to make up for. As the bus pulled away, leaving Hilltop behind, Joel forced himself to stop worrying, he forced himself to think positively, to look at the night ahead for what it was. A night out with his friend, for his birthday, with nothing to do but whatever they wanted.

Before the bus even pulled in Joel could feel the energy of a city center on a Saturday night. It was raw thing, a flow of bodies, in high spirits, the night before them spread out and ready to be whatever they could make of it. Joel itched to be a part of it. Frank, being more worldly and urbane, was casual about it, and Joel tried to follow his friend's lead, a look of calm nonchalance, but found himself agitated with the need to be going somewhere, doing something, as the rest of the city seemed to be.

"Where to?" he asked eagerly.

"I had a thought," Frank told him.

"Wouldn't be the first."

"Might be a little maudlin, though."

"I'm planning on killing myself. It doesn't get more maudlin."

"No, it does not." Frank laughed his agreement. "I'd like to go see the Royale."

Something arty and cultured no doubt, but since Joel and his potato-like soul had limited experience of such things, he had no idea what exactly it was. His face betrayed his confusion.

"It was my favorite theater," Frank told him.

"Was?"

"They shut it in the late nineties. I was devastated. Probably for the best in the long run, the place was falling down."

Joel could see the nostalgia showing in Frank's eyes and recognized its intense familiarity. He'd been basking in it lately. The memories of better times.

"Let's go, then," he said.

The two dapper gents made their way through the bustling city, away from the main hub of activity, the crowds thinning out as they moved from the trendy, newest parts of the town into the older neighborhoods. Joel remembered a time when these streets hummed, and the evidence of their one-time popularity showed as he recalled what the buildings had once been. A bowling alley now an industrial laundromat; a large residential block where he could remember an old movie house. He'd gone there with Lucey more than once. During their courting, and later in life when Eva had become a young lady, keen to be anywhere but in her parents' company.

Smack in the middle of the street sat the old Royale, its rounded front entrance still standing. It had been there so long Joel had stopped paying attention to it. Theater had never been his thing, and so he'd never bothered to pay it any mind but now, as he stood before it, he noted its old elegance, even in its dilapidated state. The building seemed to hold a memory of former glory that couldn't be ignored even with its boarded up windows and graffitied front walls. A large "Sale Agreed" sign stood out from the façade.

"It's quite lovely-looking, isn't it?" he remarked to Frank.

"Is that a little soul I see sparking in Joel Monroe?" Frank asked.

"I'm not completely dead inside," he retorted.

"No, my friend, quite the opposite, I think."

"What do you mean?"

"Never mind."

"How do we get in?" Joel asked, noting the fencing around the main entranceway that blocked them.

"Round the side, there's a back door. No one ever bothered to lock it. Rats don't pay much notice to locked doors."

"There's rats?"

"You afraid of a few rats?"

"Not overly fond of them, no."

"You're a funny man, Joel. Apparently not afraid to die, but damned if you'll share an old theater with some rodents."

"I suppose they can't be any worse than you," he said without breaking a smile.

Frank grinned for the both of them.

"Shall we, then?"

As Joel and Frank carefully picked their way down the narrow side alleyway, it struck Joel that he'd very quickly developed a real knack for sneaking around. Afraid of his shadow when they'd left Hilltop in a cab the week before, here he was sneaking his way down rat-filled side streets after a breakout from one institution so he could break into another.

"You been in since?" he asked.

"I come here every now and then. She was good to me in her day."

He sounded melancholic. So unlike Frank that it gave Joel pause.

"Don't go stealing my bit," he told his friend.

"What's that, now?"

"I'm supposed to be the sad, pathetic one. You're supposed to be the funny one. We can't both be sad. That'd be too much."

He heard a light chuckle from up in front. It was too dark to make out Frank's face in the little run, but he hoped there was warmth there.

At the back there was a little clearing and some steps leading up to a door. The area was strewn with trash, empty bottles and cans here and there.

"I suppose some misfortunate homeless person has been in and out, but once upon a time I came to this door for smokes. I'd smoke a cigarette in between scenes. The other actors used to hate it. You know, in case I missed my cue or something, but I never did."

Sure enough, the door opened, creaking slightly as Frank stepped up to it and into the theater. They were in what Joel assumed was backstage, the old exposed brick of the back wall now covered in graffiti. High above them the fittings for hanging the long black curtains he knew were part and parcel of a set. A tall partition separated them from the stage, and as they stepped around it the streetlights outside the windows, high up on either side of the theater, illuminated them just enough for Joel to make out the ruined remains of the stage and the battered, cloth upholstered seats that had once been the Royale Theatre.

Frank smiled wistfully to himself as he stepped out into the middle of the stage, shooting a look over his shoulder to invite Joel to join him. It was a peculiar moment for Joel, stepping into the center of the stage. Frank's grin had given way to a full-blown smile as he watched Joel absorb the feeling. Their shoes echoed through the room as they walked out.

"I was King Lear here," Frank told him proudly. "And Dr. Dysart, and Willie Loman and Ajax."

Joel scanned his friend for traces of regret, of melancholy, of anything really, but all he saw was happiness.

"Do you miss it?"

"Of course I do," Frank told him as he stepped away from the center and made for the short stairs down into the audience. "But maybe I'm not done. Maybe *The Unfortunate End of Joel Monroe* will be onstage someday. Maybe when whoever bought this place is finished, it'll be an even better theater than it was, and I'll get another shot."

"Or maybe it'll be a shopping mall."

"There you go again, glass half-empty."

"What's the cost of a building like this in a city center?

Couple of million? You think the gang that have that kind of money to throw around give two hoots about old theaters?"

"We live in hope," Frank told him airily as he sat down in one of the old battered seats. "You look good up there, you know."

Joel realized he was still center stage with his audience of one smiling up at him. He shuffled quickly off to make his way to his friend and accidentally kicked something. It was small, and he wouldn't have noticed it if it hadn't skittered across the stage so loudly. His back and all his joints protested all at once as he stooped over to pick it up. A little button. With a pin on the back. A badge. "Save the Royale," it said. That he had picked it up from the ruined stage of a very much unsaved Royale seemed a little sad to him. Another aging monument that someone had once loved allowed to fall to ruin because not enough people cared. He pocketed the badge, and made his way down to take his seat next to his friend, the two of them staring up at the dimly lit stage.

He imagined Frank up there, his voice rising and dipping in that way that only his could; his big booming laugh filling the room, hitting the back wall. Joel didn't know who Dr. Dysart or Willie Loman were, but he imagined Frank would have been perfect for them.

"You know, I wish I'd seen you. One of those times that Lucey and me went to the movies, I wish I'd gone to the theater instead, and seen you do a play."

"Go on," Frank told him, "you'd have been bored out of your mind."

He was mocking, but there was a little catch in his voice.

"No, really. I wish I had. Wouldn't that have been something? If the two of us were sitting here and you could say that you were Dr. Loman or whatever and I'd say, oooooh, I remember that, that was excellent."

"Dr. Loman?" Frank asked, amused.

"Or whatever," Joel told him dismissively.

"I wish you'd seen me too, my friend. It's a funny old thing…"

He started, and then paused. Joel watched him carefully. No de Selby mask now, pure Adams, and a new look on his face, one Joel hadn't seen before. An expression both hard and vulnerable all at once. He was clearly fighting to keep the emotion under control.

"Go on," Joel almost whispered.

"I had so many friends. So many. Friends all over the world. I performed in New York, in London, in LA, in Paris, in Dublin. I was everywhere. And they loved me, Joel, I mean they really did. And now you, my dear old cranky man, are all I have."

His voice cracked again, something itching to get out of him. Joel felt his eyes sting as tears welled up unannounced, unwelcome.

"They loved me, but I never loved them back. I wanted to. I truly did."

Frank couldn't stop the tears now; they burst out in between words, fracturing his fixed smile as he tried to keep looking happy. As he tried to keep performing.

"But I always felt that they loved me for what I showed them, you know? A sort of a comic version of me. Never really me."

"De Selby," Joel whispered again, "not Adams."

Frank seemed to ponder it for a moment, his new face flickering as he fought to keep the smile on.

"You're a remarkably clever man sometimes, Joel," Frank told him with a laugh, though he wiped a little tear from the corner of his eye as he said it.

Joel squirmed at the compliment and tried not to show his own tears.

"A thundering idiot other times of course, but now and

then… Yes. I think you're right. I never liked Adams myself, so they got de Selby, and they loved him. So I was him. But de Selby can't love anyone because he's not real."

He was still gamely trying to keep his smile on, a new type of smile, not the de Selby one, something else. It didn't seem to want to stay on through his tears.

"Why didn't you like Adams?" Joel asked.

"I don't know the answer to that, my friend. I wish I did. I wish I knew it fifty years ago when it would have done me some good. I let a beautiful man get away from me because I was afraid to hold his hand in public. I didn't want to kiss him where other people could see me. Then he'd come along to the parties after the shows and watch de Selby in his element and wonder why I couldn't be that with him. I missed out on so much."

The new face crumbled with the effort of trying to smile through his tears. It struck Joel why it was such a new face. It was Adams, but for the first time it was Adams not trying to hide from himself.

"I cheated myself, Joel," he sobbed. "I cheated myself out of a life. I think I do hate Liam after all. Isn't that funny? I hate him because he has what I never had. He's so comfortable in himself. He's so willing to be himself. He's brave and I'm a coward. Have been all my life."

"You're no coward," Joel growled through his tears. "You're no coward, Frank Adams. You're one of the kindest people I've ever known, and I won't have you say that about yourself. I won't have you say that about my friend."

"I'm sorry, I'm never like this."

"You be whatever you want to be. Whatever. Don't mind me."

"I try so hard not to be like this," he sniffed through gritted teeth, still trying to control his emotions.

Joel gripped Frank's shoulder hard as though he could communicate his feelings through the strength of his hand.

Frank's shoulders shook under the grip.

He wasn't crying, though. With something close to shock, Joel realized the man was laughing.

"Well, what on earth is so funny?" he asked angrily.

"I don't know," Frank told him, still laughing, sniffling and wiping his tears. "I don't know actually."

Joel's anger at the sudden change of pace gave way to confusion, and his face must have shown it as Frank's laughter redoubled.

"I'm sorry again," Frank told him, now laughing and still sort of crying.

The confusion gave way to mirth as Joel found himself smiling at the absurdity of his friend crying and laughing simultaneously.

Frank looked at him with his vulnerable Adams face, laughing and crying at once, and Joel found a little laugh creeping out of him, too.

Once he had started it was a dam breaking, and he couldn't stop.

His laugh bellowed out of him, not like the suppressed laughter in the car with Eva a few days before, but a release of tension that seemed to liberate them both. The laughing echoed off every wall in the old abandoned theater and bounced around the stage and back at them so they heard themselves laughing. Frank gripped onto Joel's arm as he doubled over.

"*You there!*" a voice shouted at them from behind. "What the hell are you doing in here?"

The two men turned in their seats, surprised, but not enough to stop laughing. All they could make out at the top of the aisle was torchlight bobbing at them as the carrier descended toward them.

Joel tried to sputter the word *sorry* at the man, but it came out as a strangled laugh which caused Frank to laugh harder.

"Saving the Royale," he tried again, but it came out as "saying to boil" in his mirth.

"What's the meaning of this? You can't be in here!" the voice told them from behind its flashlight.

Joel tried to say sorry again, and for the second time in the night wondered if he might die of laughing before he had the chance to kill himself. The two old men shook, trying to compose themselves as the torch bobbed impatiently at them.

"I mean," the voice said, now all over with confusion, "I expected junkies or something. I didn't expect…"

He didn't expect two overdressed elderly gents laughing themselves to death in the audience.

"I'm sorry, young man," Frank eventually said, standing and composing himself. "We were just going to be on our way."

"How did you even get in here?" the torchlight asked.

"We've always been here," Joel piped up. "We're ghosts."

"Now, now, old boy," Frank chided. "There's no need to frighten the man."

Joel couldn't see the face as the light had obscured his vision, but a little part of him liked the idea of frightening whomever it was. Two ghosts laughing it up in the theater. He expected it was the kind of thing that Frank might like to write about.

"All right, all right," Joel told them, hauling himself out of the seat. "You'll show us out?"

They were escorted back out to the main entrance and found themselves back where they had begun. Frank looked lighter on his feet now, the moment of melancholy apparently over.

"I'm terribly sorry about that, old boy," he said as they walked, his de Selby mask firmly in place. "Sometimes that place gets the best of me."

"It's fine, it's fine," Joel told him. He wanted to say more. He wanted to tell Frank that it was okay. That he was here for him. That he valued him, that he was glad to know him.

He didn't say any of that, and cursed himself for his cowardice.

He was going to kill himself at some point, the words would have sounded hollow anyway, but for all of that he wished he had said them anyway.

"Shall we have a drink?" Frank asked with an easy smile.

21

They settled themselves in the first pub they passed, a newly decorated place designed to look old, with overhead lighting that belonged in an age even before theirs. Frank smiled at the room as he walked in. It had once been a watering hole for theater makers and actors and various other creative types. The kind of people Joel had never known. It had a history for Frank, a swirl of memories and faces that had come and gone from his life over his seventy-nine years. It was fitting that he'd come back to this place on this auspicious occasion. Fitting that they should be here after they'd been in the Royale.

For Joel it was a blank slate. Like so much of the new experiences and new feelings that he had found himself swimming in since his decision that his own life was better off ended, this was one that Joel felt he had missed out on, something that he had allowed to pass him by, and for a moment he cursed himself for missing out, cursed his own rigidity, his own damned stubbornness. His own deliberate exclusion. He delved into his pocket for his pin, and stuck it to his chest.

"Save the Royale," it said. He thought some of the patrons might get a kick out of it.

The bar itself hummed along nicely with guests moving here and there. They grabbed a spot by an empty raised table and levered themselves up into the tall bar stools. They were still both a little sore from their escapades. It had been a long time since either of them had run anywhere, and being used as a stepladder was a first for Frank. They ordered their drinks and sat themselves down in the bustle and hubbub and smiled at each other.

Outside of town someone would be looking for them. Somewhere in the city there was consternation at their absence. It no longer bothered Joel the way it once had. Instead he studied his friend as they waited for the drinks to be delivered. Frank was still looking here and there, still smiling. Joel checked for signs of the melancholy that had overtaken his friend but didn't see it. Instead he felt something new between them. Something special.

He knew what it was.

He had seen the real Frank Adams. Joel felt an enormous pride in that. Frank had shown him something that he rarely showed to anyone at all. He smiled at his best friend.

"Happy birthday, pal," Joel told Frank, raising his glass.

His friend smiled back at him as he clinked his glass.

"I'm almost positive Liam saw us," Joel told Frank as they sipped their pints.

"He didn't see us, you dolt, or he'd have stopped us."

"I'm damn near positive about it," Joel retorted. He remembered seeing Nurse Liam look their way as they crept into the undergrowth.

"Make up your mind, will you? You hate him, you love him, you hate him again."

"Rich coming from you. All things considered. You should just admit it to yourself. You're in love with him."

"I am no such thing," Frank spluttered indignantly, adjusting his scarf.

He had removed his suit jacket, and it dangled on a hook under the bar, but the scarf stayed on, twisted and tied in a rather delicate manner. Joel was again struck by what a pretentious ass his friend was, and how fondly he thought of him.

"Well, you fancy him a bit anyway," Joel persisted, sipping again.

"Look at you, all urbane and cool. Two weeks ago you couldn't say the word for fear of catching it off me, and now you're telling me who I fancy."

It was Joel's turn to bristle now. Mostly in embarrassment. He had behaved like a top-quality ass when Frank had told him.

"Ask you a question?" Joel proposed, trying not to be embarrassed.

"Jesus. This is going to be rough, already I can tell."

"What was with the 'thank you' thing you guys did the other day?"

"What 'thank you' thing?"

Joel gave him the look as hard as he could.

"I continue to underestimate you, Joel. You really are smarter than you look. Almost have to be really, wouldn't you?"

"Thanks," Joel told him drily.

"It's hard to explain."

"Try me."

"He was just, sort of telling me that he knew."

"That you fancy him?"

"No, you colossal dolt," Frank replied. He got tremendous mileage out of the word *colossal*. "That I'm…"

He hesitated.

All that was Frank Adams was in that hesitation. The de Selby mask could wear scarves and tell jokes with strangers and shake the hands of the theater makers and poets, but underneath it lurked Adams, and Adams couldn't even say the word *gay*.

Joel wanted to know, he wanted to understand that part of Frank's world, that little slice of who he was that made him so miserable that he made a new name for himself to wear so that he could cover it up. Joel wanted to, but he didn't want to also.

He reached an arm out and patted his friend on the shoulder, comfortingly. He was as awkward as ever, but in the true spirit of friendship Frank recognized the gesture for what it was, one of Joel's few means of communicating support and love and consolation. He had inherited his father's uncanny ability to botch affection. Frank smiled back at his friend, a wan, weary little smile, but grateful nonetheless.

"Enough of that," de Selby said, shaking it off and reaching inside his jacket for the notebook. "Tell me all about *The Unfortunate End of Joel Monroe?*"

Joel had been thinking on it, reading ancient plays and newer ones, searching for the right way. He had ideas.

"Death by Cop," he told Frank.

"Go on."

"You star heavily in this one," Joel told him.

"I like it better already," Frank replied.

It wasn't an overly complex idea, but it had a lot of moving parts. Joel fancied that some part of his suicide would have to have a religious component. He had been raised with it all: the church, Jesus, eternal damnation, confession, nuns, vicious priests, kind priests, Sunday mornings, beatings from his father, the word *sinner* ringing in his ears.

He had wandered away from it after Lucey died. Not a conscious, deliberate thing, but in the lethargy that had grabbed a hold of his life after her, he had simply let it all slide. By the time he started to contemplate it again, it seemed so useless to him. So vague in places, so bizarrely specific in others, like a manual for how to live your life that doesn't tell you how to live with yourself. As his anger had grown, so had his disgust, until he had arrived, unhappily, at the conclusion that he had been lied to.

The religious component for the new idea was that it would take place in a church. He'd go in one day and he'd take a "hostage" with him. The role of hostage was to be played by legendary soap opera actor Frank de Selby. Joel would rig himself out with a fully fake suicide vest, or some form of false-looking bag of explosives. They'd be rigged to look real, but actually be stuffed with confetti.

When the police arrived to get him, he'd make a list of demands. Among them, that society must care for its elderly in a more sincere and reasonable manner. That loneliness and isolation and treating senior citizens like second-class citizens must stop.

They'd give him a platform, and opportunity to address the nation. He'd be all over the news; word would get out. And when the moment was right, he'd make a final charge.

He pictured himself in slow motion, bursting out the front door of the church with an animal roar, his finger on the trigger of a fully fictional bomb or gun or something threatening. They'd empty their clips into him, and he'd drop stone-dead. As his corpse hit the ground the confetti bombs would detonate, and the whole place would be showered in it.

In his head the music of that terribly sad Bocelli song was playing as they riddled him. Afterwards they'd all realize it had been a hoax, but by then his words would have gripped the nation.

"So some cop kills you?" Frank asked, pouring cold water all over Joel's slow-motion fantasy.

"What do you mean 'some cop'? I'll have set it up that way. It's extremely dramatic."

"Why the cops?"

"They represent the state, and the state has a dreadful track record of caring for the elderly."

"Color me impressed. Logic. It's still crap, of course, but at least there's thought going into it."

Frank delivered his stinging criticism as he scribbled into the journal. There were so many words in there that Joel was sure that *The Unfortunate End of Joel Monroe* would be a play seven and a half hours long.

"Why crap?" he asked, deflated.

"Everyone hates terrorists, that's why."

"That's it?"

"Yep. Confetti or no confetti—that's a nice touch by the way—you've just joined the regrettably long and exclusively awful list of terrorists. Won't matter to anyone that it was a hoax. It'll be remembered as a terrorist act perpetuated by a man desperate for attention, and all the sympathy in the world will be reserved for me and the poor police officer that killed an angry old man."

It was painful how correct he was. Joel took a long drink from his pint.

"This was supposed to be an easy decision, you know," Joel told him angrily. "Life's shit, kill myself, done."

It had become complex. Frank had made it so.

"It's your call, pal. I just think a man of your stature and caliber needs to exit in the appropriate manner. With dignity and a touch of flair."

The compliment was designed to soften the blow; Joel knew

that, and it worked. He resisted the urge to preen himself a little.

"I'm running out of time here," Joel told him.

"You have the time you have. That's all anyone has. Don't rush it."

"But what if they—"

"They're not locking you up, jackass."

"They might."

"They won't. You might think that daughter of yours is some kind of monster, but she's not. She wants what's best for you…"

Joel scoffed at that remark.

"…and there's no way she's going to allow you to be sectioned."

"You still think I should be going to see the bloody psychologist?"

"I think it's not going to do you any harm, but ultimately that's not the point. I don't think you should be made to do anything you're not comfortable doing."

Frank was animated by the time he finished. His easygoing nature and his casual attitude toward people often masked his sharp, cutting intellect.

"You're not going to talk me out of it?"

"No, you jackass. I think you should be allowed to do whatever you want. Kill yourself, don't kill yourself, therapist, no therapist, ice cream for dinner, burgers for breakfast, whatever you want—you're a grown man."

"You know what I really want?"

"What?"

"Another pint."

In a world of internet and mobile phones it's hard for some people to untether, but for Joel Monroe, who barely understood the former and didn't know how to work the latter, disconnecting from the world was as simple as being outside the gate of the nursing home that housed him. As they strolled between bars, two well-dressed elderly men on the town on a Saturday night, it struck Joel that Hilltop would be frantic searching for them, and would have absolutely no means of knowing where they were.

They drank more beer, they talked about food, about their mutual inability to function in a kitchen and how they regretted it. They talked about their achievements, the great big moments in their lives. They talked about the downsides, the moments that they let pass them by. During it all Joel kept thinking of Eva and, strangely, of The Rhino. They had been his antagonists for so long, and yet the image of Nurse Ryan in her conservatory with what Joel assumed was her child stood out to him. She was engrossed, smiling in a way he had never seen. Why had he never seen it? Why did she represent such a threat to him, such a malevolent force? And Eva, his own daughter, how could someone whom he loved so much represent so much that he hated about his life? A life that bored him to the point that he had developed a deep and abiding hatred of it, and a desperate need to get away from it.

As they talked of all their lovely moments, she was at the center of most of Joel's. Pottering around his workshop, helping him fix the cars, doing her homework after school quietly in his office as he changed oil and replaced parts. The warm feeling of company she brought to his shop, so that all he had to do was glance her way during his shift to feel like everything was okay in the world. That little girl, and the same young woman, had been replaced in his head. In her place was the woman who scolded him like a child, who refused to allow him outside into a world that he had become increasingly distant from.

They brought these conversations from bar to bar, and as

Joel felt the drink take a greater hold on him, he became increasingly, almost worryingly morose.

"That's the one that Lily goes to," Frank told him, cutting through his reverie.

"Sorry. What?" Joel replied, confused.

The two of them had left a trendy evening spot full of young people and their cocktails in search of something more their pace, and were strolling down a wide busy avenue, the giddy surge of people intensifying as the night progressed.

"This club," Frank gestured at the door of a nightclub they were passing. "It's the one that Lily goes to on Saturday nights."

"How do you know?"

"Because I asked her."

"When?"

"When you were sulking and not paying attention."

Joel let that slide. He looked through the gates into the wide open courtyard that served as a smoking area for the club. It had a fountain in it, and chairs and tiny straw-topped shelters scattered about it. It positively teemed with people.

"Let's go in," Joel suggested.

"You what now?"

"Let's go in. It's Saturday. Would be nice to see Lily if she's here."

He remembered the face of her. The respect. The admiration. She liked the person she saw in her grandad in a way that she hadn't done since she was a tiny one. He had been too distant for too long. Lucey had been everything to those kids.

Frank grinned at the idea, adjusting his scarf and fixing on his best de Selby look.

"Let's go, then," he announced, striding purposefully toward the door.

Standing at the wide oak double doors into the courtyard

of the nightclub were two young bouncers. Joel guessed at early thirties. They seemed jocular enough, sharing a laugh. Both were gigantic men, one tall and broad, easily six and a half feet tall, with an almost ginger beard; the other shorter, but more powerfully built man was clean-shaven, a fresh-faced look about him.

"You sure you have the right place, gents?" he asked. He looked embarrassed. They both did.

"Of course we have. Are you suggesting we're senile?" Frank asked.

His voice took on an edge as he said it. Joel couldn't tell if it was affronted or another classic de Selby performance.

"Eh… No. Just that…" The bouncer paused, searching for a reason not to admit two elderly, possibly drunk men into a club full of twentysomethings.

"Ah, I think I understand," Joel offered. "You think we're below the minimum age. An understandable mistake."

"Wait…" The bouncers looked at each other in confusion. "The management reserves the right to refuse admission," the shorter one said, shamefacedly. It was clear that neither bouncer had any wish to stop them, but neither had they any wish to take responsibility when management asked what two seventy-odd-year-old men were doing in their club.

Frank drew himself up and prepared to lambaste both of them, before Joel stepped in.

"Is this because we're gay?" Joel asked, almost quietly.

The jaw of the taller bouncer dropped in a most satisfactory manner. The other one scrubbed a hand through his short hair in consternation.

"Gents," the younger one started, "it's nothing like that…"

"Not homophobia? So then what, ageism?"

Joel and Frank stood arm in arm, eyebrows raised, waiting for a reply. They would stand their ground. Over one hundred and fifty years' experience between the two of them would be more than a match for any obstacles.

After a protracted moment while the bouncers tried to imagine a way around it, the smaller one eventually stepped to one side, and with a shake of his head and a wry smile of defeat, invited them in with a gesture. Frank blew him an exaggerated kiss as they passed, and the two old-timers were in.

From the outside the club courtyard had seemed busy, but nothing could have prepared Joel for the manic energy of the inside. In all manner of clothes, mostly fancy, some almost nonexistent, the young people glided by each other, the drunker ones in their heels staggering a little. A young man in a corner seat was trying to keep his eyes open and head up, on the verge of stupor.

The music thumped at them, humming through Joel's clothes, through the soles of his shoes and into his bones. There were drinks everywhere, a pall of cigarette smoke that hung above the heads of the revelers, and here and there kissing and groping.

He tried to take it all in calmly, and he felt that his fairly significant buzz was helping, but it was a long time since Joel Monroe had been in the thick of such a crazy swirl of humanity. He glanced to Frank for support only to realize that the older man was loving it.

The difference between the two men might have been summed up in that moment. One a lover of people, an extrovert, energized by a crowd, the other a quieter man, solid, and though he only realized it in this very moment, a man not fond of large groups of people.

"I think I need a drink," he shouted at Frank.

"What?" Frank roared back.

"I said I need a drink," Joel tried again, lifting his voice in the din.

"I have no idea what you're saying, but let's go get a drink," Frank told him.

The bar was, painfully, all the way at the other end of the courtyard, through the mass of people. A part of Joel worried about how they'd be received; two elderly men. Would they be considered perverts? Lurkers among a crowd much too young for them. Would they be mocked? Two relics out of time and out of place. To his great and pleasant surprise, he saw no judgment. In fact, as they moved toward the back of the bar, he found that most of the young people, those sober enough to notice them, offered a quiet deference, moving aside ever so slightly to let them pass.

A beautiful young lady smiled warmly at them as she gently pushed her unknowing friends out of the way. A path cleared for them as they made their way down the back. Joel had intended releasing Frank's arm once they were in the door, but being intimidated by the crowd, he had not, and so they made their way through the tangled mess, arm in arm.

Blessedly, by the bar, farther away from the speakers, the volume levels weren't so loud, and the two could hear themselves think, and hear each other talk, albeit by almost shouting.

"What can I get you gents?" the bartender asked. He was young and handsome and smiled encouragingly at them.

"Two pints of stout, please," Joel asked.

"Sorry, gents, cocktail bar only."

Joel looked at Frank in dismay only to realize, again, that Frank was delighted.

"We'll have two cocktails please," Frank told the man.

"Any particular kind?" the man asked patiently.

"It's my birthday. Surprise me," Frank replied, and he winked.

Joel couldn't help himself and laughed. Here was de Selby

in his element. When the drinks arrived back, and Joel reached for his wallet, a young hand stopped him gently.

"Grandad?!?" Lily asked, staring incredulously at him.

She had clearly spotted them from somewhere across the bar and wandered over to see if her eyes were deceiving her. Now standing in front of her grandfather, she was gobsmacked. Joel channeled his inner de Selby and smiled nonchalantly at her.

"Hello, love," he said, and planted a kiss on her forehead.

It was a perfect moment for him. Frank burst out laughing at the synchronicity of it all. Joel tried not to laugh, but it must have shown on his face as Lily soon broke down, too.

"Wait until Chris sees this," she said as she got her breath.

"Your brother is here, too?"

"Yeah. With a gang of his friends. Does Mom know you're here?"

Joel tried not to look angry at the question. It was innocently asked. It annoyed him that he was expected to have permission, but all things considered, he knew she wasn't trying to offend him.

"No, love. And I'd take it as a kindness if you'd keep it to yourself."

"Of course," she said, dismissing the suggestion that she'd tell.

Her face was beaming at him. This is what he had come for. This is what he wanted out of his beaten-up and drawn out and utterly pointless life. He wanted respect, and love and admiration, all the things that come from a relationship between two equals.

"How did you get out?"

"He used me as ladder," Frank told her.

She looked from one of them to the other in surprised delight as she paid for their cocktails and then guided them toward a spot inside the club, a booth, half-full of young adults enjoying themselves, "celebrating their lives," Joel thought Frank might say.

In the middle of the gang, overdressed with his highly styled hair, was Chris.

"Grandad!" he exclaimed, his mouth agape.

"This is your grandad?" a young lady immediately asked.

"Yes, I'm his grandfather," Joel told her.

Chris grinned at him from ear to ear, while Lily began exclaiming to all of them about how she had spotted them across the courtyard ordering cocktails. Frank introduced himself, and Lily began telling them all about his friend's acting career, prompting a flurry of mobile phones and googling and searching for Frank in corners of the internet.

Joel was proud of himself. Proud of the fact that he was here, proud of the fact that his grandchildren were glad to see him, proud that he could have a life even if other people were trying to stop him.

When their cocktails ran out they had more. When someone suggested it, they took to the dance floor, the booze stripping them of any inhibitions. Joel danced awkwardly, clumsily, and Frank wasn't much better, but a crowd had formed around them, a minimob of young people jumping and dancing and gyrating and taking photographs of the two of them, and neither of them cared how they looked. During one particular song, Chris swung an arm up and around his grandfather's shoulder and Joel, full of drink and high spirits, felt that he might burst from the small act of affection.

Several songs later and Joel was feeling drunk, and weary and overexcited. For a long, dangerous moment, he stood on the dance floor and waited for his legs to fail him. He felt dizzy, disorientated. Hadn't he felt like this once before? When he fainted in the pub several years beforehand? He hoped it was just dizziness.

On dangerously unsteady feet he made his way from the dance floor and toward the bar. What he needed was water. Along the way several of the dancing crowd who had broken away saluted him; one stopped to take a selfie with him. He hoped he wasn't smiling too drunkenly. The bar manager served him, with a great, warm, affectionate smile. Joel chugged back the water, one hand gripping the bar tightly, and let the dizziness pass. The bar manager clapped him warmly on the shoulder. Joel was poleaxed by the effusiveness of it all. That the world wasn't shutting them out, but welcoming them in.

When the music ended, and hordes of late-teens and twenty-somethings burst like a drunken wave out into the city streets, the two bouncers smiled knowingly at the two senior citizens, their adoring public all around them. Frank even signed some autographs while young people showed off pictures of him from his soap opera days.

The fresh nighttime air cooled Joel as he stood, drunkenly, in the middle of the street. His ears were still ringing from the sound of the music and the shouting, and he felt like his bones might still be vibrating under skin, but he felt deliciously, gloriously alive.

They reeled down the street in a group, chatting, laughing, stopping briefly while one young pal or other threatened to throw up but didn't, and came to a stop outside a kebab shop.

"Kebabs?" he asked Chris.

"Never had a kebab, Grandad?"

"Never."

"First time for everything," Chris told him as he led him to a chair in the crowded restaurant.

The group was large enough that it had to spread itself over three tables with Joel, Chris and two pals sitting at one, and

Frank sitting behind with Lily and two young ladies who apparently couldn't stop taking his photograph.

"What possessed you, Grandad?" Chris asked around a mouthful of kebab.

"My friend's birthday," Joel told him, trying to sound cool about it. Trying to sound like he hadn't been secretly hoping he'd get caught as they climbed out the window.

"And they have no idea?" Chris asked, still hugely impressed.

He had impressed them this night, and in doing so had built a moment with them, something special and wonderful. For the first time since they were tiny children, he felt connected to them.

"I think, my dears," Joel announced as he rose from his seat, savoring the word *dears*, "that I may be a little bit drunk."

His proclamation was met with heartfelt cheers. Frank laughed out loud.

"And," Joel continued, "it may be time for me to go home."

These words were greeted with a chorus of boos and hisses. Frank threatened to throw a foam container at him.

"Settle down now," Joel told them, all authority, and to his great surprise they did. "We can do it all again next week."

More cheers. Joel beamed at his audience.

"You'll be okay getting home?" asked one young lady with concern as they got up from their junk food.

"I'll get you a cab," another young man said.

"No, I'll get it." Chris jumped up and flagged the first light he could see.

Joel muttered his gracious thanks, still a little overwhelmed, but had to bark at Frank to make him stop posing for photographs and charming the young people.

"Killjoy," Frank told him as he wobbled into his seat in the back of the taxi.

"Attention seeker," Joel countered, without malice.

"Back to face the music," Frank noted absently.

"S'pose we had to at some point."

"Worth it. What a birthday treat."

They settled into silence as the taxi propelled them toward Hilltop, passing down long streets with tall buildings looming up either side, passed gangs of young people and old people, drunk one and all, getting fast food and delaying the end of their evening.

Facing the music was precisely what they'd be doing when they got back. The nurses would be up in arms. Someone had certainly called Eva. He'd have questions to answer, they both would, and then some, and on top of it all, they'd be lectured endlessly as if they were stupid teenagers sneaking out of their parents' homes instead of two grown men allowed to do what they want.

Just as Joel was realizing he wasn't quite ready to face the music, the cab crossed the bridge, and in a split-second decision Joel was calling out, "stop."

The cab pulled in alongside a tiny park that sat on the river. It had little wooden benches and sculptures and flowers in it. During the day people stopped there to photograph the skyline of the city across the river and to admire the water rushing by or the elegant old castle that he and Frank once spent an afternoon in. At night it was lovely, but a different kind of lovely, a quiet, little bit moody lovely, with the sounds of water serenading the benches.

Joel asked the driver to wait, and, drunk, full of nostalgia and brimming with sentimentality, he climbed from the cab to sit by the river.

"Everything okay?" Frank asked, as he perched himself on the bench next to Joel.

"Fine. Just fancied a moment."

"Was a little bit hectic back there all right. You looked like you might faint at one point."

"You know, I didn't realize it until tonight, but I don't like crowds."

"Unsurprising."

"You think?"

"You don't like anyone."

"I like you."

The sincerity of his words wasn't lost on either of them. It was spontaneous and heartfelt and only a tiny bit motivated by all the alcohol. Lucey had been the last real friend he had, and she was the love of his life. Since her absence he'd wandered through his days on his own, killing time, watching the hours tick past him and just trying to get to nightfall so he could go back to bed. Now he had a new friend. He was glad to have someone again.

"I like you, too. You're a cranky bastard, but I like you."

Joel let the moment wash over him. He'd rushed through too many important moments in the past. He let the sound of the water and the faint noises of the city drift around him as he sat there and absorbed the view.

The water called to him. If he wanted to he could just end it now. There'd be no music to face. He could easily climb the railing that separated him from the cool waters of the river. He realized that he had always wanted it to end in the river.

He could slide in, float away, let the waters take him away from his anxiety and his uselessness and his fear of death. He could simply go.

He'd have to leave Frank to do it. He didn't really want to leave Frank. Not right now. And it wasn't the end that either of them were looking for. It was too prosaic. Too, as Frank had once told him, undignified. His hand twiddled with his

"Save the Royale" badge. The Royale, it seemed, was safe for one more night at least.

"You think there's a heaven?" he asked Frank eventually.

"Fucking hell."

"Come on, you've read all them fancy books. You're all philosophical and all that. Simple question."

"You think asking someone if there's a heaven is a simple question?"

"I just want your opinion on the matter."

"Why?"

"Because what if there is one and I'm not going because I've killed myself."

"You finding religion again?"

"Not really. I'm not sure I ever had it in the first place. Just, sort of went through the motions."

"I don't think I'm qualified to answer."

"Why not?"

"Because apparently I'm not going there either."

"Why? You gonna kill yourself, too?" Joel asked incredulously.

"No, you blithering idiot," Frank admonished. "Because, well, you know…"

He still couldn't say it. Even drunk at three in the morning sitting by the river, Frank Adams wouldn't let himself say the words.

"We'll have fun in hell together, then. Me and you."

Frank laughed openly, tipping his head back. Joel hoped it was Adams laughing, and not de Selby.

"We can escape out of there, too," he told Joel.

"I don't think there are any rocks in hell that are big enough."

They sat there for a moment in comfortable silence. The shadow of the castle across the river standing out in the night. Their first day out had been there.

"Ask you a question?" Frank said, cutting through the silence.

"Go ahead, caller."

"You had fun tonight, right?"

"One of the best nights of my life."

"So maybe things aren't so bad?"

"What are you driving at?"

"Maybe if things aren't so bad… You know?"

"No, I don't know."

But Joel did know what he meant. He thought about it for a moment. Maybe things weren't so bad, maybe there was reason to stay here. Maybe Lily and Chris and Una Clarke were enough, and as long as he had Frank…

Then he remembered what he was doing. Sitting on a park bench by the river in order to delay the scolding he was going to get for staying out too late. The dressing-down, potential disciplinary action, the tsk-tsking and disappointed head-shaking from the woman he had raised. All because he wanted to go out. In the end, no one had saved the Royale. It had died.

Yet it was there all the same, a glimmer of hope. If he could salvage a relationship with his grandchildren this late in the game, then maybe there was a chance.

"Maybe it won't be so bad," Frank ventured. Once again he had read the look on Joel's face and saw right into the heart of it.

"Maybe it won't," Joel agreed.

"You'll think about it, then? You'll think about the suicide thing?"

"I sure will."

22

The first noticeable thing when the cab pulled up to Hilltop was the presence of a squad car, its flashing lights in-
considerately still reflecting off the walls of the home as they
rotated on the roof of the vehicle. A policeman loitered nearby,
a little bored-looking. The next thing was a silver Primera,
Tony's car, which meant Eva was here. The lights were all
on, as well. Joel could see his bedroom light on through their
window, and the main reception, and the common room. All
visible from the gate. He pressed the buzzer pugnaciously and
waited for an extended moment. Clearly no one was manning
reception while the hunt was on for the two missing residents.

"Hilltop," came the slightly breathless voice of Nurse Liam.

"Liam, old boy," Joel said, forcing some joviality into his
reply in a rough approximation of Frank.

"Mr. Monroe," came Liam's voice. Neutral. Not happy, not
unhappy, with a little sigh at the end that might have been relief. Then the buzz as the gate began to swing open.

Joel and Frank had disembarked from the cab back up at
the bus stop and walked drunkenly to the gates, which meant

they faced a long climb up the hill. They had barely started it when he saw Eva heading toward him, her hair in disarray, power walking, a thunderhead.

"Easy now, Joel," Frank told him. He could see what was coming.

Joel tried to fix the smile on his face, but he knew it was slipping.

"What on earth do you think you're doing?" she asked as she stormed toward them.

"Walking, my dear," he replied.

"Don't you dare…" She seemed to stumble on the words, her frustration evident. "What do you think you are doing?"

"I went for an evening stroll," he replied casually.

"Until three o'clock in the morning? We were worried sick. We called the police. Nurse Ryan is beside herself."

"I somehow doubt that," Joel replied.

"Anything could have happened to you out there. Anything. Do you realize how stupid and irresponsible you were being?"

"Stupid and irresponsible? A man can't go for a drink with his friend now?"

"No, Dad, a man can't go for a drink with his friend without telling a soul, slipping out in the dead of night without so much as a word."

"If I told you you'd have said no."

"That's because you're not supposed to be out, Dad, for Christ's sake."

"So what on earth would be the point in fucking telling you?" he shot back angrily. Profanity. He didn't care. He wouldn't apologize.

Eva failed to see the ingenuity in his argument and seemed unaffected by the swearing.

"Oh, so this is my fault?" she asked. "You vanish without

telling anyone, working us all up and terrifying me, and this is my fault?"

"Not entirely yours, no, but mostly."

"Mostly my fault? You selfish man, you selfish, self-obsessed man."

The others were making their way out now. Another police officer, Nurse Ryan and Tony. He hurried his step when he saw Eva's temper coming to a steady boil. Beside Joel, Frank stepped uncomfortably from one foot to the next. Joel had never seen him so lost for what to say or do. He didn't have time to marvel at the moment, though.

"Selfish? It's so dreadfully terrible that I might want to get out a little bit every now and then, is it?" Joel asked, slowly working himself up a little to match his daughter. "I'm a selfish bastard for not wanting to be cooped up in this prison all day and all night from now until the time I die, is it?"

"My God, you're so dramatic, you could have visited us anytime you want, but you were too busy sulking."

"Oh, visit you, is it? For what? To sit in your house being ignored by your children for a few hours on a Sunday? Well, that just makes everything better now, doesn't it."

"If you weren't such an asshole to them all the time, maybe they wouldn't ignore you."

The words were hastily spoken and quickly regretted, Joel could see that, but he knew better. His grandkids liked him now, respected him.

"Well, that doesn't matter because they like me now, and they respect me, and that's more than I can say for their mother."

"This might be a good time to call it an evening," Frank tried to politely interject.

"Shut up, Frank," Joel said, just as Eva snapped, "Stay out of this, Mr. Adams."

"I think maybe he's right," Tony tried, but there was no stopping them.

"I have tried to provide you with everything," she told him vehemently. "I've tried to be nice. You just complain so completely constantly that it's a challenge to be in your company."

"Oh, stop, just stop," he replied, his anger now seething in him, a raw thing, mixed up with drink. "You preferred your mother and we both know it. You enjoyed coming here until she died, and since then you've been just waiting for me to check out."

"How dare you?" she said, tears springing to her eyes.

"I dare because it's true. That's why I'm here, isn't it? To wait out my days? To pass the time until I'm dead?"

"You're not just selfish, you're a mean, vicious man," she shot back, her fury stilling her tears as she scrubbed them away with the back of her hand.

"Yeah, well, the truth hurts," Joel shot back.

Her tears got to him. He hated to see her cry.

He remembered her first major breakup. Lucey had done most of the talking, but Joel had held her in his arms as she sat, knees folded up to her chest on her bed, and cried. The tears were taking the wind out of his sails, but he was determined not to yield. Instead he brushed past her and headed for Hilltop.

He passed The Rhino on the way. Half in uniform, half in her casual clothes, her hair still tied back in the ponytail that somehow made her less intimidating, less threatening, more human. The look she gave him, though, eyes hard as agates, promised retribution.

Of course, he thought. *Punishment for not being a good corpse and refusing to just lie down and die.*

It was a dramatic thought. He knew it was. Perhaps Eva was right. Perhaps Frank was contagious. The police didn't try to stop him; they merely acknowledged his presence as he stomped past them. He didn't look back at Eva; he wasn't sure he could see her crying again, but he heard Frank trailing in his wake as he headed for their room.

As they lay in their respective beds, Joel still boiling, his temper kept up by his elevated heart rate and the feed of cocktails and pints of stout, they listened to the sound of the fall-out happening a short distance from the window. Joel heard Nurse Ryan talking, though he couldn't make out the words. Then there was Eva, and Tony. Another voice, presumably a police officer, mumbled something, and then one by one car doors opened and closed and engines gunned and gravel was stirred as they made their way down the hill. There would be consequences. He knew that. Serious consequences.

At the sound of footsteps Joel shut his eyes and pretended to sleep, fearful that The Rhino was coming for him. The feet shuffled about the room for a minute and Joel chanced a look. It was Nurse Liam. He stood at Joel's bedside, waiting. There was a little gleam in his eye. His face was arrow-straight. Too straight. He placed some water and some painkillers on the nightstand by his bed.

"For the hangover," he said, and Joel thought he saw a little smile. "Happy birthday, Frank," Liam said, as he withdrew.

At least one person was on their side.

The first and most significant consequence of a major night out in which the police have to be called, is still the hangover. It had been a long time since Joel had a major hangover, and all at once he was reminded why he had never been much of a drinker. His head pounded. He could still taste the kebab, and his stomach rolled every time he stirred in the bed. Through bleary eyes he could see his bedside table. "Save the Royale," the little pin said. Joel fervently wished that someone would come into the room and put the Royale out if its misery. The

May morning poured sunlight through their room, and it stabbed him in the brain. Inevitably, though, things got considerably worse for Joel.

"Mr. Monroe," the voice said. It was a stern voice. A commanding voice. The Rhino's voice. "I'd like a word, please."

Joel shifted in the bed, feeling his stomach twisting in his gut, and tried to sit up.

"Can I help you?" he tried to say. It came out as "cun I hep oo?"

She raised an eyebrow at the state of his disrepair. This morning, back in her pristine uniform with her hair in the usual severe bun, she looked authoritarian again, terrifying again.

"Mr. Monroe, how did you get out of Hilltop?"

"I flew," he told her, stretching and wincing at the same time.

"Mr. Monroe, I'm asking you a question."

"Not being an idiot, I'm very aware of that, Nurse Ryan, but I have no intention of telling you anything."

"Perhaps not being an idiot, you'll think better of that decision and explain to me how you got out of Hilltop."

"I used a grappling hook and climbed up over the north wall."

"Perhaps then you'll be more willing to speak to the psychologist we've contacted."

And there it was. The consequences.

"I assume you and my daughter have decided what's best for me, without consulting me at all?"

"Your daughter and I have your best interests at heart, Mr. Monroe, and we're both now quite concerned about you. I'm concerned that Hilltop is inadequately resourced to take care of a man who's clearly suffering as you are."

Concerned about his suffering. Unlikely. Expulsion is what she wanted. If the old man won't behave, we'll kick him out.

"Sure you are."

"Have I ever given you reason to believe that I don't have the best interests of the residents here at heart?"

He checked that statement. It was difficult since his brain appeared to not actually be working. To his surprise he couldn't find an example. He knew there were plenty, he just knew it, but for the life of him, he couldn't recall a single one.

"You're the warden in this prison, aren't you?" he concluded lamely.

"Your behavior, Mr. Monroe, has been erratic, irresponsible and unpredictable. You've been having mood swings, and temper tantrums, you've been confrontational and uncooperative. These are all bad signs, Mr. Monroe."

She was right, but wrong at the same time. She was also picking a fine moment to pin him by the collar. His brain was mashed peas.

"Well, how's this for uncooperative? I'm not talking to your damn psychiatrist."

"Psychologist, Mr. Monroe, there's a difference, and the appointment is being made. You can talk or not talk, but your suitability to remain at Hilltop is what's being assessed here. So you'll have to decide how talkative you are when they get here."

"No. I won't. Because I'm sick to death of being told what to do around here. I'm sick to death of having no say in anything, of being forced to behave the way you think I should just because you think it. I'm more than that."

"We'll see, Mr. Monroe," she said ominously, as she withdrew from the room.

He sat there fuming.

He turned to get his support from the lump covered in quilts that was Frank Adams. It stirred slightly. A foot protruding out the end of the pile the only evidence that what lurked beneath was human and not monster.

"Perhaps, old boy," came Frank's gravelly voice almost from

entirely under his covers, "perhaps you should consider speaking to someone."

Joel was stunned.

"Excuse me?" he asked, infuriated.

"Look, don't get all 'Angry Joel' and start shouting, but do you not think that maybe…"

"Maybe what?" Joel snapped.

"I said don't get all angry," Frank replied, sitting up in the bed with a wince. He wore his hangover like a second skin. "Just, wasn't last night fun? Wasn't it nice to see your grandkids and all? Maybe someone can help you with all that. Relationship stuff and grief and things?"

It had been fun. It had been revelatory, and somehow addictive. He wanted more. He did not want it at the expense of his freedom and having played the good dog for long enough, he didn't want to have to beg for it.

"Where the fuck is this coming from?" he practically snarled.

"Pardon your language."

"Stop kidding around for once in your life. Where is it coming from? You're supposed to be on my side. You want me to beg for their permission? What happened to all that stuff about taking control of my life?"

"I am on your side."

"No, you're not. You're taking her side. You afraid of her?"

"God, I'm way too hungover for this," Frank sighed, passing a hand in front of his face. "I'm not afraid of her, Joel. I just happen to think she might have a point."

"You? Of all people, you? The one person I was sure was on my side. What about all that talk about me being the only friend you had left? What about that? With all your big talk about master of my own destiny."

"Oh, for crying out loud, can you stop making this about

people taking sides? I'm just saying that it might help. I'm not condemning you to life in prison."

"You promised, Frank. You promised you wouldn't make me go."

"I'm not making you go, you jackass."

"Well, you're practically making me. Thought I had one person in the whole place who wouldn't turn on me."

"Can you stop making this all about yourself for one minute? Your daughter is worried, The Rhino is worried, Nurse Liam is worried, Una is worried, fucking everyone is worried about you, and you're going to sit there telling me that no one is on your side? Are you completely fucking stupid?"

"Why don't you go to the damn psychologist?" Joel asked. "Me?"

"Yes, you. You're a gay man who literally can't say the words *I'm gay*, you changed your name so that the real you would never have to be gay. You're the one that needs the damn psychiatrist."

If Joel's brain had been working correctly that morning, he might never have said that. He might have held his tongue instead of flaying his best friend with it.

The words hit Frank hard, right between the eyes. There was no sign of the de Selby mask, just a rock hard and furious Frank Adams.

"You're one nasty, vicious bastard when you want to be."

That was the last time that Frank ever called Joel vicious.

"But since we're fighting dirty," Frank continued, "let's stop and have a look at what's really going on here. You're a coward. You're afraid of going to the therapist for fear of what that therapist will find inside that head of yours, for fear of what you might find out about yourself. This isn't about you controlling your own life. This is about you being afraid. And worst of all, you're a coward because you want to kill yourself rather than face anything."

"I'm not a coward," Joel fumed, his fists bunching.

"Then why do you want to kill yourself so badly?" Frank snarled.

The words were timed with the most awful perfection, for at that very minute, Una Clarke walked through the door with a tray of tea and biscuits. She stopped dead, her stunned face blanching as the impact of the words struck her fully.

Frank's face blanched, too. He hadn't intended for anyone to hear. The furious face dropped. Joel tried to think of something to say to cover it, something to make her not know, to take it back. A joke, a comment, anything at all...

But nothing came, and the look she turned on him was a mix of bitter disappointment, deep and profound sadness, and a white-hot anger.

With some obvious effort, she managed to carry the tray over to Joel's bedside, and she placed it delicately there, never taking her eyes off him. Desperately his mashed-peas brain struggled for something to say, anything to say that would fix it, that would take that hurt look from her lovely eyes. Still nothing came. She shook her head at him and turned away, making her way out of the room.

For a long moment neither of them said anything. Joel's confusion and his disappointment in himself turning back into anger, he stared balefully at Frank across the space in between them.

"Joel," Frank almost whispered. "I'm so sorry, I never intended—"

"Shut up, Frank. Just for once, shut the fuck up."

Joel turned in the bed and dragged the covers back up to his neck and tried to go to sleep.

He could have died that very moment, and he'd have been perfectly happy to do so.

23

He dozed in the afternoon and dreamed again. He was trying to find Una, walking across the same barren landscape as before, populated with the skeletons of Mr. Miller. Hills and boulders everywhere and low thick clouds of despair, so close to him that he thought he might just be able to reach out and touch them. The rocks that sprinkled the place were all the same shape as his and Frank's rock, but they rolled at the gentlest push. In the distance he could see Una and Frank laughing as they sat at the foot of a hill, their backs against a boulder, but as Joel pushed through the various Mr. Millers, the hill seemed to get farther away. Suddenly he couldn't see them at all.

"Where did you go?" he called out.

"They're on the other side of the hill," came Lucey's voice.

He turned to speak to her, but it wasn't her; it was The Rhino, in her casual clothes, smiling at him warmly. She reached out to grab him, and he woke.

The room was empty. There was no sign of Frank. The tea and the tray of biscuits were still there, cold now and somehow awful-looking. The tea in the large mugs looked like it was made with stagnant water. Joel had always felt that there was something terrible and pathetic-looking about a cold cup of tea. He stared through them to look at Frank's bed. It was made up and neat and tidy and looked too sterile. The halls were quiet too, missing the usual signs of life. He checked the time. Three o'clock. Everyone must have been in the common room.

The worst of his hangover had apparently passed in his sleep, but traces of it lingered in his stomach. An uneasy feeling that was part the alcohol and part his great and overwhelming remorse. He hauled himself from the bed, feeling no satisfaction from the cold on the soles of his feet, and turned on the television.

He flipped through the sports channels for an hour or so, trying to find something worth watching, but his brain wouldn't let him think or feel anything other than sad. The void was back, looming in his head, threatening to suck him in, stretch him out. Make him unreal.

By evening time, Joel gave up on television and put on his slippers and dressing gown. He walked through Hilltop, passing the residents in a kind of muted resentment. There was Mrs. Klein. She smiled awkwardly at him, a pathetic kind of hello. The word was out about their shenanigans the night before, and most of them would have heard the argument that morning. How much detail they heard was another matter. Joel tried not to think about it.

Frank had snarled the words at him, venomous, nasty, but not loudly. Surely they hadn't carried to the ears of the nurses. Would Una have told anyone? He doubted it. Still, it was a terrifying prospect. As if things weren't bad enough without people looking at him like he wanted to kill himself. The fact that he did was irrelevant.

Joel settled in the common room. Frank sat beside Mrs. Clarke; neither of them were speaking, just sitting there watching soap operas. Joel hated the damn soap operas. He sat at a small table out of the way and set up the chessboard. And waited.

He cared little how it looked, one broken-down old man sitting at a table, stubbornly not talking to anyone, stubbornly waiting until Mighty Jim ambled in. His eyes lighting up at the board.

"I obviously believe that he's an accurate representation of the human race," Jim told him, taking his seat with a friendly smile.

"Just play the damn game," Joel told him, for once not trying to decide if the man was more sane than senile.

They played to a stalemate in just under half an hour, and Jim began to reset the board. Joel didn't bother objecting to another game, or even saying anything. He had killed half an hour, so he stood up from the table to leave. Frank turned his head and looked in his direction, and for just a second he looked like he might say something. He didn't. Una didn't even turn.

Joel made his way back to his bedroom with the sense of resentment growing deep in his belly.

At some point in the evening, Nurse Karl arrived with the pills that were supposed to save him from the stroke that everyone promised was coming. The one everyone feared so much. Joel didn't object. He took the damn pills without a word, drank the water that came with them and lay down. Nurse Karl's expression never changed. Impassive. Silent. Joel was grateful for that at least.

He lay on his side, facing the window, facing away from the bed that had been his wife's, then Mr. Miller's and now Frank's. He didn't want to look at it. Instead he stared down the long drive and into the corner where the rock was.

He heard Frank come in some time later. He listened carefully as Frank dressed himself for bed. He didn't move as the sound of creaking announced that Frank was all the way in the bed, and he barely breathed as Frank clicked the lamp on his nightstand off. He just lay there and didn't speak.

When Monday rolled around the following day, as it typically did after a Sunday, Joel found himself back where he had been the night before. Back where he had been the day after Mr. Miller died. Alone, silent, full of bitter resentment and exhausted by it all. The isolation of it was awful. He wondered how he had ever lived like this. In the time before Frank. The time when being in Una Clarke's company meant feeling guilty. That terrible moment in his life between the passing of his wife and the arrival of his best friend.

He ate breakfast in bed, picking at his meal more than enjoying it, and flipped through TV channels. Game shows and documentaries. Nothing of any consequence, but at least it wasn't a damn soap opera.

He tried to doze afterwards, to pass some time, but found himself tossing and turning. So he went back to staring out the window, staring down the long drive, wondering if they had discovered his rock. He wondered if Nurse Ryan was working, or was she at home with her child, or maybe even children. He realized he knew nothing about her outside of this place.

"You're not helping yourself, you know?" Nurse Liam said.

"Leave me alone," Joel told him.

"Not this time, Joel," Liam replied.

He stepped around the bed, quietly on his soft shoes, because this was not the time or the place for loud.

"Why won't people let me be?"

"Because we're worried about you…"

"So you keep saying."

"…and this self-imposed exile isn't helping the case against seeing a therapist."

"Bloody therapist again," Joel grumbled.

"I've been worried about you for years."

That was surprising.

"What?" Joel asked him.

"Years. Una Clarke, too. I think even Mighty Jim Lincoln was worried about you. You're the only one he wants to play chess against, you know."

"Nonsense," Joel insisted.

"Not nonsense. You've been so low. So quiet all the time. So anxious and unhappy."

"No, I wasn't."

"Sure you were. Only these last couple of weeks you've come out of your shell. I remember when you weren't like that. When Lucey was here, you were a quiet old gent doting on his wife. With a polite word for everyone. You read and you watched your sports and you were nice. Then years of nothing, only for it to finally pass. It's been lovely seeing signs of life from you. Seeing you wake up a little. Hearing you laughing when I pass the room in the mornings. Listening to you and Frank mocking each other."

"That why you let us go the other evening?" Joel asked, almost tentatively.

Liam adopted a bland expression and spread his hands as he sat down on the edge of the bed.

"I didn't let anyone go anywhere. It would have been a significant breach of my duty of care if I had let the two of you sneak out. If I had seen you, I would have stopped you. But I didn't see you ducking into the tree line like two World War II vets behind enemy lines."

Joel couldn't stop the small smile from creeping across his face. It was quite an image. Not one he would have picked for himself, but a charming one all the same.

"If you care so much, how come you keep pushing this therapy thing? How come you're always on Ryan's side?"

"Joel, I mean this in the kindest way possible, but you're an extraordinary dope sometimes," Liam told him with a rueful smile.

"Well, that's not very nice."

"You have to stop thinking this is a fight. You have to stop thinking this is a prison. You have to realize that we're trying to help."

Joel tried to picture it otherwise. He tried not to see bars on the windows. He tried to picture life at Hilltop as something other than an open prison. It was difficult.

"Look," Liam continued, "I want you to try to look at this as an opportunity. It's happening regardless. You will be meeting a counselor. If it has to happen anyway, why not seize the opportunity to share a little? Why not look at this as your chance to get some things out in the open? Please understand that this isn't being done for no reason. It's not a punishment. It's not a penance. It's only because you're too pigheaded stubborn to even admit you need the help."

"You're a very insulting boy when you want to be," Joel told him, trying not to look pouty.

"And you're a very infuriating man when you want to be. A good one mostly. But infuriating."

He looked like he might say more. Instead he placed a steaming mug next to Joel. "I brought you some tea."

He patted Joel consolingly on the arm and stood up. Joel would never have admitted it, but it was nice to talk. He had gotten used to talking again, and the silence had become oppressive.

Without waiting, Joel sprang from his bed, or at least, hauled himself out of it with considerably more energy than he had previously shown, and picking up his tea, he headed out into the hallway.

When he reached her door, he tapped on it three times.

Three appropriately even taps. She must have known it was him, since Una opened her door stony-faced.

"Joel," she said frostily.

She had never been frosty to him before, and for a flash of a second he missed the days when she was unrelentingly pleasant to him, often uncomfortably so.

"May I come in?" he asked nervously.

"You may," she told him, standing aside to admit him.

"I'd like to talk," he told her.

The words almost stuck in his throat.

"Very well," she replied, still icing him with her eyes. "Talk."

He sipped his tea to compose himself. Frank would know what to say. Something clever and disarming. He'd do it with a twinkle in his eye and his de Selby mask on and she'd laugh, and then everything would be smoothed over again.

"I'm sorry you heard that yesterday," he began. "It was never my intention that anyone know."

"But why, Joel? Why on earth would you think a thing like that? What on earth is so awful about life here that you'd even contemplate doing that to yourself? You have a daughter and two lovely grandkids."

"I know, I know," he told her. "But it doesn't change anything really. I'm not happy here. Or at least, I wasn't happy here."

He had wanted it, he was sure of that, but it seemed long ago somehow, when he had truly wanted to die. Now he was unsure. His brain a confused jumble. Two nights ago he could have stepped into the river. Been done with it. At any time he could have fashioned a noose from the cord of his dressing gown and been done with it.

At any moment he chose, he could have been done with it. So why wasn't he done?

"And now you are happy?" she asked, a small hope in her voice.

He didn't want to hurt her. For all her anger and her fury at him, she still seemed so delicate, so breakable.

"I don't know, Una. I don't know what I am. I had enough, you know?"

"No, Joel, I don't know," she replied.

"I had enough of it, you know?" He almost stumbled on the words; they stuck to his tongue just a little as he started, but once they were out, he pressed on.

"The pointlessness. The utter boredom of it. I used to be useful. I fixed things. I fixed cars. People brought me their broken things and I made them go again. Even after I retired, I fixed things. All around the house. I fixed everything. Do you know, I used to hope that things would break just so I could feel useful? Lucey kept the place. She kept it clean and tidy, and I sat there like a big useless lump, complaining that I was bored instead of helping her. And the garden. We had a beautiful garden. A lovely little thing, she kept it so nice. And I sat inside waiting for something to break just so I could fix it." It was sticking in his craw again, the words bumbling and clumsy to his ears. He remembered her little garden and her earthy hands and how he could see her through the living room window while he watched the football, toiling happily in the dirt. He'd make her tea and she'd beam at him. He tried to recall when he had changed, when he had become something new, and different. When had he forgotten how to communicate? He struggled to express himself without sounding stupid, and weak, but he was rolling now.

"Even Eva, our daughter, when she needed things she went to Lucey with them, not to me. I did nothing. But at least I had Lucey, you know. And I had cousins, and neighbors and friends, not many, but I had them. And they went. One by one they went. Some moved, most died. Then I just had Lucey. And when she was gone, I thought I had nothing left. And I got so bored of having nothing, and being useless and doing nothing and I just…"

He paused, he could see the empathy in her; there was something in her eyes, some hint of recognition, some part of what he was saying was familiar to her. Maybe it was the idleness and pointlessness, maybe it was the relentless sense of loss, or perhaps that grim and terrible feeling that you might be next, that ever-invasive thought.

He had run out of words regardless and stood, stupidly, waiting for her to say anything.

"I know," she told him sympathetically. Her eyes had softened, and she rested a hand on his forearm.

"I'm sorry to burden you with all this," he said quietly.

"It's no burden, Joel, I promise. Do you still feel like you want to?"

"I don't know, Una. I honestly don't know."

"You're a dear, sweet man. Please don't leave us, Joel," she said, tears standing out in her eyes. She reached one hand out to brush his cheek with it.

The intimacy of it, the physicality…it was almost too much for him. He felt dizzy in it. Had he become such a stranger to affection that it could have such a profound effect on him?

He knew in that moment that she cared for him, cared deeply. Maybe she even loved him. He stepped in to her and wrapped his arms around her, enveloping her. She wept softly against his chest and hugged him back. He thought that maybe he should feel guilty for it. For the affection and the warmth of holding her. Like he might have been betraying Lucey's memory somehow. He didn't, though. He didn't feel a single bit guilty.

24

The following morning was a Tuesday, and though it brought no more optimism and hope in all the world for Joel, he still woke feeling better than he had the day before. He reckoned it was because he had gone to bed happier. Frank was still not speaking to him, but it was nice to know that Una was down the corridor, and just as he was dozing off he thought of her and smiled. A guilt-free smile. Which was uncommon when he thought of Una.

When he woke, Frank was already gone again, off to the common room. He was such a habitual early riser that it bothered Joel a smidgeon. In Joel's view of the world order the actors and creatives and their ilk were all late sleepers, and the morning was time for the productive people and the tradesmen like himself.

Someone at some point over the previous weekend had discovered the piece of paper in the window catch, and the previous night Nurse Karl had come in and checked the windows thoroughly before he gave them their tea. It made Joel smile and wince at the same time. He and Frank were unlikely to be trying to escape again anytime soon.

As he nibbled on his breakfast and contemplated his own impending death, or his impending visit to the therapist, a fate worse than death, he also pondered the problem of Frank. He didn't want to be mad at Frank, nor did he want Frank to be mad at him. He wanted things to go back to the way they were. When they talked and laughed with one another. He wanted Frank to look at him as he had when they had sat in the broken-down theater, like a friend, a real one, a kindred spirit for all their differences.

Bad enough he was facing the possible end of his days; he didn't fancy doing it all alone. Not after he'd made such a good friend. A friend who might be able to help him decide if he really wanted this death after all.

In the early afternoon his day was ruined entirely by the arrival of a boy.

Joel was certain the boy would argue that he counted as a grown man, but to Joel's eyes the thing before him in its non-threatening suit pants and shirt with rolled-up sleeves was a boy. He could have all the qualifications he wanted, and Joel was sure the wee thing would have bags of them, with a whole alphabet of letters after his name. Joel cared little for the letters that a psychologist might have. He looked at the cool, calm smile and loathed the creature in an instant.

Into who else's life had this boy walked? What untold damage had he done elsewhere? Where else had he gone, unwelcome, and imposed himself?

Nurse Liam showed the boy into Joel's room and pointed him at Joel. A weapon, a gun, another prison guard, maybe an executioner.

Joel could practically hear his Frank telling him he was being overly dramatic.

He clammed up as the boy dragged over a seat and smiled his most nonthreatening smile.

This boy, this adolescent creature, held the power to lock him up. To have him sent from Hilltop to some other place. A place for the mentally unwell. To take him away from the last room he had shared with Lucey. The room he shared with Frank.

"Joel, how do you do? I'm Martin. We're just going to have a little chat today if that's okay?"

Condescending ass.

It was not okay. Not that anyone was consulting him about it. He didn't want to talk to the boy. If Frank was here he'd know what to say.

Smart-ass.

Then it hit him.

Joel was inspired in a moment.

Frank would know exactly what to say. All Joel would have to do was channel his inner Frank. He tried to imagine what the old popinjay would do:

"My dear boy, I hope you'll keep it brief since I find this entire charade somewhat unnecessary."

He thought that sounded pretty Frankesque.

The boy adjusted his tie, still smiling his stupid nonthreatening smile. Joel thought his hands might get greasy just touching the boy.

"I'll try not to take up too much of your time. Now, first of all, is there anything in particular you feel like talking about?"

Inside Joel's skull the words repeated: "Don't say killing yourself, don't say killing yourself."

Frank had once told him that he had no sense of calm. Joel felt like this was an examination in calm. His face betrayed nothing, and in fact, he thought he was managing a fine job of Frank's enigmatic smile. The one that made him look like he knew a joke you didn't.

"Happy to converse on a wide array of subjects, young man, but I'll let you pick the topic since you've come all this way to see me."

Inside his head: "Don't mention Mr. Miller's little skeleton being pounded to death in your wife's bed."

In his Frank voice: "I should hate if you came all this way and I monopolized the conversation."

It was an effort not to affect Frank's drawling performative accent. The one where his voice went up and down, dropping to almost a whisper at times, yet never so low that he couldn't reach his audience.

"Okay," the boy said, a little confused. "I understand that you're none too fond of this nursing home, for starters?"

Joel recognized the need for care here. Too blasé and they'd know he was lying. Too vehement and he'd be locked up as a threat, or shunted away into some corner of a psych ward for being too angry at being old.

As if everyone else wasn't furious about that.

"Something of a misunderstanding there, old boy. I'm feeling a touch unheard."

Now that sounded very Frank. He should be wearing a scarf for this.

"I don't have a problem with Hilltop. My problem is being constantly cooped up in it. Their problem, of course, is that I've flown the coop a couple of times."

He tried for the sly smile that Frank was so fond of when he knew he was being clever. He worried that it might look wretched on him. Lack of practice smiling was half his problem. He wondered if he might look crazy if he got up and stole one of the scarves.

"And, do you think that's unreasonable of them?"

Inside his head: "You're god damn right, I do."

His Frank voice said: "This is an unreasonable world, no? And these are unreasonable times. What I'd like is for them to just grant a little bit of leeway."

They wanted to throw him out because he wanted not to spend his last moments in a prison? Fair enough that they didn't know how close he was to the end. He wasn't even sure, but that wasn't the point. The power they held over him. It was unfair.

The boy looked at him, and then at his notes. Something wasn't matching up. The Rhino, or Eva, or someone had told the boy what to expect, and it wasn't this. Joel was winning. He was beating the trumped-up little ass, with his stupid suit and patronizing face.

Could he keep it up?

"Tell me about Mr. Adams?" the boy asked.

Inside his head: "Popinjay. My best friend. A jackass. The loveliest man you ever knew."

His Frank voice said: "Now there's a man in need of a doctor. Certainly a little bit of crazy in that one. To be honest I'm worried about him. He needs to get out more. He needs some friends. He needs to learn to display some affection."

Joel stopped when he realized he was talking about himself, and then reminded himself that he wasn't Frank and the name of the game here was just not to mention that he might want to kill himself. Most important, to not get evicted.

He smiled at the boy. The boy smiled back. His face was extraordinarily punchable.

"I see," the boy said, still smiling. "And do you think you're helping him?"

"I think I've done everything I can for him. Kept him going, you might say."

Frank had done everything for him. He had kept him going. Maybe he'd kept him going too long. Maybe just long enough.

Joel desperately missed his friend. Missed his company. He wanted Frank to be here. Sitting with him. Just watching TV or reading quietly.

The boy continued to question him, probing, lightly of course, never too heavy, and Joel channeled his inner Frank to divert the questions.

The questions varied. His childhood. His father, the vicious bastard that he was. Joel dodged those ones with an airiness that even Frank might not have been able to pull off. The de Selby mask, Joel found, was a powerful way to avoid showing your feelings. His wife. His daughter. Clearly the boy was prepared.

After a while Joel found himself enjoying the game of it. He watched the boy scribble things down on the paper in front of him and nod encouragingly whenever Joel spoke, and as they wound to their conclusion, Joel fancied that he had gotten the best of the boy. Eluded him with a de Selby display.

"Okay then, Mr. Monroe. I think we'll call it a day there…"

Joel's heart leapt.

He had defeated the dreaded psychologist.

"Same time next week?" the boy told him.

Joel's heart sank.

He'd foolishly thought this would be a one-off. It must have shown on his face.

"Mr. Monroe, it's not a death sentence, just a little chat," the boy told him, with what Joel considered to be his most punchable look of the day. "See you then."

Joel stared bitterly at the boy's back as he made his way out of the room. He had been an idiot to think that they'd do this all in one go. There was always going to be more. And now he'd look properly crazy because there was no way he was going to be able to keep up the de Selby routine. When the mask dropped the boy would know, and then Joel would really be in for it. How on earth was he going to talk his way out of that one?

Time was all he had bought himself. Perhaps time enough to get the job done. Though there was doubt now, doubt that was growing inside him. The thought of leaving them behind was becoming increasingly difficult to imagine. Una stood out in his mind. And Lily and Chris. And Liam. And most of all, Frank.

Frank, his friend, who might have saved his life. He didn't want to argue anymore.

The problem, of course, was how to apologize? Joel Monroe knew little enough about apologies. As everyone seemed to be at pains to remind him, he was an infuriatingly stubborn man, and these things had simply never been part of his makeup. For that matter, neither was talking, which made both apologizing and therapists problematic. He considered the problem for a while that morning, and by midday he had come up with his solution.

That afternoon, Joel made his way to the common room. Inside, spread out among various tables in the wide open room, were the various residents of Hilltop, but sitting on the large couch in front of the television, patiently waiting for the start of his soap operas, was Frank. Joel walked directly up to his friend and sat down on the seat next to him. There was plenty of room farther up the couch, but Joel opted to plonk himself down directly next to Frank, practically hip-to-hip.

Frank grunted, and glanced sideways at Joel. It was a touch frosty, the glance, but not overly so. Joel was looking straight at the television. He pretended not to see the glance. Or Frank's narrowing eyes. From his little table behind them and to the left, Mighty Jim saw them sit and, with a gleeful, almost mischievous smile, he dropped into the remaining seat on the couch.

"There is no sun without shadow," he told them as he made himself comfortable.

Joel nodded in agreement, but still said nothing.

For the first two hours they watched game shows. No one said a word. Frank's face was unreadable. Joel's, too. He hoped and leaned into that hope, that Frank knew what he was about. Una sat nearby; Joel could almost feel her worry and her curiosity. She sat there and watched them and hoped that the gulf between them hadn't become too big to bridge.

Sometime later Nurse Liam brought them their lunches on the couch, on the trays he typically reserved for their bedrooms. He was clearly and unrepentantly trying to stifle a laugh.

They both murmured their thanks without ever saying anything distinguishable.

For the next two hours they watched soap operas. Painful, dull, extravagant, over-the-top soap operas with irritatingly dramatic performances. For the pure hell of it, Frank even flipped on a foreign soap, so Joel would have to read subtitles as well as watch people overact. Mighty Jim abandoned ship at that point. Even Jim had limits, apparently.

Joel wasn't permitted limits. Not in this game. So he continued hoping that Frank knew what he was doing. A growing sense of amusement that he couldn't show came from the belief that Frank knew what he was up to, but was going to push the boat out as far as it might go.

They continued to say nothing to each other. Una continued to watch them.

In a stiff test of Joel's resolve, Frank fetched the *Glory Days* box set from the DVD shelf and slipped it into the tray. As he retook his seat, a single eyebrow arched in a challenge. Joel met the look with calm acceptance, and into hours five and six they sat in silence and watched episode after episode of the eighties soap opera. It was painful, but Joel had to admit, his friend was the standout performer of the bunch. The scene stealer.

Shortly before dinner, Frank played the episode where he died. To Joel's amusement, his friend drastically overacted the part, the heart attack dropping him dead before he could reveal the climactic secret about how many women the local bar owner was sleeping with. When it was finished, Frank's hand hovered over the remote control.

"Had enough yet?" he asked casually.

"No," Joel replied blandly. "By all means, continue."

"Oh, for fuck sake," Frank grumbled. "Even I've had enough. Dinner?"

"Dinner," Joel agreed, trying not to let his relief show.

The two took their places next to Una and Mrs. Klein.

Una looked at the two of them in horrified turn.

"So that's it?" she asked incredulously.

"That's what?" Joel replied innocently.

"That's all? That's all you're going to do? Just sit there watching TV and then it's all done?"

"Do you have any idea what she's talking about, old boy?" Frank asked, as his dinner was placed in front of him.

"None," Joel replied, being obtuse.

"Are you honestly telling me that after all that, after all of the…with the other day, and the…" she trailed off, her jaw working furiously.

"She seems upset," Frank remarked.

"She does. Do you think we've done something to bother her?"

"Can't think of anything, old boy."

"Una?" Joel asked, as sweetly as he could manage. "Is there something the matter?"

Una reached for her newspaper and frantically swatted at Joel and Frank. They kept their arms up for protection and weathered the onslaught until Una ran out of gas. She sat there in front of her dinner, the rolled-up newspaper discarded.

"Can I have the salt, Frank?" Joel asked.

Una returned to her dinner and ate her food furiously, grumbling under her breath. Mrs. Klein beamed at them both, but deliberately avoided looking anywhere near Una.

25

It was a victory for Joel, but by no means a perfect one. The amiable silence between the two men that evening was infinitely preferable to the frosty one of the previous two days, but mixed in that silence was a great or terrible thing not being said. They didn't speak of it, because Joel reckoned he didn't know how, and Frank couldn't think of a way that wouldn't smash their uneasy friendship to smithereens.

And so throughout Wednesday, what the two shared was an awkward, hopeful, but tense friendship. Gone was the easy camaraderie of the previous days and weeks. The banter and ribbing were out and in their place casual chitchat. Joel was not a fan, but the alternative was not something he was yet willing to contemplate.

"An old game show or something?" Joel offered politely as they sat watching TV in their room that afternoon.

"Oh, anything you like," Frank replied graciously. "Might read actually, or do some writing maybe, if you don't mind?"

"Want me to turn it down?" Joel asked helpfully.

"Not at all," Frank told him conveniently, reaching for his little journal. "I'll hardly even notice it once I start."

And that was the way of their conversations.

It was all day painful. A considerable improvement on the dreadful isolation of Monday morning, a happier, less anxious world for him to live in, but this was not his relationship with Frank. This was an uneasy thing of their joint creation, and Joel stayed awake for some hours that night desperately trying to think of a way to break through the wall. To no avail.

He tried the following day too, and the day after, but he had broken it. He had broken the whole thing with his stubbornness, his refusal to talk about anything more relevant than the television or the nurses or the books they were both reading. And on Friday night, he realized grimly that what stood between them was the very thing he had been running from, the very thing that had terrified him since he had seen Nurse Angelica try to pound the life back into Mr. Miller.

Between them, invisible, silently and patiently waiting for his turn, was death. Specifically Joel Monroe's death.

Their relationship could never be fixed while Joel was waiting for the moment to end his life. It would remain broken as long as Frank knew that, at any moment, Joel might walk out of life.

There was nothing profound about it, nothing momentous and nothing worthy of statement; it was no more than a grim and deeply awful urge to be free of fear, free of the feeling of uselessness, and now that secret that had once bonded them together was what kept them at arm's length from each other.

It was particularly painful since Joel found himself in such doubt. The certainty of wanting to die had been replaced by an uneasy but growing desire to know more about his grandchildren, more about Una Clarke, more about Frank. He wasn't sure if he could leave them behind anymore, and the only person who could help him sort it out was sitting in the room with him.

Except they weren't talking. Not in any real way.

The solution to his problem, which at the time he didn't realize was a solution at all, pulled up in the car park of Hilltop on a sunny Saturday afternoon, one week to the day since they had slipped out for Frank's birthday.

It was a small little car, a neat little thing that Lily drove, and from it came both of his grandchildren. In his misery and idleness all week he had hardly thought about them, about how they might have been caught up in the storm. Did Eva know they had met him? Did she know they had spent the night drinking with him and dancing with him and that they had brought him to a kebab shop?

As he saw the car pull up he realized he didn't much care; he was far too glad to see them to care what they had come for. That they were here to see him without being cajoled, and he was happy to see them instead of bitter and resentful. How much nicer a world it was when he had that little thing to warm him. He knew that Frank was responsible for that, for unlocking in him that sense of something nice, for reaching out to him and leading him away from his isolation. He smiled at his friend, pleased to see a similar smile of delight on Frank's face.

Lily came through the door first, smartly dressed as always. It was some kind of a dress, Joel knew that, and a fancy dress to boot, but he was guessing at that. He also thought it seemed very sophisticated but was blunt enough with himself to admit that he had absolutely no idea what sophistication in women's fashion looked like. She also had on her customary smile, charming and open and friendly.

Chris followed after. His look was unsophisticated. Borderline sloppy actually, with jeans and sneakers and a jacket much too large and unsuitable for the weather, and for just a second his socks peeked out and they didn't match. Joel didn't let it get to him. At some point over previous months and years that might have occasioned comment, but this time he simply smiled at his grandson. Chris smiled back, and from inside his overlarge clothing produced a bottle of whiskey, which he promptly handed to Frank.

"This is the one you said you liked, isn't it?" Chris asked.

"This is the one I like, all right, but I don't remember saying it…" Frank told him.

"Really?" Chris asked, arching his eyebrows up in surprise. "You talked about it for ten minutes."

Joel laughed out loud; they'd get to know Frank a little better. Ten minutes was a short time for him to talk about anything.

"Don't know what you're giggling at," Chris told Joel with a smile. "You tried to teach my twenty-year-old girlfriend to waltz, you old pervert."

Joel flashed back to the previous Saturday. He remembered. The poor girl already knew how to waltz, but he wasn't having it; he was going to teach her anyway. He cringed at his own stupidity and nearly pulled the covers up to his eyes in embarrassment.

"Not to worry, Grandad," Chris told him. "She still thinks you're great."

"Everyone thinks you're great," Lily told them.

Joel saw Frank resist the urge to preen himself in the bed.

"In fact," she continued, producing something from her wallet, "the bouncers asked me to give these to the 'two elderly gay men' that I was hanging out with."

She had two cards of some kind.

"What are they?" Frank asked.

"They're VIP passes to the club, Mr. de Selby."

Joel guffawed loudly at the hilarity of that, and Frank burst into a long and loud laugh, the belly laugh that Joel had heard on Frank's first day. It bounced off walls and set Lily and Chris to laughing, too.

Lily handed the cards to Frank to keep. Joel wondered if he'd ever get to use them. He would have liked to be a VIP in a fancy nightclub. Get all dressed up this time, fancy as he could make himself, and go to a trendy nightclub. He imagined that people would be staring at him and Frank; never mind that they'd think he was gay—what did he care whether they thought him gay, or straight or bisexual or whatever the other letters stood for? They'd be looking at an elderly man doing as he pleased on a night on the town, getting to go where they couldn't, instead of it being the other way around.

"And what brings my two lovely grandchildren up to Hilltop on a Saturday?" Joel asked. "You've surely got better things to be doing?"

They looked at one another uncomfortably for a moment.

"First of all," Lily said, "we want to say sorry."

"For what?" Joel asked.

He didn't want her to say it. If she apologized for making him do something that he had done all on his own, he'd scream in frustration. If she took that moment away from him…

"For any part we might have had in you getting in trouble," she replied, and he nearly sighed with relief.

"Not at all," Frank told them dismissively. "We're old enough and long enough in the tooth to know very well what kind of trouble we were getting ourselves into."

As usual, Frank saw right into the middle of it.

"Did we get you two in any trouble at home? Does your mother know that you were out with me?" Joel asked.

They looked uncomfortable again.

"No," Chris said eventually. "But we kind of want to tell her."

"Why so?" Joel asked. He didn't want them to be in trouble.

"Because," Lily interjected, "it was nice. She's worried about you, really worried. We think she'd be less worried if she knew that you're having fun. Enjoying yourself. You know?"

Joel looked at them both for a long moment.

They looked like their mother, and their grandmother. He supposed there must have been some of their worthless father's genes in there too, but he couldn't see where. Perhaps they had run off, as well.

They were so clever, and friendly, and lovely. How had he allowed himself to let the distance between them become so great? Why hadn't he been more like Lucey? Why hadn't he cared enough to try harder?

Chris had wandered by his bedside locker, and he absently picked up the sign: "My Tools, My Rules." He smiled at it.

Joel looked at it for a long moment, and then his gaze moved to his lucky penny. He remembered the trebuchet and the bored-looking workers in their mock-up stands. It seemed long ago now, that first time out of the nursing home on his own. Really it had only been a matter of weeks. He realized how his friendship with Frank had, since then, blossomed into something profound and powerful. That lucky penny was a reminder of good times, but more, it was a reminder of Frank in his life.

Joel looked over to the Royale badge sitting next to it. He hadn't worn it since the week before. There had been something bittersweet about it. "Save the Royale." The Royale had been doomed and didn't even know it. Doomed like Joel thought he was. Watching his grandson smile at him as he replaced the "My Tools, My Rules" sign, Joel felt that perhaps the Royale could be saved after all. Not the theater, which would remain outside his realm of control, but he himself could be saved. Enough people cared. He was sure of it.

He knew then that he couldn't do it.

He couldn't leave them behind.

There was no way now that he could kill himself. There was no way he could deprive himself of whatever time he had left with them. For them he would find a way to resist the urge to let it all go.

It seemed as simple as that. He had wanted it. Hungered for it even. He had been so alone, so thoroughly bored and so scared all at once that he wanted to end his own life. Now he was not alone. Now things seemed less boring. Now the fear wasn't so strong.

With Frank by his side he had walked farther and farther away from that person, and what he had become no longer wanted death. No longer saw it around the corner. He still wanted it. He still wanted to go, but now he had something he could fight the urge with.

"You're good kids," Frank Adams told them seriously.

Frank saw what they were doing. Their little part in rescuing their grandfather. A grandfather who had been cold and aloof and cranky with them. All they needed from him was one spark of something, and they were coming charging to the rescue.

Frank had done that for him. Frank had reconnected him with the real world; with each day in his friend's company he had walked farther away from the void inside himself.

There was no way he could leave Frank either. He would find a way to fix what damage he'd done to their relationship. He wouldn't leave him behind.

The silence had stretched on too long. Joel sitting there in a sort of bemused wonderment.

"Say something, you ass," Frank commanded him.

"What do you need me to do?" Joel asked. He was all theirs now.

"We don't like seeing you fight," Lily told him. She looked so much like her mother that Joel got a lump in his throat looking at her.

"Well, I don't like fighting," he told her, trying not to sound choked up.

"Ha!" Frank commented from the bed next to him.

"I don't like fighting with real people, Frank," Joel told him acidly. "You don't count."

"I don't count as a real person?"

"Court jesters aren't real people."

"Oh, so that makes you the king, does it?"

"You're only figuring that out now? Little slow on the up-take, aren't you?"

"Wow. Joel Monroe is calling me slow. Pots and kettles everywhere rattle in protest."

Lily and Chris were smiling again, and Joel had to restrain himself from heaving another sigh of relief. They might not be broken, he and Frank, they might be okay, as long as this wasn't just another "de Selby Show."

"Carry on, love," Joel told Lily.

"We want you to apologize—" Chris told him in a rush.

"For what?" Joel asked flatly. It was one thing to decide not to kill yourself, but apologies might be a step too far.

"For scaring her, for making her worry and most important, for telling her that she preferred Grandma to you."

Joel had forgotten that.

A nasty little dig at the tail end of a nasty little argument. He hadn't really meant it of course, and whatever truth there was to it was likely more his fault than anyone else's. He had passed the buck of his only daughter's emotional well-being on to his wife. How could he possibly expect there to be a stable and worthwhile relationship when he had abdicated that responsibility so thoroughly?

"Told you about that, did she?" he asked, embarrassed.

"She's really upset about that, Grandad," Lily told him.

The idea that she might be upset was startling, and he felt unpleasant about it. She was typically so strong, so capable, so enduring that he doubted that any of his words might have an effect on her thick skin.

"Well, might have been a touch over the line," he mumbled, still uncomfortable with the position he had managed to place himself in.

"Will you come out and say sorry?" Chris asked.

He had to. If he could save his relationship with them, then maybe he could do the same with Eva.

"I will," he promised. "When?"

"Tomorrow suit you?" Lily asked.

"Tomorrow's fine."

"And you, Mr. de Selby?" she asked Frank.

"I might just let Joel take this one. I don't think your mother is terribly fond of me," he said with a smile, still appraising his bottle of whiskey and his VIP passes to the nightclub.

It made sense for Joel to go, and for him to go alone. There was no way he could take his own life, if he still even wanted to, while his daughter was angry with him. Things would have to be said, things that he didn't know he could say, words that had eluded him for a long time but were necessary and overdue. Whatever happened next he would make sure that at the very least he got back on terms with his daughter. He loved her, dearly and without reservation. She might look like her mother, but her standout traits and qualities were picked up off her father; he saw himself in her resolve and her determination and the grit in her eye.

"What time are we thinking, my dears?" Joel asked, suddenly warmed by their presence. He would leave them with something to remember fondly at the very least.

Joel spent that Saturday night in quiet contemplation. Given recent complaints about his mental health, he hoped that no one would mistake his silence for some kind of seclusion. He was, in fact, practicing what he would say to Eva the following day. Soft words had never come easy to him. He'd never known them in his own childhood, but that was paltry enough as excuses go.

Several times as Joel rehearsed his clumsy words, Frank would look at him sideways from across the room and scribble something into his journal. He did this conspiratorially, dramatically, and Joel knew that the dramatist desperately wanted to be asked what he was up to, so Joel smiled to himself, said nothing, and continued practicing his speech.

When Sunday rolled around he dressed himself well. Better than he had done in a long time. He showered and gelled his hair and spit-polished his brown leather shoes, and when he was done he appraised himself in the mirror.

"I've seen worse," Frank told him in a lukewarm declaration of support.

"It's okay?" Joel asked.

"Better than that. It's very nice."

Joel adjusted the collar of his shirt and the suit jacket lapels. Frank was still looking at him askance, their tentative creeping efforts to return to their friendship were still strained, and Joel vowed that he'd take care of that after he'd spoken to Eva. Frank had filled all the roles of all the friends that Joel had somehow missed out on in life. Joel felt he owed him more than he could repay, but at the very least he would make it clear to the older man that he was grateful.

For Frank's part, he seemed to realize that something important was stirring in Joel. That this was more than merely putting on his suit and sprucing himself up. This was no mere dinner with the family; this was going to be a seminal moment for his friend. Joel was heading into mostly uncharted territory, and the first steps of the journey he had begun taking with Frank only weeks previously were now becoming huge leaps, leaps of faith and leaps into the unknown, but important to the old man in ways that he was only beginning to understand.

Frank climbed out of his bed and fixed the collar that Joel was struggling with. He smiled broadly at his friend, patted him on the shoulder and climbed back under his covers.

The children escorted the prisoner through the halls of Hilltop that afternoon. One of the consequences of displeasing the warden was his more or less constant supervision. It had been deemed that neither he nor Frank were trustworthy. Which Joel accepted was probably fair enough, since he didn't intend on giving up his lovely rock just yet. There was time, not much, but just enough for one more night on the town if his plan went the way he expected it to.

Nurse Angelica smiled a weak smile at him as the trio made their way out the door. She was still wary of him. Fair enough, as well, Joel thought; he had earned that one, too. It was, in its own, slightly watered-down way, a liberating feeling driving through the gates of Hilltop and out into wide-open society. It looked different now; the bus stop had significance it had never had before, and the walls of the grounds of Hilltop looked smaller from the outside than he had remembered them being. They passed the front of the houses that lined the road up to Hilltop. He had seen some of their back gardens as he trailed along the path under the trees to his rock.

He wondered if The Rhino was at home today, playing

with her child, her hair down and normal-looking, human-looking.

"Does your mother know I'm coming?" Joel asked.

"Yep," Lily told him, her voice chipper, upbeat, hiding something.

"She's not happy about it," Joel ventured.

"Of course she is," Chris chimed in from the back.

Joel tried to twist in his seat to fix his grandson with the look, but couldn't, so he settled for a loud harrumph instead.

So that's how it was going to be. Him on his way to apologize to her, and her waiting to flatten him with a frying pan. He supposed he had earned that, too. Life lessons all 'round it seemed.

The house his daughter shared with her two children was what some might have called "modest." A semidetached three bed in a part of town that had never been part of the soaring house prices of economic boom times. It was, in Joel's opinion, a wonderful neighborhood with wonderful people, but not exactly sought after.

Parked outside the house was Tony's silver Primera, in the driveway Eva's small hatchback. Joel levered himself out of Lily's car with some work, helped by Chris's steady arm. He swung an arm over the man's shoulder after he was upright and was pleased to find Chris lean in to his casual embrace. When had he last really hugged his grandson? When Chris was eight? Nine? Joel couldn't remember.

The door to the house opened up, and Tony stood waiting to receive them. He wasn't a particularly tall man, just shy of Chris's height, but in tremendous shape for a man in his late forties, slim and yet muscular. His tousled brown hair was thinning a little, but he had a long way to go before age took away the handsomeness and left him withered and broken down. Like Joel often felt.

"Mr. Monroe," Tony said formally, by way of greeting.

Joel had done that. Enforced it. Tony was an interloper as far as he had once been concerned, and Joel had bristled when the man used his first name.

"Tony, please, call me Joel," he told the younger man.

Lily and Chris hugged the man who had sort of replaced their father. He hugged them back warmly. It was nice to see their relationship was a positive one. How had Joel managed to exclude himself from it for so long?

"I brought wine," Joel told Tony, holding out the bottle they had stopped to pick up en route.

"Lovely," Tony replied, clearly awkward and uncomfortable around a version of Joel he had never met before.

"Dad," Eva said, announcing her presence at the top of the hallway.

She looked so stern, so authoritative, with a wooden spoon in her hand and the smells of cooking wafting from the kitchen. She was becoming more like her mother every day. It might have hurt Joel at another time, but now he just enjoyed seeing so much of the woman he loved in the woman he had helped to raise.

"I brought wine," he told her quite lamely.

"Thank you," she replied, grudgingly.

"Might we have a word?" he asked, beginning to feel the first grip of nervousness. You can rehearse these things all you like, but when you've been raised not to talk about your feelings, the only way you can feel about deep and meaningful conversations is uncomfortable.

She nodded at him, her face already softening. She could see his awkwardness and, he hoped, his sincerity. They sat in the living room, while the children and Tony departed for the kitchen.

"He's a handsome fella, isn't he?" Joel asked, trying to delay.

"Excuse me?" Eva asked, taken aback.

"Tony. Handsome fella. Suppose he'd have to be. You're a beautiful woman yourself, you know."

It was all delivered so inexpertly, so clumsily. Compliments were not his wheelhouse.

"Thank you, Dad," she replied, smiling a little at his blush.

"And those kids of yours, they're..." he hesitated. He tried to think about how he and Frank talked. That was usually easy. They had talked about big important things, and it had typically come quite easy to both of them. "They're fantastic is what they are."

"They're very fond of you too, Dad," she told him, softening to him; the stern glint in her eye, the one he had earned not just in the last few weeks, but in the last few years, was beginning to vanish. He wondered if she could see the man he used to be when she was little.

"Well, can't say I've earned that," he confessed, looking at the ground.

She said nothing. Perhaps she didn't want to tell a lie by correcting him, or perhaps she was just as awkward as he. Probably the former, he concluded.

"I owe you an apology," he told her after a long and uncomfortable silence.

"Look, it's fine, Dad—" she started to say.

"No, please, let me say this..."

He drew a deep breath.

"I'm sorry I was a bad father," he told her.

"No, Dad—" she started, sitting forward in her seat.

"Please, Eva," he said, stopping her. She looked at him for a long moment. He thought she might be able to see it, see the need in him to get this out. She sat back.

"I see how you are with the kids, how you always were with them. Mother and father at the same time. Did a great job. I didn't really, you know? When it was convenient, sure, but I let your mother deal with the difficult stuff. Told myself that it wasn't my job. Earning was my job. Told myself that I didn't have the tools to cope with that stuff, you know? Let your mother do it all. Shouldn't have done that. Mean on her. And mean on me, you know? I missed out. I missed out on learning about you, on learning who you were. Missed out completely. Shouldn't have done that."

She had tears in her eyes. He had some in his, for that matter.

"I miss your mother. I miss her something awful. No excuse for being an asshole. Frank says I'm a vicious bastard sometimes. He's right. Usually is anyway. Got very lonely, you know? Very selfish. Kind of scared. And I didn't deal with it well. Maybe…maybe if I'd known you better, if I'd done more raising, spent more time with you, then we'd have had something, you know? I guess I didn't realize it until too late, and then I just thought I was all on my own. I'm sorry about that, too."

She moved from the armchair to sit next to him on the couch. She put one arm over his shoulder. He brushed away a tear that trickled down to his jaw.

"It's hard for me," he continued, "it's hard for me to be so alone, to feel so useless, to feel like I'm just waiting to die."

He drew a breath.

"That's what I feel like. I feel like I'm just waiting to die. And I'm sick of waiting. I'm sick of looking over my shoulder for it. A cough that turns into pneumonia, a lump that turns out to be cancer, a headache that might be a brain tumor, this stroke they keep shoving all these pills at me for, or I could go like your mother, just one minute the switch is hit and I'm gone. And all the while I feel like I've no reason to be here, no reason to keep on bothering."

She looked at him differently now. Profoundly differently. Like she could see something she had missed before.

"I'm so sorry, Dad," she whispered.

"It's not your fault. It's mine, but it's okay. I want you to know that I'm going to be better. There's a therapist involved... I'll talk it out. I've got Frank now, and Una, and those kids of yours, and I want to have you back, too. If it's not too late? But you have to trust me. You have to trust that I know what's best for me. That I can make my own decisions and that I still have a life to live. Can you do that for me? Can we do that together?"

She cried and hugged him, and he cried and let himself be hugged.

26

Joel returned to Hilltop refreshed. The sense of feeling something, really feeling it after many years in the doldrums of his own life was empowering, invigorating, and yet Hilltop still felt like a prison to him. The wide gates swinging open to admit him seemed as ominous as ever, and the sense of regret saying goodbye to his daughter was tangible. She looked different to him now, fresher, younger somehow. The memory of the little girl he had once known seemed to shine through her, and her smile as she waved him goodbye was genuine and heartfelt. He desperately wanted to ask her to just sit a while in the car, just to chat about nothing, just to spend some time in her company feeling out the edges of their newfound relationship.

Back in his room Frank sat up in his bed, sipping from a hot mug, looking thoroughly pleased with himself.

"What's made you so happy?" Joel asked.

"I could ask you the same question, old boy."

"Nice Sunday dinner with the family. Hardly fought with anyone at all."

"The wonders never cease."

"And you?"

"I've Irished up this coffee," Frank said, clearly delighted.

Joel laughed out loud.

"Had many of those, have you?"

"Probably more than I should. Want one?"

"Absolutely."

Joel called for coffee, was served decaf, but decided not to make a point about it. He was behaving himself now, and if the staff decided that he was too old to be drinking caffeine after seven in the evening, well at least he could take satisfaction in the fact that they had no idea he was going to be drunk in no time.

The two of them sat in their beds and sipped whiskey in decaffeinated instant coffee and watched game shows. Joel still felt the distance between them. It was the same discomfort that would remain between them as long as Frank feared for his friend's life. There was no way he'd speak on any subject larger than television in case he touched a nerve, or sent Joel down a dark road.

The distance between them, Joel decided, was unacceptable.

"I'm going to see the therapist," he told Frank.

For a moment, nothing was said as Frank absorbed the news.

"Why?" he asked eventually.

That took Joel by surprise. He had been expecting congratulations, a warm and enthusiastic round of applause for his healthy and very grown-up decision-making.

"What do you mean why?"

"I would have thought that question was self-explanatory."

"Well, it's not. What do you mean why?"

"I want to know why you're doing it. Why now? What's changed?"

Joel heard the questions Frank was asking, but more important, the questions he wasn't asking.

"You want to know if I still want to kill myself?"

"You're only two-thirds as thick as I think you are," Frank told him with a broad smile.

"I'm going to see the damn therapist," Joel said indignantly. "Shouldn't that tell you enough?"

"I want to hear you say it."

"Well, I won't."

"Hahahaha. You're a mule of a man. You know that?"

"Sorry."

"Don't be. It's simultaneously your most infuriating and your most endearing quality."

"Look…"

"You don't have to."

"I want to. Sort of."

"Give it a shot, then."

"I still want to kill myself," Joel confessed. "I just don't *want to* want to kill myself."

"That's a start," Frank told him, climbing from the bed and wobbling on unsteady feet across the room. He clearly had a massive head start on Joel. When he reached the bed he planted a kiss on Joel's forehead. "I'd hate for anything bad to happen to you, old man. I really would."

"You're getting sentimental in your old age."

"Only for you, you grumpy old bastard."

He said the words with such affection that Joel worried he might start crying again. Frank toddled back to his bed, and his coffee, with a smile. Joel's melancholy lifted. They were back. His friend was back. There was reason to keep going.

His idea returned to him as the two of them sat in contented silence.

"One last hurrah before I take the plunge?"

"Go on," Frank urged him with a sly smile beginning to creep across his face.

"It's this new leaf I'm turning over, the new me and all that. I saw the therapist already. Pretended to be you and got away with it."

"Pretended to be me?"

"Well, I just acted like you."

"And what exactly does that look like?"

"You know, smarmy and overconfident."

"Point to you."

"But when I see him on Tuesday I'm going to have to tell him the truth."

"Sooner the better, if you ask me."

"All right, all right, steady on," Joel admonished him. "So what about one last bash before the new me starts, and I'm no fun anymore. What about we take those VIP passes and go have ourselves some fun?"

Frank barked a laugh.

"First of all, you've never been fun. You're too cranky, but now I think you might actually be crazy."

"Come on," Joel urged him. "One more night on the town. I've never been a VIP before. I wasn't a famous actor. I don't think I've ever even been an IP before."

"Tomorrow night?"

"They won't be expecting it."

"We'll need a reasonably good escape plan."

"So you're in?"

"Wouldn't miss it for the world."

It felt wrong, a little, to be scheming again, but this time he'd write a note, or ten, or he'd call his daughter and tell her it was happening, or he'd do something to offset the damage, but he wanted it too much. He wanted one more chance to be a man on his own steam. He hoped, he hoped to the bottom of his toes, that the therapist wasn't going to drug him, or lock him up, but it might happen. He might never have the chance again. He could be dead tomorrow.

They planned, drunkenly, until the nurses came to turn out the lights.

27

Mighty Jim's birthday was a considerably more conspicuous occasion at Hilltop than Frank de Selby's had been. In the afternoon the former mayor was brought out, whether he was aware of the date or not, and a forlorn-looking hat was placed on his head. The other residents gathered around to partake of the various treats and drinks that were served in little plastic bowls and cups trotted out for just such occasions. Joel knew his was coming, six days until his birthday, and they'd get to go through all this again. He wouldn't object this time, nor would he have a temper tantrum. Instead, he hoped, he'd have Eva and Lily and Chris and even Tony come to visit, and they'd sit around with him and Una and Frank, and Joel thought it might even be a passably good time. As long as he kept his end of the bargain.

He tried not to worry about the possibility that he'd be heavily sedated, or that he'd be moved to a psychiatric establishment for his own good. He tried to tell himself that the chances of it were slim, but the niggling doubt played in his head, stayed in his head and refused to leave. He refocused, and remembered that he had a job to do.

When the cake emerged, surprisingly ornate and delicious-looking, it was placed delicately on top of Mighty Jim's chessboard, to his immense confusion, and he was sat in front of it to blow out the candles. By the time he realized what was going on, the confusion was replaced by happiness, a pure and unadulterated joy that seemed to shine out of him. He clapped enthusiastically. Joel had remembered pitying Jim for that ignorance many times; now he envied it.

As the singing began, Joel took the opportunity to slide out of the room, nodding at Frank as he passed. He carefully watched all angles, checking the corridors. Scanning for a sign of sentries. Finding none, he proceeded through the corridors of Hilltop. "Happy birthday to you…" echoed off the walls behind him as he carefully picked his way to the nurses' station.

The station itself was set in a small cubby, barely large enough for three people, though it was typically only occupied by one at a time. The front of it was a small glass window panel that slid back and forth. Just large enough, he had surmised, to fit his frame through the glass.

Nurse Liam was waiting at the station.

"Can I help you, Joel?" he asked.

Joel couldn't be certain, he was way too paranoid to be certain, but he thought that Nurse Liam looked like a man who knew that Joel was up to no good.

"I don't think Frank is feeling terribly well," Joel told him. It wasn't a complete lie. Frank had a touch of hangover about him, a queasiness in his stomach and a throbbing pain in his head.

"Oh?" Liam asked blandly. He suspected something. Joel guessed that whatever he and Frank did for the rest of their lives together, someone would be suspecting something.

"Might have been something he ate?" Joel suggested.

"I see," Liam said and he didn't move.

What Joel wanted was in reach. He was sure of it, just inside the sliding panel, but Liam wasn't budging. He couldn't tell him to leave; that would only confirm Liam's suspicion that Joel was up to something, which he was.

"So…" Joel said lamely. "Just thought I'd let you know."

"Keep me up to date," Liam told him casually.

Oh, he was sharp all right.

Joel made his way back into the common room and stood next to Frank.

"Get sick," he told his friend.

"What?"

"I need you to actually get sick. Like, throw up."

"Here?"

"Here, our room, wherever."

"Why am I getting sick now?"

"Liam's wise to us. Told him you weren't well. He wasn't buying it. You get sick and he'll come running."

Frank looked at Joel with a long, flat, unfriendly stare.

"Only one shot at this, pal. It's got to be while they're here."

The singing at the party had started to die out; the staff had begun to mill a little. In a moment or two they'd be heading back to their various tasks. Frank grimaced. It was way too late to come up with a new plan.

"For he's a jolly good fellow…" he began to sing.

The staff and residents joined in. The end of the celebration delayed, and then, without warning, Frank stuck a finger back his throat and threw up the treats he'd been nibbling at. Some of the vomit landed on Joel's shoes. He was fairly sure that was intentional.

Without waiting, he slipped out of the common room and

back to the nurses' station. Liam was still there, scribbling on various forms and leafing through clipboards.

"He threw up," Joel told him.

The rather bland look Liam had been wearing vanished in a most satisfactory manner, and he was moving immediately.

For just a second it looked like he might leave the door to the nurses' station wide open, but he had the wherewithal to throw Joel one last suspicious look before he pulled the door shut behind him. The second he rounded the corner into the corridor, Joel himself was moving.

He slid back the panel of glass in the partition and stuck his head into the little cubby office.

The clipboard with the monthly door codes hung on a little hook on the inside wall. He reached a hand in, his fingers brushing the board. He stretched, his fingers gaining purchase but not enough for him to lift the clipboard clear.

He checked the corridor again, glancing left and right before going again. This time he shoved his head and arms through the small gap, as he had guessed, just wide enough for him to fit through, at a squeeze. Leaning on the desk inside he hauled himself up and hunched over, his legs now dangling out of the tiny window slot, his left shoulder on the desk. He reached out and lifted the clipboard clear, his eyes rapidly scanning the page. His eyesight wasn't what it once had been, and so he had to adjust the position of the board several times to get it in focus. And there it was: ground floor code: 3266D. Clumsily and with tremendous effort he managed to rehang the clipboard on the wall and slide himself awkwardly back out.

Una Clarke stood in the hallway facing him, one eyebrow raised.

"Una," Joel greeted her. Aiming for casual innocence as if

his arse hadn't been stuck up in the air, with his legs dangling behind him a few seconds beforehand.

"Aren't you in enough trouble?" she asked almost wearily.

"I don't believe I know what you're talking about, my dear," he replied, and then, aiming for some de Selby charm, he added, "but aren't you looking lovely this afternoon?"

She smiled in spite of herself but shook her head as she did it.

"Honestly," she told him. "I don't know which one of you is worse."

He offered her his widest smile and an arm. She linked his, and the two of them began walking back toward their bedrooms. As they passed the common room Frank was being helped, whether he wanted the help or not, back to the bedroom, too. He scowled at Joel.

"I hope you're feeling better," Joel told him calmly, and tried not to let his amusement show on his face.

"I hope you shove it up your arse," Frank replied, still dabbing his mouth with a handkerchief.

They spent the day playing it cool. Relaxing in their bedroom, eating dinner in the common room, counting down the minutes until their last night of fun.

Joel hoped that Eva wouldn't be mad at him or, at least, not too mad at him. He needed this. One last time before they made him confront himself in a way that he had never done before. One last chance to be a VIP before he was forced to begin therapy, before they figured out that he was suicidal, that he had enough of being alive. And when they did figure that out, and they would, he was certain, it would be drugs or a section or something, and then who knew what his life would be? The very last he knew of Joel Monroe was in this night, because from the following day on, he'd be something else, someone else, and the thought terrified him.

He promised himself he'd write her a note. All of them a note. He'd even apologize to Nurse Ryan.

As the moment approached he felt himself less concerned by what other people thought, or who'd be mad at him and why. He had loved his first taste of freedom ever since he and Frank had stolen out one Sunday afternoon some weeks beforehand, and he had been hooked on that feeling ever since. He had stared down the yard at his rock and thought of the wonderful feeling he had discovered when his feet touched land outside the wall.

Quietly and with a suppressed excitement the two men began to plan their night on the town. Without being asked and without waiting to request permission, Frank began to select Joel's clothing for the night.

"What's wrong with what I pick?" Joel asked grumpily.

"We're VIPs, you colossal dolt," Frank told him. "Not the same thing as OAPs."

"But we are OAPs."

"That right there is exactly your problem, old man," Frank replied airily.

"You're older than I am," Joel replied incredulously.

"Don't go telling people that. I don't want anyone thinking I'm over a thousand years old."

"Ouch. I have feelings too, you know," Joel told him.

Frank looked for a moment like he might have another pop at Joel, but instead he just turned to him with a smile.

"I know you do, my friend. I know you do."

Joel hadn't intended for the comment to be taken in any way seriously, but there it was. The tenderness of the moment felt awkward to him, despite the collection of them he seemed to have been building up lately.

After lights out, when the nurses had done their final rounds for the evening and closed all the bedroom doors behind them,

Joel and Frank stole from their beds. The note Joel left for the staff was addressed to Eva first.

Eva,
My love, don't you be worrying about me tonight. Tomorrow I start my therapy and all that, and I just wanted one more night of freedom. One more opportunity to have a drink with my friend. I've never been a VIP before. I'll be home later on.

Nurse Angelica,
That top part up there only applies if you call Eva. I wouldn't bother her if I was you. We'll be home later on. We just fancy slipping out for a little pint or two.
    Sorry if this causes you trouble, really.
Joel Monroe.

He smiled at it. They'd be beside themselves wondering how the two elderly men managed to Houdini themselves out of the nursing home for the third time that they knew about. The two men dressed themselves as sharply as they knew how and appraised each other in the dim light of Frank's reading lamp when they were done.

Frank was in his one and only suit, tan in color with its complementary brown waistcoat and a dickie. Joel was in a navy pin-stripe suit, one of the few he owned but never wore.

"Good enough," Frank grumbled, looking Joel up and down.

"Too bloody fancy," Joel told Frank with pursed lips.

"Oh," Frank said suddenly. "One more thing."

He fished around in the coat stand by his bed and produced a brilliant sky blue scarf in silk with a white trim. It was a magnificent piece of ostentation that Joel doubted he would have

ever worn in his life, had he not met Frank Adams. He let the
smaller man loop the scarf over his neck and adjust it on him.

"Now slightly better than good enough. But only slightly."

Joel let him have that one.

Between the low light and failing vision Joel fumbled to
find the security panel. They both winced loudly at the sound
of the latch unlocking and held the door open just an inch
as they waited for the sound of footsteps. None came. There
was no way they'd be able to explain themselves out of this,
if caught in the full of their regalia.

Outside their bedroom the corridor was quiet. Almost eerie
in the nighttime hush. Joel realized he'd never been in the
corridors after bedtime save for coming home drunk the week
previous. There was a ghostly quality to them and a bizarre
sense of familiarity. It was somehow the same feeling he got
when he saw the barren landscape of the dreams he kept having. The sensation was alarming and unsettling.

"You okay?" Frank whispered.

"Shut up, you jackass," Joel whispered back.

Somewhere up the corridor, past the common room and
in the reception area, a blue light lit the walls, along with a
low murmuring noise. The night nurse was watching television. The two would-be escapees moved silently down the
corridor, into the common room and, slowly, carefully, silently opened a window into the cool night air. The common
room itself jutted out from the building at the front, and as
such was close to the window of their bedroom, despite being
some distance down the corridor from their place. Joel went
first, helping Frank behind him, and within minutes the two
of them were free.

At the end of the drive they picked their way into the
bushes and trees that marked the wide perimeter of Hilltop,
and slowly they made their way to their rock. Out later on

this night than on their previous escapes, the darkness was a welcome shadow for them to move in. When they cleared the rock and found themselves once again on top of the wall to Nurse Ryan's house, they found themselves once again looking into the conservatory below. The lights were on, but there was no one there.

"Move your old ass," Frank whispered at him.

They executed their escape maneuver, both more comfortable now that they had some practice. Frank touched down first and offered his back as a platform for Joel to drop down to. Joel felt the familiar giddiness sweep over him. He wondered what exactly The Rhino's face would look like if she were to walk out into her back garden now, and catch Joel Monroe using Frank Adams as a stepladder so that the two of them, as fancy as they could make themselves, could enjoy a night on the town.

"Stop giggling," Frank told him as he lowered himself down. "You'll make me giggle."

Before either of them knew it, they were standing at the bus stop, brushing each other down and adjusting their scarves for departure.

"Gents," the bus driver greeted them with a smile as he pulled in. "On the town tonight?"

"We absolutely are," Frank told him as they climbed aboard and left Hilltop behind them again.

28

They found a pub by wandering in a small circle for about fifteen minutes before eventually picking a door. It seemed to be Frank's method. Walk around a little bit, go this way and that and when you've had enough of walking, stop at the first and most convenient place.

"What do you think will happen after I've seen the shrink again?" Joel asked as they sat by their table sipping.

"I don't know, old boy. I suppose that depends on what they make of you."

"What do you think they'll make of me?"

"Usual," Frank told him glibly, "cranky, short-tempered, paranoid, crazy old man."

"Come on. What do you really think?"

"I really think you need to stop acting like this is the end of the world and you're on your deathbed."

"But what if it is the end of *my* world? What if they lock me up?"

"They're not going to lock you up, you crazy old bastard. That's not what therapists do, Joel."

"Then who's in charge of locking up crazy fellas?"

"Okay. So sometimes it's what they do, but mostly they don't."

"So there's a chance?"

"For fuck sake," Frank sighed.

"Have you been to a psychiatrist?" Joel asked suddenly.

It had never occurred to him that his friend might have needed one, after all that had happened to him.

"No, never been," Frank replied. "Got nothing against it, mind. Knew a few psychologists in my time. Not the same as therapist or psychiatrists, mind, but similar field."

"Are they not the same, no?"

"No, you—"

"Colossal dolt," Joel finished for him.

"Yes. That."

"So what's a therapist?"

"Anyone who performs therapy."

"Stupid question, stupid answer," Joel concluded.

Frank laughed at him.

"Ever think about going?" Joel finally asked.

"I don't need one," Frank told him casually.

"I didn't think I needed one, but you're all so damn adamant."

"Well, to be fair, you are suicidal."

"Fair enough. But, it's not like you couldn't do with getting some stuff off your chest."

Frank stared into his pint. He didn't look up. There was no eye contact. He barely even moved.

It was wrong to Joel. Fundamentally and undeniably wrong that Frank Adams/de Selby should have such a problem with who he was. It was people like himself that were the problem, Joel concluded. The Joel Monroes of the world with their shortsightedness and their ancient old-time stubbornness and their refusal to bend, to accept the world around them. Those

Joel Monroes were the people who beat up Frank Adams when he was still a boy. Those Joel Monroes slapped him in hospitals when he fell in love. Those Joel Monroes were the reason that Frank Adams wore a de Selby mask everywhere he went and couldn't say the word *gay*.

"I wouldn't change you, though," Joel told Frank.

Frank looked up at him questioningly.

"I wouldn't change you for the world. Shitty thing that happened to you. Real shitty. Suppose fellas like me don't make it any easier."

"You did ask me if I was gay for you," Frank reminded him.

"Yeah. Well. Colossal dolt and all that," Joel agreed with a smile. "Just really, though. You did it. You reached this age having had to encounter the likes of me all your life. It's different for the kids now. Now most people don't give a shit, and the ones that do all look like raving lunatics. In our day it was different, you know. No excuses or anything, still not right and all that, but we were brainwashed, you know. They hammered that into us, while they were beating us black and blue in school. And you came through it. You did it. And now…"

He paused again. Too many times in too few days. He was getting into the habit of talking. Of sharing. It was alien to him, but somehow refreshing. He decided to just dive right in.

"And now you're the best person I've ever met. You did that all on your own. Became the best person in the world despite your own family telling you that you were supposed to hate yourself. I'm proud of you. Is that weird to say? I'm proud of you, and I'm proud I know you."

"It's not weird to say," Frank whispered.

He scrubbed at his eyes with the back of his hand.

"Come on," Frank said. "Let's go be VIPs."

★ ★ ★

They walked through the streets passing pubs and restaurants and cafés and diners, all brimming with life, a city center with a lively, beating heart. There were elderly people mixed among the crowds but few, and you had to look for them. Joel sought them out with his eyes. He wanted to make eye contact, to say, *I see you. I'm glad to see you.*

Mostly it was young people. He had feared them a little bit until quite recently. Now they were all Lily or Chris to him. Some variation or other of his grandchildren, and as he watched them move in their flocks from bar to bar he felt an urge, unfelt for a long time, to take care of them. To take them by the hands and show them what was good for them and what wasn't, what they needed to do better. He hoped it wasn't too late to impart some of that wisdom on to his grandkids.

They meandered here and there, and Joel was near certain that Frank had gotten them lost again when they rounded the familiar corner with the wide double doors that led to the courtyard of the club.

There was only one of their two bouncer friends when they rocked up to the door. The shorter one, the one Joel reckoned was the leader of the two. Joel adjusted his fancy scarf and tried not to look too self-conscious about it. The bouncer offered them a welcoming smile and stood to one side to allow them through.

"Evening, gents," he offered as they walked up.

That was more like it, thought Joel. A little respect. None of the display from the week before where they had to practically beg to be accepted. He offered a gracious nod as they walked past, instead of the lambasting he might have offered some weeks before. Frank practically glided in beside Joel, in as much as any man of his age might be said to be gliding. The fact that he had been used as a stepladder earlier in the

DAN MOONEY

evening took some of the grace out of his movement, but he propelled himself along nicely anyway.

Inside the main door of the club a woman sat at a small desk, taking payment from customers and such. As the two elderly gents approached she stood up to greet them with a smile.

"Gentlemen," she said warmly.

The noise of the club getting into its stride was loud, the music, the thumping of the bass, it sent a shiver up Joel's leg, a jolt almost, but it was invigorating, something about it suggested life and vitality. The woman stepping up to greet them, the handing over of their VIP cards and her knowing nod, it all felt like some kind of movie. He felt like he was walking through a film, where he and Frank were the main characters, powerful men, men of influence and culture and character, and wherever they went people were glad to see them and glad to know them.

They followed the young lady toward the VIP section, along the inside of a velvet rope that separated the clubbers from the VIPs. They passed the first arrivals to the club, young people with plenty of drink already taken, and Joel tried not to look too smug about his status. Some of the young people were watching them, and Joel's sense of being in a Hollywood film redoubled. "Who are those two important men?" he imagined them asking themselves.

At the entrance to the VIP section another bouncer stood. He checked their cards and then checked them. It was a long check. An insultingly long check. They stood there eyeballing the bouncer who stood there double-checking that there wasn't some mistake.

Joel felt his cheeks heating up with embarrassment. Eventually the bouncer stood to one side, and the two of them thanked the young lady and walked by the giant who had blocked their way.

The VIP section, a little secluded from the main club, was quieter, though certainly still loud enough that Joel would have to raise his voice to be heard. The furniture, all plush couches and armchairs around solid oak furniture, looked new and expensive. Potted palm plants added a sense of the exotic to the room, but other than the bar at the end of the room with two staff members idly polishing glassware, it could have been the waiting room for some expensive doctor's surgery.

"What an asshole," Joel fumed as they headed for the bar.

"Don't get all worked up about it," Frank insisted. "He's just doing his job."

"You see that, though? We had some VIP passes, and he still looked like he was going to turf us out."

"So what? We're in here now." Frank shrugged at him.

"He was going to stop us, though. Why? Because we're old?"

"Speak for yourself. I'm not old."

"Really though, why was he going to stop us? Is it because he thought we were gay?"

"Have you gone and lost what little was left of your mind?" Frank asked him.

"I just want to know what his problem was."

Frank sighed again, and then stopped just short of the bar. He turned to Joel and, looking up at his friend, he grabbed a hold of both of Joel's arms.

"Joel, old pal, you have to stop making everything that happens into some kind of personal crusade."

"I do not," Joel spluttered, but he could feel that his friend wasn't wrong.

"You do, though. Pretty much everything. All the time. Sometimes you're being wronged—in fairness to you, probably more often than not—but sometimes you're just encountering an asshole of a doorman who feels like being a prick tonight.

And when that happens, it's not about you, it's about someone else, and the only way to be happy is to just get fucking over it and get on with your life."

In an instant Joel revaluated his many gripes and complaints over the previous month or so since Frank had arrived. So many insults that he now wondered if he might have gotten wrong, that he may have taken completely out of context. Poor Nurse Liam, he thought, that man had been on the receiving end of several boots.

"Everything okay, gents?" one of the bartenders asked.

"Just fine, my good sir," Frank replied, slipping easily into de Selby mode. "My cantankerous old friend here was just having a little rant about your doorman out there."

"What, Gonzo?" the bartender asked, gesturing toward the offending bouncer. "Don't mind him, he's a prick."

Joel and Frank both laughed out loud. Gonzo the Bouncer was a prick. Joel wondered if perhaps people had occasion to say that about him. He hoped not, but it was as likely as not. He had, he concluded as he continued to scan back through the various encounters and rows, been a particularly difficult resident.

"Do you think that some of the people at Hilltop think I'm a prick?" he asked Frank.

"Probably," his friend told him glibly.

"Really, though?"

"I don't know, Joel. You've been difficult. Poor Angelica is scared shitless of you. I imagine Karl wouldn't mind the chance to punch you in the head a few times, too."

"Liam?"

"For some reason that man seems to like you, can't imagine why."

"Neither can I," Joel admitted.

"A rare moment of honesty from Hilltop's resident basket case."

"I'm not wrong all the time, though," Joel insisted.

"No, you're not, pal," Frank assured him as he reached for the cocktail menu. "Just wrong about how you deal with it."

Joel wanted to reply with something clever to put Frank back in his box, but he had already moved on and was scanning the menu with incredulity.

"What's wrong?" Joel asked.

"Are these prices correct?" Frank asked the bartender.

"Afraid so," the bartender replied, apologetically.

"And the names?"

The bartender looked somewhat embarrassed, his eyes down.

"What's wrong with the names?" Joel asked.

"Sex on my Face?"

"Excuse me?"

"One of these cocktails is called 'Sex on my Face.'"

Joel couldn't stop himself and snorted with laughter. It was as much for Frank's unexpected prudishness as for anything else. If either of them had been likely to complain about crass wordplay in a drinks menu, Joel had thought it would have been him.

"Keep going," he told Frank.

"Cock Sucking Cowboy?" Frank asked, looking at the bartender as if he personally blamed him for the names and the prices.

Joel burst out laughing again.

"Merciful hour," Frank breathed as he realized how much it cost, "for that amount of money, it would have to…"

Joel thought he would choke laughing. The bartender somewhat guiltily joined in, and Frank couldn't help himself.

They ordered a pair of "Royal Fucks" and sat sipping those as the VIP section began to fill up.

The other attendees came in all shapes and sizes. Young, old, male, female, some that Joel couldn't quite decide were which. The world, he concluded, was moving on without his generation. It had always been that way, he guessed, but harder to accept when you're on the receiving end of it.

He had watched as his father's generation was left behind by the rise and rise of television, of a planet that shrank seemingly year by year. Now it was his turn, or rather their turn. Their turn to be left behind, by a generation that had embraced technology like no other, that had created virtual worlds for themselves that he was excluded from because it was no place for his generation. Sure, there were a select few who had managed to learn the way, but mostly, his kind had no place here. This generation had forged something special for themselves that his generation had never managed. More tolerance, more acceptance, more diversity. More power to them, he thought.

If they were lucky they'd reach a point where they weren't viciously beating the shit out of their children for daring to be the person they had been born to be. Maybe they'd reach a point where their fathers didn't casually beat them all about the house just because they felt like it.

He realized he was becoming morose. Two pints and a Royal Fuck apparently had that effect on him.

They ordered Slippery Nipples while trying not to laugh out loud, and the barman greeted their childish enthusiasm for rude cocktail names with a smile and tremendous patience. Joel wondered what Lucey would make of it all. Him, in a bar sometime after midnight, with a gay man drinking Slippery Nipples and laughing and telling bawdy jokes. He thought that she'd love it. Somehow he just felt that she would laugh long and hard and rub her fingers through his hair and say something like, "Joel Monroe, you never cease to amaze me."

Their Slippery Nipples arrived in fancy shot glasses, reserved, Joel surmised, for the VIP section. He popped his empty one back up on the countertop, but Frank glanced around the bar, rubbed the glass quickly with a napkin and slipped it into the inside pocket of his jacket.

"Hey," Joel sort of barked at him.

"Don't be such a Gonzo," Frank replied airily, turning in his seat to take in the room again.

They attracted a crowd with their good humor, as other VIPs came to see who these two well-dressed old gents might be. Joel told them he was a retired mechanic, and they didn't believe him. He wasn't lying, but they assumed he was anyway. Frank told them all who he was, and they believed that, so he kept telling them. He spoke at length about the small parts in the small films he had worked on, and the awards he had picked up, and the great actors he had shared a stage with, and the crowd loved it. They mostly ignored Joel, who, several drinks in now, insisted to anyone who'd listen that he was a retired mechanic. It was important to him that they believe him. They still didn't.

Sometime around two-thirty in the morning they made their goodbyes and walked out into the warm summer night.

"Home to face the music again?" Frank asked, slightly slurring his words.

"I'll delay a little if you don't mind," Joel suggested.

He hoped they weren't all furious at him. He wanted one more chance to be himself, to be a VIP and have people look at him like he was somebody. He wanted to feel like somebody and not like a waste of space, taking up room in the nursing home where he lived, extraneous, superfluous, unnecessary.

"Kebab?" Frank asked.

Joel remembered tasting the kebab for the entire day over a week ago and shuddered.

"How about that little park by the river?" Joel suggested.

They shared a cab there. Sitting in companionable silence all the way out. Joel felt a little melancholy dragging at him, but only a little. It had been a fine way to pass the evening. A fine way to round out his quest for freedom.

They sat on the same little bench overlooking the river again. The sound of the water rushing by them was hypnotic, somehow musical, and in the dark the swirling eddies that rippled by them under the streetlights looked somehow inviting, appealing. He watched the river flow by him and just enjoyed it.

"Remember when you told me you were gay?" he asked suddenly of Frank.

"I remember telling you I fancied Liam," Frank replied.

"I got such a shock."

"You were quite the extraordinary ass-hat about the whole thing," Frank agreed.

"Caught me off guard. I'm better about it now, though, aren't I?"

"You want a cookie for not being an ass-hat?"

"No, not like that. Just…" he hesitated. The drink was making it difficult to form the thoughts coherently. "I thought it was too late for me to get better, you know? Like I might be beyond that somehow."

"Nonsense."

"I know, I know. And I hate when people even suggest it, you know? Like because I'm old I'm incapable of being responsible for my own thoughts, you know? But there it is. I thought I might be too old."

"So you want a cookie for growing up a little?"

"If you have one to give I wouldn't say no."

They both chuckled at that. It wasn't a lie. Joel was a little bit proud of himself for managing to come around. Even he had thought that Joel Monroe was too old and cranky for life-changing perspectives.

"No cookies, my friend, but you can have this," Frank told him, reaching into his jacket pocket and producing the fancy shot glass his Slippery Nipple had been served in.

"A filthy shot glass," Joel remarked. "You shouldn't have."

"You're not nearly as good at sarcasm as you think you are, you know. Take it. For your collection."

"Collection?" Joel asked, confused.

"The little knickknacks on your bedside table."

Joel smiled as he took the shot glass. It was frosted and heavy in his hand, and, he decided, a fine addition to his collection.

"Remember when," he continued, "I told you that I was going to kill myself?"

They didn't chuckle at that.

"I remember," Frank said lowly.

"I've had some time to think about it."

"Conclusions?"

"I don't think I'm going to bother anymore."

By the streetlight he could see Frank grinning happily.

"Well, that's nice."

"It's because of you, you know?"

"Me?"

"Yep. I think I'd sort of forgotten that people are okay. I've never had a best friend that wasn't my wife before. Now I have one. It's nice."

"What about when you were a child?"

"Nope. My father wouldn't let me out of the house. Strict man. Religious. Very religious. Didn't have many friends."

"That's shit."

"Not great all right," Joel agreed. "Still better than the shit you had to put up with."

"Fair enough," Frank told him. "So you're not going to kill yourself. That's nice."

"It is actually."

"I can't think of many things nicer than not killing yourself, to be honest."

"There's a few all right."

"When did you decide this?"

"I guess I've been coming around to it for a while. I think the first time that Lily looked at me like I wasn't wasting oxygen that could be put to better use. I think around then I decided that's not such a bad feeling, and maybe it might be worth sticking around for."

"Then Lily did it?"

"She helped. Mostly you, though. Thank you."

Frank smiled and patted his friend on the shoulder.

"Came up with a top-notch suicide, though."

"Oh?" Frank sat up. "Go on…"

"Did you bring your notebook?"

"Left it at home. Thought having it with me was encouraging bad behavior."

"You've stopped writing the play?"

"For now, but I'll get back to it."

"Why'd you stop?"

"At first I thought it would be fun to write, then I thought it could be used to talk you out of it, but eventually it just made me sad. Don't think I could have made a play about a man who I knew really wanted to kill himself."

"But now that you know I'm not?"

"Oh yeah, absolutely. I'll dive right back in."

"Okay, so it had to be something religious."

"Why?"

"I think it always did, you know. My father was a religious man. Vicious bastard."

"But you're not religious, and you're not vicious. You're not him, you're a perfectly good man."

"No. I think that was part of it, though. I didn't have to be him. The statement, you know," Joel said.

Frank nodded at him comfortingly, a little look of encouragement and belief.

"So, we'd need to break into the castle to start with…"

The castle had been their first day out together. Joel didn't know what a trebuchet was then. He really had come a long way.

Joel imagined that he and Frank could steal in there. The visitor center on the far side of the castle could provide them access outside of office hours, if they were savvy. Joel would admit that there may have to be some research done to up-skill on his breaking-and-entering abilities, but he didn't see it as being significantly problematic.

Worst case scenario, they could simply walk in during the day, though that may attract unwanted attention that perhaps they didn't need to be drawing on to themselves, on account of the nun's outfit.

Joel had decided that he'd be dressed as a nun for this suicide. In a nun's habit, preferably one with some kind of ceremonial cape. If there were no habits that came with capes, then they'd just have to add one themselves, because it would be a matter of crucial relevance.

Inside the grounds of the castle the trebuchet would be waiting for them. The old medieval catapult could heave huge rocks through the air and fire them tremendous distances. Joel would make his way in dressed as a nun, but underneath his habit he'd be weighed down with rocks. It might be a bit heavy to have to drag them, but he reckoned he could manage.

He imagined himself having his stoic, ever so slightly tear-ful farewell with Frank. The two men clasping hands, as Joel, fully bedecked as a nun, climbed into the trebuchet. Frank, in his sharpest getup with his fanciest scarf, would wait until Joel had positioned himself correctly, and with a shake of his head, marveling at his friend's bravery, he'd cut the rope that held the cup in place, launching Joel high into the air and over the castle walls right in between the two bridges.

Joel could see himself sailing through the air, a flying nun, as people stuck in traffic on the bridges or on the opposite quay whipped out their camera phones to snap blurry images or take short, shocked videos. The flying nun would arc grace-fully through the air and splash into the water. Weighed down with all the rocks, Joel would sink to the bottom.

He could see headlines now, and grainy front page pho-tos, as the search for the flying nun intensified. They'd ask, sometime later, what he had been trying to prove, what was his message, what did he want to tell the world, and that itself would be the message. Question things. Puzzle them out. Un-derstand that there's a motivation for most things, analyze it.

They would find no reason. And that would be the lesson. Pointlessness.

Joel decided it was quite simply the very best plan he had come up with.

"So what do you think?" he asked Frank as soon as he had finished regaling his friend.

Frank said nothing.

"I'm not going to do it anyway, so you don't have to worry about that. So tell me what you really think, and don't be get-ting all unnecessarily critical."

Frank still said nothing.

"Okay, so maybe the point isn't very philosophical, and I sort of just made up all that stuff at the end, but you have to admit it would be hilarious, and a real blaze of glory way to go."

Frank said nothing.

In a curious moment, an instant really, Joel thought he tasted tea in his mouth, or rather, the memory of tea, before he realized the familiarity of the situation he was in. Frank was being silent. Not quiet. Silent. There was no noise coming from him. He sat upright still, but his head had nodded forward. Joel would remember afterwards that there was a tiny little smile playing about the corner of Frank's lips. His usual smile. Like he knew something you didn't.

"No, no, no," Joel begged as he began to shake his friend.

Lucey had been sitting up in her bed. Talking one minute. Gone the next.

"Not you too, please, please, oh Christ if there's a god please no." Joel began to sob, still shaking the unmoving Frank Adams.

"You can't now, not you, you can't do this to me, Frank. Up please," Joel cajoled Frank, as he lifted his eyelids.

Frank said nothing. He did nothing.

"Fuck you now, Frank, wake up. Please. Please don't go, Frank. Please don't leave me," Joel pleaded as he lowered Frank down onto the hard brickwork pathway that led around the little minipark.

Joel didn't know how to do CPR. Not really. He had seen it on TV. He had also seen Nurse Angelica and Mr. Miller. He checked for a pulse.

"Please please please," Joel whispered, even as his fingers probed Frank's neck. Nothing.

He leaned in and pinched Frank's nose and tried to breathe some of his own life back into his friend's body. It wasn't just breath, mere oxygen. Joel Monroe tried to empty his life force and his spirit into what was once Frank Adams.

His hands pressed roughly on Frank's chest. Pushing it in the rhythm he had seen Nurse Angelica work at. He feared pressing too hard. He feared pressing not hard enough.

"Breathe," Joel shouted at the limp thing that had once been Frank Adams, better known as Frank de Selby. "Breathe please breathe."

He pinched the nose and tried again, forcing his life force into the corpse's lungs. He pushed on the chest and begged it to breathe some more.

Eventually, after an eternity, or ten seconds, or somewhere in between those two, Joel Monroe stopped. He could feel the little body, already seeming so frail where it had once been full of energy, wilting under the pressure of his hands. He hated that feeling. He hated the feeling that somehow he might be hurting Frank. Though he certainly was not.

He had been lying on his side, dozing lightly, facing out the window, when he heard Lucey whisper for a cup of tea. He had never heard her voice again. Never knew that sound again.

Now he looked down at the still form of Frank de Selby, once known as Frank Adams, and he bawled his grief and sorrow at it. Some part of his brain desperately searched for the last words Frank had said.

You're a perfectly good man, Frank had said.

Joel would never hear the voice again. It would be lost to him. A remembered thing, no longer real. No longer present.

He bawled again then, in a sort of animal grief he couldn't control. The voices he'd never hear again. The voices that had left him behind, alone, again.

It wasn't until a passing couple on their way home from a night out heard the sounds of sobbing and moaning that anyone called the police.

Joel barely saw them. He cried and desperately fought to remember the sound of Frank's voice.

29

Joel lay on his side, facing out the window of Hilltop, wrapped in a blanket of grief and shock, staring at the spot where he knew the rock was. Behind him the shot glass sat among his little collection, his gift from Frank. Lying on his bed, in between the rock and the shot glass, Joel stared down the yard at the former. He had no idea why he was staring. The rock's magical grip on him was gone. He had no more interest in it now than he had in the whispered conversations of the staff and residents of Hilltop going on behind his back. Behind his back, where the bed was. The bed that had been Lucey's and then Mr. Miller's and then Frank De Selby's. There was nowhere to put Frank's personal effects. No one would be coming for them. There wasn't even a number to reach them, nor any way of knowing where they were, if they cared. Even if Joel had the energy or the wherewithal to reach them, he wouldn't have. They didn't deserve Frank's possessions, meager as they were. They didn't deserve all those books and those scarves and whatever other memorabilia Frank had accumulated.

Joel had known Frank a mere four weeks. But in that time he had really come to know the man. They had shared with one another. Loved one another. Joel felt he had more right to be allowed to look at Frank's possessions than any of his friend's lousy, rotten family.

When the police had arrived at the scene the night before, they had considered arresting Joel. They didn't say as much, but dimly, somewhere on the edges of his consciousness, he was aware of it. They thought Joel had killed his friend. The only witnesses were a couple of drunk twentysomethings who had stumbled onto the scene when it was already too late. The police had argued quietly about whether or not there had been a murder. Joel could tell them nothing. What on earth would be the point?

The ambulance had arrived next and the paramedics knew shock when they saw it. They wrapped him in a blanket and spoke to him in loud and slow sentences. He remembered the shapes their faces made when they were saying the words, but had no idea what they had been telling him. He thought one of them looked a little like Chris. He focused on that. He looked at the Chris paramedic until the man looked back at him. When their eyes met, the paramedic had offered him a look of such pity that Joel began to cry all over again. The lady paramedic who didn't look like anyone Joel knew wrapped her arms around him. It was a warm and caring gesture. He sobbed into her shoulder until she carefully passed him on to someone else.

Even in his grief he recognized the smell. He didn't have to see her; he felt his daughter wrap her arms around him and he sobbed again.

He wanted to ride in the ambulance that was bringing Frank to the morgue, but the paramedics told him he couldn't, and his daughter urged him away with gentle hushing noises until he was in her car. When the gates of Hilltop opened before him, he stopped sobbing. He didn't know why he had chosen that moment to stop, nor why he should suddenly no longer feel the need to express his grief; he just didn't. So he climbed out of the car and shuffled to the main building. Shuffled. Like a broken old man, shoulders down, head down, feet dragging the whole way in. He had never in his life felt so old.

Inside his bedroom he had curled up on his bed, with his back to Frank's bed and to the shot glass and stared out the window. He woke, some hours later, in the same position. Curled up, eyes forward, the bed behind him; and at the end of the garden, down the winding driveway and behind the stand of trees that marked the boundary of Hilltop Nursing Home, was the rock.

He had curled up in the bed and wished he was dead. All over again.

"Joel," a voice whispered. A soft voice. Kind. Caring. Liam's voice. "Can I bring you some breakfast?"

"No," he heard a voice croak back, and he supposed it was his own.

"I'm so sorry," Liam told him. There was a catch in his voice when he said it. A hint of a sob suppressed.

Joel wanted to roll over and face the man. He wanted to tell Liam that Frank had loved him. Or at very least fancied him. And, Joel reckoned, envied the man, too. Saw in him the life that he was not allowed to have. Joel wanted to do it, but instead he just lay there.

Eva came back that morning, too. She hugged his bony old body, still curled up on the bed, and whispered soothing things to him. He tried to smile at her to say thanks, but his face wasn't his own. It didn't do what he wanted it to. It did whatever it wanted to. And it didn't want to smile at her.

That was the morning after Frank Adams, mostly known

as Frank de Selby, had died. For a whole day Joel lay on his side, and he thought about Mr. Miller, and he thought about Lucey and he thought about his friend. And he wanted to die.

He went to sleep that night, after everyone had come and gone with their kind words and their condolences and hoped, as he closed his eyes, hoped desperately that he wouldn't wake up.

The following morning was a bitter disappointment to him.

Not only was he still alive but he had to use the bathroom. Which meant he had to get off the bed, and that meant he would have to acknowledge the empty bed behind him. He struggled to sit up on the edge of the bed. He still had his back to the bed behind him. He sat there for a moment, trying to build the will to move. He found that he was in something of a race. Building the will to move versus the building urge to urinate. Eventually biology beat him, and he stood to his feet.

It was just a bed. He was disappointed for the second time in the space of mere minutes. The bed looked ordinary. Frank's things were still there, for which he was grateful, but the all-terrifying bed that he had been so reluctant to look at was still just a bed. He had wanted it to be something more. Something profoundly ugly, or profoundly beautiful. Something significant. He blamed the bed. It had taken people from him. It haunted his life. Silly that something that haunted his life should look so ordinary. It deserved spikes, or chains or barbs or something.

He walked past it in disgust. Bed didn't even have the good grace to look impressive.

He found the same was true of his reflection, when he cast his eye on it after he had relieved himself. It was a very unimpressive face. He tried to remember the last time he had looked at it and been proud of what he saw there. He had always thought that he looked older than he felt; now he felt as old as he looked. Ancient. And a little bit broken.

"Monroe," he addressed the reflection, "why aren't you dead yet?"

He waited to see if the stroke would finally get him. He almost prayed for it.

"No, Mr. Monroe, not yet, please," Angelica said to him quietly.

Her voice was almost a shock to him.

She had obviously walked in to check on him while he had been doing the necessary. He washed his hands quietly and waited for her to leave. He felt embarrassed in her company, and uncomfortable. Her meaty hands still scared him a little. The memory of her body compressing Mr. Miller mixed with his memory of trying to push the life back into Frank and made him well up. He brushed the tears away with an angry hand. Crying like a child again. He wouldn't do it. Not here.

He took his time drying his hands and listened for the sound of her exit. It never came. He wanted to wait in the bathroom, but that simply wouldn't do. There was a line even Joel Monroe couldn't cross, and hiding in bathrooms was apparently it.

She was standing there when he emerged. She looked frightened of him. Still. Even after everything else that had happened, she still looked like he frightened her.

"Not yet, Mr. Monroe, please," she said again in her soft accent.

"Why not?" he asked her, hearing the bitterness in his voice.

"We don't want you to," she told him. It was a kind thing to say.

He smiled a weak little smile at her. His face was almost his to control again.

"I'm tired, Angelica. I'm very, very tired."

"I know. Sometimes I am, too. Sometimes I'm exhausted. I've been working here for eighteen years. Did you know that, Mr. Monroe?"

He didn't. In his selfishness he had never bothered to find out. He bet that Frank had known that. Una certainly did. She was here nearly three times longer than he had been.

"I didn't know that, Nurse Angelica. I'm sorry, I didn't take the time before."

"It's okay, Mr. Monroe. I understand."

The look she gave him was filled with understanding. He was surprised by it, and yet it made sense. In a way that he had never considered before, it made perfect sense. She had been here for eighteen years; the corridors here were packed with the ghosts of people she had cared for, people she had known, some well, some others not so well. She understood because she was tired of it, too. She looked different to him all of a sudden.

"How do you do it all the time?" he asked.

"You just do," she told him. "Or what else are you going to do?"

"What if I can't?" he asked her.

"Mr. Monroe, if anyone else asked that I would have to think about my answer, but I never met someone before like you. I think that if you want to do anything, you can do it. You've broken out of here three times—"

"Four," he absently corrected her.

"Four," she said, smiling. "You just have to want to keep going. Please, Mr. Monroe, you just keep going for me, okay?"

He smiled at her again, a little more warmly this time, but still a wan little thing.

"I think I'd like to go back to sleep," he told her, as he walked past the very ordinary bed.

★ ★ ★

He dreamt again that afternoon, as he dozed. Another barren, hilly landscape populated by skeletons of Mr. Miller and Mr. Adams. He was looking through the crowds of bones trying to find de Selby before it was too late. In the distance Lucey and Una pursued him, calling for him; he dodged about the skeletons, evading them, he was staying in front of them, even beginning to put some distance between them and him when a low rumbling sound filled his ears. He looked all about him and realized the rock from the end of the garden was rolling down every one of the hills, rolling toward him, getting bigger as they rolled, smashing Mr. Miller and Mr. Adams skeletons as they inexorably closed in on him. He spun on the spot, looking for an avenue of escape, but the rocks were all around him until all he could do was put his hands up in the air and wait…

He was shaken awake by the gnarled hands of Mighty Jim. The ancient old man was staring straight at him, dead in the eye, his face only inches from Joel's.

"Boundless grief is too heavy to bear," he told Joel. He looked serious. Certain. His eyes were clear and bright and not clouded over as they so often seemed to be.

"I was having a nightmare," Joel told him, trying to shake off the feeling of impending doom.

Mighty Jim looked at him expectantly. Joel noticed the boxed chessboard in the man's hands. A lovely gesture, if the man was mentally capable of such. Joel thought that he might be. He had no interest in playing regardless. So he just shook his head.

He didn't eat that day either. Nurse Liam looked at him with concern as he came to collect his dinner that evening. The plate had gone untouched.

Lily and Chris came to see him. They brought chocolates

and flowers. Lily forced a jovial demeanor as if by pottering around the room with force and vigor she might infect her grandfather with the same. It didn't work. Chris tried to talk to him. It was banal stuff. A question about car engines that he had prepared at home in the hope that the old days might knock some life into the old man. It didn't work either.

Before he went to sleep that night, Una came to see him.

"I can't bear to see you like this," she told him.

"I'm sorry," he told her, and he meant it.

"We're all heartbroken, Joel. All of us. Did you know he had breakfast with me every morning? While you slept in, he and I had breakfast. He was my friend, too."

"I'm sorry," Joel told her, and the urge to cry began to creep up on him.

Of course Frank went for breakfast with her every morning. It was a typically classy gesture from the man. Taking his neighbor out to breakfast every morning, even if taking her out meant walking to the common room. Joel had wondered what the old rogue was up to with his early mornings.

"We need you now, Joel," she told him earnestly. "This is how communities work. We share in life and we share in grief."

He nodded his agreement at her. She was right. He lay down and curled up and faced out the window so she wouldn't see him crying.

He slept all night that night, a deep and dreamless sleep, and woke exhausted and weak. His head was swimming in itself, and he could barely pull himself up in the bed.

Nurse Liam was there again. Another shift. Another day. Joel wished that he could be stronger for the man. For all of them. They weren't nearly the terrible gang he had made them out to be.

All of them were gold.

He wished he had it in him to tell them that. He wished that when he was really alive, for those brief, beautiful weeks when he felt like somebody again, when he walked taller and laughed loud and shared dinner with his friend, that he had told them all that he was very fond of them.

He wished he hadn't been such a selfish bastard for so long. Such a vicious bastard. Maybe they'd remember the good times when he was gone. He hoped so.

"Joel," Liam's voice came to him from a tremendous distance away, like the voices that haunted him and chased him in his nightmares. Floating through the ether. "Have some breakfast, please."

There was a note in the voice, a note of command and authority. The voice he'd normally use when he was calling Joel Mr. Monroe. Liam expected the voice to cut through the malaise, to reach the part of Joel that sometimes reluctantly did what he was told. The voice did not. Joel offered a look to the nurse. He hoped the look said how sorry he was, and how much he appreciated what the young man was doing for him, and had been doing for him for a long time.

"Joel, if you don't eat we're going to have to get a court order and make you eat, or a drip or something. Please, Joel, don't make us do that. No one wants that."

The boy arrived again. The therapist. With his shirtsleeves rolled up. He was a flimsy little thing really, insubstantial. He wasn't smiling patiently now, he wasn't practicing his non-threatening look; he was solemn.

"Mr. Monroe, I thought you might like to talk today."

"You thought wrong," Joel croaked at him, his throat cracked and dry.

The boy poked at him a little with his questions. Joel sat in the bed and stared through him. Now he didn't care if the boy knew that he wanted to kill himself. He became more insubstantial by the minute, like his form was coming apart, a ghost of a thing. Had Joel really been frightened of this in-consequential creature once?

When he left, Joel tried to go back to sleep. Tried and failed.

Joel wondered if this was how he would die. Not some elaborate suicide catapulted out of a castle or the angry-man suicides of a man possessed with vigor, energy and more fury than he knew what to do with, but a simple wasting away, too tired and fed up to do anything, too lonely and sad and afraid of his death to do anything to stop it coming to take him away.

Nurse Liam looked like he might be on the point of tears as he took away the tray of untouched breakfast. Joel slept again.

Then Eva was there. Sitting by his bedside. The Rhino was there, too. She was in her uniform, but only half the way and her face was painted with a sad concern. She looked too human. Too sad to be herself.

"Dad," Eva said softly to him as he woke from his daze.

He looked at her and tried to smile. She looked so solid. So real. He had always known she would grow up to be a force to be reckoned with. A tough woman. Soft in her own way, but so very capable. He was at least proud of that.

"Dad, look, I didn't want to tell you this…" she hesitated. Her hands were restlessly playing with a little book.

Joel looked at the little book. It was Frank's. He recognized it.

"Dad, I know how sad you are. I know this is devastating, but please…" She hesitated again. She looked so earnest. So worried. "I know I'm tough to deal with sometimes," she told him. "I know I could have made this easier for you. I didn't and I'm so sorry about that. I got so caught up in myself."

She was saying the words to him that he desperately wanted to say to her before he went.

"But I thought we had a chance to make it right," she continued. "I was so glad when you came to me the other day. If you didn't..."

She didn't finish. The implications were pronounced enough for both of them. He might have died before they ever fixed themselves.

"I don't want to take from his memory. I know you loved him very much. I know you did. And we didn't want to tell you this, because we didn't want to hurt you, but we're so worried now. We think you should know..."

She was still playing with the little book. He knew what it was. *The Unfortunate End of Joel Monroe.*

"Dad, Frank was a terribly lonely man. We think he was going to kill himself."

"What?" Joel asked incredulously.

He sat up in the bed.

Their faces registered shock at him speaking, then some spark of hope.

"We found a little book he was writing. It's full of ideas for how he might kill himself. He's filled it up. He was very unwell, Dad. He talked about shooting himself and hanging himself from the clock tower. I know it's terribly sad that he's gone, but it was probably for the best that he went this way."

They found *The Unfortunate End of Joel Monroe*, but since Frank had never written the title, or identified the characters in any way, they had assumed it was autobiographical and that Frank wanted to commit suicide.

They assumed that Frank wanted to kill himself in the stupidest ways imaginable.

Joel burst out laughing.

It was a weak laugh, lacking in the vitality he had let slip from his body in the days previous, but it was heartfelt, real, substantial.

He laughed and laughed until he wheezed, and his eyes watered. For a split second he thought he might choke to death laughing, and wouldn't that have been just peachy, but he didn't. Instead he sucked in great big breaths and tried to stifle another laugh. He reached out for a drink of water and found the shot glass. It drew another laugh from him. The guilty little glance about the room before Frank stuffed it into his jacket. A shot glass in lieu of a cookie.

Eva and The Rhino watched him laughing and coughing in utter bewilderment.

He gathered himself.

"Oh no, love," Joel assured her, trying to sit himself further up in the bed and shaking his head from side to side. "No, no, no."

"But," The Rhino protested lightly, gesturing at the book, "he wrote it all down here."

Her voice wasn't cold. It was warm. Concerned. He imagined she used that voice when she spoke to her children. He found it lovely in a way he never thought he would.

Joel tried to picture Frank in any of the absurd suicide situations Joel had pitched to him. Frank with the suicide vest on. Frank charging the police. The absurdity brought on a fresh batch of the giggles. They might have thought he was going insane. He reached out to the shot glass again and picked it up, rolling it in his hands as he spoke.

"No, my dear," he told her, smiling from ear to ear. "Frank de Selby would simply never have killed himself. He enjoyed his life too much. He loved it. Nearly every minute of it."

"But why would he write this all down?"

"It's a story. A play. A writing exercise. Something he was working on, but not real," he told her. "Frank had some problems. His family were a pack of bastards, and they scarred him a little bit, but Frank de Selby simply loved his life too much to do that. He loved living. He loved people. He loved facing life head-on. There was nothing he couldn't overcome."

"Dad, everyone sometimes…"

"No, love," he told her gently but firmly. "Not Frank. I promise you, not Frank. You see he has a skill. A great skill. He wasn't inhuman, or some kind of superman or anything like that. He was just excellent at being Frank."

He looked at them to see if they understood. Eva still seemed bewildered, but not The Rhino. The Rhino was looking at him with an expression he had never seen before. There was a sparkle in her eyes.

"I don't…" Eva replied, confused.

"He was as miserable as anyone else, you know? He had the same problems anyone else had, worse than some, but he found a way to live through them somehow. And to love living through them. He watched the soaps and he did all the other stuff everyone else does around here, except he found a way to take tremendous joy out of it. He loved it. All of it…"

Joel trailed off as it dawned on him.

Frank did love everything. He approached his days with enthusiasm. Even his lazy days he valued for their laziness. He loved drinking pints in bars as much as he loved having breakfast with Una behind them. He might have even thought of Hilltop as a prison, but instead of raging against it, he just enjoyed being in prison.

He had sat in the room with Joel every day and listened to Joel complaining about his life, and somehow Frank Adams had found a way to make that enjoyable, too. He saw life differently. He saw everything differently.

Better still, he had dragged Joel kicking and grumbling and complaining into his way of life. He had done everything he could to delay Joel's demise as Joel marched, slowly, stupidly, to a better place in his life.

It was doubly heartbreaking, the realization that he was gone, but Joel felt something profound and magnificent in his moment of realization. He felt an enormous sense of gratitude for Frank's life.

The day before the funeral, Joel sat in the common room at the chessboard with Mighty Jim.

"I should have put him in his proper face," Jim told him as he moved his first piece.

"Clever opening gambit," Joel told him and placed a piece.

It wasn't a considered tactical decision. He just moved the knight into a square.

Mighty Jim's eyes narrowed quizzically. He pondered for a moment before moving another piece.

"Bold move," Joel told him as he moved another piece. Again he moved the piece before he had time to consider it.

They played like that, back and forth, but as the game progressed, Jim took longer and longer to decide his moves, and Joel found himself enjoying the game more and more. He moved his queen into a killing position.

"Absurd…" Jim said, scratching his head in confusion.

He considered the board for a very long time, so long in fact, that Joel decided to pay attention to it, too. Checkmate in six moves. There was no way out of it. Jim reached for a piece, then stopped. Then another, but stopped again. He withdrew his hand and took a long look at Joel.

Then he smiled at big broad smile, warm and happy, and simply got up from the table and wandered over to the television.

"Just like that?" Joel asked him.

Mighty Jim paid him no notice. The soaps were on.

On the day of the funeral Joel dressed himself soberly. Una Clarke helped him. She wore a look that was one part relief,

one part irritated, like she wanted to scold him but couldn't.
She did take the opportunity to fuss over him a little more
than was necessary. He took it in good humor. The least he
owed her really.

At the appointed time, he stood outside on the gravel of
the front yard waiting for the car to pull up. There were cars
arriving in twos and threes, and the residents of Hilltop were
out in their somber finest. It was a sunny day. The kind of
day made for wandering around town in circles until you gave
yourself a thirst, and Joel smiled at the memories of it. They
hurt him a little, cut at his heart just a tiny bit, but they came
with a great surge of affection. He held Una's hand in his as
Lily and Chris pulled up to collect them.

The grandkids were clearly relieved to see him restored to
some kind of health, but the conversation was stilted, forced
almost. His decline and the recent tragedy had taken something away from all of them. Joel wasn't about to let it get further away from him. Frank wouldn't have let it either.

"You ever meet Gonzo the Bouncer?" Joel asked them from
the back of the car.

"Gonzo? In the club?"

"Yeah. Big guy. Dopey-looking."

They looked at each other in surprised amusement.

"Yeah, I know him," Chris replied.

"Am I wrong or is he constantly a prick?"

Chris guffawed loudly.

"Not wrong," Lily told him. "And a creep, as well. When
did you meet him?"

"This past Monday," he told her.

He regaled them with the story of the nightclub and Slippery Nipples and the Cock Sucking Cowboys, describing
Frank's unexpectedly prudish reaction in detail. They laughed
at the story and added their own. Lily passed her phone back
to Una to show her the dozens of selfies she had of Frank

with all of her friends, up to his neck in drink, dancing on the floor of a crowded city center nightclub at one-thirty in the morning. Una chuckled at them all, particularly one of Frank and Joel together.

Joel stared at that one for a long time, his eyes brimming slightly.

At the graveside Joel stood alone. Alone and yet surrounded. Frank Adams, credited for stage and screen as Frank de Selby, had a biological family somewhere. They weren't at the graveside. Instead there was a different kind of a family. The residents and staff of Hilltop stood side by side with a smattering of theater folk and the producer of *Glory Days* as well as half the cast past and present. A throng of people turned out to see off Frank de Selby, and yet when the moment came and the celebrant asked if anyone wanted to speak, no one stirred. Frank hadn't been lying in the Royale Theatre; his de Selby mask kept most people at a discreet distance. It was just as well for Joel. He didn't want these people talking about Frank anyway. He knew that it was he who knew Frank best. A paltry four weeks together, and yet this was undeniably true. People nodded encouragingly at Joel in turn as he stood forward to deliver a eulogy of sorts.

He didn't say much. He wasn't sure he had the strength, but what he did say was full of sadness and humor and sincerity and warmth. The crowd that attended warmly applauded, and as they began to lower his friend down, Joel felt himself overcome again. Grief heavy and thick settled on him, but with it love and community and friendship and all the other things that he thought he had left behind him a long time beforehand.

And one by one they came to him to show him that they cared. The Rhino was there first, hugging him warmly while he softly wept. His grandchildren with tears in their own eyes.

The young men shaking his hand gruffly since they thought that's what they were supposed to do, and the young women with gentle kisses on his cheeks. His daughter, so warm and compassionate, kissed him and told him everything would be okay. The residents, the nurses, old theater folk shaking his hand and professing their grief while he tried to hold back gentle sobs.

Finally Nurse Liam and Nurse Angelica. They were both red-eyed from crying, from sharing his grief and their own. A final gift from his old friend, a community that he didn't know he had. Joel smiled down at his pal even through his tears.

When it was done the crowd milled about in a hushed, almost reverential silence. No one knew what to do next. It struck Joel that it was a most un-Frank atmosphere. Something he wouldn't have stood for. He'd have rescued them all from their gloom somehow, with some generous act of humanity. Joel guessed at what it might be.

"Shall we go for a pint?" Joel asked them.

EPILOGUE

Joel adjusted his scarf for the fiftieth time. He was nervous. He knew that. He was also unused to wearing scarves.

"Get you anything, Grandad?" Lily asked from the door of the living room.

"A different therapist?" he asked. "One that doesn't look like he's twelve?"

The boy, Martin, sat across from him, preparing himself for their weekly meeting, smiling wryly. Eva had arranged to have the meetings at her house, since she reckoned it would put Joel at ease. It had been an improvement on Hilltop. He liked it better here, in her house, in her comfortable living room with its comfortable furniture. He found himself becoming more and more at ease talking to Martin as the weeks went on. He even liked him a little. Though with Joel it was sometimes difficult to tell who he liked and who he didn't like. Easier than it had been, for certain, but still a little difficult.

Lily laughed as she moved away down the corridor, calling out to the people in the kitchen as she went.

As Martin sorted his things out and made himself comfortable, Joel strained to hear the conversation happening in the kitchen. It was early evening, there was cooking going on, and that came with its own sounds and smells.

He could hear Eva talking, her voice soft and command-ing all at once. He could hear laughing, too. Lily and Chris. Probably mocking their mother lightly. They enjoyed that. They were sharp. Not as sharp as Frank had been, but not far off either. He was proud of their wit.

Una's voice was there, too. Melodious and pleasant. She had come with him for dinner and to hold his hand through the difficult early stage of his therapy. She had literally held his hand up to the door. He pretended to be annoyed at the fuss she was making, but he hadn't removed her hand either.

She knew what Eva didn't. What the kids didn't. She knew he had been suicidal.

Had been.

He wasn't anymore. He thought.

Martin knew, too. Joel had told him. The boy had nodded at him sympathetically and then carried on. He didn't lock Joel up. He didn't judge. He didn't do anything except ask more questions. He always started with the same one.

Joel didn't mind. The gift that Frank de Selby had given him was a new perspective. He feared a little less now. He was definitely less bored. He had started a chess club.

The walls of Hilltop had stopped being so terrifying to him. He played games against Mighty Jim. He won now as often as he lost. He joined social media. He didn't un-derstand it, but he held out hope for himself that he would eventually. Lily and Chris posted his pictures online. Com-plete strangers in places he didn't know liked the photos. The world had shrunk itself down for the new generation, and Joel grabbed their coattails, determined to ride them for as long as he could.

Nothing was as terrible as it seemed, and indeed, though Joel was still slow to admit it, things might even have been described as good. Many things were a great deal better than they first appeared.

"Mr. Monroe," Martin began. "Do you still want to die?"

"No, my dear boy," Joel told him, adjusting his scarf again. "Not just yet."

★ ★ ★ ★ ★

ACKNOWLEDGMENTS

It took a village to raise this little child of mine. I couldn't have done it without all the constant support, encouragement, love, (occasional criticism) and so many coffees.

First and foremost, Pete Moles. This story wouldn't be half of what it is without you. You helped mold Joel and Frank, and I'm tremendously grateful. Ding ding ding.

Mam, Dad, Ciara, Jean, Paul, Tara, John P, Mike Sr., Ellen, Mikey, Emily, Grace, Joe, Megan, Maeve and Daniel... Wow. That's a large immediate family. Thanks for always being patient with me. I love you all. For the aunts and the uncles and the cousins and the people who it turns out were never related to me but I always called my uncles, aunts and cousins, thank you for the support.

My eternal admiration and respect is kept for Alex Dunne who has once again been an inspired editor and Grainne O'Brien who's just plain better than me. There, I said it.

Lauren Parsons and Liz Stein and David Forrer and in fact, all the people at both Legend Press and Park Row Books. I loved how much you all cared about this book, and I even more loved when we were finished. Thanks for all the effort and consideration you've put into this. I hope it lives up to expectations.

For the test readers; Eadaoin O'Neill, "Chilli" John Kearney, Maureen Mooney, Jean Mooney, Emma Langford, Kennedy O'Brien and, of course, Christine Burnell. Thanks for the feedback. Mostly lovely, occasionally brutal. Which is how feedback should be, I think.

To Ross, who seems to be a bigger exponent of my work than I am. Your endless belief in me is as impressive as that eye-roll you do when you think I can't see you.

Eric Kelleher, my thanks for the website and explaining things so that the idiot could understand them.

To the WritePace gang in Limerick, all of whom are inspirational as writers, bakers, chefs, sports pundits and friends, I thank you for your time and your ears. I started this book in your company and finished it there too, so you're its godparents. Whether you like it or not. Special thanks to Sarah Moore Fitzgerald and Bob Burke who helped Joel and Frank bust out one Saturday morning.

To all the other gangs and clubs and societies; my work colleagues in the Shannon Control Centre for patience and goodwill even when I'm boring them to tears. The Torch Players and the College Players who don't seem to mind if I'm overly dramatic. The Banter Brigade who I hope never change, Young Munsters RFC, Limerick FC, MRSC and more besides.

Will and John; why haven't you changed yet?

To Paul in Copy That, formerly Moviedrome. I'm grateful for the help and the reams of paper and the patience to put up with me.

Finally for Christine, who encourages, supports, pats me on the back, tells me I'm pretty and has been my personal rock for this entire book. I don't have enough thanks for all you do for me. I love you.

Writing acknowledgments is harder than writing a book—I'm terrified that I've left you out. If I have, I'm sorry and you can demand pints/coffees off me in Charlie Malones. I've never really gotten anywhere on my own. It's always taken your help. Whoever you are.

Stand Up and Fight.

QUESTIONS FOR DISCUSSION

1. It's Joel's improving relationships that ultimately save him. Which relationship is most important in stopping Joel from wanting to commit suicide? That with his daughter, his grandchildren or his new friend?

2. Joel takes a number of items "home" to remind him of the world outside: the old garage sign, the lucky penny and the pin to save the Royale. What do you think these represent?

3. Joel and Frank both have their own problems to deal with. Which of them is more affected by their problems, and which of the sets of problems is more challenging?

4. Joel believes the world is out to get him. Do you think he's right, or is his perspective colored by his suicidal thoughts?

5. Joel and Eva argue over his seemingly childish behavior which Joel blames on her for treating him like a child.

Do you think he's being unfair to her or is her attitude toward him dismissive?

6. Frank and Joel's relationship has been described as "unlikely." Do you think this is true? How much do they share in common?

7. If Joel had gotten his wish and met Frank earlier in his life, do you think they would have been friends?

8. Is Joel's ennui and fear of the therapist a sign of a much deeper mental health issue that's gone undiagnosed?

9. Death is a prominent unspoken character in the story. What impact do you think that character has on the supporting characters (i.e. those who are not Joel and Frank)?

10. Is Frank and Joel's rapidly growing relationship a sign of their openness or is it informed by Joel's impending death and his need for comradeship?